UNDER ANOTHER SUN

D.M. SICILIANO

This book is a work of fiction. The names and characters are a product of the author's imagination, and any resemblance to actual persons, living or dead, is purely coincidental.

Edited by Amelia Beamer. Interior art by Riccardo D'ariano

ISBN: 9798635755877

FOR

My Father

2000 RAVYNN BRADLEY

"The world is falling down." Ravynn had no idea what had urged that from her lips. She slumped in the backseat of her parents' station wagon as it crossed the bridge to take them home. A sense of melancholy gripped her and wouldn't let go. She wished her twin brother Ray was with her. He always understood her the way only twins could.

Ravynn belched and swallowed the taste of bile. She cranked the window down all the way. Placed her arm on the window frame, set her head on her arm, and sucked in the fresh wind that raced at her face and caused her to squint into the night. Her raven-colored hair danced and flipped over her face in the cooling air. The lazy moon tried and failed to slip its light through the hazy clouds above.

"What was that?" Her dad called back. She caught his eyes in the rearview, brows raised in question.

"I—"

She never did get to answer him.

A woman stood in the middle of the road. Dark hair shrouded her face, and she wore nothing but a thin, white gown. The aura surrounding her was like she'd stolen the light from the moon itself. Ravynn saw the woman's lips moving, but there was no way she could've heard what she uttered. Yet, in her ear, like a whisper, Ravynn heard the woman say, "*A crack in time saves ninety-nine.*"

Headlights from up ahead stunned her, momentarily blinding her to everything- her father, the woman, the road- all of it swallowed up by the lights.

Her mother cried out from the passenger's seat, "It's in our lane!"

Ravynn's father slammed on the brakes and yanked the wheel to the right as he tried to avoid both striking the woman in the road, and the car coming straight at them. The force sent her smacking into the back of the driver's seat, then spilled her onto the floor of the car as it skidded off the side of the road.

The tires screamed in a way that Ravynn should have as she lost her breath. Slammed into something hard. Crunching sounds. Metal ripping. Still they kept moving.

Then the world went lopsided.

The car lurched forward at a hopeless angle and thrust her against the back of her dad's seat. Lights danced across Ravynn's vision, like thousands of little fireflies.

Her mom said something, and then she screamed. But her parents already seemed so far away. Like Ravynn was all alone, pitching downward in her metal prison toward the unforgiving water below the bridge.

The world was darker than before, despite the little fireflies that flashed their stunning brilliance at her.

She didn't scream.

Not until the car hit the water. That was when time slowed to a crawl.

Her jaws and lips yanked wide open, as the most terrifying sound she'd ever heard came from her own mouth as the vehicle broke the surface of the water. Her jaw slammed shut from the impact, rattling her teeth. Water pulsed and thrummed up over the station wagon, but within those initial nanoseconds, Ravynn had already reacted. Those first few drops of water trickled over the side of her open window, into the car, still too slow to be real-time. It didn't matter. Her body had vaulted to the side, flinging herself out the window, into the cold, dark water of the lake.

She never once thought of Mom or Dad- because in those moments- no one else existed.

In shock, Ravynn robotically tread water the family car sank to the bottom of the lake. The lake was some strange live thing as it greedily devoured the car like a starved beast. She registered this unemotionally, as if her feelings had been frozen by the cold of the waters.

Then, something from behind brought her attention around; a woman who stood, or floated there, above the lake, in a spinning vortex of water. It was as if the water were a protective funnel, bending and swirling around her, keeping her above the hungry reach.

Ravynn knew what she needed to do. Where that melancholy had come from, because it had returned. A looping deja-vous stole across her mind and she remembered being here before, in this exact moment. A recurring dream she'd had thousands of times, so often that Ravynn blurred the line between reality and dream. This woman had always been here. Her dark hair spun around her head, in the same motion that the funnel of water spun in. The white flowing dress billowed, twisting and turning along with the rotation of the water.

Ravynn needed to go to her.

The woman opened her arms in welcome.

2021 RAVYNN BRADLEY

R avynn was tired.
Tired of the fights with her estranged husband, Matt, who grew drunker by the day. Tired of the secrets and lies, all of which were her own doing. As the days and weeks and months went by, she came closer and closer to *The Day*, and in turn she withdrew more and more from everyone she loved. She could see no way around it. No one would understand. She didn't entirely understand it herself, but she readily accepted it.

Since that inauspicious night when she was thirteen and narrowly escaped the end her parents suffered, Ravynn was on borrowed time. Knew she was never supposed to leave the water that night. Knew the *Woman on the Water* who came to her meant to take her home. Where she belonged. But fate stepped in that day in the shape of a young man by the water's edge. He'd witnessed the whole accident unfold and swam out to save what he thought was a drowning girl in need of rescue.

She hadn't needed rescue that night, nor did she now. Ravynn sighed, the past and present interweaving and enswathing her in their weight. She grew tired of the same conversation that led to the same fight.

"Let it go, Matt. Please."

"How can I? It's not right, not healthy. Maybe it's not my place anymore, since we split, but... if you won't talk to me, at least call your brother."

She shook her head in the negative, not willing to budge, unable to give an inch.

He paced the bedroom floor roughly, and Ravynn was certain he would wear footsteps into the carpet. He tried to reason with her yet again. "But you two always... you know... you always..." His frustration tripped his tongue and he couldn't complete his thought. That was always a tell that he was on edge. The problem was, she couldn't pull him back; he had to do it himself. And lately, he rarely succeeded. She knew most of it was her fault. She couldn't give him what he needed most- answers. His drinking was half the reason they were newly divorced, and of course, her secrecy the other half. It would be so much easier if she didn't love him, but she did. Always had.

Ravynn hugged the journal to her chest, keeping her secrets close to her heart.

Matt paced harder across the floor. "I just don't understand that journal." He stopped long enough to shake an accusatory finger. "Those entries don't make sense."

He curled the fingers of his right hand into a fist and covered his mouth with it, as if to hold back his words. It didn't work. She heard him mumble, "What is— who are the ninety-nine?"

She peeled the corner of the journal back in frustration and rolled eyes. "Nothing Matt. You don't *need* to understand. Just- let- it- go. Please, honey."

Terms of endearment had long since gone between the two of them, and yet old habits died hard in stressful times. She bit her tongue and hoped he wouldn't notice.

He tipped his head back to stare at the ceiling, searching for either the composure or the words to continue. He groaned and looked down, unyieldingly into Ravynn's eyes, and at that moment, she felt his heart break. Felt it more than she should have. More than any human should. It had been that way since she was thirteen, like some sort of switch had been flipped and she had been activated, her sense more alive than ever before. Plus, *more* senses.

He didn't speak, but the look he gave her told her everything. She read his heart. It called to her, imploring, *"I can't do this anymore,"* clearly as if Matt had spoken the words aloud. *"I love you so much but it's killing me. Eating me up inside. Chasing me back down into the bottle, and I'm afraid I won't be able to come back out."* His eyes searched hers for something. They were so desperate, staring at her. The weight of them straining on her heart. She was stuck. She was reading him, and it took all of her energy. The vibrations came off him in unsteady waves, pulsing at her in uneven beats that she could tactilely feel, like heavy raindrops beating on her skin. The connection, the love between them had always been too strong.

The minute fragments of him which used to be whole skittered about within the vibrations like wild, untamed animals. Frightened. Weakened. The fear poured out of him so expeditiously it assaulted Ravynn's senses and challenged her ability to stay standing. She raised her hands in front of her body, as if to fend off an invisible onslaught. Ravynn saw now that Matt not only feared for her, but he feared her. *"Maybe she's sick,"* she read those frenzied thoughts. *"Her father was schizophrenic. Maybe she is too. How did I miss the signs? I should tell Ray."*

Ravynn didn't think before she spoke, "Don't tell Ray."

The fear she sensed congealed in the air between them. Like some heavy, emotional sludge made real that she couldn't pull herself free of. Instead, she pulled her arms in tight, stroking her own shoulders. "I'm not sick."

Matt recoiled, either from her words or from the emotional turmoil undulating through the air. He staggered and stepped backward, until his back hit the wall. His eyes welled up with tears, and all she could sense coming off him now was dread. Pure terror. No longer love, worry, or hurt.

"What?" he asked. His voice cracked. "How?" He tried to take another step back, but his heel kicked the wall, a solid reminder that there was nowhere to go.

Ravynn didn't answer him. As much as it pained her to watch him struggle, she could do nothing to assuage him.

He reached to the side, fumbling for the door handle, as if poised to make a hasty retreat. "Explain," he beseeched her. "Explain the journals. The events. The dates." His eyes were wild, they raced about, searching her face and trying to find the woman he knew somewhere within.

"We've been over this, Matt. You know I can't." her words came out glacial and apathetic. Even to her ear, it made her cringe. It had to be that way.

He snarled, 'I know you *won't.* It's madness! You know that, right? Most of these dates and events you've marked down haven't even happened—"

"Not yet, they haven't." She regretted it as soon as she said it.

His eyes grew incredulous. He leaned forward, but still gripped the door handle as if it were a safety line. He swallowed hard, and Ravynn could see his Adam's apple bobbing roughly before he began again. "What? You think you're Nostradamus? Some sort of prophet? What?"

His face scrunched up in disgust as if he had tasted something appallingly bitter. The one look hit her like a slap across her face, and she turned away to stare out the window instead.

"You should have never read any of it in the first place," she said while staring out the window at the redwood tree beyond the window.

Full night had snuck upon them while her attention was elsewhere. Lazy long summer days often took so long to pass by, the sun making its leisurely stroll across the sky to finally set completely. The darkness outside now crept in through the windowpane and into her. The tree stood oddly still, as if it didn't want to upset the delicate balance between the contentious couple inside.

Ravynn felt the need to open the window, to reach out and touch the tree to see if it were alive or made of stone. She knew without moving, without testing the air outside that it was heavy and dead. Like everything held its breath, waiting. *Perfect earthquake weather*, she thought as she glanced out on the dimming horizon. People always said that about nights like that one. In reality, Ravynn knew there was no such thing as earthquake weather.

"But I *did* read it!" he exclaimed.

Instead of engaging, which was futile, she walked straight up to him and reached out to remove his hand from the doorknob. "I need to check on Amelia," she said as calmly and unwavering as the tree outside.

"She's in bed. Just went down. Leave her be," he said, his hand recoiling, falling away from the knob at the slightest brush of her hand.

Matt stepped out of Ravynn's way too brusquely, giving away his odium. With one fluid movement, Ravynn moved through the door, forcing herself not to look at him, not to see the fear that was plain on his face. In less than a breath she was across the hall, pushing her way into Amelia's room, where the six-year-old slept soundly.

"I saw today's *event*. But today is almost over— and nothing. You need to talk to someone," he called out softly. "No earthquake. Not even the slightest tremor. Nothing."

Ravynn didn't have time for her anger. "The day is not done yet," she said simply. Not waiting for a response, she closed the child's door behind her and climbed into bed with her daughter. Wrapped her arms around the child and cradled her protectively, careful not to wake her.

It started slowly, barely detectable at first. Ravynn kissed her daughter's forehead and tucked a pillow against her other side. *Ready*, she thought.

Tiny figurines on Amelia's dresser began to jitter and skitter across the surface. They shimmied like they were at a dance, excited movement gripping them all. A few fell to the floor, already tired from the din, as the earth let out a low groan as it shifted beneath.

Matt raced through the door, eyes peeled open in terror and

awe. Ravynn met his gaze and reached out a hand, beckoning to him, all the while remaining unfalteringly neutral. Amelia's lamp jumped over the dresser and shattered into pieces on the hardwood floor. It reminded Ravynn of the shattering relationship between her and Matt. What once was whole.

Amelia startled awake, but her mother cooed at her and wrapped a hand behind her head and pulled her closer. Matt curled up next to them, pushing the pillow back against the headboard. All the while, he stared at Ravynn. Calm, composed, knowing Ravynn. She reached out her free arm to him, over Amelia, but he didn't take it. He held still, searching her face. The look on his face broke her heart, but there was nothing she could do about it. So, she held tightly to her daughter as the earth slowed back to stillness.

Tomorrow would be new day, but the day after... well, that would be *The Day*. She knew it. She wasn't quite sure how much of the journal Matt had seen, but if he'd read it through, he too knew what that day would bring.

RAVYNN leaned on the precipice of night, waiting for *The Day* to come. She had known about this day since after the car crash when she was thirteen years old. After that tumultuous night, she could see things more clearly. Things she knew normal people couldn't see. No, she wasn't sick like her father, Matt was wrong. She was more like her mother and grandmother than anything else. Amelia had shades of it too, and even her twin brother Ray, but he was too stubborn and blind to see that he could be special as well.

The entry had been correct in her journal foretelling the 6.0 earthquake from the previous day. That would be nothing in the grand scheme of things. So much more to come. Tomorrow morning would bring another larger quake, just off the coast of northern California. What would follow...

Under Another Sun. Ravynn held onto that thought and the

image of the *Woman on the Water* that had been imprinted on her mind since she was a teen. The longing in her heart she felt every day afterwards kept her focused and kept her sure it was all very real. She had missed her window then. But tomorrow? It would all be different. Change was coming.

Matt had been skeptical and hesitant when she'd invited him over. Invited him to spend the night even. It had been weeks since the divorce and he'd last slept in his own house, his own bed, with his own wife. His voice sounded leery over the phone, but he'd accepted.

Ravynn felt guilty for playing on his feelings like that, but she needed to see him one last time. Needed him to be there with Amelia when she left. Her mouth had said all the right things that morning, and Matt believed her. She put on her happy face and grabbed her new camera. It was time to go back work, after all, she'd told him. Too long had she leaned on him and neglected her art and her work.

Matt had been all too agreeable and eager for any sort of improvement on her part, she knew it. It was selfish, undoubtedly, but necessary.

The sun had set upon a tumultuous day, and darkness disguised the mess it had left behind. Everything felt still and calm and right as she kissed Amelia goodnight. The girl was already asleep when Matt leaned in and tucked the blankets up high under her chin the way she liked it. Ravynn slowly laced her fingers around his. He froze at first, as if his fingers didn't know what they should do. She rubbed her thumb over the back of his hand and his softened, letting his fingers intertwine with hers. His hand felt so very warm around her cool digits. His strong hands had always given her comfort, and she felt it now. Slipped her thumb in between their hands and caressed his palm, rough and calloused from years of manual labor.

She waited there, just holding his hand, letting him ease into it. He turned his head to look at her and she could see the millions of questions on his face, in his eyes as they searched hers. Pulling on his hand, she urged him to turn and face her. She grabbed his other hand and held it too as she stared into his eyes. She wanted to soak up this moment, capture it, take a picture that would last in her mind forever. "Come to bed with me," she whispered. Her heart wanted to drink him in one last time.

His lips parted as if to speak, but nothing came out. She could both hear and see the breath catch in his throat as his chest rose but did not fall. As if he were holding his breath, afraid of what might come next. He shook his head, face a mask of confusion before he spoke, "I don't understand."

"Just for tonight, Matt. Come to me." She could feel the corners of her mouth tugging downward, and she forced a smile. "Come with me." She didn't wait for an answer but turned to leave the room, giving his hand another tug to follow. At first, he didn't budge, but then finally followed her across the hall.

Inside, she shut the door behind them, stared up into his face. Lifted a finger and traced the crow's feet outside his eye. Ran her finger and across his lips, as if to shush him before he could protest. Her hand moved to his temple, then up into his hair, stroking the salt and pepper hair back away from his face. The gray grew in faster the last few months, but she didn't care. She thought it made him even more attractive.

Again, she tugged his hand, moving them closer to the bed, and this time he protested. "What are you doing? What are we doing?" He took his hand back from her and placed it still at his side.

Although she hadn't wanted to read him, she ended up doing it anyway. The confusion radiated off him like a furnace, pushing its heat out toward her. The fights were too fresh, the wounds still too open and raw. The journals, their unnerving accuracy of them rattled Matt to the core. The fear in him remained.

"Make love to me?" Her body pressed in close to his, keenly aware of his trepidation. His hand stayed at his side.

"You know I love you, Ravy. And I always want you, but…" he shifted his gaze past her, no longer looking at her.

"Just tonight," she pleaded softly.

He shook his head in the negative while his hand came up to stroke her arm very lightly.

She pulled him closer, and sat on the edge of the bed, him leaning over her. She crawled onto her knees and put her arms around him. "Come hold me then." She looked up at him hopefully. She pulled him into bed, their bed. Clothes still on, above the blankets, he tucked his arm under her. Put her head on his chest and listened to his heartbeat. Every time she spoke, he could hear and feel the beats pick up. She kissed his chin, his bottom lip, his mouth. His breath came out unsteady, shaky, and his body was rigid, unwilling to trust and give over to her. She couldn't blame him. She buried her face in the crook of his neck and breathed him in. Always loved the way he smelled; he never wore any cologne. Natural. Pheromones and sweat mixed, intoxicating her. She wanted to inhale him and hold onto it forever.

She ached to make love to him one last time, but she'd broken him, and nothing could be done about it. She breathed softly on his neck as she kissed him and felt him quiver and sigh. He wrapped his arms around her and pulled her close. There they slept, in each other's arms all night.

In the morning, she woke too early. Anxious to begin her day, her journey. Full knowing what she must leave behind. Rolled out of Matt's arms and gazed out the window as the sun hinted its pinkish glow from behind the clouds and over the horizon. The clouds swept across the sky in a single brushstroke.

A rustle of blankets behind her brought her attention around. "Come back to bed?" Matt's voice was groggy.

"Can't. Into the shower. Then off to work. You know." She gave him a smile. Her body blocked the sun from Matt who was shrouded in sleep and silky morning shadow.

"You can." He lifted the blankets and held them out as a welcome. "Let's start over. Crawl in together. Start right now, Ravynn."

"That's what I'm doing, Matt." She walked across the room to the bathroom. Left the door open, lingered a moment while her eyes drank him in. "I do love you, Matt."

WITH morning still in its early beginning, Ravynn stepped out of the car at the beach. She kicked of her shoes and left them there in the sand, not bothering to toss them into the car. There was no need. Glanced up at the baby-blue sky and thought it looked so fresh, like new beginnings. She breathed in the damp salt air and knew that it should be happening about now. *Off the coast…*

The cool sand trickled around her toes as she pressed them in, deeper, disappearing them into the beach. The sensation pricked goosebumps over her flesh. Ravynn closed her eyes and imagined the earth speaking to her, whispering its secrets. Change is coming. More every day. Faster and faster until it can't be stopped. She wiggled her toes and a vibration came up to tickle at the bottom of her feet. The earth shifted below, agitated. Still undiscernible to the layman, Ravynn used her senses to feel what was coming.

She never even took her camera out of the car- had never meant to. It was all a ruse, an excuse to get her here. The waves were choppy, gray-blue and spirited, dancing and slapping at one another. Not many people on the beach this early, and rarely anyone but surfers in the water anyway. The water this far north was mostly too cold for play.

Off in the distance, several surfers were atop their boards, sitting, waiting for the next decent wave to catch a ride. They dipped and rolled in and out of her sight. Their presence made no difference to Ravynn.

A colony of seagulls took flight at once, frantically darting off the beach and into the air, screeching and moving inland. The sanderlings, moments before doing their skittering dance to avoid the water while searching for food, also darted inland and took flight.

It's coming.

Birds shrieked and cried high in the sky, moving far away from the beach's edge. As if some strange fissure had sprung up from deep within the earth and burst into the sky, rupturing what was normal from what was about to happen, the clouds began to move in an unnatural way, colliding into each other, as if devouring one another. Then, they'd disappeared as if plucked right out of the sky. Ravynn looked to the ocean, and the surfers appeared to be moving farther and farther out to sea without any effort. One of them, though she couldn't tell from this distance if man or woman, began to wave their hands around frantically in the air. Shouting something, but what, Ravynn could only imagine.

Tsunami.

The shore receded, and suddenly everything seemed like it was moving in slow motion. Perhaps it was, Ravynn thought. Everything was changing. From a few feet away, pushing up out of the retreating waterline, a funnel began to spin. First just a foot or so in diameter, is spun and pushed up out of the ocean and toward her. It reached up and out until it rested above the water, floating. Water spun and flowed around in a circular motion, and an opening began to generate from inside it. It grew until it stood about six feet tall, tall enough for a person to walk into. A female figure came clear, standing within the funnel; at first the woman seemed made of water. The shape of her familiar, so strikingly similar to the one that stood within the funnel when she was thirteen. As the figure became more solid, Ravynn could see the woman moved, as if gliding over the floor of the funnel to its edge without lifting a foot. Her dark hair flapped around with the motion of the funnel. The woman's green eyes became clearer to Ravynn as she found herself walking toward the gateway. Though no words were spoken, those eyes called to her, summoning her home. And this time, nothing would stand in her way.

As she walked across the damp sand, where moments before there had been water that would have been to her waist, she could hear the screams around her as the realization hit the others on the beach. But they were muted, as if she were already gone. In between worlds, Ravynn stepped up onto the water funnel's edge. She looked down and saw what didn't make sense; she was standing solidly on a spinning cycle of water.

The woman reached out a hand to her, and she took it, stepping away from the beach, away from the life she knew, and into the funnel.

1

2022 RAY BRADLEY

The world wasn't what it used to be, but Ray wasn't sure what it had become. He anxiously stared out the window into the inky night. Clouds blotted out any chance of stars and pressed the horizon down closer to the earth. A bolt of lightning danced across the sky, momentarily lighting up the dim bathroom that provided him no reprieve from the storms outside or within.

"One one-thousand, two one-thousand…" he whispered.

Thunder banged and crackled, shaking the floorboards beneath his feet. He looked up to the skylight as the rain pelted down harder. The sound of rain, usually a comfort, grated on him like fingernails on a chalkboard. Ray tried to recall, but he was certain this was *the rainiest summer he'd ever seen. Northern California summers never looked this way.*

Ray was pretty sure he was going crazy. The alternative was too strange to believe. He'd had almost a full year to sort his grief out, yet the circumstances of his sister Ravynn's death haunted him. He couldn't let her go.

The rain slammed down on the skylight above, making him flinch with each big drop. His nerves were frazzled, on the edge. He knew, when he did finally drift off to sleep, she'd be there. She was almost always there. The dreams grew more frequent and realistic by the day; sometimes he wasn't sure he was asleep when he dreamed them. The lines blurred more every day. Harder and harder it became to keep reality straight, so much that he was sure his dreams of Ravynn were a type of reality.

If the dreams were the only strange things that happened lately, he might be able to cope, might be able to find some peace, some sleep. Over the past year since Ravynn's death, so much had happened; she was dead and gone, after all. Yet why did she haunt him? Why was she always in his dreams, what was she trying to tell him? Not only Ravynn plagued his mind, but the ever-increasing natural disasters that popped up everywhere. Ray wondered if it had always been that way, or if he only started paying attention after that disastrous tsunami.

He blinked, and let his eyes stay closed a moment. A quick reprieve, although his mind wouldn't let him rest. His hectic brain scrolled through the news stories he'd read and heard about over the past year. A few months back, there'd been a limnic eruption near Rwanda, causing hundreds of people and animals to suffocate as dissolved carbon monoxide suddenly erupted from deep within the lake.

He'd never known of such a thing before.

As he glanced out the window, the wind changed direction, making the rain come down sideways. The trees, heavy with leaves, shook and swayed. He couldn't hide in the bathroom forever. At some point, he'd have to go back to the bedroom, to the bed where his wife still hopefully was sleeping and face another night of unrest. But not yet. The idea of climbing back into that bed gave him anything but calm.

His brain pulled another file, reminding him of the meteorite that hit in Argentina a month ago. And the volcano that erupted two weeks ago. Since the beginning of time, these things had been happening, though. Mother Nature's way. Nothing strange about any of it.

He shook his head, disagreeing. From the window to the sink he moved, turning on the faucet. The water poured out to fill the basin and hypnotized him. Glancing up, he caught his reflection in the mirror; a barely recognizable man stared back at him. At thirty-five, he looked more like fifty. This past year had aged him so. Still staring in the mirror, he wondered when that light sprinkling of gray took over and spread, like a plague through the rest of his hair. Eyes, bloodshot and tired, dark circles under them even darker than yesterday. *I look a lot like Dad.*

Sleep was no longer his friend. Fearing it nightly, he rarely found true rest anymore. The dream was always there, waiting. The water, the devastation, Ravynn. He lived in fear that the next night, the next dream, would finally push him over the edge. Some nights, he was right on that edge, balanced precariously. Problem was, he wasn't sure what would happen there. Would he fall? Might he jump? Or would he cross some line he might not be able to come back from? Possibly end up like his dad.

"I've got to get some real rest," he whispered to his reflection, before looking away into the water filled sink. He startled to his sister Ravynn staring back at him. He backed up so far and so quick he slammed his back into the closed bathroom door. "No, no, no."

Rubbing his eyes, he tried to free himself from what he just saw. He took a deep, shaky breath before summoning the courage to move forward, to look back into the water. Hands on the rim of the sink, he braced himself.

"Ravynn," he whispered. His voice was raw, full of a year's worth of pain and loss.

Her image reappeared faintly, rippling through the water. She smiled at him. "Hello, Ray." Her smile faded as quickly as it appeared.

"No," was all he could manage as he shook his head back and forth. "No. This is crazy."

"Listen, Ray. I don't have much time. I am here. You are not crazy." There was a determination in her voice that forced him to listen; a tone he'd known very well since they were kids.

"But how?"

Another flash of lightning streaked into the room, giving Ravynn's visage a ghostly glow. A boom of thunder pulsed through the air, shaking the floor. Ravynn's image faded, jostled by the storm, then reappeared.

"I can't explain now," Ravynn continued. "It's all so much bigger than that."

Ray was frantic. "Bigger than what?"

"The world is falling down, Ray---"

A knock on the other side of the bathroom door interrupted the conversation. "Ray, you okay? Did you call me?" Feet shuffled by the door. It was Elena, Ray's wife.

Another clap of thunder rumbled through the house. The vibration pulsed through his body, or maybe, he thought, it was the chilly sense of foreboding in seeing his dead sister. He turned to reach for the door, to make sure it was locked.

Elena asked again, "Ray?"

The lock was on, much to his relief. He sighed and leaned into the door, body pressing against it. "Give me a few minutes, please." The plea in his voice sounded too desperate, even to his own ears.

"Okay," Elena replied.

Ray leaned his head against the door, waiting for footsteps move away. When he was sure she was gone, he went back to investigate the basin. Nothing. Nothing but water.

"I'm definitely losing my mind," he said to the sink. He reached in and splashed chilly water on his face, hoping to wash it all away.

ON the other side of the bathroom door, Elena tried to talk herself out of her concern. It hadn't always been this way.

She used to be so laid back, stress free, carefree. Until Ray's twin Ravynn died. Within an instant she went from being just a wife to being a mother to Ravynn's eight-year-old daughter Amelia. Not only had she become Amelia's caregiver, but somehow, Ray's too. Now she kept waiting for the other shoe to drop, adrenals in a constant squeeze.

Not that marriage should be easy. It never was, but Elena had never bargained for this. A woman can only be pushed so far, can't she? And pushed away. As Ray's mental state worsened each day, Elena feared the rift between them would only grow larger and harder to mend. Sleep had been a problem for him that had worsened over the year, but now he was being secretive, hiding in a way. How many times had she heard him talking when no one was around lately? Was he going to end up like his father?

She backed away from the door as fears raced through her mind. So much more than grief, so much more than nightmares. He was talking to her. *Ravynn.*

Elena shuffled to the bedroom window and pushed the curtains aside. The backyard had become a pool, unable to soak up the heavy rains. The picnic table where they used to host so many BBQs had a puddle of water streaming underneath. Amelia's swing-set had a swing rocking eerily back and forth with the wind, as if giving a ride to an invisible guest. Ray forgot to put the cover on the grill, again. She stared at the mess outside and couldn't help but compare it to the mess inside their lives.

The chill deep inside her had burrowed its way in, like a vole digging down inside the earth, making a home. Over the past year, it had worked its way in, tunneling through her mind and body, taking up permanent residence. Ever since Ravynn died. Elena knew he talked to her, his dead sister. Like her ghost wouldn't leave him alone. Not a ghost. He was losing his mind, Elena was certain.

A double flash of lightning chased her away from the window, pulling her from her thoughts. Thunder growled behind, loud and rolling, like an angry dog giving warning to a stranger.

Elena headed for the bedroom door, intent on checking in on Amelia, afraid the storm might have frightened her. She glanced at the clock by the bedside. 2:18 a.m. She sighed, knowing yet another night was passing without being able to sleep all the way through. She wondered how long she could maintain this level of sleeplessness before it started to affect her daily routines. Down the hall, she pushed the child's partially opened door further and stuck her head inside. The glow coming off the bunny-shaped nightlight revealed Amelia with her eyes closed. She waited a moment longer to make sure the child was asleep, and Amelia rolled to face away from the door. The little girl let out a sigh and tucked her head into the blankets.

Satisfied, Elena backed into the hallway in tiny steps, careful to pull the door back to its prior position. A mumble escaped the child. *Something about the sun?* The words themselves meant nothing to Elena, yet they stuck with her as she headed back to her bedroom.

Back in their own bedroom, as she waited for Ray to come out of the bathroom, Elena climbed into bed, grabbed her glasses and her book, *The Last Man* off the nightstand. She flipped through the pages, unable to focus on the words, her eyes flitting over them again and again, forcing her to go back several times to re-read a passage.

The words didn't have a chance to soak in as the bathroom door opened and Ray trudged through into the bedroom. Elena tried not to look at him, but she couldn't help it. She dropped her book into her lap, tilted her head down and shifted her eyes up over the top of her glasses. Held her breath and waited for him to speak first.

Eluding eye contact, he said, "I'm beat." The bed gave to his weight as he sat on his side. "I think I'll sleep well, soon as my head hits the pillow."

Elena tried to bite her tongue but couldn't manage. "Who were you talking to in there, Ray?" She was pretty sure he'd been talking to Ravynn. But what information would he offer her? She wasn't quite sure she was ready to challenge him.

He shrugged, finally facing her way. "Must have been the storm." As he said it, he bit the inside of his cheek, like he was trying to hold the truth from sneaking out. Or like he had to chew on the answer a bit, roll it around in his mouth before finally spitting it out.

What a crappy poker player he'd make, Elena thought. What a tell. *Always does that when he lies.*

"Uh-huh," she said instead.

He leaned in and kissed her on the cheek. "Love you." He flopped his head down on the pillow and said no more. Within seconds, he was asleep. Elena hoped and prayed it would stay that way, through the whole night.

RAY stands utterly still, not breathing, hypnotized by the foreboding, dark gray-blue mountainous mass in front of him. The sand pulls gently around his feet, like some master puppeteer is trying to pull the ground below him with invisible strings. The wet saltiness looms in the air above him. He knows something isn't right, but his brain can't process it all. The eerie silence is gone, chased away by the coming onslaught. His eardrums pulse with the deafening roar of what he now recognizes as a wall of water barreling toward him. His heart slams, too fast to count the beats, too fast to be safe. A sickness overcomes him as his stomach seizes. He's sure he will vomit. At the same time, a warm stream slides down his pant leg.

All of it feels like minutes, long dragged out miserable minutes. Like he has all the time in the world to decide what to do. That's not the reality of it, only his mind's interpretation of that horrendous event. A few blinks of the eye and the disaster is upon him.

His arms come up, a hopeless attempt to shield himself, protect his face. The weight of the water hits him, the cold harsh force striking him, and he jumps awake.

He bolted; body pulled upward to sitting. There he was, once again, sitting in a pool of sweat, next to his terrified wife.

"The dream again?" She always knew. He didn't need to say. He couldn't answer anyway; his voice was stuck in his throat. He nodded instead.

"Let me get you some water, honey," she murmured.

Sliding into her slippers, she took off for the kitchen. She returned, her feet a soft, quick shuffle across the bedroom's hardwood floor. She handed the glass of water to Ray and sat beside him with a towel, wiping sweat from his brow.

"That's the second time this week, Ray." Her voice was laced with worry.

He nodded again, eyes unblinking, as he tipped the glass back and drained it dry in two long gulps. Thunder ripped through the silence, causing Ray to shudder.

Elena smoothed her hand over his back trying to soothe him; but they both knew, when the dreams came, there was nothing he found soothing. His mind still gripped the trauma of the dream, as his body tried to adjust to being awake.

Yet Elena sat very still, very patiently, rubbing his back in calm, soft strokes, likely more to ease herself than him. He faced her, and her lips pursed. His voice came out, crackled, "I'm here."

She didn't miss a beat. "I'm right here with you, honey."

"I'm sorry," he whispered.

She cooed, "Don't apologize, it's not your fault. Shh."

Ray put his hands over his eyes, and dragged them down over his face deliberately, causing his entire countenance to pull downward. He breathed in and let out a ragged sigh. Raised his hands up to his head, running them forcefully through his sweat soaked hair. Ashamed, he forced himself to look at his wife.

She put her hands over his. Took his shaking hands out of his hair and set them in hers upon her lap. She stroked them over and over, saying, "It's okay, honey. It was just a dream. Just a dream. You're here now. You're with me. You're safe. We're safe. Say the words with me, come on, Raymond."

They spoke the words together, like a mantra, the words so well-rehearsed flowed out of both in unison, "It was just a dream. I'm here. I'm safe. It was just a dream."

2

At 6:00 a.m. the alarm went off with a torturous blast, shattering the last few minutes of restless sleep this morning allowed. Ray pulled the pillow over his head and smushed it against his ears, trying to drown out the sound of the man's voice on the radio:

--- another day of storms ahead. Yesterday's deluge left parts of the normally sunny Northern California coast in miserable conditions for the evening drive home. Expect similar conditions today, as this massive storm system shows no sign of slowing---

When Ray failed to smother the sound, he reached his hand out and missed on the first attempt, his arm flailing wildly. Letting out a groan, he swung again, this time connecting with the ill-fated alarm clock. Not only did he hit the button, but sent the clock flying off the nightstand. Mildly satisfied with the result, Ray turned back over and tried to go back to sleep. This time, the interruption was much gentler.

"Un-cle Ra-ay," a small voice sing-song whispered in his ear. "Uncle Un-cle Ra-ay. Time to get u-up. Break-fast. We got eggies and bacon and me-lons."

Ray reluctantly turned toward the voice in his ear,

squeezing his eyes shut tight before prying them open to face the day and his niece Amelia. Her face beamed with joy, and that was all Ray needed.

"I'm up, little one. I'm up. I'll meet you there is a sec."

Satisfied, Amelia jumped off the bed and raced out of the room.

Ray sat up and ran his hands through his hair. Shook the covers off and stepped out of bed clumsily, his foot a tangle in the sheets. He plodded across the hardwood floor to the bathroom and right to the sink. Brushing his teeth, he looked up to assess the evidence of last night's lack of sleep in the mirror. Another night, another dream. He mouthed the words so softly to himself in the mirror, "Okay, let's do this day thing. Ravynn is gone."

Faintly, a whisper stole into the room, the words indiscernible, so soft he couldn't be sure he heard them at all. *"Must have been the rain,"* he told himself.

Shutting the water off, he glanced over his shoulder. Someone was standing beside him; or so he thought. The air trickled across his skin, inviting the gooseflesh. Finding no one there, he headed down the hall to his two very real ladies waiting in the kitchen.

"Good morning," Elena said. Her eyes were full of concern, as if holding so many questions.

Wearing a stoic smile, he walked over and placed a soft kiss on her cheek. Knowing at least one of the questions in her eyes, he said, "I'm good. Just need some coffee."

Elena grinned, and Ray was relieved she let it go with that.

"Extra shot of espresso in yours this morning?"

He nodded. "You know me too well."

"Auntie E said that I don't have school today but you both do. That's not fair," Amelia crossed her arms and pouted.

Ray laughed, but it quickly faded when he realized how serious his niece was. "Well, you are finished for the year. Preschool is a little different than middle school. Auntie Elena and I still have a few days left. But you get to go spend the whole day with Auntie Becky and your cousin Carrie. That's probably better."

Elena chimed in, "I hear Auntie Becky is taking you to the museum today."

"The one with the dinosaurs?"

"Yes, that one exactly." Elena said.

Amelia shrugged, slowly giving in. "I guess, if I can't go to school, the museum is ok."

"Good, I am glad it's ok," Ray teased. "How about finishing that yummy breakfast that you woke me up for?"

"Uh, ok Uncle Ray. I like the green melons the best."

"I gotta finish getting ready for work. You two enjoy the rest of your breakfast. Time to put my face on," Elena said, snickering.

"You're silly, Auntie E. Your face *is* on," Amelia replied through a burst of giggles. This little joke got her every time. A happy little girl, especially considering all that she'd been through. Ray wished he could say the same for himself.

The first few months after Ravynn died were the worst. Amelia cried every night. The sound of it broke their hearts, especially Ray's already fragile one. Elena had been a saint in those months. Ray wasn't sure how she did pulled it off. Scuttling back and forth between their bedroom and Amelia's, consoling both Ray and the little girl. But that was ages ago. Elena eventually worked Amelia into a nice bedtime habit and things were much better for her. Too bad Ray couldn't conquer his nighttime fears.

"When you are all done with school, will *you* take me to the park? And to the store? And maybe the zoo? And oh, oh how about the beach? I love the beach!" Amelia played with her breakfast, making a piece of bacon dance on her plate.

"No, not the beach," Ray replied sternly.

Amelia dropped her dancing pieces of bacon and stared at Ray with incredulity.

Anyplace but the beach, Ray thought. A chill ran up the back of his neck. He hadn't meant for it to be so harsh, and he softened. "We can definitely go to the park, and the zoo. Other fun places too. Promise." Changing the subject, he asked his niece, "Did you hear the storm last night? All that thunder? That was something, huh? We definitely don't get much of that excitement around here."

Amelia sat, eyes wide, listening to him speak, as if he were telling her a fairytale, and not the real events of last evening. "I didn't hear anything, I was sleeping." She popped the last bite of melon into her mouth. "I saw Mommy."

Ray's toast got stuck in his throat. He coughed, hoping not to choke. Clearing his throat, he asked, "You mean, you had a dream about your Mom?"

Elena's voice interrupted from down the hall, "Come on little bunny, hop hop. Auntie Becky is gonna be here in ten minutes!"

Amelia jumped out of her seat and ran screeching down the hall, "I need my shoes! What shoes can I wear?"

"It's raining outside and there are puddles everywhere, so its rain-boots today," Elena answered.

"I wanna wear my fuzzy boots! I never get to wear them!"

"Not today. Rain-boots on. Safe and warm and dry."

"But fuzzy boots will look better! I wanna wear them. Pleeeeease?"

Ray cringed at the sound of his niece's begging. Her shrill tone jangled his nerves and reminded him how little sleep he got. If a little girl could rattle him this much, the rest of his day could prove a bigger challenge. He was losing concentration and patience not only at home, but at school as well. It was just a matter of time before it became evident. Realizing the time, Ray hastened to the bathroom to shower and get ready for work, and to put on a face of his own, leaving the girls to debate the appropriateness of shoes.

STEPPING outside to the car was a challenge. Immediately, they got pelted by a steady stream of large raindrops. "Watch your step!" Elena yelled, but not in time.

Ray looked down a little too late as his foot smacked down in the middle of a giant puddle. The cold water ran into his shoe and soaked his sock.

Amelia giggled, pointing at Ray, as he stood in the puddle, defeated.

"I'll be right back, quick change. I can't go to work like this." He didn't wait for an answer.

Back outside, he waved goodbye to Amelia as Elena finished getting her buckled safely inside Becky's car. Elena shut the door, waited for the car to pull away, then hurried to her own car and jumped in the driver's side. Ray hustled to the passenger side, careful this time to avoid the puddles.

"Ray." Elena said his name in a way that sounded like a painful question. Her tone was like pinpricks on his skin. "They are getting worse, aren't they? The dreams."

Ray paused, listening to the sound of the rain beating against the car, and the wipers on full speed. Something about the combination made him both anxious and sleepy at the same time. He replied, "Yes and no honey. I mean, do I sleep well? No. I think the storm last night made things worse, though."

"But I mean," she hesitated, licking her lips, "you have them a lot. And it's been a year since she passed. Maybe you could go back and talk to Dr. Sheffield again."

"Honey, I know you are trying to help, but Dr. Sheffield didn't help me. From trying to treat me for anxiety and depression, none of his meds worked. You know it made me feel worse."

"Well, maybe you could try someone else? It's getting bad, Ray."

He knew what she was dancing around and hoped she wouldn't say it. Maybe Dr. Sheffield missed the diagnosis. Maybe what he thought was grief was so much more. Maybe the old apple didn't fall far from the tree. Maybe Ray would end up like his dad. Just like his schizophrenic dad who talked to Jesus and trees. Sure, his dad's illness was treatable. He'd done really well once they found the right dose of medication, but up to that point, he'd been a mess.

They'd originally missed Ray's dad's diagnosis as well. Soon after Ray and Ravynn were born, he seemed stressed out all the time. What first-time father wouldn't be with two brand new babies? But then he became detached. From stress to detachment in the blink of an eye. Of course, Ray's mom thought that was how he dealt with the stress at first. Almost like meditating, taking himself out of a room or situation without leaving the room.

Even his calm conversations out in the backyard with the trees didn't necessarily phase Mrs. Bradley right off. Not until it became that there were full-on conversations happening- and that the trees were 'speaking back' to him.

After getting help and medications, his mental health improved, for a while. Until he stopped taking the meds, claiming they dulled him. Made him dull and not feel. How many times had dad stopped his meds only to go back to talking to things and people that weren't there?

How many times had he said he could see an angel hovering over his wife and daughter's shoulders?

Ray shook the thoughts away. "I think once we wrap things up at school in a few days things will settle down. I'll sleep in a bit to catch up. I'll start running more like I used to. You'll see. I think things will shift this summer."

"I really think there's more to it than exercising. You need to talk to someone. Maybe you can try some different medications. Maybe even a more holistic approach."

He wished she would stop. How many nights had he spent looking up his 'symptoms' on WebMD while she lay asleep? How many nights did he play over scenes with his father, on and off his own medications? "Maybe. But I think I can get this under control myself. Really."

"But I hear you talking…" she said this softly, Ray thought, like a child expecting to be scolded, "talking to her. Ray—"

He cut her off. "I don't know what you think will make it all go away. I've tried the psychologist. And his drugs. I've tried acupuncture, yoga, and meditation. Nothing did one damn bit of good, Elena."

"There must be something. If not Dr. Sheffield, then someone. You need to talk to someone about this… someone other than Ravynn. Don't lie to me."

"Like I said, I will sort this out when school's done. It's nothing but grief. Dr Sheffield knew it wasn't schizophrenia. He knew. So do I. I'm not my dad."

"That was then. Maybe things have changed. Maybe he missed something. I'm not saying you're your dad, but… I think you just need some help, Ray."

"Maybe nothing. Elena, please drop it and focus on the road, please."

Her face grew stern. "Maybe I coddle you too much. Give you too much leeway. Too afraid I'll be the one to push too hard and—"

"You think I am crazy?" he asked, balling his hands into fists by his side.

"I never said that."

"And yet…" he trailed off. He took a deep breath before responding, "I've got this, Elena. I'll work it out, myself, my way."

"What a typical man thing to say, Ray. 'I can fix it. I don't need help. I don't have to stop for directions.' You can't do everything yourself."

"I'll be fine."

"You are not fine. I am not fine. Thank goodness Amelia is fine! Will you wait until it affects her before you do something?"

"Really, we need to drop it Elena."

"It's not just you, Ray, you have a family now."

His voice softened. "I know that. I love you both. I'm grieving, my own way. There's no time limit on grief, Elena."

To Ray's surprise, she let it go. For now, at least. But how much longer could he pull it off for?

TWO more days to go; Ray could get through them. With sweaty palms and heavy eyelids, he somehow maintained enough focus to get the kids through exams, and himself through the day. Almost.

Before heading home, an impromptu meeting with the principal was called. An *unplanned* meeting. Even as a teacher, Ray knew it was never good to be summoned to the principal's office.

On the way to the office, he swung by Elena's classroom. Her door was open, and she sat at her desk, furiously correcting tests. For a moment, he thought about leaving her alone, but realized it would be foolish in the end. At some point she'd notice the time and that he hadn't shown up and go looking for him. He regretted having to interrupt her. That, and he didn't want to be quizzed about the meeting when he himself had no information to give; at least nothing concrete.

"Knock, knock," he said softly.

Elena lifted her head at the sound of his voice and pushed a stray piece of hair away from her face. "Sorry, I got swept up. I thought I'd get a head start and grade some work before you got here. You ready now?"

Ray hesitated, then did his best to deliver his words as nonchalantly as possible. "Gotta swing by Cynthia's office first. Just wanted to poke my head in and give you the heads up. Why don't you just keep grading while I finish up?"

"I didn't know you had a meeting scheduled." It sounded to Ray more a question than a statement.

That was what he wanted to avoid. Concern. "It won't take long. Be back soon."

Elena absently sent her pen to her mouth where she began chewing wildly on the top of it.

Ray cut off any chance for questions by turning quickly and heading out the door, leaving Elena with both her thoughts and her pen to chew on.

HE pushed the door to the principal's office open, and to his surprise, not only Principal Cynthia O'Conner, but also Assistant Principal David Finch and guidance counselor Jessica Worthington were all seated, waiting for him. He stood, frozen in the doorway, still holding the door open, as if ready to make his escape.

Cynthia cut through the silence, gesturing to an empty chair. "Ray, thanks for coming."

Still holding the door, Ray asked, "Did I miss something? I didn't know this was a group meeting."

"Have a seat, Ray," David said sternly.

"If it's all the same to you, I think I will stand, thanks." His heart raced. Had he said something, done something? He knew he should be sleeping better. Maybe they'd seen the circles under his eyes lately. Ray racked his brain, trying to guess what this was coming to.

"Then shut the door, at least." David leaned back in his chair and crossed his legs. He raised one arm to rest on his hip like a parent about to dole out punishment and the other elbow he put on the arm of the chair, bringing his hand up to rest his chin on.

Condescending prick, he thought, seething.

Cynthia was seated behind her desk, while both David and Jessica sat to her right, leaving one lonely, empty chair to her left for Ray. The positioning of the seats unsettled Ray. This wasn't going to be any ordinary meeting. Looked more like an intervention. He stood just inside the closed door, facing Cynthia with his arms folded. His posture became rigid, guarded. "What's this all about?"

Cynthia made a weak attempt a smile. "Ray, listen. We've had this discussion before. When your sister first passed. About your work. I know...we all know," she made an inclusive gesture with an open hand to the two seated on her right.

34

David corrected her, adding, "We've had this discussion several times. Over the past year."

Cynthia held up her hand, and David stopped.

"We know that losing your sister was a terrible blow," Cynthia offered. We sympathize, we really do."

"But..." Ray interjected. "There's a big fat BUT coming." *And it's a small one compared to the one attached to you,* he mused to himself.

"It's not like that, Ray. We have to look out for the best interests of these kids. It's not an easy decision. You know how much we all love you here. You have been an amazing teacher, a fantastic asset here at Walter Mathison Middle School for quite some time now."

"Are you firing me right now?"

"No, no, nothing that drastic," Cynthia insisted. As I have said numerous times, we value you and everything you've given this school. But we all believe you perhaps need to take some time off." As she said it, she looked to both David and Jessica sitting to her right. They nodded in agreement.

Ray thought they acted a lot like good little puppies.

She continued, "To re-focus. Take this summer break to think things over. To heal, take time for yourself. That lovely niece of yours. Be with your family. Before this next school year starts back up, let's revisit this conversation. We need to make sure your focus in the fall will be one hundred percent on the education of these children. If that's something that you can't do, well then we need to find an alternative."

"An alternative?" His pulse quickened again. The room grew hotter and suddenly smaller. He tried not to let his disdain show through. He looked around as they all stared at him. As if waiting for him to break. All because he lost his sister. Yet, here they were, being blatantly insensitive.

David elaborated, pointing directly at Ray, "Yes, an alternative. As in if you can't get yourself together over the summer, it would be best if you do not come back in the fall. The alternative would be to hire someone in your place."

"I can't believe this," Ray said, shaking his head.

"Really, you can't?" David raised his eyebrows. "This is coming as a surprise to you? Come on, Ray. You haven't been yourself this entire school year. You lack focus. You lack enthusiasm. You look like you don't even sleep. You 'drift off' more and more these days, spacing out in your classroom. Did you notice your students' grades have been markedly down since last year? Did you think this was just a coincidence? You have to know there is a direct correlation." He looked to Jessica for agreement, and she dutifully nodded her head. "You are not present. We need someone who is. Nothing personal. It's in the best interest of the students."

Ray bit his lip hard. After all, they weren't wrong. Maybe being a bit harsh, but Ray was slipping. "I'd like to believe that it's not personal, but somehow everything coming out of your mouth David, seems personal." It was true. David used to be one of Ray's best friends. Until a woman came in between them. Elena, to be precise. Since the early days of college, they'd competed for Elena's affections. Ray had won, but ever since then every dealing with David was like putting two roosters in a cage together, full on cockfight.

"Okay, enough. We are getting way off track," Jessica attempted to reel it back in before the words got too ugly. "It's true, Ray. These kids are suffering because of your difficulties. I have had it come up more than once in meetings with the students and parents."

Cynthia folded her hands on her desk and leaned forward, clearing her throat before speaking. "The decision has already been made, Ray. I am sorry. I am not a fan of ultimatums, but we are down to the wire here. We need you to be the teacher you were, and if you can't... well, we'll talk again. Just take care of yourself."

"I thought I was coming here for a discussion, not a directed verdict. Not a big fan of the ambush." Shaking his head in disgust, Ray momentarily imagined a scene where he stormed out, slamming the door behind him so hard it rattled the door frame. Instead, he bit his lip and nodded, turned and exited the room with a cool he didn't really have. He walked straight down the hallway to Elena's empty classroom, where she was waiting.

"So, what kind of meeting was this?" Elena asked.

"Not a good one. Had their pitchforks and torches and everything."

"I thought it was only a meeting with Cynthia?" She dropped her pen and looked straight at him; the questions and doubts painfully evident in her eyes.

"So did I. But I walked in to her, David, and Jessica, all waiting to attack."

"Wanna talk about it?" She sucked in her bottom lip and bit at it.

"Not now, I'm too pissed. Can we get outta here?"

"That's a shock." Elena grumbled. "You don't wanna talk about it, huh? You don't wanna talk about much these days, do you, Ray?"

Ray gnashed his teeth together to keep from losing his temper. He tried to remind himself that it wasn't *her* fault. She wasn't the enemy, and she didn't deserve to be treated like one. He took a deep calming breath before continuing. "We'll talk later about it, I promise."

Elena shook her head at him, packing up all her papers and well-chewed pens and not saying another word.

3

Ray shifted his gaze out the window. Even though Elena sat right next to him driving, even though he could've reached out and touched her, he felt miles apart.

The silence was palpable. On that long fifteen-minute ride home, he sat and stewed, part of that old Irish anger welling inside him. Targeted and betrayed. How could they have done this to him? Threaten his job? See a man going through a hard time and that was what they did.

A tiny little Ray-brain voice snuck in as they pulled into the driveway. It's whispered to him, *"You know they're right."*

He couldn't accept that. Ravynn was his sister. His twin. Shared so much. Shared their mother's womb. The same eyes, same nose, the same...

Ray remembered hearing his late father's voice, "I swear sometimes, you two share the same brain. I ask one of you a question and you both give me the same answer in unison." Ray's dad would shake his head at them as he said it, but more out of bewilderment than anything else. And, of course, the two of them would answer, at the exact same time, "cool."

The idea had always made him happy; like somehow he and

his sister had superpowers, like that cartoon they loved in the 80's: *Wonder Twin* powers, activate. Form of, a pail of water...Water.

Ravynn.

"Ray, did you hear me? Ray?" Elena's voice erased the childhood memories and drew him back to the present. "Ray, I was talking to you. Did you hear anything I said?"

"Yeah, sorry. Just thinking." But he hadn't heard her. Wasn't really aware she'd been speaking.

"Uh-huh." He hadn't been listening, but he wasn't dumb. The irritation in her voice was easy to read. As much as it frustrated him to do it to her, all he wanted was an escape. For a bit. To be alone, not have someone question him, doubt him, look at him like he was about to break.

"Think I'm gonna head to the gym for a bit, run it off, ya know?"

Pursing her lips, Elena huffed, "Not really. I can't know until you tell me."

"I will tell you. But I gotta go blow off some steam. We'll talk about it later. Promise. I don't have the words right now, honey."

THE car sat in park in the driveway. Elena put her hands firmly on the wheel, eyes staring hard forward. Never once did she look his way.

She opened and closed her hands on the steering wheel, her grip making a little squeaking sound on the leather. "Fine. I'll pick Amelia up and we'll go shop for dinner." Still looking forward, she added, "I should go and get her now, I think." She nodded. "Amelia's going to be sad we can't grill out tonight.

Dumbfounded, Ray responded, "Why wouldn't we grill out?"

Elena turned to face Ray, the irritation and befuddlement in her eyes obvious. It made Ray realized he liked it better when she was staring at nothing. Elena answered his question, "Because of all the storms. Hadn't you noticed?" Dramatically, she nodded her head towards the outside, and glanced back to him. "You know. The rain? Soaking wet yard? Puddles everywhere?" She leaned forward, her hand in front of her in a sweeping motion, calling attention to the soggy day that had begun its wind-down. No evidence of a sun poking through the heavy clouds. The light was dimming too early for this time of day; a permanent gray splashed across the caliginous sky.

"Oh, it'll be fine. The thunder and lightning are long past. I'll grill out, and we'll eat inside. No big deal." He grabbed his satchel and hopped out of the car.

BEFORE he slammed the door, a gust of wind blew rain into the car. The cold slapped Elena in the face as Ray scurried into the house like a rat trying to avoid being drowned. For several minutes, Elena sat in the car, gripping and ungripping the wheel, using it like a stress-ball.

She finally let go of the steering wheel and hit the call button on the Bluetooth. She knew better than to call him, knew the trouble it could stir up, but her desire to know what happened in the meeting took precedence over all else. She knew *he*, unlike Ray, would tell her. "Call David Finch." She put the car in reverse and backed out of the driveway, heading to Becky's. Her mind on other things, she remotely made the familiar drive to her sister's.

The phone rang. Elena panicked, wondering when the last time she called David was. Would he even take her call?

She was about to hang up when a familiar voice came on the line. "Hello, this is David."

Elena paused, unable to speak. Why was she calling him? Because She had to know what happened and he'd tell her. He didn't have ill feelings towards her, after all. Just Ray. Yes, their history had been colorful to say the least, but in the end, they were friends, weren't they? Elena talked herself into that justification.

The voice repeated, "Hello. Elena?"

"Hi, yeah, it's Elena." Her voice was unsure, mousy, even to herself. She wished she could have a take-back and answer more cheerily.

The car splashed through a large puddle in the road. The car hydroplaned, careening, gliding, and she eased off the gas pedal, regaining control. She flipped on the windshield wipers to clear the mess that splashed up.

"Elena, is everything okay?"

"Yes." Again, her voice above a whisper. She cleared her throat and continued, "I am okay. Yes. I just... well, I just wanted to call you... to ask you... I dunno—"

"About the meeting. With Ray?"

"Well, yes."

"What did he tell you?" He was sincere, caring.

Elena tried to hold back the tear that crept from the corner of her eye. If one fell, she'd never be able to stop the rest of them. Deep breath. "Nothing. Not yet. He's pretty upset. And I'm worried. Maybe I shouldn't have called." Her fingernails dug into her palms, wrapped tightly around the wheel. She imagined the tiny crescent marks forming in her skin as she pressed harder.

His voice had become gentle. "No, it's okay. I'm sorry you're so worried. To be honest, we're worried too. Do you want to meet for some coffee? Talk in person?"

"Oh, I can't. I'm on the way to pick up Amelia. Thanks, though. It is okay I called you, right?" She doubted it as soon as she asked.

"Of course." The calm in his voice suggested it was good that she called him. That he might help her understand what was happening. If only she could harness some of that calm for herself.

She lifted her left hand from the wheel and shoved her middle finger to her mouth. The terrible nervous habit took her over; chewing on her nail, tearing away at each new hangnail she created. Finger still to her mouth, she mumbled, "The meeting was bad, wasn't it? I just need to know what happened."

"Are you gnawing on your nails right now?"

She let out a nervous chuckle. "Yeah, how could you tell?"

"I remember when we were in college, and you were studying for a big test. You'd be so nervous you'd chew off all your fingernails. You never knew you were doing it then, either. You'd talk while your fingers were still in your mouth. All mumbly-like. Remember what I'd call you?"

"Stubby." That gained a giggle from both and eased things for her. In an instant, she was flung back to a time when she and David were dating in college. When the biggest worries on her mind were exams and passing grades. What she'd give now for such small worries.

"So, listen Stubby. You can call me anytime. Don't worry, okay?"

Elena pulled her hand away from her mouth to speak. "Okay, thanks. Can you give me the abridged version?"

"We're concerned. And yes, Ray lost his sister. Everyone's aware of that. And we have all been kind and considerate and empathetic, but… I don't want to sound cold, but it's been a year, Elena. And he doesn't seem like he's grieved and moved on. At all."

An audible sigh escaped her.

David persisted, "This isn't just about him. It's about those kids. His grief is affecting the kids, their schoolwork."

"I know. But he does care about those kids. He loves his job." Her words did little to convince even herself. He needed help. It was only getting worse.

That's not the point, Elena. I wish that was all that mattered." There was a long pause, and Elena wasn't sure what to say. If there was anything she could say. David wasn't wrong.

"So do I."

"Cynthia told him basically to get his head together this

summer. If he can't do that, then perhaps we need to find someone more focused for the new year."

Surprised, Elena choked the words out, "David, you can't!"

"This isn't up to only me. It's gone too far, Elena. I'm sorry. He needs to talk to someone. He needs to move past all this. I can't tell you how many times I've caught him sort of spacing out. I don't know if he's sleeping with his eyes open, thinking of his sister, whatever. But he just fades out."

A defensive urge came over her. She wanted to protest, even, but it was futile. Heat rose in her face. "He doesn't sleep well," was all she could say. How many times had she seen Ray doing that? How many times had she wondered recently where Ray was when he stared off into nowhere? Elena wrung her hands around the steering wheel.

"I can see that. He looks like crap."

Another tear built in her eye, and this time she couldn't fight it back, as another one snuck in behind and pushed it out, streaming down her cheek. The rain outside had finally tapered off, but the rain of tears falling down her face grew more intense by the second. She wiped the back of her hand across her eyes, smearing her eyeliner.

"Are you still there?"

"Yeah, I have to go, David. I am almost to my sister's. Thanks for talking to me. Thanks."

"Anytime. I mean that. Call me, anytime."

"Okay. Bye David."

"Take care, Stubby."

As she disconnected, a pair of seagulls came into view, headed straight toward her car. She had enough forethought to remember her dad's voice in her ear, "*Never swerve for the little creatures on the road. If you hit them, they'll probably die, but if you swerve and hit someone in oncoming traffic, you might die. Better them than you. And that critter's not gonna pay your insurance deductible, either.*"

She held strong and straight and true in her path, braking ever so slightly, but only one of the birds lifted up in time to miss the car. The other was on a suicide mission, like a kamikaze pilot, flying right into the middle of her windshield. Beak first hit, as a sickening flesh and bones sound thudded against the glass. Her mind reeled with images of its poor bones breaking and she prayed that it died instantly. Elena held her breath and hoped the glass didn't crack from the impact. When she was sure it was safe, she pulled over to the side of the road to inspect the damage. As she got out, she stepped in a puddle, splashing cold and muddied rainwater up onto her slacks. Cursing under her breath, she glanced back up at the reason she stepped out of the car in the first place; the windshield. There was a small hairline fracture in the glass, and a bloody smear streaking down the glass. On the pavement beside the car, the broken seagull lay in a heap. In the not too far off distance, caws of crying seagulls filled the foggy late afternoon air. She would've thought the whole thing was odd if she wasn't so worried about Ray.

Back in her car, she hit the windshield wipers and fluid. Dazed and relieved, she stared as the washer fluid did its job, wiping away the stain. If only the crack were that easy. A couple more seagulls darted and dipped in front of her car. "Crazy birds, what is your problem today?"

View now unobstructed, she finished the drive to her sister's, realizing how close she was. She silently chastised herself for not paying attention, doing the whole drive by rote. Maybe that was why she'd hit the bird, after all, she tried to justify. She took the familiar turn left and then a quick right and three houses down on the left, she pulled into the driveway. Glad that the rain had ended, she took her time getting out of the car. Hesitating, she sat for a moment, door open, one foot in, one foot out. Flipped down the driver side mirror and did a quick make-up check, wiping off some of her smeared eyeliner. Pulled some lip-gloss out of her crowded purse, hoping the shimmer of her lips might distract from the evidence of teary sadness of her eyes. Convinced this was the best she could do, she headed to the house.

With a quick rap on the door, Elena's eight-year old niece Carrie soon appeared. "Hi! Come on in! We're playing." Carrie flung the door wide open the rest of the way and took off running down the hall.

Elena let herself in and shut the door behind her. She walked down short the hall, her heels on the hardwood floor clicking all the way. In the kitchen, she found her sister Becky sitting at the table on her cell-phone. "Yes, I'm telling you. This is the fourth one she's dragged in in the last two hours. It's weird, and gross."

Becky looked up at Elena and gestured for her to wait with the wave of a single finger. "I don't know, Dax. She never does it anymore. And seagulls? It's creepy... Alright, I gotta go, Elena is here to pick up Amelia. See you in a bit." She put down her cell and got up to greet her sister. With open arms, she pulled Elena in for a big bear hug. "You look tired. You sleeping?"

"Some nights better than others."

"And how's Ray doing?"

"Fine." She changed the subject. The phone conversation she'd overheard had her disconcerted. Coincidences with seagulls? The day grew stranger by the moment. "What was that conversation all about? Sounded weird."

Becky rolled her eyes dramatically. "Oh, yeah. Snowball has been doing some serious hunting and gifting today." She opened her mouth and stuck her finger in, mocking-vomit face.

"I didn't think she did that anymore. She's getting old, isn't she?"

As if on cue, a big, fluffy white cat came stalking into the room, rubbing her head and tail on Elena. She let out a delicate meow and waited, green eyes beseeching. Elena bent over and gave Snowball a scratch behind the ears.

"She's twelve. I dunno what that is translated from cat to human years, but yeah, she's getting older. Anyway, she started a couple hours ago." She turned to call the cat. "Come here, baby, come to mommy." She squatted down and petted Snowball's back, watching the cat flop over to expose her belly. "Mommy's gross little baby." Becky gave the fluffy tummy a rub and lifted her head back up to Elena. "All of a sudden I hear this crazy screeching sound and she comes flying through the cat door with a dead seagull in her mouth. I freak out, I'm squeaking like a freaking mouse," she said through a giggle," and finally throw the thing away, then she comes back about twenty minutes later with another one. Then another, and another. That cat has never been wily enough to catch a seagull. I mean, she was never the greatest hunter, period." She stopped rubbing the cat and walked back to the table, reaching for her purse. After a moment's search, she pulled out hand-sanitizer and doused her hands, then offered it to Elena. "Honestly, and this is super-gross, but I think some of them were already dead. No way she killed all of those."

Elena accepted the sanitizer, rubbing her hands over and together. "Okay, that is extra weird, considering."

"Considering what?"

"Come outside." Elena made a bee line for the front door and her sister followed her to the car, dodging little puddles along the way. Pointing to the splintered windshield, she asked, "Guess what did that?"

"You've got to be fucking kidding me. If you say a seagull, I am gonna lose my mind." She crossed her arms over her in a defiant posture.

"Then I won't say it. You should make sure Snowball has all her shots and stuff." As she said this, she rubbed her hands together, over and over, making sure she'd cleansed herself of touching Snowball. "What if there are a bunch of sick seagulls around? I wonder if that would explain all this." They both stared quietly at the windshield. "I gotta run, though. We still have to go to the grocery store. Thanks for watching her."

Becky crinkled up her face in disgust. "You think it might be a thing?"

Elena tried to appear unflustered. "Nah. I'm sure there's a logical explanation." She didn't believe it as soon as the words left her lips and wondered if Becky had.

"Amelia, time to go!" Becky shouted back toward the house.

"Mo-o-om, nooooo," Carrie whined. "We're still playing!" The two little girls appeared in the driveway. Amelia was wearing a cowboy hat with a plastic gun at her hip, and Carrie wore delicate slippers and a tutu. The tutu sat crooked on her hips, and Carrie kept hiking it up as she walked.

"And don't get those shoes wet in this mess!" Becky added, eyeing the slippers. "Go back inside. We're making dinner soon!" She shook her head as she turned back to her sister.

"Come on, Amelia. Give Carrie her things back and let's go shopping." Elena moved closer to her niece, reaching her hand out.

"I'm a cowboy! Stick'em up!" Amelia pointed the fake gun at her cousin.

Elena scrunched her brows together. "What did the little Princess Carrie do to you?"

Amelia squinted her eyes really small, as if trying to be intimidating. "Not all little girls are princesses. I teached her!"

"*Taught*, not teached." Elena couldn't help but chuckle a bit. "You are a tough one, yes you are." She pulled the hat off Amelia's head. "And you're right. The days of princesses are all but over. And we've got dinner to do."

She turned to wave at Becky and Carrie already in their doorway and the smile fell off her face as she spotted the fear on theirs. A loud screeching tore through the air above Elena's head. Her eyes followed Becky's hand pointing above her and caught sight of two seagulls in the sky. Flying above her head. Although they were not flying. They were falling and one was headed right towards Amelia.

"Amelia, in the car!" Elena shouted. She hurried the child into the backseat and one of the birds just missed. The second one thudded down onto the roof. Both were dead.

4

The salty whiff of sweat hung in the air as Ray entered the gym. Weights clinked in the distance and a spin class was in full swing nearby. The wheels turned at a dizzying speed as the instructor called out, "That's it! Keep going! Come on!" The techno music blared on while the class pushed and pedaled faster.

Past them he went, straight to the treadmills hoping to run out his frustrations. He used to run all the time. Before Ravynn's death, he loved to run up and down the beach. Afterward, the beach had taken on an entirely different atmosphere for him. No longer held the lure of peace and meditation, but sadness instead. Every time he pictured the beach now, his mind would create horrifying images of what happened that day. Had she seen it coming? Did she try to run? Did they all scream and panic, knowing there was no way to outrun the treacherous wave that devoured everything in its path?

Up until that point, Ray had always thought of tsunamis as some exotic problem that other countries might face, but never the US, never his home in northern California.

For a while, he seriously considered packing the family up and moving somewhere else in the country. Montana, Colorado, one of the Dakotas even. Somewhere away from the ocean. In the end, though, Elena's vote won out. She wanted to stay close to her family. Both her sister and her parents owned homes here, and she never dreamed of moving away from them.

He began a steady walk. His teeth ground as he replayed the final conversation at the principal's office earlier. Unaware of his quickening pace as he absently pressed buttons, he moved along, deep in his thoughts. That self-doubting voice crept back in again:

"They were right to do what they did. You need to step away. You're no good to your students. You're distracted. The nightmares are driving you crazy. Things are different now, and you know they'll never be the same."

"Shut up," he said. He cringed at the realization that he answered his thoughts out loud. He shook his head, hoping no one noticed. He focuses on the sound of his feet pounding on the treadmill to drown out his humiliation.

"You okay?" A woman's voice magnified his embarrassment, confirming his fears that someone had heard.

He didn't bother to look up. Pushing his pace harder and faster, he muttered, "Fine, fine. Sorry."

He grit his teeth harder, this time talking only in his head, *"I wish things were simple again, I wish you were still here, Ravynn. This is too hard without you. I'm am losing my grasp. Losing control. Lost without you."*

Ray remembered when that was a big joke. When they were kids. Inseparable. *Joined at the hip.* Mrs. White, their third-grade teacher used to say that all the time. Ray never understood exactly what it meant. Back then, he used to conjure funny images of him and Ravynn actually being physically joined at the hip. They'd have to synchronize their walking steps so they wouldn't trip. They'd have to move through doorways sideways. They would even have a special desk in their classes that looked more like two desks, fused together, with two desktops that they could easily slide in and out of together. He didn't think it would be such a terrible thing. Kind of cool, actually. Think of all the attention.

Slamming in his chest, his heart threatened to break free of its confines. A pound, pound pounding sound rang through his ears. For a moment, he was afraid it was the reverberation of his heart, about to burst, and he dropped his head to his feet. Each pounding beat in his ear matched his footsteps, hammering on the treadmill. His knees buckled and his legs became like spaghetti. He stumbled, catching himself on the handles. He hit the stop button and jumped off the treadmill. Sweat rolled down his neck and face, his shirt clinging to his chest and back. He stared down at the treadmill, hypnotized as the track wound down to a stop. *Where the hell had I just gone?*

The memories finally released him, letting him come back to the present. Too much time these days had been spent anywhere but the present. He reached for his towel and wiped himself dry. Looking up, he recalled where he was: in a gym full of people, bad music blaring in the background.

"Dude, you done with that?" A man impatiently hovered next to him.

"Oh, yeah, all yours." He wiped the machine down and walked away. Shaking his head at his lack of stamina, he remembered a time he could run for hours without a care. It seemed so long ago now. But time and grief had had their way with him, breaking him down.

AT home, he found Amelia and Elena in the living room, playing. As soon as Amelia spotted him, she ran to him, jumping in his arms as he lifted her sky high.

"Yup, getting bigger," he said to her. "I can feel it."

She gave an approving nod and he pulled her in for a hug.

She crinkled up her nose at his sweaty neck and shirt. "Why

are you all wet, Uncle Ray?"

"I went for a long run, little one. Sorry. I'll hit the shower."

Elena appeared next to him suddenly. She stood perfectly still. Ray wondered how she had snuck up on him. "Hey," he said. "Quick shower and I'll fire up the grill."

When she didn't respond, he pressed, "You ok? You seem... off." Her eyes were a bit distant, as if she too was caught in a memory. Her skin was a paler shade than normal.

"Got a crack down the windshield. Birds. Seagulls. Smashed right into it like they didn't care." Shaking her head, she added, "Becky's cat has been dragging in dead seagulls all day, too." She shivered.

The confusion got him joking. "Glad we never got a cat then, huh?"

Elena frowned, and Ray realized his error. The seriousness of her day became apparent as she continued, "When Amelia and I were getting back into the car to leave, a couple more fell out of the sky and almost hit us. It was... unnerving to say the least."

Not knowing now how to respond after his feeble attempt at levity, Ray apologized. "Sorry, that's awful, and—"

"The birds know... about the changes," Amelia said out of nowhere.

Ray and Elena looked up at each other in stunned silence. Not only haunting, Amelia's words rang true to Ray, though he couldn't imagine why. *Things are different now...*

"What did you say, little bunny?" Elena wrapped her arms around herself, as if needing comfort from the ominous words.

Amelia flapped her arms like a bird and repeated, "They know changes." She headed out of the room before anyone could say more on the matter.

AT the dinner table, all seemed well, at least on the surface. Quiet, but Elena thought perhaps the run had made the difference. She hated that he was struggling but here wasn't anything she could do besides be there. Torn between wanting to support him and being bitter with him for not taking the initiative and doing something before things got worse.

Conversation was light and a bit playful. Much to Elena's chagrin, Ray challenged Amelia to a corn contest. Of course, the corn needed to be eaten in a very specific way that qualifies as both fun and the rules for winning. The method was called "type-writer". It involved holding the corn with both hands up to your mouth. Then, starting at the left, and working your way to the right, you eat the corn. When you got to the right end of the cob, you'd say, 'ding', turn the cob about an inch or so, and start back from left to right, repeating until the corn cob was clean. Even though Amelia had no concept of what a typewriter was, the game tickled her to no end.

The sound of Amelia's laughter helped Elena settle into a bit more ease. Thinking about the odd day with the birds gave her the willies, wondering if there was some bigger picture she'd missed. Birds don't just fall from the sky and children don't usually act like it's no big deal. So, why had Amelia? What did she mean when she said that the birds know changes?

While what happened at school today had obviously been unpleasant, it now seemed that Ray may have worked himself through it. Too bad she wasn't over it. She felt a little guilty for calling David, but she needed to know, and Ray was taking too long.

After the typewriter corn eating contest, Amelia was declared the winner and still reigning champion, Ray started the conversation casually. Out of the blue, he announced, "So, I think I'm gonna maybe take a little time off from work."

Elena, baffled, fumed, "Time off? We have two more days left this year, Ray. You've got the whole summer off." A heaviness started in her chest and worked its way into her stomach. She had a bad suspicion this was all going south real quick. "Please tell me this is another attempt at humor," her voice was shrill. She clenched her teeth together and tried to hold back a verbal attack.

"After summer. Next school year I mean. I think I might take the whole year off, spend some time at home, maybe pull a 'Mr. Mom'."

Thoughts raced through Elena's mind at the mention of time off. When was he going to consult her on the decision? Weren't they a team, after all? The one-sidedness of his actions lately had her embittered. As if they could even afford such a thing. Her blood pressure rising, she was ready to explode. Elena slammed her hand down on the table, unable to contain her frustration. Amelia jumped and dropped her fork.

"Sorry, sorry. Dropped my hand rather hard, huh, little bunny? Clumsy me." A forced smile made its way to her lips before disappearing.

Ray's words were too casual, too lax. Elena bit her tongue. Even though she was aware of what happened, she couldn't tell him. He'd be furious if he found out she talked to David.

Amelia chimed in, "Yeah, Auntie E. Me and Uncle Ray are not going to school anymore."

"But you love school." Elena tapped her fingers on the table.

"But there's no more school." Amelia got serious. "And we'll have a lot more time to play."

"We would, wouldn't we?" Ray asked.

"What's going on Ray? Where is this idea coming from?"

"On my run, I thought it all out." The way it came out of his mouth sideways, as if he'd been chewing on those words before he spit them out, filled Elena with doubt. "It will be a good choice. I'll exercise more, get back into great shape, and in turn that will help me sleep better. Spend more time here around the house doing handy things." As if the money wasn't important. As if they could afford to do anything around the house if they both weren't working. Where was his head?

"Amelia, put your plate on the counter and go to your room to work on your letters, okay? I'll be in in a minute and check on you," Elena said firmly. She bit her lip and tried to disguise her tension. She added, lightening her tone, "Then, maybe I can dig up some ice cream for dessert."

"Okay, Auntie E." Amelia picked up after herself, then made her way to her room, timidly glancing back at Ray and whispering, "No more school." Again, the child's words made Elena think there was more to what she was saying, but how could a seven-year old know?

"When she was sure Amelia was out of earshot, Elena tried, but failed to maintain a cool tone, "What's going on Ray? Really."

"It's time for a change, honey. It might actually be long overdue."

"Does this sudden change have anything to do with your meeting this afternoon?"

"Well, sure it does," he agreed, almost too lightheartedly. "No big deal."

"Cut the BS, Ray. Come on."

He rolled his eyes and tilted his head back, looking up at the ceiling. He brought his hand to his jaw socket and rubbed in a circular motion.

"It's just," he began thoughtfully. "Well, with everything that's gone on it would be best for me, and for the school, for me to take a little time away. A little 'me-time'. And more time to be with you both."

"So, they've called you out." She got up from the table, angrily pulling plates and silver off to the sink.

"Yeah, something like that," he admitted, his hand still massaging his jaw.

She placed the plates carefully down in the sink, then gripped the edges of the counter for something to squeeze. "Well, what else is it like?" Her tone escalated. Deep breath in, she tried to calm herself before turning around to face him. The anger in her was heavy in her stomach, making her nauseated.

Ray dropped both hands to the table and clasped them tight. "They said my head's not in the game, the students are suffering because my instability. Allegedly… grades have fallen off because of me. They say I am distracted, not present. That it might be best if I took the next year off to properly deal with my loss."

"And what did you say? I can't imagine you took it in stride." She leaned back against the counter and clutched her belly as spasms wreaked havoc on her insides.

"No, I didn't. They made it seem like they were giving me a choice in the matter at first. Once I gave them my opinion, they told me straight out the decision had already been made, they were only doing me a courtesy, the way they looked at it."

"Well, this is too much, Ray. When are you going to see that this is a big deal?" She pushed off the counter with her backside. "What part of dual income do you not understand? It's not entirely fair to assume that I can carry the financial burden solo. Did you ever think of that?" She took a step forward, then decided to stop, not trusting her proximity to him in that moment. "Forget the monetary pressure, what happened to this marriage being a partnership? Discussing big choices together *before* making them?"

"I think, in some way, it will end up being a good thing. And I never discounted you, not as a partner, not in any way. But it's for the best. Really."

"Ray—"

"Elena. It hurt to hear. Really. And I was ready to stand up and flail my arms around and yell that they were dead wrong, that I was giving it my one-hundred percent, that I've been sleeping just and not having terrible nightmares that wake me up in a cold sweat..." he took a deep breath before he continued, "but I couldn't. Don't you see? That little voice in the back of my head agreed with them. They were spot on. And it isn't fair to all those kids. They deserve my all, they do. I hate to admit this out loud, but I can't give it to them. Not now. I should step away. Re-assess. Get my head straight- and some much-needed sleep."

Elena was about to open her mouth and weigh in more on the matter, but she bit her tongue instead. They were right. He was off. She did think Ray was jumping the gun a bit in giving up. David made it sound like they were only giving him a warning.

"I know you're disappointed, honey. I'm sorry."

"Don't be sorry, Ray. Just… well… take this time to make things better. Make you better. I love you Ray. But I do want my old husband back. I miss you."

"Aw honey, I miss you too. I will figure this all out. I promise."

Left with not much of a choice, Elena let it go, for now. There wasn't much more she could argue without risking telling him about David.

Without a word, Ray wisely chose to clean up while Elena checked in on Amelia.

Instead of practicing her letters, she was playing with her dolls. Elena froze in the doorway.

One doll in one hand, and another doll in the other, Amelia flung one up in the air and slammed the other one hard into the ground. Toys were scattered about the normally organized room. She grabbed her owl stuffy and threw it hard at the wall.

"Amelia?" Elena's voice was muted, her surprise catching her. The scene was not what she'd expect from the girl. Elena studied her hard as Amelia took both hands and slipped them under the toys on the floor, randomly flipping some up and aside.

"Mrrrrrr…. Grrrrrr…. Eeeeeeeee," Amelia groaned and screeched.

Seeing enough, Elena stepped into the mess in front of Amelia and put her hands out to pause her. "Whoa! What's happening here? Did you get upset?" Guilt coursed through Elena about having had the conversation with Ray in front of Amelia.

Amelia looked up at her aunt and smiled. "What you say, "Auntie E?"

"Are you ok, sweetie?" The smile was unnerving, and Elena took a step back.

"Uh-huh."

"Why the mess with the toys? Looked like you were flinging them around in here."

"The earth was mad," Amelia replied, in a simple, matter-of-fact tone.

Elena crouched down to eye level, tilting her head? "What do you mean?"

Amelia bit her lip. "It's mad. So it shakes—"

Elena interrupted her, "The earth was mad?" She gently ran a hand down the girl's arm and laced her fingers through Amelia's delicate fingers.

"*Is* mad, Auntie E. Still mad. Birds get dizzy. Fish get lost. Day gets confused." Amelia yanked on Elena's hand as if to drive home the point.

Quizzically, Elena peered at Amelia. The child was steadfast and seemed to fully believe in what she was saying, which made it all the more unnerving.

5

"Pour me another drink, Rick. This one's about done," Matt slurred to the bartender.

He stuck his index finger into his drink and pushed the single ice cube down into his Maker's Mark, then let it bob back up to the surface. As it broke the surface, so did a memory...

Under the bridge he stood in the waning light of day. Dusk had settled in, the sun neatly settling in for the night over the horizon. He breathed deeply as it disappeared, tucking away into its slumber. Fishing rod in his hand, out for a peaceful moment to clear his mind, he tried to resist the lure of the booze. The urge was strongest at night.

First, the sound caught his attention. Screeching. Brakes slamming, car reluctantly sliding across asphalt. Metal on metal. Matt looked up to the bridge in time to witness the two cars meet, one thrusting the other over the side of the bridge, into the waters below.

Matt dropped his fishing pole.

Something bobbed up out of the water. Farther out, where

the car went down. A person. Treading water.

Matt didn't think. He acted.

His feet hit the water and dove in. Moved with purpose through the cold, moonlit water, towards the figure bobbing in the distance.

With a determination like never before, he swam hard and fast. The young girl called out, facing away from him. "I'm coming," she said.

There was also another voice, a woman's voice. Her words were muffled and indiscernible; strange sounding, like when you're under water and try to talk.

The water grew colder and darker around him in that instant. Perhaps the chill came from inside, from witnessing some supernatural event unfolding before him.

The girl swam toward the sound of that voice, away from Matt and dry land. Matt pleaded with the young girl, "Wait! I'm coming for you. Don't go! I'm over here!" He tried to make himself seen in the water, waving his hands at her.

She didn't even seem aware of his existence. Like she had a singular purpose.

The Woman on the Water.

Matt's eyes locked onto what the girl was swimming to. She didn't look real though, this woman- more ethereal- like an angel. Her hair darker than the night itself. A long white flowing gown billowed around her in the evening air. It appeared as if she was lit up from behind, almost glowing, yet transparent. As she beckoned to this young girl, she held out her arms while standing on the water. No- just above the water. There was something like a funnel of water, floating, holding this woman inside, creating the appearance that she was standing on the river. Matt filled with dread, somehow realizing that if this girl reached this woman, she'd be gone forever. He didn't understand how he knew this. Harder and faster he swam, his breath coming in quicker, shorter bursts. He reached out and wrapped an arm around the girl. Still facing the other way, she was oblivious to his presence. He tried to swim in the other direction now, with this girl in tow, but she didn't budge. Something had a hold on her; it seemed like he was trying to drag her from thick mud. Struggling as he tried to free the girl of this invisible hold, he began to panic. As he glanced back up, he could still see the *Woman on the Water*, perhaps closer now, her arms open.

"I said, last one." The bartender poked Matt in the shoulder and placed a drink in front of him. "God knows you don't need it. And I'm a jackass for pouring it." He shook his head and turned back to polishing the glassware.

Matt tilted the near empty glass of Maker's back, polished it off, and grabbed at the new one clumsily. He should have called Ray but he was a coward. What would he say anyway? He laughed at himself. He was turning into some kind of conspiracy-theory man. He took a long pull on his drink and faded back into his thoughts as the liquid sloshed around in the glass. He wondered if she bobbed like that then- so many years after that- before she died…

He remembered her face that day, before she left for the beach. Her eyes were so full of happiness, they actually twinkled.

"I'm gone in a few. Gonna kiss Amelia goodbye," she had said.

"Don't wake her, you know she'll never go back to sleep. And it's too early in the morning," Matt said, following her down the hall to Amelia's bedroom. The summer dawn light trickled in through the windows, teasing the walls with its dancing light patterns.

Ravynn's hair had grown longer that summer. She pulled it back into a haphazard braid, spilling down to the middle of her back, loose strands brushing the side of her face. She tucked a few behind her ear as she leaned over Amelia, asleep in her bed, to say goodbye. Matt regarded them from the doorway as her lips gently brushed the child's forehead. A strand of hair came free and tickled Amelia's face, causing her to scrunch up her tiny nose.

Ravynn turned back to Matt staring at her from the doorway. She gave him a smile twisted with effort, as the weight of their arguments had taken their toll and now there was so much distance between them.

"I told you I will be fine watching her. Jim's at the shop, I am not going in at all today. Daddy and daughter day, all day."

"No alcohol. Not even a beer," Ravynn warned. Her face was stern, her brow creased. Matt thought those creases in her brow were growing heavier every day.

Matt cringed at the implied accusation. Yes, he'd been drinking, and pretty heavily since their divorce had been finalized not even three weeks previous. It was still hard for him to imagine that he'd lost his family over those stupid journals. Why did he have to question her? Why couldn't he let her have her secret? Even if the contents scared the living hell out of Matt, why couldn't he just love her and let it go?

Because it wasn't natural. It defied reason.

So, he'd buried himself in the bottom of a bottle. But he was no fool. He wasn't going to drink today. For Amelia, today he'd make it a good day.

"I can call Ray and Elena. It's not too late. Today's Saturday, after all, and they'll be around. Tell me if you can't do this—"

"I will be fine. She's my daughter; you know how much I love her. How much I love you, I just—"

She cut him off abruptly, "There's no time for this right now, Matt. I love you too, I do." she shook her head, now standing inches in front of him in the doorway.

She wasn't wearing perfume. She rarely did, but she always smelled so good. Like lavender. His nostrils hungrily filled with the scent of her. She pushed him back away from the doorway, away from sleeping ears, and into the hallway.

"I'm sorry," she said, her voice strained. Those two words held more meaning than she was letting on. They sounded so heavy.

He put a hand up to her shoulder, then reached up to brush those loose strands of hair from her face. His hand grazed her skin and she sighed. "I can't, Matt—"

"I'm sorry. I know I screwed up. With the journals, pressuring you, questioning you. And then the drinking. I shouldn't have. I should have trusted you. I just couldn't understand..." his voice trailed off when she frowned. "I should have said yes last night. I just— it was too hard. It wouldn't have been right to pretend, I think."

She nodded slightly.

"I just don't understand how we got here. Those fucking journals."

"Language, Matt." She peered around him, towards Amelia's room, but the door was closed. "I don't understand it either." She shrugged, but there was nothing nonchalant about her posture.

"And the *Woman on the Water?*" he asked her for the hundredth time. Who is she? What is she? Why you?" He wrestled with what he knew and what he suspected. And tried to rectify it all with reality. It was all connected somehow. That day she almost drowned, the *Woman on the Water*, and Ravynn's journals.

"I have to go. Take care of Amelia. Take care of yourself, Matt. And if you need any help, Ray and Elena are there, ok?"

"We'll be fine," he assured her. He hoped he sounded convincing. He was unsure of most things these days.

Sadness ran across her face. It was fleeting, but Matt sensed it was something more, like a melancholy lived there, behind those eyes. Whatever secrets she held; they wore her down.

"I hope so." She patted his cheek and took off down the hall, not looking back.

"She never did look back. Like she knew," Matt mumbled, glass to his lips. "What if sseee-shee knew..." Bad sign when it's still daylight and the slurring has begun.

"What did you say?" Rick asked. He leaned over the bar towards Matt, still a glass in his hand, ambitiously polishing.

"She fuggin' knew." Matt forgot the glass in his hand, and dropped it on the bar, shattering. He startled.

"Okay, Matt," Rick said, cleaning up the pieces. "You gotta go."

"But I haven't not even finnisshed my last drink."

Rick pointed to the shattered glass on the bar, saying, "That drink? Yup, looks pretty done to me. Go home, sleep it off. Get it together, buddy."

Matt reached into his wallet and pulled out a wad of cash and slapped it down on the bar.

Outside of the old tavern on 5th Street, Matt stumbled into the late-night air. Surprised the full dark of night was upon him, he glanced up, blinding himself in a streetlight. Hadn't he only been in there an hour or two? He only meant to have one little drink. Went in during daylight, and then....

At the corner, deep in his thoughts, not looking where he was headed, he tripped, bumping into a teenage couple holding hands. The teenage boy shoved at him, yelling, "Watch it, loser! Why don't you crawl back into your cardboard box and sleep it off!"

Matthew lost his already shaky balance and fell to the pavement. The pavement came up on him quick, and he scraped the palms of his hands trying to catch himself. The teen's girlfriend erupted in a fit of giggles and pulled her boyfriend in closer to her as they walk on by, looking down upon Matthew with disgust.

Matt wasn't homeless. One couldn't tell though by his appearance on these drunken days. He wore a pair of well-worn blue jeans, scuffed and torn, which could've been seen as either fashionable or homeless depending on who was wearing them. His shoes were a pair of comfortable but tattered old brown loafers that he'd had forever. A gray t-shirt lay underneath a lightweight red flannel shirt with one sleeve rolled up past his elbow. His brown hair was overgrown and disheveled, occasionally flopping over in front of his left eye. He carelessly flipped it off his face, to no avail, as it fell right back down.

Too much on his mind today. A tough day, for sure. He deserved at least one drink. That one drink had led to another, then another, until here he was, stumbling around, as day turned so quickly into night before the unsuspecting Matt. Now he was trying to find his way home. He hadn't meant to get drunk; he just wanted a little liquid courage so he could call his estranged brother-in-law. Matt hadn't spoken to Ray in about a year. Since the last time he'd tried to have a conversation like this. He was drunk then, too. Showed up at Ray and Elena's after Ravynn's funeral, drunk, slurring, knocking things over, including himself, and scaring the hell out of his daughter. Matt couldn't remember all of that day, but he did remember telling Ray that Ravynn was crazy. Told him she wasn't herself. Like she was possessed by something. And she apperceived things. Wrote things down. About the future. Things no one should know.

He'd handled that poorly, that was certain. It was his chance to talk to Ray and finally unburden himself of the reasons for all his suffering and eventual divorce, but instead he went on a confused, drunken rant that chased him right out of all of their lives. And rightly so.

He wasn't even sure what he's going to say.

A drunken mess, sleeping was the most important thing now. He could call Ray tomorrow. *Hiccup.* Yeah, tomorrow.

He fumbled and stumbled to the curb and hopped into the third cab he tried to hail.

At home in bed, his mind wandered again. Her voice still echoed in his ears. He was lost in thoughts of Ravynn. His head on the pillow, eyes closed, he slipped back in time once again…

"Hello? Hey, is anyone around? My car broke down and I need it fixed, super quick. Hel-looooo."

Matt could hear the voice but couldn't see the woman who spoke, he had himself tucked underneath a car, hard at work. At the sound of her calls, he rolled the creeper out from under the car, and there she stood. At first, he could only make out her outline. Dark long hair framed her face, a sundress fell softly around her form. Her visage was framed by light all around, and he thought for the second time in his life, he was before an angel. He lay there, dumbfounded on the creeper, staring up at her.

"Hi there. I need some help. I had my car towed in, and…" she paused as a look of recognition crossed her face. "Do I know you?"

Matt made his way up to a standing position, now inches away from this woman. He saw her face clearly, and some recognition passed through him as well.

"I think I do know you?" He hadn't meant for it to come out in a question.

She laughed. A pleasant sound. It made him smile. He reached out a dirty hand. "I'm Matt." She did look so familiar, like a woman he'd once seen, but where? Maybe in a dream, she was too lovely for words, for reality.

Recognition lit up her face. "I do know you! Matthew Higgins, Hero!"

He was taken aback by those words. He hadn't been called such a thing in almost ten years. Not since the accident. Now it was his turn to remember.

"Ravynn Bradley? Little Ravynn Bradley?"

"All grown up." She made a playful curtsy and bowed her head.

He was speechless, taking in the beautiful woman in front of him. He didn't want to gawk, but that was exactly what he was doing.

She let out a little laugh, and said, "Well, you look exactly the same. You really do. I don't know how it's possible, after all this time, but you do. You look great."

Matt couldn't help but blush. He shook his head, trying to hold himself back from what he wanted to say to her, tell her how beautiful she looked, but his mouth betrayed him, "And you… you look… I don't have words."

"Did I take your breath away?" she playfully teased.

He shook his head several times before answering, "I think you did."

Matt fell asleep in a pool of his own drool on his pillow.

In the morning, his urge to call Ray and confess all he'd known about Ravynn and her secrets had disappeared along with his courage, completely overshadowed by his massive hangover and the remnants of his dream. He forced himself out of bed and to the kitchen. Grabbed a glass of water and a bottle of ibuprofen. Tilting his head back, he brought the bottle of pills up to his lips, not bothering to count how many spilled into his mouth, and quickly washed them down with the water. A steady, strong tap, tap, tapping, sound began. At first, Matt thought it was his hangover, pounding away in his skull. Over at the window, he pushed aside the blinds. Hail was falling from the late summer sky. With a pot of coffee now brewing on the countertop, he headed back to the kitchen table and sat down. Cringing at the glow of the computer screen as he fired it up, he typed a few words into the search bar: *Woman on the Water.*

6

*R*ay stands, staring into the face of it. That cold hard slap that will surely devour him, take him away from this world forever. Here it comes, that inevitable mountain of water barreling toward him with unthinkable speed. Everything in its path will be decimated.

But this time, it's moving too slow. He's watching now, he realizes, the events unfolding slower than reality. That was the way of dreams, though. Piecing the parts all together, watching the scene unfold. Yet unable to change the outcome.

Each second ticks by like a lifetime. Ray sees each individual wave, each crest folding into that one big wave. Oh, the detail, like he's never been able to see before. Why now, he wonders. What's different?

Gazing up into the sky, the clouds are so clear. He never noticed them before, but they were always there, had to be. They pull him in, now completely entranced. As his gaze lingers, the clouds, the world around him begins to blur. Kaleidoscope distortion, colors wrapping and bending into each other.

Through the fuzzy lens, he sees these clouds becomes confused. Not moving as normal clouds do. Each one, instead of following each other across the sky, crash into the next, from left to right, up to down, each cloud seemingly eating the one next to it, as if once one meets another, they *fight to the death, absorbing the other into itself.*

Then they do the strangest thing, as if what was occurring wasn't odd enough; randomly they would go poof, and disappear, as if sucked out of the sky by a huge invisible vacuum. A spinning, transparent vacuum.

Ray begins to panic, shouting to the sky, "This is not real! This can't be how it happened! The world doesn't work this way..."

Ravynn's voice floats through his mind, as if carelessly riding the disappearing clouds above, "You are finally beginning to see—"

Like the screeching sound of someone dragging the needle of a record player across the record, a man's voice busted into his brain, pushing away all the clouds and water. "Ray?" Nothing. The voice grew louder, "Ray?"

Ray snapped to, discovering he'd been daydreaming. He was in the teacher's lounge men's room at school. The sound of rushing water from a sink made him look down. Water running full blast hitting the sink, splashing out, up and over the sides. Water pooled around his feet as well.

He must have turned the water on and started daydreaming about Ravynn, completely losing himself. He retraced his steps, remembered going into the bathroom to splash some water on his face to wake up, and...

"You ok?" The same voice interrupted.

Ray looked up from the sink into the mirror and caught the reflection of the man behind him. He turned to face David.

Trying to sound as casual as possible, Ray replied, "Oh yeah, sorry. Didn't hear you with the water running." He held his breath, hoping that will be the end of it. He looked David in the eyes, searching for some recognition or acceptance.

David stared at him, unblinking. Crossed his arms in front of him. "Your shirt is all wet."

The neck and chest area of his shirt were indeed wet. He scowled. *Son-of-a-bitch!* He didn't remember it happening, though, which worried him. He didn't remember much except Ravynn invading his work world.

David leaned forward, as if waiting on the tip of his toes for Ray's response.

Ray reached for the paper towels and scrubbed his shirt, trying to make light of the situation, and avoid David at the same time. Shaking his head, he lied, "Ridiculous. I was a little clumsy with my coffee, and it ended up on my shirt... and, well, I made a mess."

David looked uncertain, as if weighing Ray's response. He tilted his head to the side, still staring at Ray sideways, squinting. "Your face is all wet, too."

Bringing the towels up to his face, Ray dried it sloppily. "Well, I was in a hurry to get that coffee off, I didn't really care. If you've ever ruined a shirt with coffee stains, you'll understand."

David shook his head, giving Ray a look of disbelief, his eyes squinted. "Sleeping any better?"

"I'm good, thanks." He turned his back to David and continued scrubbing the imaginary coffee off his shirt, all the while wondering how long he was stuck in that daydream, and how long David had been standing there. He was pretty sure David didn't buy his excuse, but he didn't care. He had one more day of school left. One more day to fake his way through it. What happened after that was best left to worry about another time.

Perhaps content with Ray's response, David walked out, leaving Ray with his wet mess.

ACROSS town, Matt sat at his kitchen table, staring at the computer screen, sucking down his fourth coffee of the day. His search for the *Woman on the Water* had led him down a rabbit hole. Eyes were straining, and his back cramped from sitting in a hunch. The hail had tapered off a while ago, but he barely perceived this. Too wrapped up in his search. The next big swig of coffee caused a burning sensation in his esophagus. Like a volcano about to erupt, the acid pushed up, up, into his throat as he belched. The acrid tang of it made him nauseated, and he pushed the cup away from him clumsily, the contents sloshing around and slapping over the side, spilling onto the table.

"Mother fucker!"

The words written on the mug stared him in the face and made him blush: *World's Best Dad.*

The picture underneath those words tugged at his heart. His daughter, Amelia, big smile painted on her face. A present from Ravynn for the Father's Day before she died. Not so long before...

He remembered laughing at Ravynn's attempt to let the little girl help wrap the present. He had to give them both credit; he had no idea what that ball of wrapping paper was. They had used about a yard of it to wrap the normal sized mug. So much tape. Amelia had wrapped it around and around the gift. So much tape that he couldn't unwrap the present; he actually had to cut the gift out with scissors. *World's Best Dad, my ass,* he thought to himself. *I hope you know how sorry I am, Amelia. I hope you know how much I miss you. You're better off with them though. Better off than with a drunk of a father...*

He pushed himself and the chair back from the table as the legs screeched across the floor. Wincing at the sound it made, he got to his feet and made his way to the paper towels on the countertop. He ripped off a long handful and shuffled back to the table, mopping up his spill. He plopped back into the chair, pushing the hair out of his eye and the memories from his mind, and skimmed through the articles and reports:

-Brooklyn Bridge. A young man, later identified as Joseph Milano, twenty-four, apparent suicide. No body was ever found, but a connection was made when his car was found abandoned nearby, and his sister discovered the suicide note in his apartment.

When interviewed, his sister spoke through tears, "He suffered from delusions for years, but he'd been better. He was doing good. But even when he was a kid, he'd see people that weren't there. We thought it was an imaginary friend thing at first. But then he got older, and he kept it up. I used to hear him all the time, in the bathroom, talking to someone. But no one."

Joseph committed suicide by jumping off the bridge to the waters below. Witnesses said they saw a figure, somehow standing or hovering on the water below, arms open, inside a tunnel of water.

-Northern California. Mitchell Abrams. A couple out for a joyride on their new boat capsized, and it turned into a night of terror for the wife, Casey. When interviewed, she replied, "It was cold. And dark. Something was in the water with us. A shark, I think. And then it was gone. When I turned to find Mitch, he was swimming away from me. I called to him, but he ignored me. And there was a man there. On the water. Yes, on top of the water, like, standing there. I know it sounds crazy, but... He was in some sort of funnel of water that was floating. The tunnel started to get smaller when Mitch got to it, and then... then he was gone. All of it gone. It's crazy, I know."

-Mexico. Raul Martinez, seventeen. Vanished from a lake while swimming with friends. His friends hadn't noticed him swimming away, until it was too late. His girlfriend heard him calling out, "Mom, I'm coming. Mom!"

His girlfriend told police that Raul's mom had died two years before. She was even more baffled when she saw what appeared to be a tunnel with a woman standing inside it, hovering above the water. By the time Raul got to it, all of it, including him, disappeared.

Matt leaned back, stretching his long legs way out under the table and clasped his hands behind his head. Why now? There were pages and pages on the strange subject. Why revisit all that madness? All the sadness? She's gone.

He brought his hands over his head to rest on his eyes and rubbed at them, trying to get the sting of staring at a computer screen for too long out.

Because there's more to the story. And she knew. And all that time he'd been ignoring it didn't make it less real, didn't make it go away.

7

The school bell rang, dismissing the students for the final time this year. Doors to multiple classrooms flung open in synchronicity, the hallway coming to life with the buzz of the excitement of summer. Chaos and hormones rushed through the air, as the stench of gym socks and Axe body spray mingled in the mix.

A student dropped her backpack a few feet from Ray, spilling the contents to the floor. As she reached to shove everything back in, another student rushed past, causing her papers to scatter in a flurry. The girl scrambled in vain, red-faced, to gain control and finally gave up, leaving the mess to the janitor for later, no doubt. It was summer, after all.

Laughter pealed through the hall as the hustle and bustle continued. The kids fled the building as if it were on fire.

"Slow down, slow down! No running in the halls!" David tried with little hope to keep some order long enough for the students to make it outside the front doors. "Summer does not start until you are home. Who wants to start their summer in the principal's office instead of at home?" A few kids slowed to a hurried shuffle. Once they got past David, though, the threat disappeared, and they returned to their wild behavior. At the door, one boy turned and flips David off, to the amusement of many.

"Anthony Milburn! I'll see you next year!" David shouted.

Ray shifted his gaze to catch Elena stepping into her class doorway, leaning against the frame. He had a moment to appreciate her beauty, something he hadn't done for some time. Blond shoulder length hair pulled off her face by a braid that was coiled over the front of her hairline. He smiled, knowing she always liked it that way, so her bangs stayed out of her eyes. The hairstyle made her look younger than she was, reminding him of when he met her in college. Her glasses set high on her nose made her delicate face look even smaller. Her mouth came to a pucker as she viewed the departing kids, clearly amused by their behavior.

She was beautiful. Girl next door kind of perfect.

He caught her eye and she smiled. She pushed her hip off the door frame and strode toward him. He couldn't hear the shouts and giggles any longer, all of it was drowned out by her, the mere sight of her, walking to him.

"Always makes me laugh, watching them scurry, so excited on the last day of school. Takes me back there. I remember how I felt on the last day, summer on the horizon," she said through a smile.

"Ah, I bet you were sad, no more homework, no tests. My little nerd," he poked.

Elena gave him a playful punch on the arm. "You're not completely wrong. I did so love getting the time to read more over the summer."

"Cutest bookworm I ever met," he added. "So, are you happy for summer, or sad you can't give out any more tests for a few months?"

She shook her head as a student bumped into her from behind, causing her to lurch forward into Ray.

"Max Shafer," Ray's voice took on a serious-teacher tone. "You are still in school for a few more minutes. No knocking teachers over, please."

Max looked back and nodded, slowing his pace. He took a few more steps, then broke into a run.

"Max!" Ray shouted after him.

"Oh, let him go. No harm, no foul. They're excited." She looked around the hallway at all the madness. A football went flying past her ear, and Ray reached up and snagged it, one-handed. "I'm going to head back to my room and get some things put away. Catch back up with you in a bit."

"Okay, I'm going to try to keep these kids from running each other over on their way out." He tucked the ball under his arm.

"Good luck with that," she said, giving him a wink.

She walked away, and the same enthusiasm as he had when she walked to him not long ago danced over his skin. His smile faded, though, as David came down the hall, following her into her classroom.

"Mr. Bradley, um, can I have my ball back?" Ray turned to see the quarterback of the football team in front of him. Ray looked down and found his hands digging into the ball.

"Does this seem like an appropriate place to throw a football?"

"Probably not." Those words incited laughter from two boys standing off to the side.

"What's so funny?" Ray asked, turning to face the two.

One of the boys replied, "Guess he can't hit his target. He needs some practice. No wonder we lose a lot of games." He fidgeted with his baseball cap, pulling it down low, his eyes disappearing underneath. "That was a sweet interception though, Mr. Bradley."

Ray couldn't help but let a small laugh escape him. "Thanks. Now take this outside, please. You only have about twenty steps to go. You think you can make it?"

"Yeah, sorry," the quarterback replied as Ray handed him back the ball.

The boys high-fived and turned tail to escape the school and all its rules. Ray eyed them with an empty sensation he couldn't quite put his finger on.

"I, FOR one, am thoroughly looking forward to summer break. I've got a few trips planned and I'm counting the days." David's voice floated through the almost empty classroom.

Elena looked up from her desk, boxing up paperwork and ridding her desk of its school year clutter. "Where you headed?"

David sauntered fully into the room and stopped in front of her desk, placing a hand on her stapler. "Off to San Francisco for a couple days and then Napa for some wine. Lots of wine. A friend of mine works for one of the big wineries out there." He tapped on the head of the stapler, making it make a clicking sound. "Tuscany on a budget."

Elena took the stapler from him and tucked it away. "Huh?"

"Well, Italy is a little more expensive of a trip, and farther away, but the rolling hills of Napa and Sonoma Valley look pretty similar, I'm told. Plus, there's wine," he added. "And the weather will be great." He pulled out his phone and pointed to the weather app.

Elena didn't look up. "Are you checking in on me, David? Making sure I'm ok?" She closed the lid of the box, set in on the floor and grabbed another. David didn't respond. She didn't look up. Couldn't. Part of her was afraid if she looked up into those puppy-dog eyes of his staring down at her, she'd buckle. Ray was so back and forth and hot and cold these days she wasn't sure she could trust herself, or her history with David in a weakness. "Don't worry, really," she added. When she finally glanced up at him, his attention was diverted, lost in the glow of his cellphone. She was at once relieved and also a bit irritated he hadn't been staring desirously.

"Holy crap!" he exclaimed. "That can't be right."

Elena leaned over the desk to try to see what had caused such a reaction. "What?"

David's eyes were larger than normal. "They just had two tornadoes touch down in Sonoma. That's nuts."

Elena came around the desk next to David, stealing a peek at his phone. "They don't get tornadoes there, do they?"

"Nope. Floods, mudslides, earthquakes for sure. Wildfires, too. But not that." David slanted his phone to show Elena.

Elena mumbled under her breath, more to herself than anything else, "that bird thing was weird, too. I wonder..."

David startled. "You noticed that, too? Thought maybe it was a fluke thing. I still haven't heard any official word as to what happened."

Shaking her head, Elena responded, "Broke my windshield. Poor bird was so disoriented. Then later they seemed like they were just falling out of the sky. Dead."

A voice from the doorway interrupted, "Need any help, hon?" Ray stood; arms crossed in a defensive posture.

"Did I interrupt your conversation? Sorry." If his posture didn't betray him, surely his tone did. The tension in the room was palpable.

She did her best to smooth things over. "David was telling me about the tornadoes in Sonoma. Did you hear?"

Ray walked in and slid a hand on Elena's back. Pure male posturing, but she accepted anyway. It somehow made her feel better that her husband was jealous. With all of his attention diverted lately, this was a bit chauvinistic, but a welcome move.

"Look." David handed his phone to Ray, who peered at the thing like it was a gift from the devil. Elena leaned in over his shoulder to check again. The whiff of Ray's aftershave still lingered.

Ray took the phone and scrolled through the weather updates. "Lot of strange weather lately. California alone. Hail. Those terrible thunderstorms. Even the bird thing. And now torna—
"

David brought his hands up in the air and made his fingers do the creepy-dance. Woo-hoooo, Ray. The world's coming to an end. Look out," he stifled a derisive laugh.

Elena caught the deadpan serious look Ray gave David. "Boys, boys. I thought the teens had already left the building."

That elicited a smile from Ray and sliced the tension in half. The smile was cut short. "Another tornado in Alameda County." He handed the phone back to David.

"Global warming." David shrugged and headed to the door. He stopped short after a few steps and called back, "maybe you guys should take a trip too. Good stress relief." He disappeared.

"I really don't like him," Ray murmured.

Elena reminded him, "Once upon a time you were the best of friends." Sadness crept in as she remembered a time when life was so much easier. When they were all friends. Life was full of promise and dreams still to be dreamed.

"And then I stole you away from him and now he'll never forgive me."

"You didn't steal me, I went willingly." She leaned on her husband as she said the last. In the back of her mind, a little seed of doubt crept in and whispered in her ear, *what if you chose the wrong man?* She shook the thought away. "Maybe we should plan a trip. Get away for a bit this summer." Her heart filled with hope.

"Maybe." The hope began to dwindle with his words.

Elena observed Ray shiver. "Are you feeling okay? Cold?"

"I, um, I just had a little chill," he answered.

8

After dinner, Elena found Ray in the living room flipping through the news channels, soaking up the details:

"Residents of Sonoma County were in for a big scare today when a tornado touched down, sweeping across a farm before it disappeared. About an hour later, two more tornadoes touched down in Fresno County, ripping through a fruit farm, and destroying acres of fruit trees. So far, no reports of injuries..."

"Ray, what are you watching?" She shook her head when he didn't respond. She tapped him on the shoulder, and recognition crossed his face.

"What?" he asked.

The news continued:

"This comes only four days after several severe tornadoes touch down in Melbourne wiping out nearly half—"

"What are you watching?" Elena wasn't even sure why she was asking, it was obvious. Her nerves were getting the best of her. Tornadoes don't occur in California. Birds dropping out of the sky wasn't exactly normal, either.

Ray responded, not looking away from the TV, "News. Tornadoes. This is nuts."

"Well, it's definitely out of the ordinary, but—"

Ray interjected without shooting her a sideways glance, "But nothing, Elena. Everything that has been going on…" his voice trailed off.

She gave up. She wasn't ready to dive in to the conspiracy theories or whatever he was going to go on about. She didn't want to feed into his neurosis. "I'm going to take a shower, and get Amelia tucked into bed. Enjoy the news, I guess."

"Uh huh." His attention was already fully back on the TV.

She didn't want to hear any more. She couldn't. Somehow, he would try to tie all this strangeness to Ravynn, and she couldn't let him go there. Better to walk away then to deal with all of that. Had the weather been odd lately? You bet. But did it mean the second coming of Ravynn? It wasn't right. Wasn't just grief.

Down the hall, she turned on the shower, as hot as she could stand the water. She slipped out of her clothes, slowly, deliberately, observing each new ache in her body. It was amazing how stress manifested itself physically. She massaged a kink at the back of her neck that had been residing there for some time, ever growing as the days and stress continued. She noted the tension in the opposite shoulder. She pushed down roughly, and the giant knot resisted her. She wondered how long it had been there. As if in answer to her own question, she thought, *how long has Ravynn been dead? Just over a year.* Each new knot had seemed to take up residence every time she heard Ray whispering at night. Every time he tried to tie everyday events into something meaningful coinciding with Ravynn's death.

She lamented over his unilateral decision to take time off from work. Expecting her to not only emotionally carry him, but now financially as well. When would her back break? When would the tears stop from running over? Even more frightening, when would the tears dry up because there were no more to cry?

That final thought cut her more than any other so far. What

if everything going on pushed her too far, pushed her right out of love. Or right into David's arms?

She cringed at that last thought and stepped into the shower, the sting of the heat greeting her. Ducked deep under the stream, letting it rain down upon her. Initially, her body tensed at the shock, then released into heat. On the exhale, she gave over to the much-needed reprieve. Hanging her head to her chest, she let the water beat down on her neck and shoulders, hoping the tension would ease away. She cupped her eyes as teardrops caught her off guard. *Let it out, let it out,* she coaxed herself. *Be strong out there but let go in private.* Sobs began to rack her body, and she sank to the floor of the tub.

Twenty long minutes passed in the shower, and her sobs finally faded into light whimpers, stuttered breaths, and then disappeared entirely. The water lost its heat and no longer gave her relief or solace. She shut it off and climbed to her feet. Wrapped her towel tightly around herself, for comfort as well as warmth. *That helped.*

She took her time towel drying her hair, methodically, combing out each tangle, and dressed in her robe and slippers. In the mirror, the evidence of her crying was plain to see. She dabbed a few small dots of eye cream under her eyes, blending it in smoothly.

It would have to do. The cream hid nothing. The puffy dark circles under her eyes betrayed her.

AT the door to Amelia's room, Elena practiced her smile, and entered. "Okay sweetie. Let's get ready for bed. It's getting late. Quick, quick, like a bunny, into your pj's."

Amelia giggled. "Bunnies don't wear pajamas." She scurried to her green stuffed bunny and lifted it high in the air as evidence. "See? No pj's on Mr Bigsy. Bunnies don't wear pjs!"

"Are you sure, little one?" Elena teased.

Amelia replied in her know-it-all-child tone, "They wear

fur."

Elena reached for the pajamas she has laid out on the bed for Amelia, but Amelia ignored her, tossing Mr. Bigsy onto the bed and walked right past her, straight to her cartoon themed dresser. On one side was painted a princess, and on the other, a cartoon dog.

"Whatcha doing, sweetie? Pajamas are right here." Elena pointed to the pajamas waiting on the bed.

"Can I wear my bathing suit to bed tonight, Auntie E?" She pulled out several of the dresser drawers, looking for her swimsuit.

"Well, why would you want to do that? Pajamas are for sleeping, and bathing suits are for swimming."

"'Cause I'm gonna see Mamma tonight in the ocean," Amelia replied.

Those simple little words sent goosebumps all up and down Elena's back, chasing away any warmth that was left from the shower. "Why would you think that, Amelia?"

"'Cause Mamma and I meet on the beach sometimes at night when I sleep. She looks so pretty."

Ice coursed through Elena's veins. Chilled to the core. Part of her wanted to ask Amelia questions, to glean what the child was talking about, but the other part of her was too afraid, and didn't want the answers. Of course, on some level, Amelia was aware her mother had died as a result of an accident while she was at the ocean, but was that all it was? Of course, it was. Elena was a logical woman. The only reason Amelia's words cut her tonight were because of everything Elena herself was going through. The rawness that made her aware of every little thing lately. Her nerves were wound too tight, too easy to be affected. Like the tiniest shift in the balance would throw her off completely.

Amelia continued as she rummaged through the dresser looking for her bathing suit, "I think Mamma lives in the big turny water wave. Or maybe..." She trailed off, flinging a pair of socks to the floor.

Elena was so surprised by those words she swooned. She

sat down on the edge of the bed, perfectly still. Mr. Bigsy went tumbling off the side of the bed, though no one noticed. It was as if the words struck her paralyzed. Her mind re-played what Amelia said. Once her brain told her body she could move again, her initial thought was to run to the living room and tell Ray what happened, and then she thought better. That would shove him right off the edge. It was just a dream, a crazy coincidental dream. Kids dream all sorts of strange things. She probably overheard Elena and Ray talking recently anyway. That was probably how the idea got planted in her little head in the first place. No big deal.

Amelia continued on, "Mamma is so smart, she knows lots of things. She told me about the dizzy birds, and the rain, and the windstorm thing, and the snow and the mountain..." Amelia brought her hands together and pushed them up into the air quickly and made a whooshing sound. Her voice trailed off as the list went on.

Elena was still speechless, not sure how or if she could respond. A lump of fear sat in her throat and no matter how hard she tried; she couldn't seem to swallow it down. She spotted Mr. Bigsy on the floor and picked him up, pulling the big fluffy bunny in to her chest, as if he would provide some sort of comfort.

After a pause, Amelia's list continued, "Oh, and the dolphins on the beach, and the ground rumbling..." she brought her fingers up to her mouth, her brow crinkling as she thought. "Did you know the sky isn't blue there? It's not like here." Amelia flung a few items of clothing out of a drawer in her continued search, her demeanor growing more desperate. "Where's my bathing suit, Auntie E?"

Elena remained quiet for a bit longer, until she could muster the courage and strength to finally say, "You don't need your bathing suit." She moved to the dresser and pulled some random clothes from Amelia's hands, putting a halt to the child's search. "Now let's put all these clothes back. Nice and neat, see." Folding the clothes, she tucked them into their drawers.

"But—"

"No but's Amelia. You wear your pajamas in bed to sleep." Her voice was stern, and she wished she was as confident as her tone suggested.

"But Auntie E—." Amelia turned to face her aunt and stomped a foot.

"Ah-ah-ah, time for sleep. Enough," she said, firmly. "Pajamas are for sleepy time, and its sleepy time. Come on little bunny."

With that she got another little giggle, as the girl finally gave up and put on her pajamas.

"I'll try not to get my pj's full of sand."

"Okay, very thoughtful Amelia, now climb into bed. Tuck time."

Elena tucked her in, nice and tight, so the bed bugs wouldn't bite. She kissed her on the forehead, and then gently padded to the door, as Amelia was already falling asleep. She left the door open a crack, like she always did, and before walking away, stole one last look at the sleepy child. Their conversation ran back through her mind, and she found herself pulling her robe tighter around her, as if she had developed quite a chill. She headed back to the living room, where Ray still sat watching TV. Stopping in the doorway of the living room, she stared distantly at him, her robe huddled tight around her as the TV droned on, seemingly so very distant, like she wasn't even in the same room, the same world:

"Breaking news. Yes, this is just coming in. Yet another tornado has touched down in California. This one ripped through Universal Studios, not long ago. Significant damage is being reported, but we don't yet have all the details. We'll get them to you as soon as we can. It's a lucky thing this one touched down after the park was closed for the evening…"

Elena sneezed, and it was enough to break Ray away from the TV.

Ray turned his head and his gaze fell heavy upon his wife as she leaned in the doorway. Her arms were wrapped tightly about herself. "You cold?"

Elena heard him but didn't respond; she was far off in her thoughts.

He asked a bit louder, "You okay, honey? Elena?"

She blinked a few times in quick succession and came out of her stupor. "What? Oh, yes. I'm sorry, what did you say?"

Ray gawked at her with a goofy, baffled grin. "I'm supposed to be the one who spaces out like that. Can't have both of us doing it or they'll lock us both up."

She gave him a burdened smile; it was all that she could muster. He always had a way of making things feel lighter, even if for a fleeting moment, even if it wasn't entirely appropriate. It was one of the things she loved most about him. Back in college, David was always so serious. He was the type of person who couldn't multitask with emotions. No empathy when he was absorbed in his own emotional state. At first, Elena thought that was a quality she loved and admired, but as time went on, she realized that was something that bothered her about him. He couldn't see past his own feelings when he was upset or overly focused. Then Ray came along. Sweet, thoughtful, aware, Ray. She was doomed. She fell hard. Though she fought those urges every step of the way.

"Are you okay, Elena?" he asked again, each word very deliberate.

She pondered the question, ever so briefly, and decided to say, "Kids. They say the darndest things, don't they?" She didn't wait for any response and didn't offer anything more. She exited the living room for the kitchen to put on a pot of tea to warm her chilled bones.

9

In the garage, Matt was a man possessed by the sudden overwhelming need for answers. Almost twenty years of questions and mystery gnawed at him, weighing heavy on his mind. Why would Ravynn narrowly escape that car crash only to die in a tsunami? Did Matt himself cheat her death that first time only to have fate swoop in later on and steal his wife from him? Was there some sort of Universal balance that needed to be righted? Or was there something more *supe*rnatural going on?

Boxes stacked against the back wall, not forgotten, but untouched since he had packed them away a year ago. He told himself he'd never open them, and yet here he was, intending to do just that.

One by one he pulled them down off the stack. He couldn't remember where he kept the one that he needed, the one that held Ravynn's journals locked away from the world. Five boxes now sat before him. Sad to realize that a once vibrant life could be reduced to the contents of boxes. He peered over the top of each of them, wishing that in his grief-ridden haste to pack up all her belongings, he'd at least labeled them; alcohol and his mourning had gotten the best of him.

He opened the first box and pulled out an old photo book. Overcome with melancholy, he sank back on his knees and rifled through the pages. He was struck by a picture of his beautiful bride, her eyes so full of life, possibility, and happiness.

He remembered as he looked at the pictures, Ravynn walking down the aisle toward him. Her long flowing gown back then had conjured an image, a fleeting moment of something like deja-vu. Something ethereal, otherworldly: The *Woman on the Water* with her hair and dress billowing in the night air. It was the third time in his life he thought he'd seen an angel. How much Ravynn looked like her, that woman who had hovered there above the river all those years ago when he was twenty-two, a young man trying to save a thirteen-year-old girl.

He'd questioned that sense of deja-vu then, and he questioned it again as it crept up on him like a hairy little spider as he sat in the garage. He slammed the book shut and reached for another album.

Why torture himself with the pictures? What good would it do?

The second book was already open in his hands, and this one took him back to a family trip to the beach, only two years previous. As he turned through the pages, a heavy smile washed over his face. One particular picture caught his breath. The setting sun behind Ravynn, causing her to look more like a shadow of a figure than Ravynn herself. The outline of her form was clear, but he couldn't make out her face. He understood it was her, knew it for a fact because he had taken the picture. He also saw the other woman who had haunted him for so long. The *Woman on the Water* could be Ravynn standing there on the beach. The likeness was uncanny. Hadn't he seen it then? He had, yes, he had. That was when he first stumbled across her secret journals. Just after that trip…

"You coming to bed?" Matt had asked her as he stepped into the bedroom, his tone full of innuendo. "Amelia is down and out, tucked snug as a bug and all that."

She didn't respond. She sat in a chair beside the bedroom window that faced away from the doorway, and Matt. She used to sit in that chair every night when Amelia was a baby, reading her off to sleep.

Now, instead of a baby, there was a journal in her lap, and she was scribbling away in it like a madwoman.

Matt stepped further into the room and tried again, "Hey, you hear me, Ravy? Honey? Amelia is out."

Still nothing.

He moved in front of her and tried again. "Hey bebe, it's sexy time." He waggled his eyebrows at her but gained nothing from her. Not a gesture, she kept on writing.

"Ravynn? You-who…"

Finally, she startled. Her face scrunched up, clearly confused by his presence. "When did you come in? I didn't even hear you." She looked as if she'd been yanked out of a dream. "What did you say?" She peered down at the open journal and Matt staring at it, and snapped it shut as his fingers reached out.

"What had you so intense there?" He pulled his hand back like a man almost bitten by a dog.

"Nothing," she replied with a slight waver of her voice.

"What are you writing?" he asked her.

"Ah, nothing important." She shrugged and pulled the journal to her chest.

Matt wasn't willing to let go though. There was something so odd about it all. "Seemed pretty important a second ago. You didn't even hear me talking to you. Just scribbling away in that thing, all intense." He pointed an accusatory finger at the journal.

Her tone stiffened. "I said. It's nothing. Let it go. Nothing." Her words took on a staccato effect.

"So you keep saying," he said. He tried to keep the conversation just that, and not a confrontation. With his finest English accent, he said, "Methinks the lady doth protest too much."

Not entertained, she pushed past him and out the door, still clinging to the journal like a life-raft.

That was the beginning of the whole mess. How many times did they fight about that journal? How many times did Matt walk in to find her hunched over, writing so fast at times her hand was a blur? It was like nothing else existed in those moments but her and that journal.

He put the photo books back in the box with a renewed determination. He knew what was inside the box he sought but wasn't sure which box it was. On the fourth box, he struck gold.

He pulled it to him and sank into the ground like a puddle. Time seemed to freeze, like the world itself waited, holding its breath.

He tore the box apart. Instead of peeling back the tape, he shredded the box, fingers clumsy and awkward, as if they too were afraid of what they'll find.

Then he hesitated, knowing the contents and all that it held. Not just journals, not just words on paper. He told himself he'd never look at those again. So why did he keep them? He wished he'd never seen them, never knew of their existence. Maybe they would never have split, maybe she'd still be alive... so many maybe's.

A tear fell down his cheek as his mind drifted to that night she found him, her journal in his hands, invading her most private writing.

"What are you doing with that?" her voice had snapped

through the silence of the bedroom. Matt had thought he was alone. He hadn't considered himself sneaky, or what would happen if he was caught. He hadn't really thought about it at all, yet there he stood with Ravynn's journal in hand, reading her private entries. Frozen, dumbstruck by being caught red-handed, he couldn't respond.

He shook his head and opened his mouth to speak, but no words came out.

"What are you doing, Matt?" her tone became more frantic as she stared at the open journal in his hands.

"I just... I don't know. I came in, it was here, I didn't think..."

"So, you picked it up and started looking through it?" Her face worked itself into a frightful mix of panic and tears. Her eyes squinted, her brows furrowed, her lips fought to maintain some semblance of control over the little sobs that emanated from them. "How could you?" Hands at her sides, she stretched her fingers out, then clenched them into little balled up knots. Starting at those fists, her arms began a slow shake, working its way up her arms to the sockets. She looked like she was going to explode.

He'd never seen her so frantic. "I'm sorry," Matt said. His mouth expressed his sincerity in those words, but his body was saying something else entirely. He held a hard stance, frozen with the journal still open in his hands. Like a deer in the headlights, he was unmovable, struck by the surprise of being caught, and the fear of what he read. He hadn't had time to make sense of any of it. Mad scribbles and ramblings of incomplete thoughts. Dates. Events. All of them catastrophic. Some dates had already passed, but some had yet to come.

"Give it to me!" She raised one of those shaking arms out to him. "Give it back now!" She was screaming. She was berserk, despite Amelia sleeping down the hallway.

"Whoa, Ravynn. Calm down, honey. Please, Amelia is asleep."

"Give it back to me and I will calm down!" she yelled. She

stood there still, arm outreached, waiting.

Matt closed the journal and walked to her and placed it in her hand. Now holding the journal, she shook it at him.

"How dare you? How could you read this? It's private. Mine." Her eyes were filled with both disappointment and something else. Embarrassment. "How could you?" Her voice softened now, choked by a sob. She took a deep, shaky breath and composed herself.

Matt chose his words carefully. He didn't want to upset her any further, but he was so confused and frightened by what he read in those few brief entries he glimpsed before she walked in. "I don't understand," was all he managed to say.

"You don't have to. It's not for you." She shook her head at him and repeated, "It's not for *you*."

"Who is it for? Help me understand, Ravy."

"No."

"But these entries, they—"

She cut him off. "Leave it alone, Matt."

"But how do—"

Again, she cut his words short. "I can't explain it. Let...it...be." She didn't wait for a response this time. She clenched the journal tight, hugged it into her chest, and left the room without another word.

She left Matt there to wonder about the entries he found. The dates, the events, some having recently passed, but some that had not yet come to pass. Storms, natural disasters, all listed and dated. A log of terrible happenings, that was her secret. Matt was unsure of the accuracy of most of them; he'd need to check them against records to be sure, but one recent event flashed in the front of his brain like a neon sign: The locust plague a month previous. The Dakotas and Nebraska had been overwhelmed this summer when trillions of locusts hatched and ran amok, taking to the skies and blotting out the sun for hours at a time. Turning normal traffic into gridlocks, causing multiple accidents on the highways and bringing normal life to an almost full stop for several days. How could she have known? How could she see those things before they happened? There had to be some other explanation...

As he shook himself from the memories, he took a calming breath and steeled his nerves, summoning the courage to do what he needed to do.

He bent forward, peering over the edge and spotted a stack of journals. His heartbeat escalated from the excitement and fear. With his fingertips, he reached in and lifted them out so very gingerly as if he were to be too rough with them, they would crumble like some ancient text into a million pieces.

He took the top one and set the rest back down. He opened the cover and turned the pages slowly, and then stopped upon a date: The date was days away....

10

"R ay," her voice whispered. "Raymond."
Her voice, her breath tickled his ear. *Ravynn.* He was still asleep, unable to move.

"Ray, wake up," her voice rolled in and out, like a calm ocean wave. "We need to talk. Need water."

Ray snapped awake, his body responding to her request before his mind could process what was happening. *"Need water,"* her last words pushed him to act. As if led by a consciousness not his own, he reacted. Quietly, he crawled out of bed, gently enough to not wake Elena. He almost cartoonishly tip-toed across the floor to the bathroom and closed the door behind him without a sound. Plugged the sink with the stopper and filled it with water. When there were a few inches in the basin, he turned off the water, placed both hands on the side of the sink and leaned forward, his head just above the water. Closer now, as he thought he perceived some kind of movement in the water. A reflection? No, that couldn't be. Of course, he knew it could. She told him to do this, to come to the water. She called him, and she came.

The water took on a shape, or at least the reflection of a

shape. Familiar, a face he recognized so well. Logic and reason meant nothing in that moment; he didn't question the possibilities.

He stood, mesmerized, as the water hazed and cleared. Her face. Her dark hair. Her green eyes twinkling against the backdrop of the water. Lips moving, but he couldn't make out what was being said. No sound, only movement.

Frustration bubbled to the surface as he leaned forward, desperate to hear her. There was a hush, a faint murmur from her lips. He cocked his head to the side, just a few inches above the water, at an angle where he could no longer see her. His voice wavered with nerves as he whispered to her, "Ravynn, I can't hear you." Such desperation and pain in his voice, it frightened even him. "Ravynn. Where are you?"

The words rolled forward, as if off another ocean wave. "Under another sun."

He mumbled to himself, "I must still be dreaming."

"You… awake… Ray," her voice fading, as if a storm crept over the ocean and drowned her out. "…attention. Disruption… can't communicate."

"No!" Ray exclaimed, slamming a hand against the side of the sink. He pleaded, "I'm losing my mind."

"No," her reply was firm. "It's starting. Once it starts…" her words were lost. "…the world."

The water rippled, though nothing could have made it move. As if a breeze blew through the room, impossibly shaking her attempt at communication.

"World… down…"

Only those words. Her lips moved, but nothing else came though. Agitation stirred not only the water but his emotions. Sweat formed at the back of his neck and the top of his lip, as it always did when he was anxious. "Ravynn!" His voice cut through the silence of the heavy night- no longer a whisper.

"Mistakes." Her words again soft, as if trailing the winds of a storm. "Eclipse. Dolphins. All speeding up…"

A knock at the door startled him. "Ray? Honey? You ok?" Elena held a steady knock on the door, a frantic pleading.

"Honey, open the door."

Ray had forgotten himself, where he was, and who was asleep in the next room. The reality smacked him. "Go back to bed, I'm fine," he called through the door.

Too late. The doorknob was turning. "I'm coming in, Ray."

His voice filled with unavoidable anger, "I'm fine! Don't treat me like a child." He looked down at the water, but that was all it is was. Water in the sink. Nothing else. Panic rolled over him with the realization that Ravynn was gone, and the goddamned doorknob was still turning. "I said, stay out!"

With the last word, Elena popped her head through the door with trepidation. Her eyes were wide- concern laced with fear. Her mouth puckered, almost to a pout, as if she was holding back the tears.

Ray cringed at his own harshness. He'd never been so angry with her like that before. He chastised himself internally. She was just concerned, and rightly so. She didn't deserve that kind of response.

He pulled the door the rest of the way open, letting her see him. "I'm sorry, babe. I don't know what came over me. I shouldn't have shouted at you.

"Are you alright?" she asked gingerly, as if another angry response would harm her physically. "I heard you yell. Say her name. I got worried, that's all. I am sorry if I upset you, Ray."

"No, I'm sorry. I was upset. I had another dream, of course. I didn't want to wake you, so you'd have to hold my hand like a little baby. I wanted to let you sleep. No need for us both to be awake because of my bad dreams." He managed a smile.

"You said her name, while you were in here."

He took a moment to think it through. "I was just shaken and frustrated from the dream, so I came in here. I was sweating, so I filled the sink and splashed water on my face. I was cursing her name. Cursing her for haunting me so. That's all, babe. And I'm sorry I startled you."

"If you're sure that's all," she said, though her tone suggested otherwise.

"Yep. Let's go back to bed." He left the water in the sink,

took his wife's hand, and led her back to the bed. They each crawled into their own side of the bed, and onto their backs.

"I love you, Ray," she said, as she stared at the ceiling.

"I love you too. Come here, let's spoon. He pulled her hips to him. She curled her back to him, and he wrapped his arms and body around her, enveloping her. The perfection of it, of her, wrapped tight filled him with such a bittersweet heartsickness. Why didn't he hold her like that more often? Because of that look in her eyes. She probably wasn't aware she did it, but that look, so full of judgment and fear. Like every time she looked at him, she expected him to finally fall to pieces. Like Ray was made of glass, and she had to tread with caution. He wished she'd just look at him the way she used to. With love, pride, safety.

She snuggled back closer and tighter, and he kissed the back of her head. Within moments, she relaxed completely and gave over to sleep. How many nights had they gone to sleep this way in the past? In the beginning, they'd always done it. Fell asleep holding each other or at the very least touching in some way. But recently, the distance had grown, making it seem some nights their bed had grown larger and larger. At times, lost in a sea of blankets, unable to reach out and find each other, find solace.

He was glad she fell asleep, though a little envious. No more sleep would come for him tonight.

The World Is Falling Down. That's what Ravynn was telling him. He wasn't exactly sure what it meant yet, but it wasn't good. Sleep wouldn't make it any less real.

SLEEP finally overtook him around 5 a.m. Thankfully, there was no early wake-up; no Amelia jumping on the bed, no Elena poking or prodding, no alarm clock blaring. He finally lifted a heavy eyelid and focused on the clock. 11 a.m. He sighed. A moment of panic, of *why didn't the alarm go* off shook him, but then he remembered: school's out. Pulled the blankets up and shielded himself from the light of day. His breath came back in his face as he exhaled into the shroud of blanket.

Remember the eclipse. The dolphins.

Much of what Ravynn said to him was unclear, but that much he recalled. A lot of good that did him. He had no idea what any of it was about. His mind started racing and forced him out of bed.

The house appeared empty as he walked down the hall to the kitchen. While brewing a pot of coffee, laughter trickled in from the open kitchen window. Peering out, a soft breeze caressed his skin as he spied Elena pushing Amelia on the swing-set. Amelia's laugh warmed him more than his coffee would. Smiling, he scooped up a cup of coffee and strode to the living room, plopping himself down into the sofa. He opened his laptop and searched: Eclipse.

No results.

The giggles in the background grew nearer as Amelia and Elena came into the kitchen. Elena appeared in the doorway of the living room alone, leaning against it. "Up at last," she said.

Momentarily pausing, he lifted his hands from the keyboard and gave her his full attention. The memory of the scent of her hair while they cuddled last night distracted him, and he almost forgot what he was doing. "Felt good to hold you last night." He smiled at the beautiful woman standing before him.

"Almost normal," she said. Her words probably weren't meant to be cutting, but with tensions high and nerves raw, they stung.

Ray's focus shifted. He couldn't help it; he was like a dog with a bone. "Do you know anything about the eclipse today?"

"I don't think so," she replied, shooting him a curious look. "Where did you hear that?"

He ignored her question and continued, "No, I am positive there is an eclipse today, but I can't find the info anywhere."

She shook her head. "Okay, whatever you say."

He went on absently, ignoring her growing frustration with him. "I tried several different searches. Can't find anything."

"Well, maybe you got the date wrong?" She moved into the room and glanced over his shoulder at the computer. She placed a warm hand on his shoulder and rubbed it gently.

He hadn't meant to, but he shook off her touch. He didn't want to be distracted.

She pulled her hand back and placed it on her hip. "Since when do you care about that stuff, anyway?" Her tone had shifted from delicate to biting.

Since Ravynn started sending him messages and warnings, that was when. The bitterness of those words scraped the back of his throat and he choked them down with a swig of coffee, glad to not have said them aloud He bit his tongue and chose not to answer.

11

Giving up on any chance of conversation with Ray, Elena headed back to the kitchen.

At the table, Amelia was eating a banana. She looked up at Elena, one eyebrow raised. "What's an e-lips, Auntie E?"

Elena paused, thinking of the best way to describe the event. She picked up and apple and an orange from the table.

"Eclipse. When the moon passes in front of the sun and blocks the light." She showed Amelia what she meant by holding up the orange. "This orange is the sun. And this apple..." she said as she picked up the apple with the other hand, "is the moon." She slowly made the orange move behind the apple, blocking it from Amelia's view. "So, the sun gives off light, making it daytime, but the moon blocks the light, making it look dark, like night."

"Oh," Amelia acknowledged, putting the banana down. "When day turns into night."

Elena shook her head. "Not quite. Not like when the sun sets at the end of day and night begins. This is different."

Amelia poked at the banana. "Like nighttime, but in the daytime. Only for a little while, right?"

Surprised by Amelia's comprehension of the subject, she

delighted her with a smile. "Yes, very good Amelia." Her teacher's joy beamed.

"Yup, Mommy told me about that too." She picked the banana back up and took another bite.

Elena, dumbfounded, found herself stuck between an apple and an orange, and couldn't respond. Like Amelia's words had blocked out all her light.

BARELY another hour passed before the eclipse happened. Even though Ray was aware of what was coming, he was surprised, nonetheless. Still twiddling on the internet, he sat at the picnic table waiting. The sun's warmth spilled down his neck and back as he hunched over the screen.

So gradually it began, and at first it was like the sun just passed behind a cloud. Ray didn't even flinch. The shadow loomed, and grew darker, dimming, dimming, forcing his eyes to the sky. A mix of excitement and dread filled him; there was not supposed to be an eclipse today. Every part of his rational mind understood that. But *she* said there would be.

The soft chatter and song of birds grew muted until they were gone. They all seemed to sense the upcoming display and took cover.

Ray lifted his hand up to the sky, to shield his eyes and sneak a peek. Indeed, an eclipse. Ray took care not to look directly at the sun.

Day folded itself into the guise of night, and his surroundings melted away into Cimmerian shade. The swing-set off to his side, and the grill not far from the picnic table, now all but faded into obscurity. Moment by moment, the faux night took over, draining the day of its light until there was none left. A total solar eclipse. Darkness.

Muted voices came from the house. The door opened, and Elena emerged with a flashlight in hand, the beam bobbing around through the newly fallen calignosity as she stepped out.

"I told Amelia to stay inside," Elena called out.

The flashlight's beam bounced around the yard and drew nearer, shedding a stream of light across the grass.

Elena continued, "She wanted to come out and watch but I told her to stay inside. I don't want her burning out her eyes staring." The sound of her feet shuffled the last few feet to Ray. "I did not think there was an eclipse today, but you were right."

Ray said nothing, stared off into the dark. He wasn't sure how long it would last or if perhaps it might last forever. Ravynn hadn't provided much information in the little time she'd communicated. The idea of a world pitched into darkness and chaos filled him with dread. He fought back a panic as the darkness crept in around him, crawled inside him, pushing on him, squeezing the air out of his lungs.

"Did you end up finding the info on the internet?" Elena's voice skittered its way through the heaviness like an insect to his ears.

Still no response. He looked down at his computer to catch the screen flicker twice and flash out. Blackout. All light was seeping away. He took a deep breath and wrapped the darkness around him like a cloak, wearing the shadows like a strange second skin.

"Who told you about the eclipse, Ray?" Whatever intonation she had in that question was lost on him. He was immersed in the dark, shielded by it.

Ray voiced one word, confidently, one name. "Ravynn."

Elena dropped the flashlight and it flickered on the ground. The silence between them gave Ray the impression he was miles away from his wife. The flashlight went out momentarily, then came back to life at the same time Elena's voice cracked. "Did you say *Ravynn* told you about the eclipse?"

Ray had no lie to tell her, no way around what he'd said. He didn't even care to try this time. Point blank, he said, "Yes, I said Ravynn." If it wasn't so dark out, Elena might have seen his unblinking eyes staring right through her. He continued with dead seriousness, "She told me the eclipse was coming."

Elena's tone sharpened. Even in the dark, he sensed it poking through. He imagined her face hardening, the soft contours falling away, edges sharp and pointed. "What do you mean? That's impossible." The flashlight sat on the ground; its beam aimed at the swing-set. A light breeze pushed the swing ever so slightly, and it creaked and swayed to and fro. Ray might've thought it an eerily timed display if a queer insouciance hadn't washed over him.

"You asked. I'm telling you. She told me last night. When you heard me in the bathroom. That's when." He raised his voice, but his delivery was still very robotic. "How else would I know about a solar eclipse when no one else did?" His dramatic shrug lost in the darkness. "I'm not crazy. There's more going on here. It's unexplainable. I don't understand. Not yet."

Elena's voice was chastising. "It's not unexplainable. We just don't have the explanation. There's a logical reason."

"Really, Elena?" Ray's voice was now charged with anger, crackling through the air like electricity.

"You must have heard it from somewhere. Someone." She bent down to pick up the flashlight, her form's shadow stretched out supernaturally through the beam. The light sputtered again and went out for good, leaving them in the full dark of the day.

"I did," he repeated, refusing to let this go. "I heard it from *Ravynn*."

"No. No. Absolutely not, Ray." He didn't need to see her face to realize her eyes had gotten small, like they did when she was angry. That her mouth was puckered and lips tight.

Ray threw his hands up in the dark, a lost dramatic gesture. "I don't know what else to tell you. But I'm not going to lie to you. I am not losing my mind. I am not having nightmares. Ravynn is trying to tell me something. And I am going to listen."

"I think I should call Dr. Sheffield," she whispered.

Ray took a moment to wonder if she meant for him to catch it and decided he didn't care. "Call him for yourself, if you need. But I am not going back there. It's not just the eclipse. There's more, Elena, so much more."

"Pray tell, Ray, what else did your dead sister tell you?" Her words were sharp and cutting, but Ray chose not to let them cut him in the dark.

"The dolphins..." his voice trailed off. There was something about standing there, in the dark, confessing his secrets to Elena that was finally so easy, so freeing. Probably because he didn't have to look in her eyes, note the disappointment, the concern, judgement. Here in the dark of the eclipse, he was free.

LIKE some kind of stand-off, Elena and Ray sat in chairs on opposite sides of the living room, watching TV, trying to find an explanation for today's strange events. Elena was sure Ray was out of his flipping mind but had been at a loss to get through to him. The evening news confirmed the eclipse, ringing out through their silence like the sound of a first shot being fired. Elena jumped at the broadcast:

Today's total Solar Eclipse surprised people all across the Western Hemisphere. Without any warning of the coming blackout, scientists were baffled. Not one has of yet offered a feasible explanation as to what occurred and how it was missed, but skeptics and conspiracy theorists alike claim everything from government cover-ups, strange experiments and military procedures, to other claiming UFO's and the end of days.

Scientists did, however, offer up possible explanations for the vast number of dolphins and sea lions washing up on shores today from Oregon to Argentina, saying it's possible that the dramatic solar event could have affected these sensitive creatures...

And speaking of creatures, a heavy swarm of Mayflies

inundated a Louisiana town today. Swarms have been known to flourish in the area, but the baffling part of this particular swarm was their behavior. Typically, the males leave the water after mating and move inland to die soon after. Strangely, these Mayflies all died within seconds of each other. There were literally millions of insects falling out of the air in unison today.

That sure will be one heck of a cleanup, Aaron.

(amidst chuckling) Sure will, Katrina. In other news, a massive storm system brewing over a significant portion of South Eastern Europe could bring a surprising amount of summer snowfall...

Coming up next, a peculiar bug seems to be sweeping the nation, and all over the world. Have you been impacted? The CDC reports that this particular 'illness' appears indiscriminate. Affecting young, old, healthy, and sick alike, this odd blend of vertigo/motion sickness has people reeling. From dizziness, nausea, trouble focusing and an inability to maintain steady balance. No serious symptoms seem to be present. No fevers, muscle aches. As of yet, the CDC does not report this as a dangerous concern, but asks if you're experiencing these symptoms, consult your doctor.

More coming up, tonight, at eleven, only on KRKW, your source for the most current and accurate local and world news...

Elena shook her head in disbelief. The news- Ray, Amelia, the whole damn day- too strange. She didn't understand what was going on, but there had to be a rational explanation, she was certain. She glanced across the room, stealing a peek at Ray who was still totally engrossed in the TV. What kind of madness was this? Was she just subscribing to Ray's fears, or was there something more going on? And Amelia, the quirky things that she'd been doing and saying...

12

Still in his slippers at two on a Saturday afternoon, Ray lazily contemplated things as he shuffled down the hall. The world, the reality of it had split. Everything he ever thought he was certain of had been challenged, distorted. It was only going to get worse, and there was still too much that was vague, undefined.

He placed a hand on the wall, as the thoughts dizzied him. Ravynn still existed. Somehow, she was trying to urge her warnings through to him.

He pushed himself off the wall and continued on towards Amelia's room- but he never made it past her doorway- something stopped him dead in his tracks. Amelia singing a song. A song he'd never heard before, yet somehow it was somehow eerily reminiscent.

"No rain for you... the sky was blue...
You're running out of time...
A crack in time saves ninety-nine..."

A haunted sensation crept over him. An oddly familiar song.

"Amelia?" He stood outside her half-open door. Leaned

into the door frame and listened.

She didn't respond. She continued.

"we spin around and around...
The world is falling down..."

She scooped up a doll and spun around with her arms outstretched, the doll flailing in her hands, crepuscular rays of sunlight shining through the blinds with a heavy orange glow that skittered and danced around Amelia like a spotlight as she turned. She took another wild spin and dropped to the floor on her back.

Ray couldn't interrupt her even if he wanted to. He was dumbstruck, and she was entranced, in that place that children go when they're playing with imaginary friends and make-believe. The sun's rays shone on the spot of the floor directly above Amelia's head, painting her in an eerie halo.

But this isn't make-believe, he thought.

Amelia got to her knees, held the doll out in front of her and shook it violently, all the while, her face maintained a calm expression.

"The world quakes... the people shake...
Hmmm-hmmm-hmmm-hmmm-hmmm"

What an odd song, he thought. *Where did she learn this? I'll have to ask Ravynn.* That one name struck him like a slap in the mouth. *I mean Elena. Why would I—Ravynn?*

The song reminded him of his sister. He tried to shake it off, like it was no big deal. He thought a lot about his sister these days. Amelia's song continued.

"The day is almost done...
Under another sun... under another sun...
We walk, we walk, we walk under another sun"

The last verse sent a shockwave through his very bones. He almost leaned himself right off the wall. Sensed himself slipping and reached out to grab the door frame to steady himself. Finally, he stepped into the room, in a daze. Opened his mouth to speak, but no words came out. His mouth was moving in the shape of words, but he couldn't make the sounds.

He knelt down on the floor next to Amelia. Put a hand on top of the other in his lap, rubbing his palm roughly. He cleared his throat to speak. There was a giant cotton-ball stuck in his esophagus, which he attempted to clear twice, then spoke, the first few words coming out like gravel.

"Amelia, where did you learn that song?"

Taking his question quite literally, as kids did, she responded, "At the beach!" Her eyes lit up as she said this, and a smile tilted the corners of her mouth.

Baffled, Ray tried to comprehend what his niece was telling him. None of them had been to the beach again since Ravynn passed. It was an unspoken rule that they all stayed far, far away.

"When did you go to the beach, sweetie?" He was vaguely sure she'd not been, and yet...she sounded so convincing. Ray found himself questioning a lot of things he'd previously known as truths lately.

"At night. In my dreams."

The huge cotton-ball in his throat came back with a weighted vengeance, cutting off not only his voice but his air too. He absentmindedly reached for his neck and rubbed at it. Gulped with a fiercely audible sound, trying to force the imaginary obstruction down. He was convinced like he was going to choke.

"You okay, Uncle Ray?" Her smiling face turned to worry.

The blockage dissipated, as if Amelia's voice held the secret remedy.

"I-I'm fine. Yes. But I don't understand. Who taught you that song?" His tone was desperate. And it frightened Amelia.

"I'm sorry." She tipped her head downward in shame.

"No sweetie. It's okay. I'm just surprised." He lightened the timbre of his voice and asked, "So you say, you learned this song on the beach. Sounds fun! Who taught you this?"

Her head lifted back up to stare in his eyes, "My friends!"

Of course, Amelia had imaginary friends. He laughed to himself for being such a fool. All children go through that phase. He chastised himself internally for overreacting. Don't be so quick to hit the panic button. Made up friends and songs of a five-year-old. Whoop-de-doo.

"Amelia continued, "My new friends, and I see Mommy too!"

Well, that almost brought on a heart attack. Imaginary friends and playful songs were one thing, seeing her mommy on the beach hit entirely too close to home. He reached for his neck, his throat again, rubbing and gulping. He took a shallow breath when he could finally find his air.

Her voice continued on, in that shrill excited voice that only little girls seemed to have, but he couldn't focus on the words. His world was spinning. If he didn't settle down quickly, he was going to have a full on panic attack, hyperventilate and pass out there in front of his niece. He begged himself silently, *"Get it together, man. Hold-it-to-ge-ther."* He found the control to take two deep breaths and it brought him back. Amelia's shrill voice started to make sense, and he could understand words now: 'beach', 'pajamas', 'water', 'mommy'. Panic attacks had always been a stranger to him until this past year. With more regularity they cornered him, like a starved pack of wolves, closing in on him savagely, more and more every day.

Amelia was rambling on now, and Ray finally listened. "And then Mommy was there. In the wave. The water. She waved at me. She was really pretty. Her hair was all floaty. Then another time, in the water, through the spinny door, that's where my new friends are. They play and run and we sing and dance. It's sunny there. Bright. Happy. And mommy swings me around and around until we're both dizzy. And we fall down laughing. And we cuddle. And giggle. That's when she tells me all the neat stuff. And the sad stuff. I see her at night. Sleeping time. But I am not sleeping, not there, on the beach with Mommy. And then I come home. Back to bed. Here." She pointed to her bed. "I told Auntie E about it and she said no, I can't wear my bathing suit to bed, just pajamas.

She said I am dreaming. But you know, Uncle Ray." She turned and pointed a tiny finger at him. "You know about Mommy too."

Those last few words hit as heavy as a ton of bricks, cracking him upside the head. Elena knew. Elena knew about all this and didn't tell him. Why? Was it because it was too similar to what he's been experiencing? The water, Ravynn. Did she think he couldn't handle that information?

This couldn't all be just a coincidence. He tried to calm himself, but Amelia's words danced across his brain. 'We walk under another sun'. Amelia sang it, and hadn't Ravynn told him that too? No, no coincidence. A burning rage welled up inside of him, something he hadn't experienced in quite some time, if ever. Like a volcano getting ready to erupt, it surged, growing, burning, welling up inside until he thought he would surely blow. He got up off the floor, leaving his excited niece to continue spouting off about the water and her new friends. Undeterred by his departure, his niece shrugged and casually picked up a couple of dolls and told them the story instead. A much more captive audience.

Ray turned away from Amelia and headed out the door with a purpose. Confront Elena.

13

Ray sat at the kitchen table, facing the door, arms tightly crossed over his chest. He was a loaded cannon waiting for her to return from the store.

Holding onto all that rage, keeping it tight to his chest, he'd unleash as soon as she stepped through that door. If the eclipse wasn't enough, this was more proof that he wasn't crazy. Amelia visiting her mother at night. Ravynn whispering in her daughter's ear, no longer only in his head. Elena could have told him, could have eased some of his worries and fears, but she kept her secrets. Why? And what other secrets was she keeping from him?

The familiar sound of the motor hummed as Elena pulled into the driveway. Ray waited for the engine to cut out, but the car sat, idling. This only fueled his fire more. He needed her to shut the damn car off. Shut it off and get in here now before he lost some of his will, some of his fire. Through the open window of the kitchen the radio came blaring in. Her soft melodic voice drifted in, too, singing along.

No, his wife singing wouldn't take away his hurt, his disgust, his rage over this betrayal. Because that's absolutely what it was. A betrayal. She purposefully withheld everything with Amelia from him. Everything that would help with the questions he'd been wrestling for so long: *Why won't Ravynn let go? Because she's not dead and you're not crazy. How much more does Amelia know? I wonder what else Elena hasn't told me. Does she not see it, does she still not believe? This is happening.*

His mind raced, blurry thoughts spinning, twisting, gnawing at his brain. Too many questions, too much hurt. A kaleidoscope of pain, all the months of frustration; fractured, distorted, shards of inner turmoil making its way out.

The car door shut. A moment later, Elena stepped through the door with two armfuls of groceries. Any other time, he would've rushed to relieve her of her burden, but not now, not today. His own burden was too heavy.

Still humming softly, Elena looked up, startled to find Ray there staring at her. She jostled the bags, almost dropping them. He didn't move to help.

"Ray, honey, you startled me," she said.

He managed a wan smile. The bitterness twisted into something strange on his lips. He wondered what it looked like to her, then decided he didn't care.

When he didn't answer, her voice quickly shifted to worried, fragile. She faltered again with the bags in her hands. "Ray?" She leaned forward and let the bags fall lightly on the table, one tipping over, and orange rolling across the table toward him. "Raymond."

He blinked slowly, trying at the same time to both justify and quell his anger. Shoulders scrunched up, tension in his neck gripped at him, tightening his throat and chest. He fought those feelings back, and unleashed. "How long have you known?" His voice cracked.

She shook her head, bewildered. "How long have I known what?" She tipped her head to the side, one eye squinting at him.

"Amelia. The dreams. The beach. Her mother." Each word had a staccato effect, like drumming a quick backbeat. He continued, "Under another sun. She said the words!" His voice was a booming thunder at the last. He was wild, uncontrollable, untrusting of what he'd do or say next. The clock on the wall tick, tick, ticked as the hands tapped off the seconds, and it made him think of the ticking timebomb that he'd become. He wasn't sure if he wanted to calm down or unleash a crazed fury that alarmed even himself.

Elena's shoulders sank to a defeated posture. Her entire countenance seemed to collapse under the accusation. Her mouth opened as if to speak, but then she shut it, unable to find the words. Ray thought she looked like some bizarre ventriloquist's puppet, trying to mouth words that weren't being spoken.

"You let me continue on like a goddamned crazy man!" The words flew out of his mouth so harshly she reacted as if she'd been slapped across the face. She flinched, eyes welling with tears.

Ray continued, "You let me carry on with these nightmares. Waking up in a cold sweat. Night after night after night! You held my hand and rubbed my back and tried to convince me it was all a dream, a goddamned nightmare!"

"Please Ray, keep your voice down." Elena managed to sneak the words in between sobs. "Amelia will hear you." She whispered, trying to catch her breath. "Let me at least shut her door."

Elena disappeared down the hall. Music floated back toward him. He got to his feet ready to face her as she reappeared. Chest puffed in the air, arms crossed, he seethed, "How could you do this to me? I have been questioning my sanity forever. All you had to do was tell me about this. About Amelia." He stepped forward, inches from her. He reached out so quickly she flinched. His hands wrapped around her upper arms so hard and so fast she whimpered. He spat, "And the fucking eclipse. You act like it's no big thing. You act like the only logical answer, the very best answer to all of it is that I'm losing my mind! When will you acknowledge that things aren't right? Things in this world are not happening as they should. There's more to this goddamned story?" He shook her, without realizing what he was doing. Like that doll in Amelia's hands, Ray shook his wife.

She managed a hand free and slapped him across the face. They both froze, looking at each other in shock. His hands fell off her like dead things, and they stood there, inches from each other, but worlds apart. His face a field of questions. Questions and hurt. A line had been crossed, and both stunned, neither knowing how next to proceed.

HEAVY moments of silence passed, baited breaths. Heartbeats pounded, hanging in the air between them.

Now it was Elena's turn to be angry. "What would it have done for you, Ray? What would Amelia's dreams have done to smooth out your shaky mental state? Tell me. Tell me!" She backed up, shaking her head, startled and afraid of her very own words. "Where's the fix here? What would have made it all better? I failed. I failed you," she added, voice quivering as she pointed a finger at him.

She didn't wait for a response. He was as shocked as she was, it was clear upon his face.

"I didn't tell you about Amelia because I thought it would push you right over the freaking edge. I thought, 'well this is just it. If he hears this, he will crack and we'll lose him forever. I'll have to call the big tough men with the pristine white coats and they'll come over here and haul you out of your bed, still in your pajamas'. No Ray, they won't even let you put on decent clothes, they'll just put you in the back of the van, most likely medicating you before you are even out that door. Dull you down to nothing. And then Amelia and I would be alone. Is that what I should have done?" Anxiety and frustration took over her body and she began to shake. She crossed her arms over her chest to try to get a literal and figurative hold on herself before she continued, to no avail.

"Should I have been the one to see you teetering on that edge of sanity, because that is where you have been for some time…" her voice raised an octave and shook with her body. "See you rocking back and forth on that ledge and just come over and give you a little shove off? Poof, presto, whacko! Coo-coo for cocoa puffs!" Sobbing now. Sobbing like a child; tears billowed out of her sockets. Tears and snot dripped down her face, into her mouth, onto her shirt.

"You do realize that they don't do that, right? That's like old-school movie nonsense."

She didn't respond.

"It's not a thing," he added.

"What was I supposed to do, Ray? There is no manual on what to do here." Her voice lowered, barely above a whisper, her eyes cast away from him, to a cobweb previously unseen tucked into the corner of the stove and the floor. "I am only human. I'm doing the best I can, without much help from you." With that, she uttered a pitiful and defeated combination of a sigh and sob. Her body melted to the ground, where she sank into a heap. She brought her hands up over her eyes and pushed down on them. She pulled harshly as she ran her hands roughly down her face, dragging first her eyes, then cheeks, then mouth down, down, down. She got to her jawline and there she held her hands, stuck for a moment like a statue. The room was so quiet, so freakishly quiet. The only sound was the muffled music of Amelia's playing behind closed doors down the hallway, and the sound Elena made to keep the snot from running down her face. She brought a sleeve up to her nose and wiped it away, like a child.

Those seconds of quiet ticked on and on like minutes turned to hours, the fine grains of sand running hurriedly through the proverbial hourglass.

Finally, Elena spoke, finding herself more restrained and strangely calm, "What does it even prove, anyway? Let's look at it logically, ok? Please. So, Amelia is having these dreams of her mother and all that goes with that. And you're dreaming of Ravynn too. So maybe Amelia picked up on our conversations and her little creative mind has run with it."

He started to interrupt, but she hushed him and continued

before he could rebuff, "Or, you both are losing your minds. In one case, it's harmless and almost a little cute. The emulation. But you being off balance and not seeking help to remedy it frightens me to the core." She shuddered.

"There's another possibility you're not mentioning." Ray finally seized his opportunity to speak. "Ravynn is trying to tell us something. It can't all be coincidence. It's too much." He hesitated. "Ravynn is still alive, somewhere. There's too much evidence here to ignore. Can't you see that? And it's not just at night, when I'm sleeping. She comes to me when I'm awake, too. She knows things. Things you simply cannot write off as coincidence. You can't do it!" His eyes were wide, imploring. His hands reached out, but fail to connect, as Elena took a step back. She snorted, actually snorted, when she heard him say that. Shook her head, as if that could change his truth. "Listen to what you are saying, Raymond. Your sister, alive? It can't be." She couldn't bring herself to look at him.

His voice was softer now, "And yet I know in my heart it is true. The eclipse yesterday. How can you discount that? No one understands, and Ravynn warned me of it. And then when I heard Amelia singing that song today, it confirmed so much for me. Such a small thing, but a big coincidence, or whatever the word for it should be." He shrugged. "She sang, 'the world is falling down' and 'we walk under another sun'. Those are exact words that Ravynn said to me in the water. It's been happening for a while. Ravynn talks to me. She tells me, foretells things that will happen. She told me of the eclipse. The dolphins. All these catastrophes over the last year that I ignored, because I thought I was either dreaming or crazy. I tried not to accept this for so long, Elena. But I had to, I have to now. It happens in the water, not only in my dreams. When I'm awake too. I know she's trying to warn us."

"Warm us what, Ray?" Elena's voice was snotty and sharp.

"I don't know. Not yet, I mean. I think, well, I think something catastrophic is going to happen. Somehow when that tsunami hit, Ravynn didn't die. She got sucked into another world." He slapped his hand over his mouth, as if not sure he meant to say it aloud. All Elena could do was frown and shake her head.

Ray continued, undeterred. "Crap, it does sound crazy saying it out loud. It scares me too, Elena. But not because I am going crazy. I've spent so many nights when I couldn't sleep, looking up symptoms of psychosis and schizophrenia, paranoid that I was headed down the rabbit hole. But crazy makes sense. This does not. Under another sun. She said that to me," he said nodding. "That's where she is. She's as real and alive as you and me. She's just not... well, not here."

Elena sighed. Her body, her mind was so heavy, so inundated and overwhelmed by everything that had transpired the past few weeks. The strength within her waned to nothing. Defeat stroked at all her nerve endings, dulling them down. The dizziness skirted her peripheral. Like she was swimming in the kitchen; the room swayed and tilted around her. How long had she been feeling this way? Didn't they mention some strange illness on the news the other night? She blinked, and the room stilled itself. "This is a huge leap of faith, Ray..."

"I know. But bear with me. Please. I need you. This is all so unbelievable, but I need you to believe. Believe in me, believe it for me. What's the alternative, anyway?" He let out a little nervous chuckle. "Crazy. That's the alternative. And if I'm wrong, and it turns out that I am indeed losing my mind, then I will go off to the doctors with the nice clean white jacket and I won't put up a fight. Okay?" He smiled, hoping his levity would help. It did not.

She shook her head slowly back and forth.

Ray rolled his eyes and dropped the sarcasm, his voice carrying his sincerity, "If I am headed in the same direction as my father, I'll go back to Dr Sheffield. We'll see about meds for schizophrenia. But until then..."

She was tired. Tired of the struggles, the nightmares, the fear of losing everything. She tried to utter even one supportive word, but she couldn't. She wanted to vomit. Not sure if it was from the vertigo she experienced or the implications of actually believing Ray, she gulped the bile back down, cringing. All she could say was, "grab the rest of the groceries out of the car, would you? I need to soak in the bath for a while before dinner."

As she walked away, she was thankful he didn't say another word, didn't reach out for her or put up a fight. She heard the front door shut, and she sighed, knowing at least this time, he heeded her request.

14

Elena slid her body down into the hot, steamy bath with a strange invisible weight that wrapped around her like cement bricks to her ankles. Not only because of the physicality of the argument, but mostly the emotional toll it had taken, and that strange dizziness. Almost like when she was pregnant, but not quite. She belched and swallowed hard.

She was starting to believe. Although she fought with every ounce of her being, her resolve, her stubbornness was failing. The coincidences, or as Ray referred to them, the facts, were starting to add up. The uncommon was becoming the common. It was getting harder and harder for her to justify the strange happenings. Maybe Ray wasn't crazy after all. So then, what was happening?

Not sure if she could take any more, she tried to weigh her options. Sit by and watch Ray fall apart, or the world around them? W would truly be more frightful? In that moment, David popped into her mind. She wanted to call him. Wanted to hear his consolations. Wanted to feel his arms around her, comforting her. Was it because of true feelings for David, or hiding from the mess with Ray?

"No." She held her breath, and forced her body down farther, the sting of the heat a combination of soothing and burning. Submerging her whole body in the bath, she released her breath in a long, ragged exhale.

The last year was quickly adding up to one big nightmare. She couldn't even remember who they used to be, how they used to live.

As the hot water embraced her and coaxed her to relax, she floated away on a not too distant memory. A memory from before Ravynn died, before Amelia came to live with them, before all the madness.

A surprise a week, that's what he promised in their wedding vows. Elena couldn't believe this week's surprise was him cooking her dinner. Not Ray, who never cooks.

A giddy anticipation enveloped her as she waited patiently sipping on a very expensive bottle of Nebbiolo and nibbling on a cheese plate.

"Drink all the wine you like, hon. I've got an amazing bottle of Amarone to go with dinner!" he called out from the kitchen.

She hadn't been allowed to enter the kitchen under any circumstance while he cooked, but the delightful smells as dinner simmered, rosemary and thyme, wafting into the living room tickled her taste buds and made her mouth water.

Ray appeared in the doorway, glass of wine in hand. He wore a goofy grin and an apron that said, 'kiss the cook'.

He was irresistible. She set her glass down and sauntered over to him, grabbed him around the waist and pulled him in close.

His eyes grew wide. Elena offered an explanation, "It's the apron." She backed far enough away for him to look down to where she was pointing.

"Oh… that." He said, raising his eyebrows in recognition.

Her lips were upon his in an instant, savoring their warm, salty flavor. As she pulled away, she let out a youthful giggle.

"I should cook more often. If this is the response I'll get… and you haven't even tried the osso bucco yet!"

"Osso Bucco. Italy, our honeymoon!" she responded in delight, clapping her hands together.

"How could I forget?" he said with a sly smile.

The honeymoon had been two weeks of exploring Italy in all its splendor. It's also where Elena had eaten her first Osso Bucco.

"But where did you…. How did you…" She struggled to find the right words.

"Sneaky, huh?" He winked. "Cooking classes on the sly. I wanted to surprise you."

"I'd say this is quite the surprise!" Her eyes filled with joy and the butterflies leapt in her chest. "Italy," she sighed.

Elena snapped back to the present. A surprise a week. That had changed a lot. This week's surprise: 'Elena, my sister's not dead. She talks to me all the time, and she's warning me of disasters to come.'

Her mind raced, unable to ascribe logic to the fantastical. She mused to herself, *Why can't I just believe? Because this is all too unbelievable. Ravynn coming back from the dead or some other world to talk to Ray… and Amelia. To warn them that some disaster is coming. Could it be possible?"*

Somewhere deep inside herself, Elena knew this was not some strange phobia, conspiracy theory, or Ray going crazy and taking Amelia with him. Too many weird things had happened since Ravynn died, most of them recent. Just because she couldn't wrap her head around the how and the why of it, she had to accept the possibility.

She pushed all thoughts out of her mind and forced herself to relax, to meditate all of it away, at least for the time being.

By the time the water cooled, she had a better sense of calm about her. She didn't realize until rising out of the tub that there were the faintest beginnings of bruises forming on her upper arms where Ray had grabbed her earlier. The sight of them snapped her back to the fight and back to reality.

RAY wisely ordered a pizza while Elena was in the bath, and the family silently ate dinner. The couple exchanged pained, forced smiles while Amelia was looking, but other than that, didn't acknowledge each other. Too raw, the remnants of their fight hung heavy in the air. Something in the relationship had ripped and there was no telling if it would be able to be repaired.

Elena disappeared to the bedroom right after dinner without a word, and Ray put on the tv and sat down on the couch next to Amelia.

With her tucked into his side, she drifted off, her head occasionally bouncing onto his arm then back up again as she fought sleep. Halfway through the show, she was out cold, so Ray scooped her up and carried her into her room, tucked her into bed, and pulled the covers up to her chin the way she liked them. He kissed her forehead softly. Treaded lightly down the hall to the bedroom where Elena reclined, reading. She didn't even spare a glance when he entered, kept her nose in her book.

Ray shrugged and headed to the bathroom. Washing his face, he could swear he perceived Ravynn's voice, but it fell off rapidly, leaving him to question if he had heard anything at all.

Back in the bedroom, he stole a glance at Elena, who either didn't see him or most likely didn't care to- her head tucked deep into a book- like it was the most interesting thing ever written, the way she stared so intensely, flipping pages with an unusual vigor.

He wanted to engage her, but decided it was best not to. Let her have this time. She'd come around. She'd believe him, eventually.

In bed, he pulled the blankets up high and turned to his

side, tucking them under him like a fluffy cocoon. There was a dull heaviness to the air that made him shudder.

He'd barely fallen asleep when Elena shook him awake. "Ray… Ray, wake up. It's Amelia." Elena turned her back to look at Amelia, pointing, and dropped her book off the bed with a thud. Ray sat up. Amelia stood over the foot of the bed, not speaking. A ghostly glimmer sprinkled across her face from the waxing gibbous moon as it shed thin moonlight through the window curtains.

"What is it?" He croaked. He wasn't not sure who he was asking but was keenly aware of the startling display before him. Amelia looked like she was in a trance. Stared past the two of them, not at them. Maybe she was sleepwalking, not awake or aware.

Elena finally asked, "Amelia, what's wrong, honey?"

Without blinking, Amelia slowly opened her mouth to speak, and the moonlight suddenly turned her soft features harsh and lined. She looked so much older, suddenly. She looked so much like her mother, her grandmother. "Mommy told me to tell you…"

Ray waited, but the tension was unnerving. He pushed back the blankets and sat up straight, the hackles on his neck raised at attention, now fully awake. "Tell us what?"

Amelia blinked as the moon passed behind a cloud. The room grew dark, disappearing the girl in shadow. She whispered, "It's starting…"

Those two words sent a shiver up his spine as Ray looked to Elena, who appeared as baffled as he was. Before either could ask what she meant, the floor shook. If they'd been sleeping, they might not have noticed it right away. The floor trembled beneath, rocking the bed. Down the hallway, cabinets were rocking and rattling. Loose items in the kitchen danced and slid around in the cupboards. Instinct seized him, and he jumped out of bed and grabbed Amelia, flinging her into the bed. "Tuck inside the pillows and blankets and stay put!" He hovered over her, an extra layer of defense if something should fall on them. Elena followed suit, hunkering down beneath her body pillow. The three of them grasped each other in the bed, shaking and holding their collective breath.

Faint words drifted out of Elena into the chaos of the night, "This is it. Dear God."

The kitchen cabinets shifted enough that Ray heard plates and glasses come free and shatter on the ground.

In a matter of mere seconds, it stopped. No rumbling. No shaking. No teetering. Stillness and quiet. Like every other mild earthquake they'd ever experienced. Underwhelming after the fact, but in the moment, the fear that somehow, this would be that big California quake.

THEY waited there in the cushioned safety of the bed for a few more minutes, not believing that there wasn't more coming. Not after Amelia's foreboding words. Ravynn's warning. So quiet, so still that all that everyone's breathing was the loudest sound. Drifting out of the panic other things could be heard now too; dogs barking in the night, car alarms set off by the quake.

Elena broke first, pulling herself free from Ray and heading towards the kitchen to assess the damage there. Raymond tried to protest, but she shrugged him off coldly. Pissed at herself for thinking this was *It*. For that fleeting moment to believe in the 'Ravynn prophecies'.

"Elena, what if there's more?"

"Don't be ridiculous, Raymond. That was it. 'The Big Quake'. Broke some dishes, woooo...."

"But honey, Ravynn's warning."

She paused her steps down the hallway and shot him an icy stare. Too bad the dark of the night disguised it. "Don't be a fool, Ray. That was it. We live in California. This happens all the time. And bigger ones than that." She shook her head in disgust, mostly because she felt like a fool for giving over to the belief, however fleeting, that Ravynn was indeed trying to warn them. Those little fears that Ray could be right leapt from the back of her mind to the very front and took over in that quake. "It was a slight temblor, nothing more, nothing less. No premonition, no warning from the great beyond or wherever you think your sister is."

In all the commotion, Elena forgot that Amelia was still there, soaking in all of their words.

"But Mommy said..." Amelia's words sliced through the tense air like a samurai's sword, further dividing them.

Elena scooted back down the hallway towards Amelia, cooing and shushing. "Oh, little bunny, I know you saw mommy. This had nothing to do with that. That was a dream. This was an earthquake, we have them all the time here. Nothing special. Nothing new. This one was just a little bigger, that's all. Let's get you tucked back into bed. My, it's getting late!"

"But Mom---" was all Amelia could say before Elena scooped her up in her arms and kissed her face all over. Amelia let out a series of giggles and gave in. "Do-over tuck?"

"Yes, little bunny. Hop, hop, here we go. Nothing but sweet dreams here on out."

"Amelia tucked her face into Elena's neck and whispered, "Yes. I'm gonna go see Mommy again."

15

Elena nervously eyed her watch. Got up off the park bench and was about to call out for Amelia, when there were footsteps behind her. A sigh escaped her as she sank back down on the bench. "Thanks for coming," she said to David without looking.

Amelia bounced around in the jungle gym. A swift breeze cut across the early afternoon and whipped Amelia's hair in her face. She giggled, stumbled, but righted herself before she fell. Elena called out, "Be careful!"

The little girl waved and smiled, and her dark hair shone in the sun. *Dark like a raven*, Elena thought. *Like Ravynn.*

He sat down beside her, though they both faced forward, watching Amelia. "Sorry I'm late."

She shook it off. "I didn't know who else to talk to about this. My family is too close... I... I don't want their pity or judgement." She nodded, convincing herself it was the right thing to do in calling David.

Elena continued with the faraway stare. "She's such a good kid. Especially with losing her mother. And now this..." her voice trailed off and she blinked thoughtfully.

"What's *this*, Elena?" He turned to face her, but Elena couldn't look at him.

"Had a huge fight last night. I guess, if I'm being honest, I think that blow-up was a long time coming. Too much happening, too much has happened. It's been a very long year." She offered up a strained smile as Amelia glanced over from the top of the slide and waved. She waved back, then tucked a stray strand of hair behind her ear.

David leaned closer, and she could feel his expelled breath touch the side of her face. The tension between them quickened her heart rate. She felt flummoxed, unable to justify these feelings. "What did he do?" His words startled her, and for a second, she was sure she'd given her anticipation away.

Elena shrugged coolly, an overexaggerted action, trying to disguise her disquiet. "I was lying to him. Keeping things from him." She pondered a moment. "He's kept so much from me, too. Not that it justifies what I did. Two wrongs and all."

David started to speak, but Elena continued as if he hadn't, "They weren't just dreams. About Ravynn, you know. He said she talks to him while he's awake." She brought her hands up and covered her eyes. The sounds of laughter and screams of the children playing in the park rang out around her and felt so mocking. The sun beating down on the left side of her body did nothing to warm the chill in her heart.

"That's crazy," David said softly.

"No, it's not." She let her hands fall from her face. She reconsidered. "Yes, I know it is. She tells him things. He said she told him about the eclipse the other day. Before it happened. He always has this sense that something else is going on."

David shifted his feet out in front of him and crossed them, leaning back with a sigh. "He's not healthy. Something is wrong. I've seen it. He needs help." His words were genuine, an old friend's concern.

She tipped her head back, letting the sunlight hit her full on.

126

She squinted. "That's what I thought too. Until Amelia told me some pretty strange things. She said she sees Mommy at night, at the beach. Ravynn tells her things. She knew about the birds, the eclipse, the dolphins, the earthquake too, I think." She let the realization sink in. "God, what else? I just don't understand any of this." He fidgeted on the bench, searching for comfort where he'd find none. He scooted a few inches closer to her and stilled.

She brought her hand to her mouth and gnawed at her cuticles.

David reached out and pulled it away. He wrapped his hand in hers and lowered them both to the bench in between them.

"How could she?" Elena whispered. It felt good to hold hands, to have some sort of physical closeness, even if it was with the wrong man. Or was he the wrong man? A feeling of presentiment clenched at her gut and a wave of nausea again rolled over her. It was becoming a more common sensation every day, but one she couldn't get used to. Yet another new symptom in an ever-changing world. "At first, I thought maybe she was overhearing our conversations and her mind ran with the ideas. Childlike imaginings and all that. But now I don't know what to believe."

He squeezed her hand. "I'm sure it has to do with all that, like you said. Seeing Ray behave this way, things he says. I'm sure she's just feeding off him."

"A lot of weird is happening lately, David. Maybe--"

"Maybe nothing," he interjected. "Ray is sick. With grief. He never accepted his sister's death and it's turning into something unnatural. He's creating some fantasy world where she warms him of what? A coming apocalypse? He's interpreting signs around him incorrectly and making something of it when there's nothing there. Confirmation bias, I think that's what they call it."

She shook her head, slowly. "And then, last night, right before the quake, Amelia came into our room and said, 'Mommy told me to tell you it's starting'. And within seconds, the earthquake hit." She glanced back to Amelia on the slide and guilt washed over her. Seeing the sweet innocent girl in front of her then, compared to the frightful ghostly image she had appeared to be last night.

He gave her hand another squeeze, and Elena felt ashamed by the comfort it brought her. For the thought that came next. She wanted to shift herself closer, tuck herself under his arm and let him hold her close, comfort her and make everything seem better, for no matter how short a time. "Listen to what you're saying. This is no End of Days. Ray has somehow poisoned Amelia's impressionable mind. These things are nothing but strange coincidences. Ravynn's gone, and nothing Ray says or does is ever going to change that. Now he has Amelia believing. And you questioning. It's not healthy. Not for any of you. Elena, please…"

David's logical mind justifying her concerns for Ray and Amelia's sanity brought her some comfort. He wasn't influenced by Ravynn and her untimely demise and the struggles that ensued shortly thereafter. "I know, I know. During that quake, I actually entertained the possibility of all of it. How could I not? But I know it's not logical. It can't be."

"No, it can't," he affirmed.

"I think I'm going to take Amelia to my sister's for a few days."

"I think that's a good idea," he agreed. "You know, whenever you need me…" his voice trailed off, as if they both knew it was unnecessary for him to complete that sentence. He'd be there for her, no matter what.

The sun dipped down behind a shadow of a tumid cloud, and the park grew dark with a minacious quality. It reminded Elena of when the eclipse came out of nowhere.

In the tree behind them, the normal chatter of birds intensified. At first, Elena thought nothing of the din. The birdsong turned to screeching. Sounds of hundreds of frantic flapping wings took to the air. Elena and David looked up to see confusion in the dimming sky. Some of the birds flew straight, some up, some around and around in dizzying circles, all the while screaming hysterically.

"Amelia!" Elena shouted and ran to the girl, David a step behind. "Amelia, down off the slide!" A bird shot by Amelia's head and crashed into the slide with a sickening smacking sound. David got to the girl first and snatched her off the slide, tucking her safely underneath. Elena scurried in beside them. Parents were yelling and kids screaming, reacting to their parents' concerns.

Two birds crashed into each other and fell to the ground feet from the threesome. There was something extra peculiar about the bird closest; its eyes were clouded over.

When she looked back up, a large black bird divebombed a thrush. The tiny little bird had no chance. Claws enclosed the thrush and it screamed, to no avail. The big black bird had the smaller in its grasp. Time was moving slow, events unfolding like a movie on a screen. Some terrible scene from the movie *The Birds*.

Amelia's voice brought her back to reality, "Look at the raven!"

The raven dropped the thrush and darted to the top of the slide and sat like a queen on her throne.

THERE was a knock at the front door.

If Ray ignored it, maybe they'd go away.

Another knock.

Silence. Ray held his breath.

Third knock was louder, accompanied by a voice. "Ray, I know you're home. I saw your car." The sound of David's voice made Ray cringe. School was over, after all. So why was David paying him a visit?

"I don't care for visitors, thanks," Ray shouted through the closed door.

David persisted, "I need to talk to you."

"Talk to you in another month or so. I'm on break." Ray laughed and rolled his eyes at the door. He turned to walk away.

"Open the door. It's about Elena."

Those were words Ray couldn't ignore. He turned back and placed a hand on the doorknob.

"Ray…"

Against better judgement, and the nagging sense that this conversation wouldn't end well, he opened the door. "Elena is not here." He motioned dramatically with the sweep of a hand for David to enter.

"I know," David said as he stepped inside. "I just saw her."

Those words were a punch in the face. Jealousy and anger welled up inside him. He flexed and unflexed his fingers, and let go. "You won't be offended if I don't offer you a drink? You won't be staying long."

Inside the kitchen, they sat down in chairs opposite each other. The stare-down was on. Silent judgements creased David's face, and Ray could only imagine what he'd say. It seemed like hours passed in silence before David spoke. "She's upset, Ray. She's worried about you."

Ray struggled for composure. "And I'm worried about you. Why are you here?"

"Because *we* used to be friends." He shifted awkwardly in his chair. "And Elena is hurting. And I'm concerned. About *both* of you."

Ray ignored his pseudo-concern. "Must make you feel good that she came to you." The blood boiling in his veins. He crossed his arms over his chest. "Now you can play hero."

The air in the room was heavy and pressed down on Ray's skin, making him shift uncomfortably.

David shoed Ray's jealous words aside with a wave of his hand. "It's not about any of that, Ray. It's about you, Elena, Amelia… your sister."

"What do you know about any of it?" As soon as the words

left his lips, he regretted them, knowing he wouldn't like the answer.

"You sister is gone. Passed. You've got to accept this. She's not coming back. She's not here. Not trying to warn you of some impending doom. She's not talking to Amelia, either." His face softened, and Ray almost thought he saw true concern. "Can't you see how unhealthy it is?"

So, Elena had told him everything. All the dirty little secrets. Ray's face flushed with heat. She still couldn't see…

His face was hot. Ray took a deep breath to calm himself. "What exactly did Elena tell you?"

David leaned back in the chair, taking in a long pause before he spoke. "Everything."

Ray bit his lip and nodded. "Ok. Tell me all that you *think* you know."

David leaned forward and set his elbows on the table, lacing his fingers together. The visual took Ray back to the other day at school, the confrontation. David cleared his throat and began. "She told me about your dreams. How Ravynn comes to you when you sleep and whispers things to you. You losing sleep over all of it. And that you told Elena that Ravynn talks to you when you're awake now, too." He brought his index fingers together, forming a point. "That was upsetting to hear. And that your sister is warning you of some oncoming disaster, and how you're so very convinced—"

Ray slammed his hands down on the table. "David, you know nothing. It's time you go." He didn't wait for a response, he headed to the door and swung it open, letting it hit against the door stop with a shuddering thud. "Please go."

David stood up, but continued, his hands splayed out on the table before him as he leaned in dramatically. "You're convinced Amelia is communicating with Ravynn now, too. It's not ok, Ray." He strode to the door with a cocky air, then paused.

Ray walked out the door, stopped, and turned back to David. "Let me walk you out then." He nodded his head in the direction of David's car and began walking down the driveway.

Following behind him, David called out, "You need to take care of your family."

Feet apart, Ray swung around to face David. The anger beat at his temples and he fought to maintain and not lose his temper completely.

He tipped his head back and rolled his eyes to the sky. "Those clouds look heavy. They look wrong." He lost himself, staring into the sky, as a black cloud passed too quickly over the sun. The heaviness in the air dissipated as the winds picked up. "Storm's coming."

In response, David said, "Pfft! It's just a little weather. Snap out of it. Pay attention to the real world. Not everything is a grand sign." The last words were a hush, drowned out by the wind rustling violently through the trees. Branches bowed and swayed. Ray looked back at David as a plastic bag floating by in the background, tossed and flipped about by the ever-increasing wind.

Looking back up to the sky, he saw lightning flicker and dance behind the darkened, bulbous clouds. The static in the air prickled at his skin.

"I don't need you to understand any of it," Ray shouted to be heard over the growing storm. "Leave my family alone. Stop trying to play hero."

The plastic bag darted and got caught in between David's feet. "She needs you, Ray. Healthy and whole. If you can't take care of yourself, take care of her---"

"Or what?" Ray closed the distance between them, so close he could smell the aftershave on David's face. "Or you'll step in and rescue her?"

David shrugged, not backing down. "If not me, someone will." The corner of his mouth slanted up into the faintest of smirks. "She's a beautiful woman."

Ray held off as long as he could, but those last few words pushed him over the edge. He dipped his right shoulder forward and plowed right through David, flinging him. They landed with a thud, the air knocked from David.

Arms up, David tried to grab Ray by the shoulders, but he was too slow, recovering from losing his breath, and Ray's fist connected with his jaw.

David grunted, managing to roll Ray off him into the grass. He scrambled to his hands and knees and sucked in a long breath.

Ray lay flat on his back, staring at the sky, entranced. "Stay away from my family." He didn't move.

David spat a mouthful of blood to the ground. "You're an idiot, Ray. I came here to help."

Ray shook his head. "Let me help you, David. Roll up your windows, it's about to rain. Better yet, get in your car and leave."

On his feet, David muttered, "Fool." He brushed the grass and leaves from his clothes and headed to his car. He opened the door, but before stepping in, called back, "Wake up, Ray."

Ray closed his eyes and laughed. "I am the only one who is awake."

The sound of the car pulling out the driveway gave Ray some relief. He opened his eyes and stared off into the foreboding clouds as they unleashed on him. He laughed, a little, to himself. His laughter increased with the rain, growing ever more intense. A light spattering of drizzle quickly turned to hail. At first, it felt almost therapeutic, like getting stuck with acupuncture needles, tiny little stinging drops waking up his skin. Soon, the rain was pelting down, too hard to withstand, and   he   retreated   to   the   house.

16

Someone was fiddling with the front door. Ray paused as he pulled a fresh dry shirt over his head and listened. Someone was definitely trying to turn the door handle. Thinking it was David, back for round two, he steeled himself. A small head poked through the door just above the knob.

Ray smiled, relieved. "Hey, little one. Where'd you come from?"

Amelia replied, "Went to the park." Her eyes flitted carelessly, darting glances around the room, landing on nothing at all.

"Sounds nice. Where's Auntie Elena?" He bit his lip. Her name coming out of his mouth made him cringe. He tried to maintain a cool his niece wouldn't be able to unmask. "Wait... did you drive home?"

Giggling, she said, "No. Auntie E drove, silly. I can't drive yet, I'm still too small." Hand still wrapped around the door handle, she turned and twisted it, waving the door back and forth.

"Yes but getting bigger every day."

"It's gonna get worse." Amelia twisted the doorknob fervently, staring directly at her uncle.

"What is?" Ray tipped his head to the side, inquisitively.

"All of the things. Look out for the mountain…"

As Amelia spoke those words, Elena appeared, reaching a hand out to still the door and paused, looking at Ray's face. "Where did you get that scratch?" she asked, glancing at the mark above his eye.

"He reached a hand up and his fingers glided across a small welt. Nodding, he pulled his hand away. "Had a visitor. Wanna venture a guess who?"

Elena turned to Amelia. "Go get your stuff like we talked about, okay?"

"Wait," Amelia interjected. "Who visited? Uncle Ray, how did you get that on your head?" She let go of the door and walked over to her uncle, pointing up at his head.

"It's nothing. I'm clumsy, just a little bump."

Seemingly satisfied with his answer, she moved past him to leave the room but stopped abruptly. She shot an all-too-adult look at Elena, her face serious well beyond her years, and said, "Are you gonna tell Uncle Ray about the bird storm?"

Elena sighed. "Yes. Now get going." Her smile was forced, but Amelia didn't seem to pick up on it.

"Bird storm? Get your stuff?" Ray stepped closer to Elena, agitation welling inside him. He sensed some unpleasant disclosure coming.

"Oh, the birds got a little flighty at the park." She shut the door. "And I told Amelia to get some things. I think it's best if we go stay with Becky for a couple of days." Her light tone didn't match the seriousness of her words. "A lot's been going on and I think… I need some distance. To sort this out." She averted her eyes from him, though his own grew wide. "I've tried to fix everything for you, but I can't fix this."

Ray interrupted, "I didn't ask you to fix anything---"

"It's eating me up, Ray. I can't wrap my head around any of this. I've tried, really, I have." She took a step back and there was a tiny falter in her step. As if she were momentarily dizzy.

"I don't need fixing, Elena. I need my wife to believe in me. Believe in things she can't see."

She ignored him and continued, "Either you're having some mental health struggles that need to be addressed, or this whole world is turning to shit..." She closed the door behind her and leaned into it, staring at him too intently, as if searching for some clue, something in his expression that could give her some solace, or answers.

He wished she didn't drop the crazy-bomb so readily. Wished she could step inside his world, in his mind for even a day. Wished she experienced life all those years ago with his schizophrenic dad, and could understand firsthand what it was like, what he was like, and that what Ray was going through was nothing like it. *If wishes were horses...*

"The world is not what we thought, Elena. I know it's hard to acc---"

"No," she replied firmly. "Stop. I can't do this. I won't. You believe. I think Amelia believes in some way, too. But I don't experience it or see it the way you do. And it seems so unreasonable... illogical. I can't make sense of something that has no sense to be made of it." She shook her head and looked at the floor.

"I get what you're saying. But honey. Come on. The world was flat until it wasn't. Just because we don't know the why or the how of something yet, doesn't mean it can't be true." He moved closer, wanting to embrace her, but she shied back away. He tried to maintain his air of calm, the tone of his voice relaxed, but as she recoiled, a picture, painted in jealousy popped into his head in full color. Elena and David openly discussing Ray's problems and their disagreements. Elena and David discussing Ray's sanity, or lack there-of. David holding her hand or wrapping his arms around her in consolation— or worse yet, wrapping his lips around hers. The anger inside him swelled and he fought to keep it down. He spoke the words, slowly, deliberately, fighting back their emotional content. "But what I don't get, is why would you talk to David about all of this? Why would you air our dirty laundry out for him to sniff at?"

The floor stole her attention. "I don't know, Ray. Maybe

I'm not thinking straight. I couldn't talk to my family. There's no way I could talk to Mom and Dad about it. They probably think God is punishing us all and Judgement Day is upon us too." She cringed at her own insensitivity. She loved her parents dearly but had beliefs that were very different from theirs. She took a more scientific approach.

"I didn't... I... I just don't know." She finally looked up at him. "It seems neither of us are perfect." She tossed her keys on the table. "I've gotta get some things together."

"Elena, please don't do this."

She shook her head. "I'm no help to you right now. Not like this. Just give me some time."

Ray hated the idea. He bit his tongue. "How long?"

Elena shrugged. "Maybe a couple days. Amelia can play with Carrie. Have some kid time."

He stuffed his hands into his pockets. "I don't think it's a good idea."

"We don't agree on a lot lately. I'm sorry." She walked past him, reached a hand out along the way, stroking his arm softly. "I am sorry."

THE front door opened before Elena could knock, and her sister Becky's worried face greeted her. Elena fought back the sadness that sat heavy on her. "Thanks for letting us stay here on such short notice."

Becky lifted a hand to shield the glare of the sun. "Of course. Any time," she replied. "You should know this." She pulled Elena in for a hug and whispered in her ear, "What's going on?"

Elena patted her sister on the back and pulled out of the embrace, contemplating the best response. Down by her right side, Amelia stood, looking up, waiting as well. Elena's tone lightened, "Well, Amelia and Carrie need to have a slumber party. It's long overdue."

To this, Amelia beamed with happiness.

Becky stepped back out of the doorway and welcomed them in. "Well then, by all means, come in. Carrie's in her room."

Amelia pranced off to find her cousin.

Becky put her arm out to block the doorway as Elena stepped inside. Becky leaned in and whispered, "but you're not getting off that easy."

"Okay." Elena ran her hand affectionately through Becky's hair, watching as the sun sneaked through the doorway and over her shoulder, running its own fingers of light through her sister's hair. "Once the girls are settled… and you have a bottle of wine open."

"Well, you know those two." She rolled her eyes playfully. "They'll entertain each other for hours. Thick as thieves, and all that. And Dax is still out of town on business. So, it's you, me, and wine." A wicked grin danced across Becky's face and she winked.

In the kitchen, Elena plopped herself onto one of the counter island seats. She looked down at a watch-less wrist and said, "Oh, it's wine o'clock already."

Becky giggled as she reached into the cupboard for the stemless wine glasses. She placed them onto the counter and pulled the cork of a bottle of an unassuming meritage. "So, I have been patient, but you've got to tell me something." Becky tipped the bottle and poured for them both. She set the bottle back on the counter. A small red rivulet dripped down the side. She brought her glass up, signaling a toast. "This may not be time for a celebration, but I can't not toast upon opening a new bottle of wine. I am civilized, after all." Raising her glass, she gave her sister a wink. "To my lovely sister. May she have the courage to tell me everything."

"That's not a toast." Elena cringed. She made to set her glass down, but Becky tsked her.

"Maybe not a proper toast, but I am not a proper lady. Now, lift that glass!"

Tension appropriately sliced; the sisters laughed. The

glasses clinked together, and both women took a sip. A long hesitation followed. Elena appreciated the restraint Becky showed in waiting, because patience was not her strong suit.

Becky swirled the wine around in her glass like a pro, aerating it, giving Elena time.

After a long pull on her wine, followed by a rather uncouth loud gulp, Elena set the glass down. "We're having some problems, is all."

"Understatement?" Becky didn't look at her sister, still swirling her wine.

The corner of Elena's mouth peeled back into a half smile. "Yes, maybe. Probably. We're just not seeing eye to eye on some big things."

Becky continued with a dramatic gesture, pouring an ungodly amount of wine into Elena's already full-enough glass. The wine made a glug-glugging sound as it left the bottle in haste. "Loosens the lips." She raised a brow.

After another much more moderate sip, Elena began, "I don't know what to say. It all started when Ravynn passed. He's so haunted. So sad. Detached."

Becky continued her swirling of the wine. "What about going back for counseling?"

"He won't hear of it." Elena paused, not sure what to say next.

There's no shame in counseling." Becky took another swig of wine and straightened her posture, flinging her hair back off her shoulders.

Elena shook her head. "Maybe I need counseling."

"Maybe you do… and maybe you just need more wine." Becky splashed more into Elena's glass, finally stopping when Elena thrust her hand out over the top of the glass.

"Whoa, whoa, slow down." Elena pulled her glass farther out of Becky's reach.

Becky screwed up her face at Elena. "You don't have to drive anywhere. Drink. Up." She set the bottle back down, only slightly covering the ring of red on the counter it left behind.

Shaking her head, Elena admitted something she'd never told Becky, "Ray's dad. He was sick. He thought... he saw..." She struggled with the words.

"What the fuck, Elena? Spit it out," Becky leaned in closer.

"His dad was schizophrenic. Not really bad because... well, he died. But maybe Ray... I mean, the doctor said not, but maybe now..." She couldn't get her thoughts out complete. She fumbled with her words and shook them all away with the wave of a hand.

"Whoa, Elena." Becky set her glass down.

"He had a hard time, Ray's dad. Took a while for them to diagnose him. Ray and Ravynn just thought he was being playful and silly. They didn't understand it while it was happening. That it was an illness. Maybe like Amelia..." She trailed off in her own thoughts, her voice dwindling down to a whisper.

"Maybe like Amelia, what?" Becky leaned back over the counter, placing both elbows upon it.

Elena sensed Becky gawking at her without glancing up. Her eyes were boring hot holes through Elena's very being. "Stop."

"Stop what?" Becky sighed close enough for Elena to catch a whiff of her hot wine breath on the exhale.

"Never mind. Anyway, Ray's dad eventually got on meds. Found the right balance to keep him straight, which worked for a while. But then he got off them again. Said they dulled him. Made him like only half a human, more like a zombie, walking around, only partially in the world. That's what Ray said, anyway. And I guess he was off his meds for about two weeks, and then the car crash..."

"And you think Ray might be schizophrenic?"

"Yes. I did. Maybe." Elena struggled with the words. "I mean, no. Not anymore. I was terrified that that was the case, but it's something else. I dunno." She set her glass down, motioning towards the bottle for a refill.

Becky obliged her, refilling the glass. Elena admired her sister's restraint. Normally, Becky would be offering up suggestions, fixes, opinions, advice or just talking to hear herself speak. Instead, she waited, giving Elena a chance to speak.

Elena took that chance to chicken out. "I don't really want to get into it, that's why I stepped away. To distance myself from everything. To think things over. To give it all time." Elena stared down into her wine glass. "I love you, I appreciate you, and thank you for your concern. Let's just drink some wine and enjoy each other's fantastic company. Deal?"

Becky gave her a sideways glance, seeming not to accept her sister's casual demeanor. She squinted and said, "Deal. Or at least, I'll try to let it go."

Elena raised her glass. "Cheers to that."

17

Matt hadn't showered in two days. He hadn't had much free time to do anything; not eat, not drink, not anything. He hadn't even gone into work.

He was preoccupied with Ravynn's journal. After digging it up in the garage, he'd been consumed by it— unable to explain it and horrified by the implications. It was something he had always feared, something he fought with Ravynn about, but never had any resolution. Now, there was no one and nothing standing in his way of getting to the bottom of it. He called Ray yesterday and left a message. A big step. An admission that all of this was too real. Too bad Ray still hadn't called him back.

He lifted his head after catching a few z's. He hadn't meant to fall asleep. His weary body had betrayed him.

Pulling his head off the kitchen table he realized he nodded off on top of the journal; his face imprinted with the rings of the binder. His watch read just after midnight.

He checked his phone. No new messages. Nothing.

After a year of not speaking, Matt hadn't expected it to be easy, but if Ray didn't return his calls, he'd have to find another way. What had he thought would happen, anyway? Ray would pick up, happy to hear from him, and invite him over for a beer? There was too much between them, and Matt couldn't blame Ray, couldn't blame anyone or anything else but his alcoholism. A cork-board stood pegged to the wall from the old days, days of family life that were now all in the past. Ravynn used to post notes and schedules for Amelia on that board. Now, it was being used for something a little stranger.

Tacked to the board were notes that Matt copied from Ravynn's journal. Dates and events lined up from the past six months all displayed in front of him. He stood, facing the wall, hands on his hips. All these dates, all the events— chillingly accurate. He glanced over the event 'scheduled' for today. Hand on his chin, he rubbed it roughly, thinking.

He scolded himself for having fallen asleep, turned back to the table and his laptop. He didn't have to look far. All he needed was a refresh of his home page to see Ravynn's prediction for today was coming true.

The first headline read:

'Mount Vesuvius Alive Again. Disaster Imminent.'

"The threat is to be taken with the utmost seriousness," Italian Geophysicist, Dr. Giuseppe Romano states, "We know from history what she's (Mount Vesuvius) capable of. We also know that she is long overdue. The activity we recorded over the last two hours is unprecedented. The 7.3 earthquake we just experienced is troubling, to say the least. This is not a recommendation. We need people to take this seriously, or it could end in terrible destruction and human loss— more than we've lost with the quake. The time to act is now."

When asked if the predictions could possibly be overblown, Dr. Romano replied, "There is always a chance, no matter how big or small, that we are wrong. I pray that we are indeed wrong. Volcanoes are fickle things. Some give you warning, some give none at all before they blow. Let us consider ourselves lucky that we have even this warning. I am very secure in saying that this evacuation could save thousands. I don't want those deaths on my conscience, would you?"

This article had his attention. No coffee needed; he wouldn't be sleeping anytime soon.

ELENA woke to soft knocking on her bedroom door. She peeled her heavy eyes open and remembered where she was. Happy to have had the rest, a full night's sleep, she sat up.

"Hey, you want some coffee?" Becky murmured through the opening door.

Elena rubbed her eyes. "Yeah, coffee would be nice."

"Righty," Becky replied, shutting the door.

Within a few minutes Elena made herself presentable and made for the kitchen and some coffee. She poured herself a cup and strolled into the living room to find her sister glued to the TV.

"Thanks for the cof —"

Becky interrupted her, mumbling through a hand over her own mouth, "Shhh, the news. I can't believe this. Italy. Volcano." Becky's voice trembled.

Elena's jaw dropped as the scene unfolded on TV, too horrific to be real; yet it was. Lava jetted up out of the volcano and into the sky. "Unbelievable. I can't believe... It can't be... not happening," Elena babbled as she brought her fingers up to her mouth and began chewing on her cuticles.

The sound of two small girls' screeches preceded the cousins running into the room. Carrie was chasing Amelia with a fake snake and the girls giggled and howled as they ran around the living room. Carrie stopped, seeing that her mother had spilled her coffee.

"Mom."

Getting no reply, Carrie spoke up louder, "Mom! You

tipped your coffee cup over, spilled all over the table. Mom!" She waved her hand around in the air.

The only person in the room completely unfazed by what was transpiring either on the TV or with the coffee was Amelia. She picked up the fake snake that Carrie had dropped and made it dance across her hand and upper arm.

The TV showed devastation of the tumultuous Mount Vesuvius and its eruption. The volcano was exploding with such force it spewed hot ash and lava high into the sky, forcing the clouds above to darken, turning day into night. Like a scene out of an apocalyptic movie, within moments, all normalcy had turned to chaos. What moments before had been a calm late morning, the sun burning its way through a thinning clouded sky, turned into an ashen gray blackout, the sun disappearing as if the volcano and its anger had devoured it. Lava raced, poured and pumped out of the volcano's top, in some places moving so quickly it reminded Elena of a human artery if, badly cut, its lifeblood pouring from the body. The volcano unleashed so quickly and violently, that those who had not evacuated the area were clearly doomed. The evacuation had started only an hour or so before the eruption, right after the earthquake. Hundreds of thousands of people were now considered to be lost or dead. Burned, smothered, buried.

Carries disappeared from the room, and within moments returned with a stack of paper towels in her hand, a trail dragging behind her. She appeared in front of her mother, blocking her mother's eyes from the TV, and handing out paper towels. "Mom, here. Your coffee."

With the images from the TV now blocked out by her daughter, Becky snapped to. She grabbed the paper towels from Carrie's hand and began haphazardly mopping up the spilled coffee. She shook her head all the while, muttering inaudibly to herself. So distracted, she missed the coffee that dripped over the side onto the carpet.

Amelia finally spoke up softly, this time seemingly aware of the weight her words carried. "Mama knew. She told me it was starting." She still held the plastic snake, it's tail wiggling as

Amelia shrugged her shoulders up high.

Elena nervously tittered and shushed the girl.

Becky's head flung up at Amelia's words. She dropped the wadded-up paper towels on the coffee table. "What did you just say, Amelia?"

Elena interrupted before Amelia could answer, "Nothing, she's playing." She smiled, a little too big, and a little too forced.

Carrie sighed and picked up where her mother left off, mopping up spilled coffee, the only one more affected by the spilled coffee than the disaster of Mt Vesuvius.

The news anchor reported in the background:

'Plumes of ash reached far into the sky, climbing to impossible heights. Pumice and ash scorched down the mountainside at an alarming rate, burning everything in its path. At least, death was likely instantaneous for all in the immediate area.' The reporter paused, took a shaky breath, and continued, 'Italy in a state of panic. Communications severed...'

Amelia continued, her voice as full of frustration with an adult as a child's voice could be, "No, the other night. She told me, remember?" Her eyes were wide and imploring, while her voice displayed her discontent and impatience.

"What on earth is going on?" demanded Becky. She was on her feet, unable to sit still.

"Nothing. Well, it's something. It's... Everything." Elena hung her head as she admitted it. "I can't get into it right now."

"Is this why you two are staying with us?" Becky asked.

Amelia headed out of the room with purpose. Elena could only watch her, still dumbfounded by the unfolding events. Moments later, Amelia returned with Elena's cell phone. She handed it over to Elena forcefully. "We need to call Uncle Ray."

"Yes, we will call Uncle Ray," she said through a daze. She

looked down at her phone to find that Ray had texted her the night previous. Elena wasn't sure if the Earth was shifting and spinning under her feet or if she was having another dizzy spell. The phone fell from her hands and she swayed.

"Auntie E, you ok?" Amelia asked.

Becky repeated the words, laced with concern, "You ok? Sit down."

Elena heeded her sister's advice and went down where she stood. No chair beneath her, she sat on the floor on her knees by her phone. The screen stared up at her brightly, like a neon sign calling attention to a sale. Thoughts raced through her mind, as quickly and unorganized as the lave spurting from the volcano: How? Didn't Amelia say something about the mountain last night? And hadn't she known about the birds, too? Only a fool would try to continue to tally all of this up as mere coincidences. There was something more happening that Elena couldn't understand, nor deny, any longer.

She gasped as she saw the text containing two simple words from the night before: Mt. Vesuvius.

"What time did the volcano blow? Do you know?" Elena asked Becky, her voice an octave higher than normal.

"They say it was after two a.m. our time."

Elena checked the time of the text Ray sent. Just before nine p.m.

"I think we need to go home," she said to everyone and no one at the same time. She turned to Becky and added, "thanks for letting us stay awhile."

Becky opened her mouth to speak but seemed unable to find any words. She shut her mouth and reached out her hand.

Amelia nodded at Becky as she dropped the snake and reached out for Elena's hand. She grabbed it and gave a tug, as if she'd been waiting for this reaction from Elena the whole time. Elena looked down, and the little girl looked back at her with Ravynn's eyes. Breath caught in Elena's chest. Everything came at her full force, smacking her in the face. Elena had chosen to be blind to all of it, until now. As Ravynn's eyes stared back at her from Amelia's face, Elena suddenly felt like the child. So many questions, so much hesitation, doubt and fear coursed through her body. But most of all, guilt. Guilt for not listening to Ray, however insistent or even crazy he acted, and not paying attention to Amelia's cryptic warnings as well.

Another tug on her hand as Amelia said, "Can we tell Aunt Becky? About what Mom said?"

Elena managed to shake her head in the negative.

Amelia tipped her head to the side, clearly exasperated. "But I told you. And Uncle Ray told you." Her eyes grew wide. "Mom knew all along."

18

A nagging sensation overcame Ray, though he wasn't sure why. Considering the recent events, Vesuvius erupting, he remained strangely calm.

He got into the car and began to drive, not even knowing where he was going at first. Let the car and that urge push him forward, control his actions.

I've spent too much time questioning my sanity and fighting against Ravynn. No more.

He found himself headed up the Pacific Coast Highway, the ocean to his left. Still, he did not flinch. He drove on until the urge to stop took over.

His breath caught in his throat as he climbed out of the car.

The beach. Where it happened.

Out of the car, he kicked off his shoes. Sank his bare feet into the soft, sun-kissed sand. The early morning sun had scarcely enough warmth to counter the cool Pacific breeze coming off the water. They countered each other, the rising morning sun and the chilly Pacific breeze, taking turns to warm and cool him.

Ray remembered why Ravynn had come to the beach in the first place that morning. Or at least why he thought she had. She had a new camera. A new job. She was so happy. She was getting herself back to work, picking up the pieces, finding her independence once again.

He walked through the sand, letting it run between his toes with each step. The smell of saltwater hung heavy in the air. A cool breeze brushed past him and faded away. The waves broke gently, a pulsing, continuous beat of water meeting shore.

I've never been here before. I vowed I'd never come...

The beach was relatively empty, save for a few sanderlings dancing back and forth, doing the jaunty dance of searching for food where the water met the sand. It seemed almost haunted. In fact, he'd heard stories over the past year that the beach was exactly that, which was why people stayed away. Haunted by the ghosts of the people who perished in the tsunami. No, his sister didn't haunt this beach, she haunted *him*.

The cool Pacific water trickled between his toes, up around his ankles, pulling him from his wayward thoughts. He hadn't noticed until then that he had stepped to the shoreline.

I should be afraid, apprehensive at least, he thought. *But all I am is calm.*

His feet carried him forward, until he was in up to his knees. The waves slapped against him, creating a steady rocking motion.

"That's because of what's happening to you," a familiar voice said, though no one was around. "Your mind is finally opening up. You're ready."

He didn't bother to turn his head; there was no one physically there. Only Ravynn's voice. He closed his eyes.

"Ravynn, I can hear you so clearly." Eyes closed, his mind open, accepting her voice playing through it.

The water continued lapping at his knees, his thighs, but he wasn't cognizant. The warmth of the sun shining upon him didn't warm his skin.

"So stubborn, Ray. It was so much easier with Amelia. She's a child, she's already open."

"What do you mean?"

"Ray, the problem is that you can't get past what you think happened. Every logical part of your brain screams that when that tsunami hit, I died. That makes the most sense. It's what would naturally happen. But I didn't die.

"Amelia has no boundaries. A child's perception of the world and what is possible is so much different than an adult's. Her little brain is more capable of accepting what happened than yours, because, well, for lack of a better way of putting it, she's not as jaded. Her world isn't in black and white. She doesn't abide by that mentality that if it's not this, then it *must* be that. She still believes in Santa, in the tooth fairy, all those things. She has no reason to believe or understand that they don't exist. She has no real concept of what happened to me— my death, if you will. She is able to see past all of that and embrace the truth of it all. She can accept our psychic connection and her ability to see what others cannot. She accepts it all without judgment or doubt. It just is, to her."

A seagull flew over Ray's head, crying out. The bird glided and played over the water. Ray wanted so badly to accept what Ravynn was saying, but doubt nipped at the back of his mind with fears of ending up like his father. Seeing things that weren't there, talking to people who didn't exist. Ray was not his father.

Ravynn carried on, "That's why you're struggling. That's why the most obvious explanation to you and other adults is that you are losing your mind. Because something like this can't happen, right? Why can't it, Ray? Just because something happens that seems unexplainable or unlikely, or even impossible doesn't mean that it is. We thought the world was flat until we discovered that it was round. Man could never have imagined that we would ever set foot on the moon, and yet we accomplished that. Or how man thought Earth was the center of our Universe, think on all that. So many things we think, we are so sure of, turn out not to be so. Just because something hasn't been proved yet, doesn't mean it's not true."

"I am beginning to see." Even as the words left his lips, they felt tainted by doubts still hanging tight.

"But you fought it. You thought you were going crazy. Thought you were turning into Dad." It was as if she'd read his mind, or his fears.

'Yes, but now it's all different," he added. He tried to push away all thoughts of his father's struggles with schizophrenia.

"Right. You're not like Dad. And your mind doesn't work like others. Neither does mine. Amelia too. We're different. It runs through the maternal side of the family."

"How could I know?"

She glazed over his question. "Mom, and grandma too. All the women in the family, on mom's side. And, then there's you."

"Why me if it's all the women in the family? I don't understand that."

"Because you're my twin. My other half, in a way. We shared a womb."

"But we're not identical."

"Doesn't matter, Ray. You have the sense. And I'm here to show you. Pay attention, this is important." Her last few words slammed into him in unison with a wave hitting his chest.

BECKY followed Elena and Amelia into the bedroom. Elena grabbed her things, hastily shoving them into her bag. Amelia's eyes bored holes through her as she waited.

"We should get home to Uncle Ray. I bet he misses us," Amelia said, tugging on Elena's sleeve.

"Yes, I am sure he does," Elena agreed. "We'll call him in a second."

"What is going on? There's something you're not telling me, and it's huge. A real doozy," Becky said from the doorway.

"I can't right now. I wish I could get into it all, but..."

Becky's voice was stern, as if she were scolding her own daughter. "Really? With everything going on right now you're gonna put me off?" Becky put her hand across the doorway and pushed her palm against the frame, blocking Elena's way out of the room. "Not this time."

Elena thought to protest but looked straight into her sister's eyes and noted her concern. "It's Ray. I thought he was losing his mind. We all thought he was losing his mind." She shrugs. "After he lost Ravynn, after she died. So many sleepless nights. So many nightmares when he did sleep." She reached for her bag. "But it was always about Ravynn. And then he told me she didn't die—"

A gasp escaped Becky's lips, but Elena continued, "She didn't. Ray knows it. Amelia knows it. She's somewhere. I don't know where, or how, but she is." Elena waved her hand through the air while looking up. Saying it out loud sounded strange, the words so foreign spilling forth from her lips. There was logic, and then there was this. Whatever *this* was. "Somewhere out there. In another place. Another world. That's what they said. Oh, I couldn't believe it, but then all those peculiar things started happening—"

"Slow down. I can barely understand you. You're not making any sense. This is crazy talk."

Elena almost laughed out loud at the irony of hearing her own previous thoughts coming out of her sister's mouth. "Exactly. But it's not. I thought it was. It is all real."

"I'm calling Mom and Dad. Elena, sit down now." Becky took her hand off the door frame and turned to leave.

Elena reached out and caught Becky's wrist and spoke with a resolute determination. "I will not sit. And you will not call Mom and Dad. Shit's going down." She realized Amelia was still in the room. Her voice softened. She rolled her eyes at her own thoughtlessness and choice of words. "Oh, I didn't mean that, honey." Releasing Becky's wrist, she turned back to Amelia. "Stuff is happening."

"Like Mommy said it would," Amelia chimed in, seemingly unbothered by Elena's cursing.

Horror danced across Becky's face, painting uneven and unflattering lines around her eyes and mouth. Mouth agape, she glanced back and forth from Elena to Amelia.

"We should go see Uncle Ray now, Auntie E." Amelia again tugged on her aunt's shirtsleeve.

Elena turned back to Becky, her eyes full of apology. "I wish I could make you understand. I don't know if I can, Becky. How could I?" She pulled her sister in for a hug, squeezing her tight. Then pushed away. "Don't worry Mom and Dad over this. They won't understand either. I'll explain it all to you when I finally understand it myself." She grabbed her bag with one hand and Amelia's hand with the other. "Now, you'll have to excuse us."

As they walked by her and out the door, Amelia said to Becky, "Be careful. Bad stuff is coming."

ELENA reeled over her thoughts, beating herself up. *What the hell had she been thinking? Why did she take so long to get on board? Unbelievable.* Because it was all so unbelievable. Yet the evidence kept stacking up in front of her. She chose not to see it. How could she? How could she push all of it aside, with both Ray and Amelia?

I've been a fool.

She loaded Amelia into the backseat of the car and then buckled herself into the front seat. She could see Becky glaring at her from the front door. She gave a halfhearted wave and dialed Ray on her cell. She hoped he'd pick up, was frantic to hear his voice and tell him she was sorry.

The phone rang a few times and when she thought it will go to voicemail, she heard his voice.

"Elena."

Rapidly, she began to gibber, "I'm sorry. I am so, so sorry, Ray. Mt. Vesuvius, all of it. I get it. I mean, I don't get it, but I want to. And I'm sorry. Did I say that yet?" The last few words came out through choked tears. "I'm so sorry."

"Elena, where are you?"

"Amelia and I are heading home to you now. Are you home?"

"No. Not yet. I can be soon, though."

"You tried to tell me. Amelia tried to tell me. I couldn't hear."

"It's okay. Really. We'll figure it all out when I see you at home. When we're all home, okay?" His voice sounded so strong, so sure to Elena. It gave her confidence and made her stop crying and regain her composure.

"Okay, I'll be home in a half hour or so," she said softly.

I'll be a little longer than that, I'm afraid."

"Where are you?"

"At the beach," he said.

A long sigh came through the phone from Elena's end. Uncertainty crept over her skin, giving her goosebumps. Why on earth would he go there, to the beach? Hadn't he banned the entire family from going there, out of fear and grief over Ravynn? "I will explain. I hope you'll believe me."

"I will try. I will really try, Ray. See you when you get home." She was about to end the call but put the phone back to her head. "Ray, I love you."

He'd already hung up.

MATT flipped through the journal, the pages angrily slapping down, making sure he had all the details, all the events correct. He glanced back and forth from the journal to the cork board, checking each one in turn.

He grabbed his cell and checked, no new messages.

Damn you, Ray. Pick up your phone. Call me back!

Matt called Ray's phone again. It went to voicemail and he left another message:

"Ray, I know this is weird. It's been too long. But I need you to call me back. I can't explain it all in a message. This is an emergency. I swear it is. About Ravynn. Call me ASAP."

Frustrated, he threw his phone across the table. "Damn you!"

He pulled up articles and pictures from the devastation of Mt. Vesuvius, scrolling through like a madman. Eyes strained, his brain frazzled. He was giving himself a migraine. He wasn't sure what he was hoping to find in all the mess. Vesuvius was small potatoes in the grand scheme of things, although so far, it was the most horrific thing to have happened. He wanted to dismiss everything, dismiss the journals and Ravynn's strange premonitions, but he couldn't. He was too smart for that.

Oh, how he wanted a drink. *Needed* a drink.

He went to the cabinet, the one he stored all his booze in. He reached, ever so slowly for the first bottle, a bottle of whiskey. His hand was almost upon it and he pulled back, as if the bottle were a deadly rattlesnake about to strike. Before he could stop himself, his other hand was wrapped around the bottle. So much for getting snake-bitten. He unscrewed the cap, lifted it to his face, and took a deep breath in, inhaling the delicious brown elixir. He flung his eyes open, somehow surprised it was so very close to his lips. *No!* He thrust the bottle upside down into the sink and warily eyed the booze as it went in a hectic swirling motion down the drain.

Swirling, turning, like the funnel. The water funnel. That was where the woman was. Floating above the water, in a most unnatural way. Inside she stood so ghostly, as a wall of water spun around her, turning, twisting.

Why was he thinking of that night? That *Woman on the Water?* He continued to wonder as the drain greedily guzzled the liquor.

Because somehow, it was all tied together. He wasn't quite certain how, though. Should have been a detective and not a mechanic. The evidence was stacking up, and all he needed to do was piece it all together.

He thought back to another time when Ravynn was still alive. A time when their fights were growing more frequent, as was his drinking.

"Why won't you let it go, Matt? It's a journal, nothing more," Ravynn said as she made the bed. Special attention was paid to the perfect fluffing of the pillows.

"Because it's too odd. It doesn't make sense," Matt replied, standing across the bed as he watched her with a growing concern. "Why won't you let me in?"

Without sparing a glance in his direction, she continued to pull up the sheets, smoothing them flat with the palm of her hand. Like it was the most important task in the world. Anything to not meet his heavy stare.

He continued, "So many things happened to us that night. That night of the car crash. So much went unexplained."

"That was so long ago. I was just a kid. You weren't much more than a kid yourself. Who knows what really happened, and what we think we remember? It doesn't matter. Water under the bridge." She released the sheets from her hands and scowled at her own poor timing of that idiom. "Besides, so many good things happened to us after that night. That should be enough." This time, she looked up, meeting his eyes. He could feel the plea in them, the need for him to let it go. But he couldn't. He had too many times before, and it gnawed at him. It wasn't going to get better, he knew this, but he wasn't sure how to get through, how to reach her and pull it out.

His voice shrank to a whisper, as if the words should remain unspoken, or harnessed a power he feared. "And the *Woman on the Water*? What was that? How can we explain that? The ghostly woman who called to you. The spinning funnel of water that you moved toward." He looked around the room, as if expecting someone or something else to be there, listening.

She shook her head. She averted her gaze from his. The neatness of the bed linens became utterly imperative again as she fidgeted with them.

"That unseen force that fought me, pulled at you when I tried to rescue you."

"Stop it, Matt."

He moved to her side of the bed, reached out and gently took her hands in his. "Look at me, honey. I love you. I always will. You can tell me anything."

Her hands were tense within his hold. Her entire body rigid, as if he were a stranger asking the most terrible thing from her. Still, she would not budge. Throughout his tenderness, she withheld.

She whipped her hands free of him, too quickly, as if she'd been zapped by electricity.

This recoiling, retreating from him filled Matt with overwhelming disgust. The look in her eyes, pupils wide and alert, made Matt question the very foundations of their relationship. Question if he understood the woman standing in front of him, doing her very best to avoid him.

Heat welled up inside him. Testosterone run amok and he broke. "What will it take?" His voice rose, too loud to be in such close proximity. Ravynn recoiled, and that only exacerbated his anger.

She turned her back to him.

"Now you can't even look at me?" His fingers balled into fists and he flexed them. Blood pressure escalating, his face was on fire. He unballed one hand and reached out for her and she must have sensed it because she spun around. He froze, then reached for the blankets on the bed. "How did this rate more of your attention than me?" he yelled. He yanked the blankets off the bed, wildly flinging them to the floor. Grabbed one pillow, then another in the other hand, holding them out, then shook them furiously. "What's so important about these goddamned pillows?" He dropped one to the floor by his feet. The other he flung past her head. He meant to miss. He just wanted something to affect her. To bring her around. To make her react.

As the pillow went by her head, she coolly turned and observed it hit the wall. She picked it up and dusted off all the make-believe dirt it had picked up from the floor and walked back to the bed. Her stillness was infuriating; she would not give. She placed the pillow on the bed, looked to Matt, and said, "Ok. Looks like you get to finish making the bed." With that, she walked out.

What made her turn to stone every time he asked? Was it something she feared, or something she didn't understand? Or something, much, much worse?

Matt grabbed the blankets and angrily yanked them back up, a messy attempt at remaking the bed. He couldn't stop shaking his head. Was she schizophrenic like her father? Was she struggling, unable to discern what was real in moments, and what was an illness causing delusions? He wrestled with his fears and wondered what it would take to get through to her.

19

The moment Ray's car pulled into the driveway, Elena flung the door open and ran to meet him. A need consumed her; the need to be assured, comforted, and to comfort her husband as well.

So opposite her personality, she had to let go. Too many things had happened that she couldn't explain, and Ray and Amelia had a much better understanding than she did.

She didn't wait for him to get the car door open, she was grabbing at it, flinging it open.

His face was painted in surprise, and the realization hit her hard, filling her with a sadness. After the last time they were face to face and so far apart. The things they said. The things she thought. Schizophrenic like his father. Overcome with grief- having delusions.

No.

No words, but her eyes revealed everything. Welling up with tears, though none fell down her face. Beseeching, searching his face for something. Some kind of recognition, acceptance, even in her mistakes.

She reached into the car and took his hand, leading him out. "I don't want to fight anymore."

He stood, pulling her in, wrapping her tight in his embrace. She gave in freely, tucking her head under his chin, melting her body into his. Clinging to him like he was her life raft; if she were to let go now, surely, she would drown.

"I'm so sorry," she whispered into his shoulder. She exhaled a long breath. "I'm scared."

"I'm scared too," he said as he kissed the top of her head.

Why did I pull away, stray away, so far from this? From him?

"I'm ashamed to admit it, Ray. But all of this…" she pulled away and searched his eyes. "It felt easier to accept that you were sick, than whatever is happening in the world right now."

To her relief, his eyes met hers and put her at ease. Tenderness, softness, forgiveness.

"I wanted to believe I was going crazy or something. Better than the alternative. Easier, but something is happening. The world is changing." He kissed her on the nose, then on the lips. "And I'm afraid there will be nothing we can do to stop it."

She shook her head, not willing to concede this defeat. "That can't be. Why the warnings if---"

"How do you stop a tornado, an earthquake?" He held her around the waist still but leaned away a bit so he could look into her eyes. "The eruption of Mt Vesuvius?" His words were so much gentler than what they insinuated.

"I don't know Ray… but Ravynn's warnings. They can't all be for naught?" She could feel the desperation welling up inside her and she fought to swallow it all down. She concentrated on his warm hands on her waist.

He dropped his hands and grabbed hers, taking a step back. Nothing but silence passed between them for a long moment. Dizziness shook her as she tried to soak up the implications.

"Why don't we go inside, honey?" His words were a delicate caress across her frazzled nerves.

"Amelia's inside. Should we speak about this so close to her? What if she hears?" Elena bit her lower lip.

His mouth creased into a tender smile, and she wondered how he could be so calm. He licked his lips. "I think it's time we take the kid gloves off, don't you? She understands more than we do. She's accepted it all along."

Elena hesitantly agreed, knowing this was one of those concessions she'd never normally make. Things were anything but normal these days, and she was trying to think differently, trying to be open. He led her into the house by the hand. Inside the doorway, she yanked on his hand, stopping his progress. He turned to look at her.

"One other thing, Ray." She scrunched up her eyes in confusion. "Why are your clothes all wet?"

"Uh," he began. "Well, I went to the beach, and ended up in the water. That's the short version of the story, anyway."

"Long version later?"

He nodded and led her forward.

In the living room, Amelia sat cross-legged on the floor watching the news.

"Hey there. I thought I left you with the cartoons on?" Anxiety rolled over her, but she smoothed her nerves back down, imagining an iron going over all the little wrinkles in a fabric. Took a deep breath, envisioning the smoothness. She walked over and sat down next to Amelia, taking the remote from her.

Amelia tipped her head to the side, looking at Elena with almost a chastising glance. In that moment, she looked more like Ravynn than Elena had ever seen her. "More important stuff than cartoons, Auntie E."

The words of the child felt chiding and embarrassed Elena. It made her wonder who the adult in the room actually was. The TV shows flashed of destruction and chaos from Vesuvius, but Elena didn't pay attention. Remote stretched out, she turned the TV off.

"I'm sorry I didn't believe you, Amelia. Auntie E sure is stubborn, huh?" She smiled at the child and ran a hand through Amelia's dark hair, tucking a few wild strands behind her ear.

Amelia turned to face Elena full on, and Elena couldn't help but note her stone calm. Her tone was very matter-of-fact as she said, "It's okay, Auntie E. Mommy told me stuff and that's why I know. She told Uncle Ray, too. But she can't talk to you. You can't see or hear her." Amelia shrugged and added, "I know."

Elena nodded. "That's true. Only you and Uncle Ray."

"Because we're special," Amelia said, a smile lighting up her face, bright as the sun.

"Yes, very special. And I love you both very much. From now on, I'll listen better. I promise. Even if it doesn't make sense to me." She kissed Amelia's forehead. She continued, more to herself than anyone else, reliving her thoughts out loud, "You knew about the eclipse that day. I didn't listen."

The little girl nodded her head enthusiastically. She lifted one hand, stuck her index finger up and twirled it. "Earth spins different now. People don't know yet. Well, they don't *know* it, but some can *feel* it." She stared intently at Elena as she spoke those words. "Mommy said some scientists know. But may be too scared to tell everyone. It's scary when you don't understand stuff. But the dolphins know. Birds too."

Elena marveled at the words coming out of this little girl's mouth. To have an understanding of such concepts, their implications. Most likely, her mother had coached her, but the amazing part was that she appeared not only to understand, but to accept it as well.

Perhaps embracing this new-found openness and sharing, Ray confessed, "I spoke to Ravynn a little while ago. At the beach."

Elena's head whipped around to face Ray. "*The* beach? You mean, where *it* happened?"

"Yes. I got in my car and drove. I had no idea why or where I was going. It didn't matter. Then I was there. Alone. Except I wasn't alone. Ravynn had pulled me there." He pointed to his clothes. "That's how I got wet. In the water." He paused, a doubtful expression crossing his face, and Elena thought, *I deserve that. He's not sure he can trust me.* He hesitated, but continued, "Explained things to me. Why Amelia and I can hear her, why she can come through to us from where she is. We have sort of a psychic bond. A bond that runs strong

163

through our family."

Elena began to nod, eyes wide and mouth shaped into an 'o', as if any moment she would ask something but never did. She became a sponge, absorbing all of the information. She thought she might vomit; her head was spinning. Too overwhelmed. She recognized she shouldn't flinch, shouldn't do anything to challenge the trust that Ray had finally given her.

When he was finished talking, she asked, "So, how did you leave it? How did it... end?"

His eyes rolled up to the ceiling and he sighed. "Didn't get that far."

"Why on earth not?" She leaned in, eyes wide, as if getting closer would help her glean the information faster.

Ray bit his lip before he responded. "Because you called."

20

Ray was asleep in bed. For the first night in a long time, he had fallen asleep without any trouble, without any fear. Arms tucked tightly around Elena, holding her close.

Ray was dreaming, and he was lucid.

Walking on a beach. I think. But, not an ordinary beach, no.

The bright coral colored sand beneath my feet feels like silk weaving in and out from my toes as I walk. Warm saltiness tickles my nostrils.

A bird cries out, a happy chirping sound, so I look up and am surprised; its wings span an impressive seven feet at least. Can that be right? I rub at my eyes and look again, expecting to find that I'd been deceived. Wonderment comes over me as it casts its magnificent shadow over the water. Its neck is long and graceful. Its body spins and rotates as it seems to be frolicking in the breeze.

I hold my breath.

Its body is elongated and elegant, silky tail feathers drape behind as the creature glides inches above the water. The strangest shade of gray I've ever seen, feathers glisten and almost shimmer in the crisp, radiant sunlight. I continue to watch and appreciate my mistake, not gray, but amber—

orange— no- brown. I can't tell. My eyes are confused as my mind tries to keep up and understand. It's as if the colors changing every time I'm certain I'm seeing them correctly.

Looking past the bird up into the sky, I swear my eyes are truly betraying me. The sky is the warmest tone of orchid.

Where on Earth am I?

"Not Earth, Ray. Under Another Sun."

I turn my back to the sea, which is so difficult because the beauty of the scene wants to hold me captive, soaking the vast beauty in forever. The waves, not unlike the sky, are a gorgeous tone of periwinkle. They mesmerize me as I stare off into their splendor.

I turn, and as always, I expect no one there. To only hear a whisper of her voice dance across the wind. But she is there. My breath catches in my throat, and I fight back a tear. In life she stands before me, despite the dream. Tall and lithe, her arms swing delicately back and forth as she walks toward me. The wind is playful with her long dark hair, tossing her locks to and fro, over her face, then away, exposing her delicate features. Emerald eyes shimmer as she looks at me. Her eyes are what smiles first, then her lips.

She looks healthier than I've ever seen. Her skin has a glow; a happiness and health that emanates from within. Although it's been about a year, she doesn't look to have aged at all. In fact, it seems, she's gone in reverse. Younger. Softer.

I lower my head, running my fingers through my salt and peppering hair. Over this past year, I've aged too much. So much worry, so many sleepless nights. I imagine what she must see and shame washes over me like a gelid wave. A burdened smile, eyes heavy. My shoulders hunch in a way I thought I'd never allow.

I shake it off as an inappropriate joke crosses my mind. "Death becomes you."

Ravynn shakes her head disapprovingly and sighs, "you know I'm not dead."

"I know. It was funny for a second. In my head, anyway."

She tilts her head to the side and raises a brow at me. I always hated that look, and this moment it was no different. Yet I am glad to see that look, regardless. A rawness prances over my heart. That look whispers a secret to me…

With a quick shake of her head, she adds, "I have something to show you. Someone."

That's when she appears. She comes up from behind Ravynn. Where but a moment ago, there was no one else on the beach, a figure emerges. Placing a hand along Ravynn's shoulder, she continues forward, letting her hand fall away as she passes her. The two turn their heads and smile at each other in passing, with the slightest of nods- a knowing shared only between them- and then Ravynn looks to me.

A wave of nostalgia washes over me like one of those periwinkle ocean waves. I feel like a child. I lose my breath. A boy of thirteen, being told of the terrible news that his parents have perished in a car accident. The realization that I'll never see them, hug them again, hear their voices, slams into me with all its force. I take a jarring step back, staggering from the blow. There's nothing to grab onto, nothing to steady my swaying.

I find myself steadied, as her hand is on my arm. She rights me. Her hand is so warm, so alive, so contrary to my reality... I find myself shaking my head over and over. This cannot be. She cannot be.

"Mom?"

She moves, coming around to face me full on, grabbing both my hands in hers. Her expression shifts from happiness to sadness in a blink. She opens her mouth to speak...

"UNCLE Ray. Uncle Ray," Amelia whispered harshly in Ray's ear. Little splashes of spittle hit him and confused him. Perhaps it was merely splashes of salt water from the waves crashing on the beach that he was on. Wasn't he just with Ravynn, and his mother? But now everything was so jumbled. So confused, perhaps it never happened at all. Amelia continued, "Get up. Up. UP." He opened one eye to see another eye, smaller, rounder, staring into his. Taken aback, he flinched. Small hands came up in front of that small eye, and Ray's brain clicked.

"Amelia?" he croaked. She was crouched on the bed, in between Ray and Elena. She scooted forward again, and her knee jabbed him in the chest. "What are you doing?" He lightly grabbed her shoulders and pushed her face away from his. "Get your pointy little knee off my chest, please."

Struggling with the darkness, his eyes slowly adjusted. He turned to face Elena as Amelia shifted her attention to her aunt, poking at her chest, trying to pull of the blankets.

"Uncle Ray. Auntie E. Get up now."

Elena open her eyes wide at him, then over his shoulder. Amelia was right there in her face, as she'd done to Ray not seconds before.

Before he could say anything, he heard Elena's worried voice, "What is it, Amelia? It's the middle of the night. You should be in bed."

Amelia shook her head wildly back and forth. Yanking at the covers, she pulled them back from Ray. "Get up! We have to go now!"

Ray startled at the last word, no longer a whisper, too close to his ear. He bolted upright to a sitting position, rubbing sleep from his eyes. "What's going on?"

Amelia emitted a sound of exasperation and pulled all the covers from the bed. "Get up! You hear it?" She sprang up out of the bed and ran around to Elena's side of the bed, shoving at her aunt.

"Hear what, little one?" Ray asked, still sleep-confused.

"Like the rumbly-rumble my tummy makes when it's hungry."

Elena draped her legs over the side of the bed. "You're hungry? Now?" She pushed a stray strand of hair out of her eyes, staring wildly at the child.

"Not me hungry. Not a tummy. Come with me." She grabbed Elena by the hand and tugged. "Come Auntie E." She tugged harder.

Elena got up, and still holding the girl's hand, let the child lead her out of the room into the hallway.

Amelia stopped dead in her tracks and turned to look back to Ray. Her eyes were wide. "You come too."

"Okay, be right there." Ray rubbed his hand over the spot

right in the middle of his forehead. For some reason, he couldn't shake this aura of sadness. A sadness not his own. Someone else's. His mother's.

Ray entered the hallway and heard Amelia asking Elena, "Can you hear it now? It tickles under my feet." Not waiting for a response, she led Elena further down the hall.

They got as far as Amelia's doorway when there was a strange growling noise, an almost grinding coming from under foot. Harsh sound of earth grating on earth, the very foundation of the house shuddering.

Ray was helpless, unable to catch up his to them in time, only able to watch as he was tossed sideways into the wall. He righted himself as Elena and Amelia were thrown about, the ground beneath betraying them, too. Elena pushed the girl forward into her room and fell awkwardly to the floor.

"Elena! Amelia!" Ray called down the hall to them. It should've sounded like a shout, especially to his own ears, but the sound was drowned out by the crunching of the angry earth.

ELENA could only compare the sounds to a giant made of metal gnashing its hungry teeth. But it wasn't a giant, rather the earth underfoot, and it could no longer be trusted.

She rolled over too quickly and a lightning pain shot up her arm from elbow to shoulder. Glancing to her right, she noticed that Amelia had fallen in a fluffy cloud of stuffed animals. She held on tight to the one she called Sally. *Or was it Shelly?*

The ground quaked and grumbled softer now, receding back to its slumber. Or so she hoped. "Stay there, little bunny," she called out to the girl. "You ok? Nothing hurt?"

Amelia responded in the negative, clutching her stuffy tight and fighting back the frown that was taking over her face.

Ray's voice shot out clearly down the hall, "Elena? You both ok?"

Elena's voice cracked as she responded, "We're ok. Where are you?"

He laughed nervously. "Got bumped. Picture landed on my head." His voice grew nearer. "We should get out of the house. In case there's aftershocks."

"Yeah, let's do that," Elena agreed.

Ray appeared in the doorway as Elena inspected Amelia. He held his head, leaning into the frame. He touched above his temple and cringed.

"What's wrong? Is it bad?" Elena reached out her hand and drew Amelia in closer.

"Feels wet. Think I'm bleeding." He pulled his hand away to check for blood. "It's not bad." He stepped forward and scooped up Amelia as she held tight to Sally. Ray snatched a blanket off the chair and wrapped the warmth around his niece. Held his hand out to Elena and they headed out, down the hall to the kitchen door. In the hallway, they were careful to step over yet another picture that had fallen from the wall in the shake-up. At the kitchen table, Elena realized her mistake, getting out of bed and not putting on her slippers. She stepped onto a broken shard of glass and it punctured her foot. Wincing, she stopped and grabbed her foot, trying to inspect the wound in the darkness. Ray bumped her from behind, tipping her into the kitchen table. She struggled to stay standing, hands braced on the table for support. She glanced up and saw most of the cabinets open. She looked back down to the ground and realized the contents had been spilled to the floor. She silently said a prayer that the wine glasses her sister bought her for her birthday somehow survived. Or maybe a piece of them was what was in her foot.

"Why did you stop?" He shifted Amelia from one arm to the other.

"Stepped on glass." Gotta get it out. Hurts like a son-of-a—"

Her words never finished. The initial movement was much gentler this time, almost like being pushed on a swing-set. Rock, rock, back and forth. "Get out, get out now!" Ray shouted.

The gentle swinging was nothing more than a trick. She hurried out and past the car, limping and turning to make sure Ray was behind her. As they got past the car, it began to shimmy and shake, a little too close for comfort. Ray pointed ahead, away from the car and into the open front yard. The glow from the streetlights was enough for Elena to see him and where he pointed. She scrambled into the yard and waited; arms held out for Amelia. He handed the little girl off and spun around and around, assessing the safety of their position. Nothing could fall on them there.

The car jumped to the side, right off the pavement. The earth rumbled and bounced, shaking everything around them, making Elena resemble a helpless rag-doll. "Ray…" Her voice betrayed her worry.

"Stay right where you are. Don't move, stay on the ground."

Elena clutched onto him and Amelia as Mother Nature unleashed her fury all around them. She was dizzy suddenly. Like being in a snow globe and having someone come by and shake the heck out of it. Her eyes juddered in her head as she fought to focus on something, but everything was moving. Her arms were wrapped tight around Amelia, who had her face stuffed into Elena's chest, blocking her from seeing anything.

The pain in her arm tore up her shoulder again, but fear and adrenaline won the fight. No matter the pain, she would not let that child go.

A loud creaking sounded from somewhere inside the house. *The floors never creaked before.* The kitchen windows burst from the pressure, the constant shaking and violent vibrations. *Am I dizzy or is the house leaning to the right now?*

Popping noises went off, like giant angry kernels of popcorn forced to explode. It seemed like it came from everywhere and nowhere all at once. The lights went out. Everywhere. Dark. Elena was absolutely dizzy.

Amelia pushed Elena away, as Elena tried to hold her tighter, afraid to let her go. Amelia fought back, pushing and crying, "Lemme go! Lemme go!"

She couldn't get out of Elena's grasp, so she stopped fighting, and threw up on Elena. Her crying slowed to hiccupping sighs as Elena brushed the hair from her forehead.

Elena cooed to the child, "it's ok. It's ok. It's slowing down, it's almost done now." She hoped she wasn't lying to her niece. *I can't take much more of this either.*

She looked around in the Cimmerian darkness, trying to make out something- anything, but everything was black. All electricity out, and her eyes had yet to fully adjust to the change. What she wanted to see, she wasn't sure. She needed to focus on something, because fear resided in the darkness.

Sounds of sirens went off all over. Police, firetrucks, ambulances all being called to action. Dogs barked and howled frantically in the dead night air. Car alarms beeped and wailed along with the frightened dogs. Elena silently said a prayer of thanks that they didn't need rescue.

She hesitated, then said, "I think it's stopped." Her voice didn't sound like her own. Too fragile, each word a tremor of its own. The acrid smell of vomit wafted up to her, and she realized there was some on her sleeve. "Should we go back inside? Stay here?" Her arm pulsed with pain and her foot throbbed and was likely bleeding from the glass lodged within.

"Let me grab the emergency kit from the car and we'll start there. I've got a lantern and some flashlights." He walked to the car which was now sitting on the lawn instead of the driveway and popped the trunk open. He called back to Elena, "I'm glad you never lock the car. It'd be a hell of a time finding the keys inside right now."

Elena accepted the backhanded compliment in silence. She could hear him rustling through the trunk, and moments later, he sparked the light of a lantern. His face was lit up with a ghostly glow as he approached.

Elena peeled Amelia's arms from around her neck. The little girl's eyes were big and alert, despite the hour. Her face openly displayed her fear. She had a permanent pout pasted on her lips that kept tilting downward into a frown as she bravely fought back the tears. *Is she too tired to cry?* Her face looked pale. Her body was tense and rigid as she sat in Elena's lap. She started to shake, likely from the shock of it all. *It's not cold out here tonight.* In fact, the air held a warm, heavy, dead weight to it. She wrapped the blanket tighter around Amelia, turning her into a little burrito, careful not to rub it against her vomit-soaked sleeve.

"Here's the lantern." Ray set it down when Elena didn't reach for it. Her hands were still full of the shaking child. "I'll leave this too." He dropped the emergency backpack full of supplies from the trunk. "I'm gonna go in and check things out. Make sure we're ok to go back in. Wait here."

Elena nodded.

He pulled a flashlight from the pack and headed to the house. From the yard, Elena saw him disappear into the house. All she could make out was a beam of light dancing around the halls in the house. *Tinkerbell. Except different.*

He was gone for several minutes, though it felt like so much longer to Elena, before he returned. The bouncing of the light signaled his return, making its way through the kitchen and out the door.

Amelia was asleep, but startled at the sound of his voice. "I can't really tell at night, but the house looks ok. I think." The doubt in his voice was palpable.

"Auntie E. Where are we?" Amelia wiped her heavy eyes.

"Still outside, sweetie. Just making sure everything looks good before we try to go back inside."

Amelia pulled back. "I don't wanna go inside. Can we stay here?"

Elena looked the question to Ray, who responded, "House is trashed inside. Cabinets emptied out all over the place. TV in the living room is toast. Basically, anything not sealed up tight is busted. I saw a small crack going up one of the walls in the living room. Most likely cosmetic, but what do I know?" He added with a shrug. "And a few of the windows are shot out."

"I don't wanna go back in," Amelia protested. "Stay here."

"That's not a bad idea, for the night. It's warm enough out

here. And safer." Ray handed Elena a shirt. "Grabbed this for you, in case you wanted to get out of that one." He pointed to the puke stained sleeve.

Elena had almost forgotten. "Thanks. That'd be good."

"I'm gonna grab the sleeping bags out of the garage, if I can get to them. We can pretend we're out camping. Ok, little one?" Elena was thankful for Ray's positive approach to the disaster.

Amelia nodded in approval.

Ray disappeared again into the garage, returning with two sleeping bags stuffed under his arms. He set them up, as Elena and Amelia looked on, all of them silent. He unzipped one bag and laid it on the ground, the other on top of it, like a sleeping bag sandwich, so they could all climb inside together.

Amelia crawled in between Elena and Ray, tucking her frightened little body close to them both. "I heard it coming," she said through sharp inhales. "It was rumbly, like a hungry tummy. I told you." Her eyes were big and round, most likely from the shock, Elena thought.

She gave the girl a squeeze. "You sure did." Elena hugged her and kissed her head. "You're smarter than everyone else here. Thanks for waking us up."

MATT was pinning another 'event' to the board when the earthquake began for him. First, the ground let out a low grumble.

He winced, body stiffening, preparing for more to come.

The grumble was followed by shaking that steadily intensified, making him question if his eyes were actually shaking around in his head. He had the presence of mind to duck under the kitchen table as he'd planned and hoped that was enough cover. Crouching on the floor, he braced his hands on the underside of the table and waited. He felt like one of those stupid wind-up animal toys that shake and jitter across the floor all crooked-like.

He clenched his jaw shut tight to keep his teeth from chattering. The ever-important corkboard hopped right off the wall as he risked a glance out from under the table.

"No!" His words held no power.

In defiance, the board toppled to the floor in front of him, cracking in two.

He covered his head with one hand, the other still braced to the table.

"Shit! Laptop!"

He could hear it dancing across the table above him, so he reached up, over the side of the table, grabbing blindly.

Contact! He grabbed the laptop and yanked it under the table with him. "Ha ha! Not my computer, bitch!"

The cupboards clattered, shook and shimmied, but didn't empty out. He said a silent thank you to Ravynn for that. If it hadn't been for the warning in her journals, he wouldn't have known to tape them all shut. Out would have flown the glasses, plates, cups, bowls, food. Even the bottle of bourbon he hid from himself in the cabinet high above the fridge. He flipped it the bird. "That's right, what else you got for me?"

In answer to his taunts, that one cupboard slammed open despite the tape, expelling the bottle to the floor, raining all around him.

Matt growled at the sad sight. Bittersweet, but he knew he didn't need that shit anymore.

Inspecting the floor around him, he saw booze, broken glass, the corkboard, and the journals scattered about.

He tried to glide forward, not lifting his knees. His hands became his eyes, feeling around the floor cautiously, trying to avoid the shards from the broken bottle. That's when the second quake hit and his hands faltered as they met spilled whiskey and he slid, hand thrust forward through the liquid, landing flat on his face. The smell of whiskey, even in this predicament, was terribly tantalizing. It was short-lived, however, as his cheek met glass, sending a shard across his flesh. The pain was sharp, then searing hot as the booze made contact.

The ground shuddered again and the whole house rattled, as if it too were frightened of the unstable earth. The very foundations being put to the test, creaking and whining in protest.

Matt scrambled in vain for purchase on the slippery kitchen floor, unable to find balance in a suddenly unbalanced world. He placed his hands on either side of his head and tucked in, hoping to last through the quake.

A loud crashing sound came from the garage. Then another, followed by a devastating blast.

An eerie calm followed, and Matt was unsure if he could trust it or not. He waited, counted to ten, and inhaled a deep breath, gathering his courage.

He drew himself up and slid out from under the table, pushing his way as gingerly as possible through the broken glass and debris. Lights were out; they'd gone out in the second quake. He made it to the counter and hoisted himself to a standing position. Pulled his cellphone from his pocket and flicked the flashlight on.

He silently thanked the kitchen table for providing him protection.

His humble shelter through the destruction was still standing. Thanks to his quick thinking and warning from Ravynn's journal, the taped cupboards all held, except that one. *Not bad,* he thought.

The coffee machine, the toaster, everything that had been on the counter also lay somewhere on the floor. So much for forethought and planning. He spotted the corkboard. Remembering how it came off the wall and split in two, he groaned at the loss. The board now sat face down in a pool of liquor and other unidentifiable liquids.

So much cleaning…

Something was running down the side of his face, and he recalled the broken glass. He finds a small shard of it sticking out of his cheek. He grimaced in pain as he plucked it out.

Searching for something to mop up the blood, he spotted

the roll of paper towels miraculously still clinging to its holder on the underside of the counter. He ripped a few off and pressed them to his bleeding cheek.

Amelia!

The worry for his daughter finally slammed into him and he dropped the bloody towel. His heart caught in his throat. He was about to call Ray again, but Ray had yet to respond to any of his many calls or texts. He dialed a different number.

But the phone was dead.

There was a sharp static hum each time he tried to call out. Finally, the line connected, and went straight to her voicemail.

"Elena, it's Matt. Is everyone ok? Is Amelia ok? Please let me know---" The phone was suddenly dead. He tried again. Nothing. Cell service gone. Not surprising after such a violent quake.

Remembering the loud crashes, he grabbed a flashlight and opened the door to the garage. Except, there was no garage. Not anymore. In its place stood a mass of rubble and one toppled redwood tree, laying on the trunk of his car.

21

Ray waited patiently as Elena tried her parents' number for the fifth time. Only once did it seem like the call would connect, then the tone died off. She brought a hand up to rub at her temple. "Did all this really just happen?"

Ray tucked the blanket over Amelia. "Afraid so, honey. I'd like to tell you that's the last of this mess, but I've got a feeling there's more coming." He reached over and massaged her temples for her.

Her jaw slackened and she sighed. "More earthquakes?"

He scrunched up his face, thinking it over. "I dunno. I mean- just more- everything."

Elena's mouth tilted down into a childish combination of what Ray affectionately called a frout: a frown and a pout.

He changed the subject, "We'll try the phone again in the morning."

Elena stuttered, "wh-what if---?"

Ray wouldn't let her go there. "Don't play the what if game. It won't help. We'll wait until the morning. In the light we'll figure everything out. Let's try to get some sleep."

"I don't think I could sleep." She scooted her legs fully under the sleeping bag, more for comfort than warmth.

"I get that. I guess at least we got a little sleep before it all started." His mind drifted, and he finally recalled the dream he'd had. "I had the strangest dream before." He hadn't meant to say it out loud, but it was too late to take it back. Nervous of her acceptance of the 'dream', he wanted to tell her anyway. Wanted to take the chance that their reconciliation was true.

"Tell me about it. I need a distraction."

Relief washed over him. Happy to have the distraction himself, and happy for her wanting to understand things instead of ignoring or discounting them as she had before. "I visited Ravynn. Under another sun. And then..." The memory of the warmth of the sun on his face hit him just like in the dream, the silky sand between his toes, and the visions of not only Ravynn, but his mother. "And Mom was with her." He recounted the entirety of the dream, while Elena listened, completely enrapt.

Finally, she spoke, "Well, now I'm really not tired." Elena tucked a few of her wild stray hairs behind her ear. They fell right back in her face. "Nope, not tired at all."

"Sorry." Ray gave her hand a little squeeze. "It's just..." Ray's brain finally made the connection. At least he thought so.

"What?" Elena let his hand go and waved hers in front of his face. "Don't leave me hanging here."

His mouth dropped open as the lightbulb went off in his head. "I had a crazy idea."

Elena flinched. "Don't use that word."

Ray laughed, and it quickly turned into a sigh. "Too soon? Ok, sorry."

She leaned over the sleeping child and gave him a peck on the cheek. "What's the idea?"

He took a long dramatic pause, let the words roll off his tongue even slower, "Got time for a story?"

Elena theatrically surveyed her surroundings and replied, "Boy, do I."

"Ok, well the whole idea is about the mysterious *Woman on the Water.*" He paused for effect, but Elena didn't speak. She was in full listen mode. Her lips parted ever so slightly at the mention of the woman, but she didn't make a sound. She placed her hands in her lap, one over the other and looked to him, waiting. So, he continued, "I never really told you about Ravynn's car accident when we were thirteen. When our parents died," Ray began.

"Yes, you did." Elena nodded slightly.

Ray closed his eyes for a long while, then blinked them open. "Not the whole story. It was so weird, the details of all of it. Now, nothing seems too weird. Did you know my family lost three generations of women to water-related deaths? Ravynn, my mom, and my mom's mom."

"I guess I didn't realize that." She pulled the sleeping Amelia in closer for warmth.

"Not one of their bodies were ever found. Not one of the three." He brought his arms into himself, almost a self-hug, a comforting gesture. "Matt and I are the only living people to know the whole story. Really know it."

Elena kissed the top of Amelia's head. "But this is all history, Ray." She hesitated. "Why do you think this is all coming up now?"

"Because so much of this is not in the past. We missed something. Something important."

Ray watched Elena fighting back fidgeting as she gripped one hand tightly with the other.

"We were thirteen. Ravynn had just finished up a swim meet. She was getting really good, you know." A smile creased his lips. "I didn't go. I had a track meet and was sleeping over my friend Steve's house that night." He dropped his head, then paused, bringing his chin to his palm, his open hand splayed awkwardly across his face.

"They went to Sullivan's for ice cream after the meet. That was Ravynn's favorite. Sullivan's was everyone's favorite. It was across the bridge." He moved his hand off his face and clutched the top of the sleeping bag, tucking it under his chin. "Sure, there were other places closer to home, but everyone knew they had the best soft-serve." He smiled. "She always got a vanilla ice cream in a waffle cone, coated in sprinkles. Rainbow sprinkles. She said they were the best. Said they tasted like sunshine." He shook his head. "They had to go to Sullivan's."

"Ray?"

He untangled himself from the web of memories dancing across his brain and continued, "On the way back from Sullivan's, they had to come back over the bridge. That's when it happened. You know, if I had gone that night instead of staying over at Steve's I'd most likely be dead." He rubbed the top of the bag across his lips, another self-soothing motion, and continued, "Coming across the bridge. That's when they got hit. Car full of teenagers, coming the other direction. Not paying attention. Crossed into the wrong lane, speeding, driving erratically, and hit my parents' car. No one knows why Ravynn didn't die in that crash. The detectives on the scene thought either Ravynn somehow got flung out of the open backseat window or had the sense after the car hit water to miraculously get out on her own.

"Ravynn never remembered. No matter how many times they asked her. Her memory of the whole thing ended the moment their car got struck by the other car and began again on the shore with the cops and Matt." Ray reached out and tenderly stroked Amelia's head, her hair.

"Ravynn didn't wear a seatbelt. She never did. My dad always wore one and drowned wearing it. My mom probably didn't wear one that day. That's what they assumed, anyway because they never found her body. They figured somehow, she made it out of the car, but what happened after no one ever knew. They searched the river. Nothing. Kept a watch on local hospitals for a Jane Doe of her description, but one never turned up. It was like she just vanished." Ray looked up to the night sky, noticing the only lights about were the twinkle of the stars in the heavens. Such a wondrous feeling, yet it made him feels so small, so insignificant. The night sky covered in hundreds, no thousands, of sparkling stars. The longer he stared at them, the vastness, the sheer uncountable number of them became apparent. Suddenly, the night felt less dark, despite all the lights and electricity being out.

"The only witness was Matt, a twenty-two-year old recovering alcoholic, son of Walter and Mary Higgins, both alcoholics. Fishing off the shore when it happened." He said this as if reading from an old police report, details distant and detached from himself. "Matt jumped in to help when he saw Ravynn treading water. She was facing the bridge, away from the car, away from the shore."

"I know about Matt, Ray." Her tone suggested he was losing her. To the old 'facts' of a story that never made sense.

Ray held up a palm to shush her. "But this is where it gets really weird, Elena. Matt said he heard Ravynn talking to someone when he got close. He heard her say, 'I'm coming'. When he looked in the direction she was looking, he saw *her*."

"Who? Elena asked. She began chewing away on her cuticles.

Ray replied, matter-of-factly, as if his answer explained anything, "The *Woman on the Water*."

"Who, what?"

"Exactly. He thought she was an angel, this woman. That's what he told the police. The way she seemed to float there, above the water."

"That's creepy, Ray. I never heard this part." She pulled her fingers away from her mouth to say the last, yet her mouth remained open. "Why have you never told me this part…" Her last word came out like a puff of air that softly carried her surprise.

Ray was intent on not stopping his flow. "And then when he finally got a hold of Ravynn to pull her back to shore, he said there was this pull. Like he had to struggle with some unseen force holding onto my sister. He was finally able to break free and get her to the shore."

Elena chimed in, "But, well, how do I put this delicately? Matt wasn't the best witness, considering." She tipped her head and hand back, mimicking slamming a drink.

"He was sober, Elena. He was there fishing under the bridge. Some kind of therapy for him. Fishing. Fight off his urge to drink. He insisted on a test to prove he was sober. Cops agreed. I mean, with a story like that, they were sure he was drunk. Talking about angels and women floating on water. But he was sober. Abso-fucking-lutely."

Elena instinctively moved a hand over Amelia's ear, even though the girl was still asleep.

Ray rolled his eyes. "Then they asked Ravynn what happened. Well, she couldn't remember, like I mentioned before. She told them she didn't know how she got in the water, she forgot all about being in the car, too. Forgot all about our parents. She was really defensive and agitated. She just remembered treading water. Later on, she said she remembered the woman and feeling the urge to go to the *Woman on the Water,* that if she got to her, everything would be ok. But at the time, nothing." He shook his head. "I'm getting ahead of myself, and the story.

"Cops tried to get more info on the woman in the water, like where she came from, where she might have gone and all that, but Matt didn't know, and Ravynn claimed to have no idea of her. No evidence of her being there was ever found." The last words left his lips like the utterance of an old ghost tale, some urban legend passed down through generations. He nodded, satisfied with its telling, and met Elena's stare.

A long few minutes of thoughtful silence passed between them, and he waited for Elena to absorb what he'd told her before continuing, "Another thing that was terribly disconcerting about the night of the accident was that in time, once Ravynn remembered the woman being there, even though she said she didn't know the woman under the bridge, Ravynn said she felt so familiar." Another dramatic pause.

Elena leaned in and spun her hand in the air, motioning for him to continue.

"As you know, we went to live with my Grandpa after the accident. And not long after moving in, Ravynn scared the living hell out of Pops.

"She walked into his bedroom late one night, telling him she couldn't sleep. Nightmares or some such. He told her to come in and sit and talk. She went to the foot of the bed and sat down facing him. When he asked her what was wrong, she never did get around to telling him."

"Why not?"

Ray continued, "A picture on the nightstand caught her eye. Like she'd suddenly seen a ghost, she froze, dumbly staring past him. Pops asked what was wrong, but she didn't answer. Just kept staring. She finally pointed to the picture and said, 'That's her'."

"Pops turned to look at the picture, the picture of his wife, our grandma, holding my mom who was just a little kid at the time. The picture was taken the same year Grandma died. Pops replied to Ravynn that yes, indeed, it was her. Grandma.

"No big deal. Not yet.

"I mean, she'd seen pictures of Grandma a million times before. There were pictures of her all over the house. Everyone always talked about how much mom looked like Grandma, but until that very moment, nothing was ever strange about their likeness.

So, Ravynn started shaking her head no, wordless. She herself became ghostly pale, and Pops thought maybe she was gonna be sick. When she did speak again, she told him that the woman in the picture was the woman she saw under the bridge the night of the car accident."

Elena gasped. "Ray, no."

Ray shook his head, eyebrows raised. "Yeah. Pops got so scared and upset he told Ravynn to get out. He raised his voice at her, something he never did. He told her it wasn't funny, and she shouldn't joke about such things.

"She tried to tell him she wasn't joking, she was as serious as could be, but he wouldn't hear any more. She started to cry, she was screaming at him desperate for him to believe her, 'That's her! It's her! Pops, I swear!' But Pops was too scared to accept it. So, she came running to my room to wake me. That's when she explained the whole thing to me."

Elena worked right past chewing her cuticles and started biting at her nails while she asked, "And what did you say to all that? Did you believe her?"

Ray dropped his head, reliving the sadness. "No, I didn't believe her. I thought she was upset, maybe even confused from a nightmare or something. I mean, I didn't say that. I just listened and nodded my head. I didn't want her any more upset than she already was."

"So, you never believed her? No one ever believed her?"

"No, sadly, no one did… Well that's not exactly true. Matt, he believed her. He always, always believed in her. He was her biggest fan. And they both saw the *Woman on the Water*."

"Why are you telling this, Ray? Why now?"

"Well, this brings me to my idea. Something is happening. I know somehow, it's connected with Ravynn's, my mom's, and even my grandma's deaths. Mom popping up in the dream in my visit to Ravynn. All this chaos that's going on right now." He beat a finger into the ground, pointing. "The world is falling down." This last thing he said without a thought. Distant, almost in a trance.

"Ray, you're scaring me."

"I need you to be scared." He raised his hand and shook a fist at the night air. "All that's happening. All that's happened. It's leading to something. We've got to figure it out, Elena. Do you believe me?"

And just like Ray did for Ravynn all those years ago when she came crying to him after Pops scolded her, Elena did just then for Ray. She listened and nodded her head.

22

Elena and Becky stood, hand in hand, looking out over two freshly dug holes, six feet down. Two caskets sat, side by side, waiting to be lowered into the earth. The bright warm summer morning sun cast its delicate rays upon them as they lingered, yet Elena couldn't help but think of how cold the ground looked. How dark and unwelcoming.

Her breath caught in her throat, and she fought back a moan.

Then shall the dust return to the earth as it was: and the spirit shall return unto God who gave it. I hope there is a God in heaven, otherwise...

A chill swept up the small of her back, and suddenly she regretted having not chosen the wooden coffins instead of the metal. Mom always said the metal seemed so cold and impersonal, but Elena worried that the wood was too porous. *The ground will be so cold down there.*

She tipped her head up to the sky, squinting against the sun. The warmth evaded her, and all that welcomed her was the coldness and permanence of the death that lay before her.

Elena could hear Becky's soft, tired sobs, as she leaned her head on Elena's shoulder. "I don't understand this. Any of this." She stifled a whimper. "Never had a chance. The house… everything gone…" Becky brought her free hand up to cover her eyes, then let it fall, as if she hadn't the strength to keep it there. Her other hand still wrapped around Elena's arm shook uncontrollably.

Elena pulled her sister closer, wrapping a hand around the side of her head and kissed her temple. Like she used to do when they were kids and Becky got a boo-boo. Except this was no boo-boo, and Elena wasn't sure if there was anything that could lessen the pain.

Dax appeared on Becky's other side, and snuck his hand around her waist, both for the physical and emotional support as Becky sobbed, her body convulsing with each breath. She crumbled into him, and sensing the load lighten, Elena let her go. Dax whispered something in Becky's ear, and she nodded. Together, they walked away from the graves, leaving Elena without a second glance back.

The warming summer day was colder now without her sister by her side. She wrapped her arms around herself and shuddered.

"You need more time, honey?" Ray's voice jolted her back into her tired body.

Elena turned her head as Ray stepped up beside her. She took a steadying breath and replied, "Not enough time." The two plots stared back at her, like dark, unblinking eyes. Death lay all around them in this cemetery and reached its cold feelers out through the ground, searching for more to grab onto.

Ray laced his fingers in between hers. "I'm right here." And here I will stay until you're ready to go."

Together they hovered in silence, at the foot of the graves of Elena's parents. She gave his hand a quick squeeze.

After some time, she tugged sharply on his hand. "I'm ready."

"You sure?"

"Positive. All those people will be there soon. At home. We need to make sure everything's ready."

Ray slowly spun her to face him. "Everything is ready. I

saw to it."

Fingers still interlocked, they turned away from the graves and to the car. Elena froze, turning her head to steal one last glance. "Good-bye Mom. Good-bye Dad," soft-voiced, she whispered into the wind. A lone cloud passed over the sun, subduing its rays, but it couldn't compare to the shadow that now burdened her heart.

THE solemn reception was under way. People milled about, exchanging pleasantries and memories in hushed tones, as the sisters sat close together in the living room on the sofa with only their sadness between them.

Elena hugged her sister. "I can't believe you guys are leaving. So soon. So far away." She inhaled the coconut-scented shampoo her sister always wore. Taking in her smell, everything about her while she still could.

"It's gonna be weird." Becky embraced Elena. "But the house is totaled from the quakes... and Dax is always in Toronto on business anyway. The offer to move us there could not have come at a better time, really. I don't think we were truly considering it, until..." She didn't need to finish the sentence.

"I'm gonna miss you so much." She drew back, her arms gripping Becky's forearms, and nodded. "It makes sense though, it does. I'm happy for you. A new beginning." The words left her mouth with a strange taste; as if she knew no matter where anyone moved, they wouldn't be free of what was coming. But what was coming?

Becky's voice cracked as she added, "No earthquakes there. I don't think I could do another one."

The sisters shared a pained smile at Becky's words. A heavy silence passed between them. Smalltalk buzzed around them like the chittering of so many bugs. No words fell heavy on their ears until Aunt Teresa.

Oh, Aunt Teresa, the Gossip. Aunt Teresa, the Shark.

The words, the memories of what Elena's dad used to say about her aunt floated across her mind, 'They need to be constantly on the move, sharks do. All the time. If they stopped moving, surely, they'd die. Then there's your Aunt Teresa. She's a gossip. She can't help it, it's who she is. Just like that shark. She keeps on gossiping, on and on, yap-yap. I think, like that shark, if she ever stopped gossiping, she'd die.'

Those words never really struck a chord until just then. Aunt Teresa's words weren't loud, she just had a certain tone that somehow carried above all others. Those words of hers jumped out over the din of the crowd and raked at Elena's eardrums.

"Damnedest thing, they say. With all those rains we had all spring and summer. I don't think I've ever seen more rain in all my sixty-five years in California, you know. All that rain, and those god-forsaken quakes." She fanned at herself as if she were overheating. "Why that house never stood a chance the way it sat on the hillside like that." She threw her hands in the air. "Landslide hit so hard and so fast; they say they probably never knew anything. Never had a chance to even wake up." She smacked her hands together in mudslide-demonstration and slid one quickly down the other. "Just gone. All those houses over there. All those pe---"

"Aunt Teresa!" Elena balled her hands into knots and her face scrunched up as she called out to her aunt. "Did you try Isabel's pie? I hear it's something to rival your own." A small win for Elena, her hands relaxed, and she forced a smile. She knew exactly what that would do to her aunt.

Subject changed. Aunt Teresa stormed off to the kitchen table with purpose, in search of the pie.

"Well played," Becky said. "She means well. It's not her fault, but she's just so damn insensitive. That's one aunt I will not miss when we move."

Elena didn't acknowledge Becky. She was too busy staring at the man in the doorway. A man she hadn't seen in about a year. Eyes locked on him as if he were the only one in the room, she rose to her feet.

Anxious, his eyes darted about the room, hands clasped together rubbing one over the other, seemingly wondering if his presence was a good idea.

"Matt." A genuine smile creased her lips as she walked across the room to meet him. His footsteps were slow and purposeful, moving with trepidation.

She reached out a hand to him, both to embrace him, and quell his anxiety. Arms wrapped gently around him, patting him on the back. "Thank you so much for being here."

"I'm so sorry. I just wanted you to know." His eyes now focused on her, he seemed calmer.

Stepping back, she gave him a once over. "You look well."

He checked himself as a laugh escaped him. "You're a terrible liar, but thanks."

Her fingers indicated his wounded cheek. "And this? Looks painful."

"Not anymore. Took a little spill during the shake-up. Just a few stitches. Did them myself, in fact. Hospitals were too busy for something so small."

"You did ok with them." She nodded her approval.

"Had a whole week to heal... has it really only been a week since the quakes?"

"Feels like just yesterday..." Elena's voice floated off subtly.

"Everyone else is ok though?" He fidgeted, sliding both hands into his pants pockets.

"Amelia is fine. You got my message? She's an amazing little girl. Maybe you'd like to sneak a peek?" One eyebrow raised with her question. "She's in her room."

Matt's eyes grew wide at the suggestion. "I... well... maybe..."

Not waiting for him to make up his mind or summon his courage, she took him by the hand and led him to Amelia's doorway.

Amelia and Carrie were inside, playing tea party on the floor. Elena and Matt looked on as Amelia arranged her unlikely guests: stuffed teddy Shelley, Princess Elsa from Frozen, a T-Rex, and one of the transformers. Elena always forgot which one.

"Only Amelia would invite T-Rex for tea. Must have gotten that from you?" Elena looked to Matt.

Matt shook his head, his entire countenance now lit up with pride. "That's all Ravynn." His face set off a glow as he continued, "She's so beautiful. Just like her mother." A tear formed in the corner of his eye, and Elena soothed her hand across his shoulder.

"She's half of you, too," she whispered.

"There you are. I was looking all over for you." Ray walked down the hall toward the duo. He continued on, seemingly unaware of who stood before him, "I thought you'd like to know David is here." Standing behind Matt, he added, "You wanna see him?"

"Yeah, and it'll give you two a chance to catch up." She pointed from Ray to Matt. Matt turned, and Ray stopped dead in his tracks. Elena headed down the hallways, casting a final look back over her shoulders, then disappeared.

WIDE-EYED, Matt spoke first. "I know. Probably didn't expect to see me. Sorry, just wanted to pay my respects." He took a few steps forward, meaning to side-step Ray, when Ray reached out and pressed a hand into Matt's chest, halting his forward movement.

"Not so fast." The stern look on his face softened and he gave Matt a bear of a hug. Pushing back and away, he took a long look at his sister's widower. "You look like hell, Matty."

An older woman brushed past Matt. He chuckled nervously and replied, "So do you, old friend."

"Haven't been sleeping well. What's your excuse?"

"Something like that."

Ray hung his head. "Sorry I never called you—"

Matt gave him a rough swat on the shoulder. "Nah. No worries. I don't think I'd return my calls either. After all this time. Thanks though, for the text that Amelia was ok. That set my mind at ease. All I could think of when that quake hit was, I hope she's ok, I hope she's ok."

"Least I could do. But I am sorry I never called. Hell of a time here lately. I can't even begin to explain. You'd never believe me, anyway."

Matt rolled his eyes to the ceiling. "You'd be surprised what I'd believe."

Ray nodded. "Thanks for coming. It was really thoughtful. It means a lot to Elena."

Matt swung his attention back to Amelia. "She's getting so big. I've missed so much." A sigh escaped him as the pangs of guilt flipped his stomach upside down.

"Is that why you were calling?" Ray shot a glance in Amelia's direction. "To come see her?" The surprise was all over Ray's face, and Matt couldn't help but feel guilty for it. He deserved that.

"It's good to see her. I was both excited and nervous about that. After all my failures." He took a step forward into the room, then placed a hand on the wall, stopping his own progress. He spoke back over his shoulder at Ray, his gaze still forward, "You don't know how hard it's been. To stay away. To know that here is where she belongs. That I'm not enough." He swallowed hard on the last words.

"You've struggled. Been through a lot."

His voice now a low groan, he uttered, "But the bottle. I can't ever seem to put it down for good." Brows furrow, eyes scrunched up in anguish. "I miss her." Those last words he choked out and wasn't sure if Ray heard him.

"Say hello to her." Ray backed further into the hallway.

Matt took a heavy step forward and paused again. A small head turned to the doorway. Beaming, she jumped to her feet. Amelia's smile melted all his fears away.

"Daddy!" she screeched.

The high-pitched sound that might normally burst an

eardrum was music to Matt's ears. The creases and worry lines of his face disappeared as if by magic. "Amelia!"

Arms outstretched to her, he waited as she ran across the room and flung herself into him. He picked her up and squeezed her tight, her little legs dangling beneath her.

Giggles flew as he swung her in the hug. "Daddy!"

"Oh, my little angel. I missed you. I'm so sorry." Tears clouded his eyes.

Amelia lifted her head and wiped the tears from his eyes, a very adult action for such a small child, he thought.

Matt was taken aback at first, then he laughed, a deep and hearty laugh as he kissed her soft round cheeks, one, then the other in turn. "I'm sorry," he repeated.

"It's ok, Daddy. I know you were sick. But you're better now."

Although it wasn't a question, he answered her anyway, "Yes I am better now. This hug made me feel so much better. And this kiss." He placed one on her forehead, then lowered her to the ground and kissed the top of her head, too.

"Wanna have a tea party with us, Daddy?"

"Daddy is thirsty for tea. He told me a while ago," Ray chimed in and winked before walking away.

"I love tea. Where should I sit?" Matt took Amelia's outstretched hand and let her lead him to a spot at her table. He grabbed a tea cup off the table, sank down to his knees, and pretended to sip it. "Oh, it's still hot. And delicious!"

He clinked cups with Carrie. Amelia clapped her hands together in joy.

ELENA met David at the kitchen door. Not exactly sure if she should invite him in, she eventually figured she'd be rude not to. She wasn't exactly sure why he was there, anyway. To gloat about the fight with Ray? Or because of her parents' passing? She weighed the options before speaking again.

"Come in?" She gestured him to step inside, but he shook his head.

"Probably better if I stay out here and don't linger. With everything." He shrugged. "I don't want to upset anyone."

She forced a smile. "Ray?" She didn't wait for him to confirm. "Yes, probably." She stepped outside and closed the door behind her, leaving them alone by the driveway.

He lifted his hand to shield his eyes from the sun's piercing rays. "I had a bunch of things I wanted to say before I got here. But now that I'm standing in front of you, all those words are gone."

"It's nice that you thought to come." She clasped her hands and let them dangle in front of her.

David looked down at a large crack that ran through the driveway. "That wasn't here before, was it?"

Elena looked up to the sky thoughtfully before responding, "There are a lot of little cracks now where there used to be none." She looked down and kicked at the split in the driveway. "Sometimes things get all shaken up, tossed around, and it's up to us to sort them out and put them back together. When we can." She glanced back down, making the slightest of eye contact, to make sure he understood.

"M-hmm," David replied. He looked away quickly.

"Sometimes it's a hell of a challenge, but then you realize the inherent value. That not everything that breaks should be thrown away. Sometimes one just needs a little patience… and maybe some glue." She waited for some recognition.

David nodded his head but didn't meet her eyes again.

She concluded, "A lot of things need mending, but I remember what's important. My family."

David reached out a hand but didn't make contact. He pulled it back into his own body. "I just wanted to pay my respects." He pivoted and walked down the driveway. "Take care of yourself," he called without looking back.

"You too, David. Be well." That was the closure she needed. She was also strangely certain that she'd never see David again.

IN the living room with the other adults, Matt found Ray and pulled him aside. "Thanks for that time. She's exactly what the doctor ordered."

"Maybe you can come around every now and then, spend some time with her." The hope in Ray's eyes gripped Matt's heart.

"I'd like that. I can't believe I waited so long, was so afraid." He bit his lip. "Especially with everything…" He carefully deliberated what to tell Ray, in the current climate. This moment was about mourning Elena's parents, and Ray and Elena were good enough to let him see Amelia, but he wasn't sure now was the time to push the envelope. How could he come out and tell Ray about Ravynn's knowledge of future events? That she was aware of her own 'demise' in the tsunami? The words, and the courage eluded him.

"What are you holding back? I can see it on your face," Ray pressed.

"That obvious, huh?" Matt didn't wait for a response. "This really isn't the time or place to talk, though. Can we meet for coffee, maybe tomorrow?"

"This *is* serious." Ray's face grew concerned, and in that moment, Matt realized how gray Ray's hair has gotten and how exhausted he looked. Time had been more enemy than friend. To them both.

"It is. Meet me at Grounded. 5:30?" After everything the past year has thrown at them, he wasn't sure his vague request would be enough to get Ray along. But all the theories he had about Ravynn, the *Woman on the Water,* and the journal were too much to spill right there.

Ray searched Matt's face for some giveaway, some clue as to what it was all about. Matt did his best poker face and Ray gave up. "On one condition."

"Name it." The one request, so small, threw Matt and he couldn't help but agree.

"Just tell me what is this about. What's so important?"

"Ravynn," Matt said, as calmly as possible.

Ray didn't respond, and Matt didn't give him a chance. Matt nodded. "I've overstayed. Tell Elena I said goodbye. I'll see you tomorrow."

"I'll be there," Ray agreed.

23

"**L**ong day," Elena lamented, setting the last glass in the dish rack to dry.

"I told you not to touch any of that. Why are you washing dishes?" Ray grabbed Elena gently by the elbow from behind.

The full impact of the day's events showed on her face when she turned to look at him. Eyes lidded, heavy and swollen from days-worth of tears. Even her mouth, her lips looked tired, no longer trying to force the smiles, they sagged in the corners, like the gravity of the sadness had finally won the tug-of-war. A line he'd never seen before, a tiny little crease in her forehead, caught his eye.

As she spoke, her lips tilted upward, ever so slightly, into a forced, weighted smile. "They're done. I needed to keep busy." Her eyes were imploring. "I needed to be occupied."

With a disapproving shake of his head, he said, "I told you, I'd do it, honey. Can't turn my back on you for a second." He leaned forward and kissed the side of her neck. "Amelia's tucked in. Out cold."

Elena leaned into Ray, the weary weight of her pressing in. "Good. I didn't have the energy for stories and bedtime battles. I'm so heavy. Like I'm not asleep, but not awake either."

Wrapping his arms around her for a hug, he said, "Looks like she's not the only one ready for sleep. Let's get you tucked in, too."

A nod of her head was answer enough, and he scooped her up in his arms and carried her off to the bedroom.

She draped her arms around his neck and whispered into his skin, "I love you, Ray."

"I love you too, honey." He placed her gently on the bed, in a seated position.

She lazily shook her head in the negative. "I'm too tired to change."

"I'm not," he said with a wink. "Arms up."

"Ray…"

"Do not protest. You don't want to the more difficult one to put to bed tonight, do you? Amelia was soooo easy." Levity was his best attempt. He didn't want to think about the day, Elena's parents, how much she must be hurting. He didn't want to think about Ravynn right then.

"I surrender." She raised her arms and let him strip off her top and unstrap her bra. "Thank you." Her smile was sincere, but weak. The exhaustion was evident.

He reached for her slip of a nightgown and guided the silky fabric over her head. Covers in hand, he folded them back to where she sat. "Now lie back."

She obeyed, and he maneuvered her skirt off as well.

Lifting the blankets, he helped her tuck her feet in, then pulled the blankets up over her. The lines and creases heavy from the past few days seeming to fade away as she closed her eyes and relaxed.

"Goodnight." He leaned forward and again kissed her forehead, but she was already asleep.

Relieved she'd have some rest, but not entirely tired himself, Ray headed to the living room to watch TV. Mindlessly, he flipped through channel after channel, not able to find what he wasn't exactly sure he was looking for. There was a niggling at the back of his brain, a nagging sensation that something had taken place. Something big. He stopped on CNN.

'That's right, Adrian. This area is not known for earthquakes, and this one definitely has people rattled. A moderate one for sure, coming a week after the magnitude 5.9 and 7.1 in Northern California. This one registered at a 6.1, with a couple of aftershocks already occurring at 4.3 and 4.8.

As you can see here, there is quite a bit of destruction.'

The camera panned around, showing New York City. Flames engulfed several large buildings, while other buildings' facades were in ruins, layers of brick strewn about on the concrete.

'Although though this is a relatively moderate quake in the grand scope of things, buildings on the East Coast aren't structurally built to withstand earthquakes, not like on the West Coast. You can see the fires in the background, and I am told there are several water mains that have ruptured as well. There's no telling what kind of cost this will be, monetarily, but most of all, in human life.'

The camera cut back to the newsroom, and the anchor. 'Thanks Walter. Stay safe out there. We will continue to monitor the devastation on the East Coast after a magnitude 6.1 earthquake struck less than an hour ago.'

Click. Off went the TV. *Can't do this. Can't watch this.*

Elbows on the armrests of the seat, he brought his hands up to cover his face. *Where does this end? All of this chaos...*

He shook it off and headed to the kitchen. Leaning over the sink, he splashed cold water on his face. *I can't do this.* More water on his face. A heaviness came over him, and the totality of the day hit. Elena's parents, Matt's strange words, all the mounting destruction.

I can't do this...

"Yes, you can. You have to." Her voice was like a cold slap across the face.

He flinched and popped his head up. No one was in the room but him. Yet, here she was once again. "I can't. I won't."

"Snap out of it, Ray. It's happening. You need to be aware."

"Why, Ravynn?" He was about to check his volume but realized there was no way Elena would overhear him or crawl out from under the covers after her long, shitty day. "Aware of what?" His voice close to a shout.

"I need to show you something. It's time. We need to move this forward. Come with me."

He tossed his hands up in the air, looking around the empty room. "Where?"

"You need immersion for this to work."

"What does that even mean? I can't take much more of this. Riddles, incomplete conversations, clues, whatever this is!"

Her voice was demanding. "Fill that sink completely with water."

Ray obeyed her command and stared into the basin as it filled with water. "What am I looking for?" He was frustrated. She didn't respond. Slowly, hazily, her face began to take form in the water.

"Come to the water, Ray."

"Seriously, Ravynn, stop the riddles. What the hell am I supposed to do?"

"Close your eyes. Take a deep breath. Then hold it and immerse your head in the water. *Under* the water, Ray."

"But—"

"No but's, Ray. This must sound scary, but you will be fine. I promise. You need to do this, so I can convey this to you properly. I need you to see."

"I can't do that Ravynn." He stepped back from the sink. "I see fine already, thank you. I can hear you clearly. Just tell me."

"No. You need to *see*. You are waking up. Your mind is

becoming more aware, but you're only halfway there. I need you to be all the way. I need to wake that part of your mind up. Like Amelia's. It is time."

"Ok. Ok. What happens after I stick my head in the water?"

"You'll see, brother, and you'll know. Without a doubt. Your logical mind is blocking you from seeing what really happened. That's why these dreams have tormented you so. All you picture is death and destruction, because you've seen it all wrong. Your mind is so stubborn, Ray. You're always so damn stubborn." She paused. "You and I are so alike yet so different. You have the ability to perceive things that others can't, but you choose not to. I need you to choose to. Let go. Your brain is trying to hold onto reason and logic, and that has no place here. You know I didn't die. You know the earth is *changing*. But you still fight reality. You block your own gift. Your true self." Her words rang true. Hadn't there been something he was missing? Couldn't he see? So often, he was certain he was staring right at the answers, but he had a shroud over his eyes, ever-obstructing his view.

Hesitation. The room fell silent. The whole house was heavy with it. Everyone else was asleep. He needed to see it through, but the fear of what might happen and what he might learn held him back still. He needed to better understand what was happening to him. What happened to Ravynn. Why the world was falling apart around his ears. And most of all, he wanted to find a way to regain security. In his sanity and his ability to take care of his family. For the past year, he'd been a burden to Elena. Like she was the strong one, the support system, the constant caregiver. And even Amelia had a stronger belief and understanding in things than him. How could he care for his family that way?

The sound of water rippling stirred his attention and he finally responded, "Ok."

Her voice more soothing now, less demanding, "You have to relax. You'll be ok. Can you trust me?"

"Yes, I trust you, Ravynn." He knew he was safe as soon as

he uttered those words. A wave of calm spread out from inside him, wrapping itself around every fiber of his being, spreading outward like the tender rays of sunshine on a warm summer day.

"Good. Close your eyes. Clear your mind. Deep breath. Put your head in the water. *Under* the water. And you'll see everything."

He closed his eyes and emptied his mind, giving over to the calm and trust. Took a measured, deliberate breath and leaned forward, pressing his face into the cool water. Pressed until the water came up over his ears. They filled with water, the pressure building, and then it all stopped. Ravynn's voice yanked him from his body. No longer aware of his face in the water or his body in his kitchen. He was fine. Not holding his breath anymore.

Her voice whispered calmly through and around him, "Come with me, Ray. Let me show you my journey."

With the last word he was flung through a memory, though not his memory- through space and time. Lights swirled around him, beams of flashing light dancing and spinning, wrapping themselves around him and thrusting him back. His body weightless, then heavy, much too heavy as the lights pushed him down, down, down to the earth. No longer in his kitchen but in the river, under the bridge, moments after the car crash all those years ago that took his parents' lives.

Though, Ray was not himself. He was Ravynn as he experienced the events unfold through her eyes, her body and sensations. Like a passenger sitting on board a plane, he couldn't control things, just sit back, and let the pilot steer this flight.

The cool, dark waters surrounded him and pressed in on him as the lights disappeared. His hands and feet aimlessly moved back and forth to keep him treading water. How effortless this body was in the water. Her body- not his. He would be panicking, fighting to stay afloat. He was not in control of this memory, this body. It all belonged to Ravynn.

Nearby, the churning of violent bubbles popped out of the

water, the glug-glug sound of air escaping from the car as it filled with water.

All of this he watched with a cool passivity, an indifference that should be shocking. And then he saw *her*.

Some sort of angel-a woman- under the bridge. Was she floating? No. She stood on something. Stood *inside* something. A tunnel? Yes, some sort of tunnel of water making an opening about seven feet high, spreading out from where this angel-woman stood. The tunnel moved itself, extending forward about another six feet or so, all the while the water within it churning and spinning.

She was so familiar, he thought. And as he thought that he acknowledged that the thought not only belonged to him, but Ravynn as well. Yes, she looked so much like Ravynn. As soon as it entered his mind, the thought floated away from him, passing like a cloud through the sky. He observed the scene unfold around him like a vast ocean in its own right.

I am Ravynn. I am One.

Arms and legs moving on autopilot, treading the water. The angel-woman's eyes upon him, and her arms open, in a welcoming gesture, to accept him. *I must go there. I must go to her.*

He found himself swimming, to this ethereal woman, filled with a peace and calm he's never experienced, and in fact should not be experiencing in a time like that.

I know if I can just get to her, everything will be ok. She will take care of me.

He swam to her with purpose, the determination in every stroke. His muscles pulsing and working perfectly as he pushed through the water more gracefully than he'd ever swam.

The funnel of water spun around her, this woman who looked so much like another version of Ravynn, black hair flipping back and forth over her face. The woman stood still, unbothered by her hair, the breeze, the little splashes of water hitting her. Like a statue, she waited, arms outreached.

The closer he got to her, the calmer he became. The less aware of his surroundings he was. Although he was paddling through the river, he was no longer wet or cold. All he apperceived was *her* radiance.

There was a sharp tug. Progress impeded.

Someone was behind him, pulling him away from the *Woman on the Water*. *No! I must go to her!* A strange game of tug-o-war ensued. Two sides, each one pulling, not willing to give up their strength, their hold on him. *Surely, I will split if this keeps up too long!*

The pull from her, from in front was warm, soothing, welcoming. From behind there was nothing but cold and dark and fear.

The arm around from behind was too strong, pulling him away. It won out over the force of the *Woman on the Water*.

Sadness wrapped its cool embrace around him, a sense of loss as he got further and further away from her. Tears ran down his cheeks, though he did not fully understand why. Dark and cold rushed over his body and he remembered at that moment that he was indeed in the water, though he couldn't remember how or why.

All he knew was the sadness of getting so far away from the *Woman on the Water*. He watched her as she faded, until finally she and the water funnel disappeared from sight. In that moment, he felt that surely his heart would break. An empty, longing sadness sank into every inch of him and his body finally stopped fighting the pull.

His body was dragged from the water and laid onto dry land.

Then, the whole scene was gone.

Swirls of light wrapped around him, tugging him away once more. Body again weightless, moving through time and space and memory, growing heavier until it pushed him down, back down to the earth.

He had to squint his eyes to shield them from the bright sunlight. Summer sun danced off the soft tan beach sand. Waves flipped shimmers of sunbeams back at him. Without a doubt, he realized where and when he was. He knew this beach although though he'd only been here once before. The

Tsunami beach that took his sister.

Ravynn. She was like a second skin he wore. Because this was not his memory.

It was very early in the day, too early for the beach to be too crowded, but there were people here, strewn about. A handful of people combing the beach, while their children taunted them by getting too close to the water's edge. A man and his pup playing frisbee in the sand. Sandcastles made, surfers waiting in the distance for a wave to ride.

An eerie silence built to a deafening roar in the background. *Doesn't anyone else notice that?* He should care, but he didn't. She should have cared, but she didn't.

Something didn't sound right, didn't settle right. He stared off into the ocean, as far as he could see, not yet knowing what he was searching for. Something was coming, he was aware of this on some strange innate level. The knowing radiated through his body and into the earth beneath his feet. Something was wrong here.

Ray struggled, wrestling in Ravynn's memories with his own doubts and fears. Difficult to grasp onto what she offered in this vision.

Where were the birds? Where did they go? The sanderlings should be skirting the waves as they rolled in, chasing little snacks in the damp sand. wings should be flapping overheard, their cries ringing out.

A pressure was mounting in his ears so strong they might pop. It was a silence that roared at him, and he almost wanted to cover his ears.

A strange sound began, low at first. Too low to be heard initially; more of a feeling. A pull. Like a suction cup clinging to a window.

The sucking built up into a whooshing sound. Was the shoreline moving? He looked to a sandcastle, built several feet from the line, and watched its distance increasing farther and farther away from the water. No. A wave of dizziness took over. Yes, the tide was moving out, and it was indiscriminately taking everything with it. A few surfers finally realizing what was happening, but too little too late. They pedaled frantically with their hands, gaining no ground no matter how frenetic they became. Slipping away, farther and farther out, melting into the horizon. Slowly sucked out to sea.

So surreal.

Frozen on the beach, struck by his own fear of what was to come, Ray saw it in Ravynn's mind, in her eyes, but he fought. Fought against the onslaught, against her calm, against the inevitable.

'*Let go*,' she urged him.

Yes, birds were screaming now, somewhere off in the distance, so far away. Where had they gone?

There was another sound, like thousands of horses racing towards him at full speed.

Those weren't horses.

Water.

Here it comes.

No time to think, no time to act. No time to avoid the devastation. 'We aren't here to avoid it, Ray. We welcome in; and in turn it welcomes us. Let go.'

Ray took a deep breath and embraced Ravynn's mind's view. He let go of his own doubt and fear and beheld what was truly before him. Something changed in this inevitable death scene; a comfort presented itself. A familiar opening began in the sand where the water was but moments ago. The funnel, the churning tunnel of water opened to him.

There was a tall woman with black hair flapping over her face, spinning around and around as she stood inside this tunnel. The racing, spinning tunnel of water lay but steps in front of him. That was his salvation. Always had been. Ravynn had known, and now so did Ray.

The angel woman beckoned to him. She looked so much like the woman standing under the bridge all those years ago; yet not the same woman. This time, not his grandmother, but his mother. She did not die in the car crash, after all. It all made sense to him, right then and there. In that instant, understanding struck him like a lightning bolt. The electricity coursed through his body. Of course! The woman under the bridge in the water when he was thirteen was his grandmother. His mother's body was never found because there was no body to find after the crash. She had gone through the tunnel, just like he'd always meant to. Like Ravynn had always meant to, until Matt had pulled her away.

There stood his mother before him.

He knew what he needed to do and did not hesitate. He stepped up on the tunnel, his foot placed on the very edge. Expecting to fall or at the least waver, he was surprised to find the spinning walls supporting his weight. He took another step up, and another. As the great wave raced to hit him, he was tucked safely inside the portal, the gateway through the rift. No longer on earth, yet not Under Another Sun. He viewed the wall of water race to meet him, sensed the rush through his hair, the salty spit on his skin, but it charged *past* him.

He exhaled a breath he'd been holding too long and it made his lungs burn. Back on shore, the water angrily stormed the beach, indiscriminately devouring anything in its path. Destruction was total.

His ears were struck deaf to the sounds, but his eyes were able to see the annihilation from safely tucked inside the tunnel. A body got tossed like a rag-doll through the water past him, their eyes meeting for a brief nanosecond, the fear and disbelief palpable on the woman's face as she reached out to grab hold of a funnel that gave her no purchase. Ray closed his eyes, unable to help, not wanting to watch anymore.

He did the only thing he could do. It was what Ravynn wanted anyway. It was what she wanted all those years ago when she was thirteen under that bridge.

He turned away from the beach, and walked through the tunnel, his mother leading him Under Another Sun. When he took his first step off the tunnel, he was blinded by the light. His eyes took an achingly long time to adjust, blinding him to his new surroundings.

"Ray, lift your head. Time to breathe." Her words rushed through his brain like the whisper of a breeze through trees. A yanking sensation came over his body, and he no longer experienced through Ravynn. He found himself back in his own body, in his kitchen, his head under water, getting short on air. He flung his head up from the water and gasped, thinking- more than feeling- he was out of air. "Calm yourself Ray," she said to him. "Your mind is tricking you. It was only a few seconds. You're not out of air."

He was fine. His breathing relaxed.

"You see now what happened to me. What I went through."

"I do, Ravynn. I knew it." He held his hands up over his face and sobbed. Hand to his heart he said, "It hurts. I felt your pain, your sadness, your ache. All that you went through..."

Her words danced over his, taking away his sadness. "When they first came to me, when I was thirteen, that's when it started. They opened up my mind. Flipped a switch, if you will. I could see things clearer than I ever had before. More than the connection that you and I always had. More than us *knowing* the next word from each other's mouths or when you were hurt. I *saw* it all, so much clearer."

"I never knew."

"No, you didn't, Ray. But I did. The moment you met Elena, for example. I knew she was the one for you. I suffered your heart. I knew you were in for a world of hurt with David."

"And you never said a word."

"It wasn't my place. There were so many things I saw. Some of them I couldn't handle. That's why I withdrew. Why I pulled away so often from so many. I couldn't rectify what was happening, especially when I was a kid."

"I'm sorry I couldn't help you." He sank down to the floor, suddenly unable to bear his own weight and the weight of everything Ravynn had set upon him. "Sorry I didn't help you."

"It's all history," she said very matter-of-factly. "Nothing that can be changed."

Ray couldn't help but shudder at the lack of emotion in her voice. The distance between her words and their meaning.

She continued, "But soon is the beginning of the future. Your senses are awakened. What we did here. It opened the pathway. You brain is able to see things now- things you never thought possible. Things you can't possibly know. Let it in, let it all come to you. This is part of your gift, our gift. What makes us so special. What sets us apart."

The last words gave Ray a chill, though he wasn't sure why.

"This is all part of your journey, and it's barely just begun. You will see so much, but don't let it weigh you down, don't let it distract you. Observe, but don't absorb."

24

In the morning, Ray rolled over to find Elena still asleep. Not surprising after the long day before. An idea sprung to mind, and he headed for the kitchen. It had been a while since he'd made breakfast for his girls. A fresh start with coffee should do the trick to get him motivated.

He rummaged through the pantry until he found pancake mix. Within twenty minutes, he had a cup of coffee in hand and pancakes cooking on the stove.

Amelia was the first to stir, likely from the sweet smell wafting through the house. "Uncle Ray, you made breakfast?"

"Don't sound so surprised, little one. I know it's been a while. But Auntie E needed some extra sleep this morning." Spatula in hand, he flipped the pancakes, one by one, like a seasoned pro. A smile crossed over his mind, and his heart ached for a moment, fondly remembering flipping pancakes just as Ray himself was doing. All sorts of shapes and sizes, Ray's dad was an artist at breakfast.

Amelia giggled at the sight and clapped her hands together. "Pancakes!"

The smile faded, her face turning serious. Her eyebrows

squished together. "You saw Mommy last night."

Didn't sound like a question. He set the spatula down. "I did. She had a lot to tell me. To show me." He spoke to her like an adult, maybe for the first time ever. No pretense, no sugar-coating.

"Now you can see?"

Ray thought a moment before answering, "I think so. I hope so."

"Good." Amelia set herself down on one of the kitchen chairs, head propped on her hands watching Ray cook.

In the doorway, a robe-clad, sleepy Elena appeared. "Good morning you two. Sorry I slept so late." Tired, the puffy circles under her eyes even more pronounced than yesterday. Her hair was disheveled, and she tried, unsuccessfully to brush the strays from her eyes.

Ray sighed at the sight. His heart ached so to witness her like that. "You needed the rest. Besides, I've got this whole breakfast thing covered. No big deal." He waggled an eyebrow up and down and flipped a couple pancakes high into the air, then onto a plate for Amelia.

She giggled again. Her smile melted into confusion. "What are they?" She tilted her head to the side.

"Bunnies, of course." Ray reached over and pointed out the ears that he thought were obvious. "Bunnies!" He waited for her approval.

"Those are funny bunnies, Uncle Ray."

"Got any bunnies for me?" Elena sat down at the table next to Amelia.

"How many you want?" Ray poured the batter into the pan.

"Mm, just one. Not terribly hungry." The memories of yesterday came back and hit her full on and she trembled and put her hand over her stomach. "Not sure if it'll hold."

Ray flipped another pancake through the air, raising the plate up to catch it. "Ta-Da!"

Elena forced a burdened smile, while Amelia remained captivated by the show.

"What can I do for you today?" Rays asked as he set her

plates down and stacked a heap of cakes onto a plate for himself.

"Nothing. I think I want some quiet. And some sleep. I feel so tired still."

"Okay, well eat your breakfast, and I'll tuck you back into bed. Maybe some tea?"

"Chamomile," she said without looking up. Her head rested on one hand, elbow propped on the table. She pushed a piece of pancake back and forth in the syrup. After eating half, she gave up and threw in the fork, pushing her plate away. "I'm full. I'll take my tea back to bed with me."

"Amelia," Ray said as he stepped away from the table. "You be good and finish up your pancakes. Be right back."

Amelia nodded as she reached for the syrup.

Elena pulled the syrup bottle from her hands. "Think you've got enough of that. Your bunnies are swimming in a pool of maple."

Ray followed Elena down the hall, tucked her in, and placed her tea on the bedside table.

Climbing under the covers, Elena mumbled, "Heard your conversation before I came in. About Ravynn."

"We can talk about that later, honey." He planted a soft kiss on her forehead.

"Your lips are sticky." She rubbed at her head. "What did you talk to Ravynn about?" The soft lines of her face creased and hardened. Her hesitation and fear came off her in undulating waves, but Ray and did the best he could to communicate to his wife without alarming her. He couldn't begin to imagine how she was processing all of this, when he wasn't processing it that well up to that point, either.

"She showed me things. About her accident. About the tsunami. I understand much better now." He sat on the corner of the bed and massaged one of her feet through the covers. "She said I'll be more aware now. I'm not exactly sure what that means, but—"

"I've got a bad feeling, Ray. Can't shake it. Things are going to get worse. Much worse, aren't they?" She pulled the blankets up to her chin, and Ray thought she looked like a frightened child.

"Rest. We'll talk after you get some sleep."

She rolled over and faced away from Ray, before adding, "What did you talk about with Matt, yesterday? Everything ok? He seemed intense."

How could he have forgotten? Matt's mysterious meeting. "Yeah, it was good to see him." Ray hesitated before adding, "He wanted to meet, this evening, to talk about something important. But I'll go another time."

Elena rolled back over to look at Ray, and spoke sternly, "Not on my account. You go meet him." Her face and voice softened as she yawned and tried to push it away, unsuccessfully, with the back of her hand. "What time?"

"5:30. For a little while." He was unsure about leaving her at all. Might be neglectful in the current situation.

"That's fine. Amelia and I will be ok on our own for a bit. Go meet him."

"You sure?"

"Yeah, don't cancel. You never know how many chances you get... I mean... yeah... just go." She closed her heavy eyes.

"Ok. Get some rest. I'll grab a pizza on the way home. Love you," he said softly, but she was already asleep.

RAY glanced at his watch. 5:20pm, and he was a few minutes early to meet Matt. Outside of Grounded Café, he remembered when this little spot used to be the only coffee shop in town. Way better coffee than that huge chain coffee place that popped up across the street not long ago. Ray was sad that the huge conglomerate was slowly putting the privately-owned shop out of business.

He stepped inside. The café had a quiet and relaxing feel. Local artists' paintings hung from the walls. Sometimes, they had a local musician in to play guitar; they'd even tried a poetry reading a few times. Anything to keep people coming in.

Only six small coffee tables lined the shop. Chairs were hard, and not the slightest bit comfortable, but it had worked for so many years, was part of its charm.

In the back table, Ray spied an older gentleman in his late sixties, early seventies who was Skyping with a relative. The quiet of the place intermittently cut through by his bought of surprised, joyous, laughter. Any other day it would have been a pleasant thing to witness, but in this setting, with a serious meeting looming, it was ominous. Ray shook off a chill and ordered a hot coffee.

There was only one other person in the shop besides the barista. A girl in her mid-twenties that Ray had seen every time he'd come in. Laptop open, head down, she furiously typed away. *Writing her first best-selling novel she'll never complete.* Every time the old Skyping man laughed, she cringed, stopped typing, then fidgeted with the set of her heavy framed glasses.

Wait… how do I know that? How do I know she'll never complete that novel?

Ravynn's voice answered in his mind, as if it were his own thought, "*Because the world is falling down. And you are waking up.*"

Ray wondered if that was really Ravynn's thought, or if he was only hearing what he thought she'd say. He peeked out the window and laughed at his own doubts. His eyes blurred suddenly, and he swooned, grabbing onto the sides of the table to steady himself. When they cleared, he was overcome by a clarity he's never had, a clarity no one *should* have. Simple scenes passed by the window outside became complicated and full.

Life would never be that simple again. Everything was changing, and fast. Ray was overcome by the realization that he'd never step back into his school in the fall. In fact, no one would. A shadow fell over his thoughts and they faded away before he could search them for more information. His palms became sweaty.

A momentary rage spiked through him and he had the urge

to slap that twenty-something girl and tell her to go outside and enjoy the sunset! Take a walk! Kiss a boy! Do something!

And that old man… that laughing man. Ray had to hold back a shout building inside him as he thought, 'get on a plane! Go kiss them, hug them while there's still time!'

But as quickly as those feelings washed over him, they dissipated. Ravynn's voice again echoed through his brain from the night before, *"Don't hold onto what you see. Observe, but don't absorb."* His mind was swimming with too many thoughts, feelings and memories, most of them not his. He rubbed his hands together anxiously, as if the action could rub all the hecticness in his mind away too.

The barista appeared in front of him as if out of nowhere with his coffee, giving him an unfeeling smile for no extra charge. He smiled back, an even less impressive smile than hers, and she rotated on a heel and disappeared.

The coffee was too hot to drink straight away, so he sat and stared out the window at all the passers-by. Life outside the window of this apparently magical coffee shop appeared to be moving at an exceptionally snail-like pace, like someone had hit the pause button on the movie, then decided to watch it in slow-mo. The movie had begun, and now here came the actors. Like an omniscient viewer, Ray identified each and every one of those people intimately, their lives, their fears, their whole damn life stories.

A woman with her child of six years old was walking by. The woman was forty-eight, her clothing screamed a professional who dressed better than she ever needed to. Her hair pulled carelessly back, having started the day in a loose bun, but had shifted around as she sped through her hectic day. Pieces of hair shot upright from her bun and some shorter pieces were falling in her face and over her eyes. Streaks of gray ran through the first few inches evenly, giving away that she'd dyed her hair in the past, but had since given up. She'd given up on so many things…

How can I see this, Ray wondered?

She gave birth to the child, Joseph Jr, at forty-two, finally having convinced her husband to have a child. What a great idea at the time; they'd reached the point in their lives where they were financially sound. It made total and complete sense. The last piece to the puzzle of their marriage, she'd told him. He left her nine months after sweet little Joe was born. He'd had an affair with his twenty-six-year-old secretary. Couldn't handle the family life, after all. So, Erica was left to raise the child all alone. She was doing the best she could, too, Ray knew this. No... he felt this.

It's like I know her, like she's part of my life.

She'd cut back on her hours at the veterinary hospital and had taken on a partner, a single woman in her thirties who was firmly set against kids and family.

To each her own. Erica couldn't blame her. Sometimes it actually was better to be the old cat lady. Ray could taste Erica's bitterness as if it were sitting on the tip of his own tongue.

Little Joe tripped on the uneven sidewalk while Erica drifted in her own thoughts. He would have landed right on his little face is she hadn't been holding so tightly. She was a good mother to Joe.

Poor little Joe. He'll never...

Ray blinked, and his eyes got all fuzzy, vision closing down at the peripherals. He was about to panic when his sight came back, in a blinding flash of light.

An elderly couple strode into view, walking past Erica and Joe Jr., admiring the twosome as only people who have children of their own could. Their families had come together to the US from Poland in 1920 to escape the turmoil and war, to make lives for themselves and future generations. Antoni and Franka, both now eighty-six, with six healthy children, thirteen grandchildren, and three great grandchildren. Been married sixty hard fought years, unfathomable in most circles.

As Antoni squeezed Franka's hand, Ray sensed the electricity running, the love that still burned between them. They were each other's strength, love, best friend and confidant... through all of the ups and downs of life, including the heartbreak of losing a child in infancy.

They passed by Erica and Joe, hand in hand every step, as they always did on their nightly walks together.

At least they're older, Ray thought...

A pang of dizziness rattled him, and he closed his eyes again. He couldn't help but feel sadness slipping into him, embracing him, yet coaxing him to continue this journey into other's lives.

When he opened them, Tiana was walking her German Shephard, Rex. Ray knew this was the route she took on Tuesdays and Thursdays, when she sometimes stopped in for green tea. She never lingered, leaving Rex outside for only a few minutes. She didn't drink coffee, loathed the taste and smell. How could she dawdle in a place that reeked of coffee?

Tiana's disgust of coffee overcame him momentarily. He pushed his coffee away, but Tiana wouldn't shake him just yet.

She left home when she was sixteen, after she told her parents she was gay. She had her eighteen-year old girlfriend Jasmine with her at the time, thinking that would help, but the company only made things worse. Tiana's parents blamed Jasmine's 'influence' and told Tiana they needed to go straight to church for confession and beg for God's forgiveness.

It was possible, they told her, that the Devil himself or a lesser demon had sneaked its way into her mind and soul and corrupted her. Only God could save such a soul, they said.

Ray sighed with relief, a relief that was not his own, knowing that Tiana's real salvation was her grandparents. They had welcomed her into their home with open arms, accepting her for the person she was and not the wayward sinner her parents made her out to be. There with them she learned what true, unconditional love was.

At twenty-one, she met Angela in college at BU. They were as perfect as two people could be for each other. Now, at twenty-four, they were engaged and planning the wedding. Unfortunately, though invited, Tiana's parents vehemently declined the invitation. That was a-ok with Tiana, as her real father- her grandfather- planned to walk her down the aisle.

But there would be no wedding...

A lone older man passed, his head down, not looking at all where he was going. He bumped straight into Tiana, finally looking up. Rex growled at the man and Tiana yanked him away quickly. They exchanged a few words as Tiana continued with Rex out of view.

The man stood, stunned, looking around wildly, not sure of where he was. Ray studied him, expecting to catch a glimpse into his life as well, but there was nothing. A void. Ray squirmed as something akin to invisible tentacles reached out through him, through the pane of glass and touched the man. Those nonexistent tentacles touched the man, and he jumped and looked straight into the café at Ray. "What the hell?" the man shouted at Ray, though his mouth never moved.

Ray jumped. How could he hear this man through the glass, through his mind? The man was staring at him now, eyes fixed intently.

Ray thought, *I didn't mean to. I mean, I don't even know how I did that. Sorry.*

The man shook his head, lips still not moving, though Ray somehow heard very well, "Ah, one of the ninety-nine."

25

Ray was so blown away by the exchange with the man that he never noticed Matt enter the café. He was too wrapped up; all those lives a sad drama playing out before his eyes. They came and they went, one after the other, rolling on past, part of something so much bigger than they could ever possibly be aware of. Ray saw so much, almost too much. The weight of it pressed down so heavily on him he couldn't breathe. Sadness enveloped him, assaulting him from all sides, threatening to smother him. He reluctantly searched through their lives, hoping to catch a glimpse of what disrupts them, but in the end, each one gives him the same answer: nothing. Whether he couldn't see that far, or he was too afraid of what he'd witness, all he knew for sure was that each and every one of their lives would be cut short.

He took a steadying breath, remembering Ravynn's warning, "*Observe, but don't absorb.*" They were just words when she said it, and now they carried meaning.

Life was moving so slowly outside that window, those people an open book, as he flipped through the pages of their lives. So many of those pages were blank. There was so much that still could be written, but never would be. He was too afraid to contemplate the implications, but they were disastrous.

That man. Why was he so different? *One of the ninety-nine.* Why did that sound so familiar?

Like a file cabinet of archived thoughts and experiences, ray flipped through his memories until he came across something of value. A little voice singing a song:

"No rain for you... the sky was blue...
You're running out of time...
A crack in time saves ninety-nine."

Yes, Amelia said the ninety-nine, too. He was certain.
"The day is almost done...
Under another sun..."

A perfect a-ha moment. The day is almost done. Amelia had so many of the answers, but did she know what they meant? Did she understand the weight of those words?

A man's voice. At first Ray let it come and go, as he let the strangers come and go into his life so briefly, as he entertained the meaning of Amelia's song.

"Ray," said the voice.

Ray didn't blink. He remained in his trance, staring out the window, unmoving. Matt moved in front of the table, blocking Ray's view of the outside world, and called out one more time. "Hello Ray."

Ray blinked. "Hey Matty," he responded.

"How's Elena?"

Ray shook his head back and forth. "Ok, considering. I think."

Matt pulled out the chair opposite Ray and sat. "I get why you didn't respond to my texts or calls. I'm sure you thought maybe I was drunk, or maybe I realized I wanted my daughter back."

Ray didn't need words to respond. Those were almost his

exact thoughts. He nodded his agreement.

"But it has nothing to do with any of that," Matt continued. "First off, I need to tell you how thankful I am that you and Elena are raising Amelia. I am absolutely sure I'd fuck it all up if I had tried. She deserves better than a hopeless drunk for a dad. I can admit that. Hurts to say it, it hurts not to be with her, but it was the only real choice. Thank you." Matt's hands fidgeted on the table as he rubbed one hand over the other.

Again, Ray only nodded. They both sat, a stalemate of sorts, Ray not wanting to be the first to spill his crazy ideas. Not wanting to address the so-called elephant in the room. It was one thing to keep your strangeness to yourself, but quite another thing to share the crazy with someone else.

Ray broke the silence, "But you mentioned Ravynn…"

"I know you're gonna think I'm crazy, but I gotta tell someone. She was your sister. And we were friends once, you and I."

Ray laughed, a nervous, uncomfortable laugh as he thought about all the 'crazy' that had been going around this past year. He leaned forward, closer to Matt, and unsteadiness emanated from the man across the table in waves. Not the unsteadiness of alcohol, though. Ray could feel himself, reaching out, with that invisible reach he'd used not long before with those strangers outside the window. He tried to steady himself, to concentrate on Matt, but his own thoughts and feelings kept getting in the way. He wasn't able to focus on only Matt. Distractions. Amelia popped into his head, then Ravynn. The waves of love and regret poured off of Matt in his grief over losing Ravynn. Ray had trouble breathing suddenly, as if someone were squeezing his heart tight.

Ray sucked in a gasp of air as a wave of anger and frustration came over him. It was so sudden and surprising, his body flung itself back in his chair. The connection was severed, but all that remained was a desperate idea of a journal. He didn't understand.

"I guess, I'll you show you my crazy, if you show me yours." He held his hand up to his head and twirled his index finger.

Matt glanced up at the ceiling, as if it could provide some assistance in what he needed to say. "I know what I want to say, what I need to tell you… but fuck, it's hard to get started. To admit this all to someone, you know?" He paused. He rolled his eyes and tripped over his words. "Say it out loud. Fuck."

Sensing Matt's dismay, Ray offered up some comfort. "If it makes it any easier, I can honestly tell you, Matty, I am in no place to judge. Things have changed. They are changing. And fast. Life looks a hell of a lot different than it used to."

The barista breezed over silently, sliding to the side of the table, appearing as if out of the blue. Matt and Ray looked at each other startled, as she set a coffee in front of Matt while raising an eyebrow, exasperation plain on her face, as if to say, 'duh, you ordered it, dumbass'.

Matt thanked her, and she gave him the same unfeeling smile she had given Ray not too long before. Matt took a long, dramatic pull off his coffee and sat back in his seat, as if getting ready for a lengthy and burdensome tale. He began very hesitantly, seemingly unsure, "She had a diary." He waved his hand at empty air. "But not a regular one. Not the kind where you recount your day, vent your feelings, or even rant about what a shitty husband you had." Matt laughed at his own self-deprecation.

That one word slammed into Ray as if he'd been punched. Diary. Not moments before as he'd searched Matt for something, a journal had briefly come to mind. He hadn't been wrong. He'd read Matt. Or had begun to.

Matt paused here, as if searching, ever so gingerly, for the precise words. Like his thoughts on the subject were so fragile, like grandma's china, and if he set them down wrong, they'd shatter. Or he would. He took another long drag from his coffee, eyes closed.

Ray sat, patiently, not touching his coffee at all. Wound a little too tight for caffeine at this point. He somehow knew what Matt was going to say. A strange deja-vous wrapped itself around him and teased at his frazzled nerves.

"It was all dates and events. Weird shit," Matt began again. "At first, I didn't realize it. I mean, I felt guilty for reading it all, so I wasn't thinking. The only reason I read it in the first place was because she left it out. Open." Matt looked to be scrambling for some sort of order to his thoughts. The desperation oozed from Matt's pores like maggots. His anxiety was palpable, and Ray struggled to not hold onto it. Matt continued, "I'm not a huge follower of current events or anything so nothing seemed odd right off. There were days of things like natural disasters and pretty morbid shit. Each event had its own page. There was a date at the very top of the page. I had no idea what any of that meant. But then further down the page, there was another date, and then an event or whatever you wanna call it. You following?"

"Not sure yet," Ray leaned forward, placing his elbow on the table. He had a decent idea where Matt was going with all of this, but he needed to hear it. Have it confirmed aloud. Ray wasn't quite sure yet if he was hearing what Matt was saying or just what he wanted to hear. Someone else confirming the strangeness of Ravynn's life and death.

Matt went on, "Well, the thing of it that I didn't realize until later was that the first date written was the day that she wrote down the entry. Typical diary stuff there. But follow me here…" he leaned in across the table and looked from side to side before lowering his voice and continuing, "this is where is gets odd. The second date was the date of the event she listed. Two different dates—"

Ray cut in, making sure he understood, "So, you mean she was journaling about all these disastrous things after they happened, like keeping a record of them?"

"That's what I thought at first, too. So, I looked closer and realized she was documenting this shit *before* they ever happened. What the fuck, right?" Matt was clearly agitated just telling the story. He shifted in his seat. "Like the explosion, or eruption of Mt Vesuvius. The entry was the date she wrote it, then the future date it would happen, along with something brief, like, "Mt Vesuvius Erupts". Not detailed at all, but scary accurate. All the dates were right. I checked them."

"Holy shit," Ray said, and slapped his hand over his mouth. Things started falling into place for him. The other night, when Ravynn told him *The moment you met Elena, for example. I knew she was the one for you. I suffered your heart ...*' Ray began to understand even more of what she was trying to tell him. She had a gift of sight. Some sort of foresight. And here with Matt, he was digging past the surface that he'd only feared might exist until now.

"Holy shit is right, buddy," Matt agreed. He tipped his coffee back and drained the last of the liquid in one gulp and set the cup down a little too hard on the table. They both sat, quietly contemplating for several minutes.

Ray's words sliced through the silence like a razor-sharp knife, "Did you ever confront her about it?"

"Yup, and it didn't go well." He slapped a hand down hard on the table, likely a product of too much caffeine, and explained, "That's an understatement. Wouldn't give me any answers. Told me it was none of my damn business. I invaded her privacy, how dare I, and all that. She cried. Like a child. Sobbing, wailing. I think she was upset at more than just me discovering it, but she wouldn't talk. Ever."

"So, she never explained any of it?"

"Nope. We fought constantly. Fucked me up big time. The prohibited conversation. I started drinking again, hard core. I couldn't deal. Then she left me."

"Wow." Ray shook his head back and forth. "I'm sorry. I never knew why, really. Why you split..." The words came out of his mouth, and Ray wished he could take them back. The sorry felt generic.

"I know, I know. Everyone thinks it was my boozing. It was... my fault in the end. But that's where it all stemmed from." He wiped a hand across his brow. "But the scariest fucking thing about it, Ray, is that she forecast her own death." He rubbed his hand across the top of his lip, that was beading up with sweat. "I mean the journal entry didn't say anything so obvious like, 'I died' or anything. She knew the tsunami was going to happen. And then, after all that stuff, there was a few more words. Different than any other entry. It said, *Under Another Sun.*"

The words shot through Ray like a dagger piercing his heart. Did she know? All that time, did she know everything? All the things she held back. Things she thought she could never tell anyone. *Not even me.*

"Do you think she knew that she was going to die in that tsunami, and went to that beach anyway?"

Ray couldn't answer. Ray wasn't sure he'd want to answer if he could. The implications were too severe. Ravynn was aware of her own death and walked freely into it.

But she didn't die, she showed him. She went there. Under Another Sun.

Matt rambled on, "Or do you think she just wrote it all down, all the events, not knowing if any of it would affect her or not? Ah, it makes my head spin, Ray. I need a fucking drink."

Unmoving, Ray sat there, a fantastic impersonation of a statue.

"Say something, Ray. Please. For Chrissake, say something."

At last, Ray lifted his silence. "Where are those journals, Matt? Do you have them?"

"I do. And I'll show you."

Ray tilted his head to the side, deliberating. "But you know it doesn't matter," Ray said with a creepy calm. He didn't realize he said it, he was so lost in his thoughts. Although Matt's revelations were a surprise, nothing was too shocking anymore. Nothing too unbelievable.

"No, it doesn't matter," Matt agreed. He dropped his head in disappointment. "But there's another thing I need to tell you. Something I've never told anyone. Not even Ravynn. After the car accident, when I pulled Ravynn out of the water, I saw a woman…"

"Yep, I know the story of the 'angel woman', the

mysterious woman floating in the lake," Rays said, air-quoting. "But there's more?"

"Yeah you know that much," Matt continued, undeterred. "Everyone does. That's not the real kicker, though. That 'angel woman' or whatever you wanna call her... well, damn... she was the most beautiful woman I'd ever seen up until that point. Stopped my breath, ya know? But she wasn't real, right?"

Ray was well versed in the story, but he listened as if it were nothing he'd ever heard before. Thanks to Ravynn, he knew the cold hard facts, too. But he wanted Matt to vocalize it. Wanted to hear someone else put the pieces together. He marveled at Matt's tenacity.

"But she was real, Ray. I did see that woman again. I saw her for real. At least, I thought it was her, at first. Your sister. Your sister, when I saw her again after all those years, she was the same woman under the bridge that night. I don't understand how, or why, or what the fuck. This all grown up Ravynn was the exact look-alike of the angel woman. I never held onto it though, played it all off in my mind, like I just remembered shit wrong. Like the lady under the bridge was the most beautiful woman I'd seen until Ravynn. Then I thought I transplanted Ravynn's beautiful face to my memory of that mysterious woman."

There came a long silence.

"Say something, Ray," Matt pleaded. His voice cracked, 'Tell me I'm crazy, a damn drunk, and to go have another drink. Or tell me you believe me. Tell me something!" He smashed his fist down on the table.

The surly barista shouted, "Hey. Take it easy or you're gonna have-ta go."

Matt's frantic pleas convinced Ray to tell him everything. That Matt could handle the truth, or at the least, he deserved to know. "It wasn't Ravynn you saw under that bridge. It was our grandmother." He hesitated, leaning farther over the little table and whispered, "Ravynn told me so. No, she showed me. Last night."

Matt's mouth dropped open, gawking at Ray in

bewilderment. Shook his head, first, slowly, then faster and faster until Ray reached out across the table and grabbed Matt's hand.

"I'll tell you. Everything." He let Matt's hand go when he calmed. "I can't believe all you knew. No wonder you drank." Ray winced at the insensitivity of his words. "Sorry, I didn't mean to—"

"It's ok. I couldn't handle it."

"I couldn't either. I thought I was going crazy. Elena thought I was going crazy. Everyone did. Elena tried to make me go back to a doctor. Tried to tell me that maybe I was suffering from delusions. That maybe I was showing signs of schizophrenia, like my father."

Matt nodded his head, as if he understood everything perfectly. "Yes. I mean, I don't know about you. But right before the tsunami, all the fights with Ravynn, and the journal, I thought maybe the same about her." He put his head in his hand.

Ray told Matt everything. Every detail about his dreams since Ravynn's death, all of her waking visits to him as well. All about Amelia's dream and visits with her mother on the beach, and Under Another Sun. How their family had a gift and that's why they could all see things differently than others, sensed more than others. He didn't leave out a single thing.

After all the battles with Elena and struggles at work, here sat Matt, a captive audience eating up every word Ray said, completely accepting every detail. What an amazing feeling to tell someone who wholeheartedly believed him. No doubts, no judgements.

Matt said, "The last entry she ever wrote, Ray, well… you're not gonna like this, but I remember the date. How could I forget something like that? It's set to happen in five days. Meaning five days from now. Like, the end of the world type event, I'm pretty sure. There wasn't just one event. There were so many listed. It's coming. The End. And there's not a damn thing we can do about it."

26

R ay pulled into his driveway, burdened by a tortured mind and a heavy heart. How could he tell Elena all that he'd learned? He needed to, but after what she'd been through, might it be too much?

His feet fell unevenly on the driveway, and he blundered over the crack made by the earthquake. *A crack in time saves ninety-nine...*

Once inside, he found Elena at the stove.

"What are you doing?" he asked.

She didn't look up. "Making dinner, of course."

Setting the pizza box down on the counter, he stepped behind her, placing his hand on her arms. "I told you I was getting a pizza for dinner, remember?"

"Oh, I know, yes." She lifted the cover of the pan, revealing a blend of seafood, simmering in a light broth. "Was craving a seafood pasta tonight. Mom used to make it when..." She didn't' finish the sentence. Couldn't.

Ray leaned over, and waved his hand over the pot, wafting the delicious aroma towards him. "Mom would be impressed."

Elena placed the lid back on and confessed, "Honestly, I

did forget. But I was feeling bored, or inspired, or both. I was sitting around with nothing to do but think—"

"No worries." He patted her arm. "Smells great. We'll keep the pizza for tomorrow."

She reached into the other pot on the stove and forked out a strand of spaghetti, blowing to cool it. "This done?" She held the fork out for him to test.

"Just right," he said.

Finally, Elena faced him. A bit more rested, her eyes didn't look so dark and puffy, although she still didn't look herself. No doubt that would take more time. Losing your parents, both at once, was something he was all too familiar with. Waking up at night, your heart wrenching as you realized your nightmare was the truth; they're gone. Gone.

"Thanks." She was able to manage a half smile. "How was your meeting with Matt? What's up with him?"

Ray was hoping for some more time to figure out how to tell Elena, but staring into her big doe-y eyes, he couldn't put it off. He had to tell her, the whole story. "It's a bit of a long conversation. Rather complicated. How about we talk about it after dinner?"

"Fine, fine," she said, her attention barely present. She lifted the pot of pasta off to drain and looked to Ray as the steam hit her face. "Mind setting the table? We're about ready here."

IN the living room after dinner, Elena sipped on a cup of tea as Ray fully recounted his visit with Ravynn the night previous. She listened, not a word of interruption, with an occasional nod of her head. She gripped the cup tightly, letting the warmth soak into her as Ray fidgeted with a journal he had in his lap. He bent the corner back and then smoothed it out, over and over, a nervous tick. He finished with trying to explain his 'water awakening'. "She said I'd be able to see more, because of our family, and the gift we have. I didn't quite understand until I went to meet with Matt earlier. While I was waiting for him, I found myself staring out the front window, watching all the people go by. Something so peculiar happened, Elena. I saw those people; I saw into their lives. I *knew* them. Intimate details about them I couldn't, shouldn't know. Like there was this secret part of my being that reached out to them, into them." Like an excited child, he spilled the details, one after the other, barely pausing to make sure she followed him.

He told her everything, all the details of his conversation with Matt. About the journals, Ravynn's premonitions within them while she was alive. How in the end, it was those things that wore them down until they split. That is wasn't Matt's drinking, not entirely anyway. That so many bigger things were going on all this time, and the catalyst for it all was the car accident when Ravynn was thirteen.

Teacup still gripped firmly in both hands, Elena sat, like the perfect picture of patience, listening. Out of the corner of her eye, a branch waving outside the window pulled her attention from Ray.

Undeterred, Rat continued, "There was one man, though, he was different." He massaged the ever-darkening stubble on his chin while he thought back. "I couldn't see his life, but I could hear some of his thoughts, and he heard mine. One of the ninety-nine." As those numbers left his lips, he still wasn't exactly sure of their gravity.

"I don't understand what that means, Ray. Ninety-nine what?" Her gaze still fixed out the window, it drew Ray's attention as well.

A storm was brewing outside, and the wind began to make a howling, whistling sound through the pane of the old window. Strangely enough, that was one of the only windows that hadn't busted in the earthquake.

Elena stepped closer to the window, pushing aside the curtain, and peered into the night sky. "Come here, look at the sky," her tone full of awe, intrigued Ray, making him momentarily forgetting the ninety-nine.

At her side, he mumbled, "Storm clouds. But not rain?"

"No, not rain." She pulled her arms across her chest and hugged herself. "I admit, Ray, I'm scared. I don't understand what on Earth is going on, but I know it's not good."

"It's not good," he agreed. He thought about the very last part of the conversation with Matt he hadn't told her yet. As if the telling conversation with Ravynn hadn't been odd enough.

Little flecks fell from the sky. A raccoon skittered across the lawn triggering the motion light, illuminating delicate snowflakes floating on the wind. "Snow in this part of California, in the summer," Ray marveled. *What is this world coming to? And end, that's what.* The snowflakes should be more beautiful than they were, but the implications were frightening.

"The ninety-nine or whatever can wait." Elena disappeared into the hallway, and when she returned, she had a groggy Amelia in tow.

Ray's face was a question that Elena answered plainly, "We're going outside, of course. She's never seen snow before."

"Sure. Why not?"

Outside, the snow was melting as quickly as the ice crystals hit the ground. The sight was lovely, and Amelia was in awe. "Where did the snowflakes go?" She pointed to the ground, disappointed.

"Melting, little one. Ground is too warm to hold them," Ray responded. He questioned himself silently, *what are we doing out here? With everything that's going on, going to happen...*

"But I want some." A frown slid over the little girl's face.

"Got an idea." Elena raised her eyebrows. Waving for Amelia and Ray to join her, she laid down on the ground on her back.

Amelia asked, "What are we doing?"

"Catching snowflakes." Elena opened her mouth wide and let the snowflakes fall as they may.

Amelia giggled at her aunt. "Eating snowflakes?"

"You said you wanted some. Lay back, open your mouth, stick out your tongue."

Amelia did as Elena directed, and giggled some more when the first flakes hit her tongue. "It tickles!"

Ray and Elena both chuckled in unison, enjoying the fleeting moment of innocence. The outdoor light shone down on them as they embraced the mini winter wonderland. The wind picked up again, rustling through the trees, causing the branches of one of them to cast distorted shadows. Branches swayed and reached out, like long arms, stretching across the lawn to grab at them. Ray's winter wonderland was losing its wonder and charm. Within a few minutes, the winds grew fiercer, and the snow quickly changed to rain.

"Ok, party's over." Elena was the first to rise to her feet, reaching down for Amelia and guiding her to her feet. "Don't want to get rained on. No fun."

Amelia scurried to her feet. "Boo! Rain! I want more snow!"

"That's all there was, little bunny. Hop, hop, into the house, and back to bed." Elena led her into the house with Ray behind.

With Amelia asleep after the snow-break, Ray and Elena climbed into their own bed.

"Nice job with that one." Ray laid his head on the pillow.

She shifted to face him, her hair spilling across her eye. "Nice job with what?"

I love when her hair looks all tousled like that. I know she likes it sleek and pulled back.

Elena leaned in closer, and Ray could smell the scent of her. Not perfume, just her. "Waking Amelia to play in the snow. That was thoughtful, and playful. In spite of all the weirdness going on."

She shook her head slowly and more hair fell over her face. "What if the world ends tomorrow, Ray? We should enjoy what we have and those we love."

Or if it ends a few days after that…

He swiped her hair from her eye and ran his hand down her cheek.

"There's too much weird going on, Ray. We have to embrace the play while we can." She batted her lashes and gave him a lascivious wink.

Understanding the innuendo, he pulled her body closer to his. "Let's play then." He kissed her, full and passionately, like it might be the last time.

27

Elena asleep beside him, Ray tossed and turned. Anxiety pulsed through his system making sleep an impossibility. Thoughts and conversations, voices pounded in his ears:

Must be one of the ninety-nine...

The End. And there's not a damn thing we can do about it...

A crack in time...

We walk under another sun...

Have to get there, have to be there, have to go...

The blankets were wrapped around him too tight, constricting like a boa, threatening to smother him. He flung them off and scrambled to his feet, barely disturbing Elena's slumber. A faint murmur escaped her; she flipped over and stilled once more.

Ray left the bedroom, closing the door softly behind him. He passed by Amelia's room and sneaked a peek inside. Despite her awe with the snow an hour ago, she was out cold as well.

Outside, the rain still trickled down. The sound was

soothing, and Ray found it calling to him, coaxing him outside, barefoot. The grass soft and wet, his feet sank into the earth like a squishy, plush carpet. His mind was still distracted, cycling, the tickertape of thoughts running over and through at a dizzying speed. Everything that led to this point, all his fears of being crazy, the confirmation that he wasn't, his conversations with Ravynn, the realization that Matt was in some way aware of everything with Ravynn- had figured everything out on his own- stunned Ray, and that the world was falling down, overwhelmed him. He had to close his eyes and breathe. When he opened them, the world around him, however deceitful, was peaceful.

Summer snowflakes. Ray found himself laying on his back in the grass, like he had not all that long ago. His body sank into the long blades like his feet had. Although the wet squishy feeling should have bothered him, it didn't.

The stars had a muted glow through the thin clouds above. Raindrops leapt across his skin, but he paid them no mind.

How do you solve a problem that can't be solved? *The world is ending.* He'd wished Ravynn's journals had given him more information, more insight, instead of teasing hints at what was to come.

"The very fabric of the Universe, of time and space has a tear from within. And it is widening, at a frightening speed." Ray didn't flinch at the sound of Ravynn's voice. He'd become accustomed to her presence as if she were still there, never having vanished. He'd come to expect the unexpected these days.

"Until it finally rips open," he added. "But what does that actually *mean*, Ravynn?"

She continued, as if she never heard his question, "But it's not the end. Not for *Us*."

"I need answers, Ravynn. I'm tired. I'm scared. I don't want to play these games any longer. Tell me everything. How can I protect my family- your daughter- if I don't understand how, don't know what to protect them from?" He blinked as a raindrop hit him in the eye. His mind was racing a mile a minute. His heart, too. He anticipated, that as usual, his connection with Ravynn would be short-lived, and he wouldn't obtain all the information he so desperately sought. Ravynn had a way of exerting herself and her need to communicate over his, so often glazing over all he'd inquired about, "I met a man today. He said, 'you must be one of the ninety-nine.' What does it mean? What does any of this mean? I see things, Ravynn. I saw so many lives today. Into strangers' lives and pasts and the futures they won't ever have." A single tear slid down his face, but it soon blended in with the raindrops.

"You always want the answers given to you, Ray. Instead of looking for them yourself. You have the power to see it all, yet you choose to be blind in so many ways. I can't do this for you."

Ray sighed, crestfallen by her response. Typical Ravynn answer, as of late that he'd come to expect. She was dancing with her words.

Ravynn's tone remained unchanged, "When I got to that beach, under another sun, after the tsunami, I wasn't alone. There were a few others that survived as well. *They* saved us, Ray."

"Who are *They*?" he interrupted, bewildered by this new revelation.

"*They* are our salvation, Ray. They are like us; from them we came. They are the teachers. Opening our minds, waking us. Because of the psychic power we have, that makes us special. Not all human beings have this quality, and not all who have it are capable of ever recognizing it. We do. Remember when we used to finish each other's sentences? Somehow, you lost yours. Lost your way. But I am here to help you get your power back. And bring us home."

"That still doesn't answer my question." His voice no longer pleaded, afraid, confused; he demanded.

Ravynn took her time with the explanation, either unaware or unmoved by Ray's duress. "They are humans, a type of human. We came from them. Long, long ago, the first human beings on earth were put here, by them. Their ancient ancestors discovered this rift and experimented and tested the potential. They had no idea of the true power; only very recently has that been discovered. But that is a different question entirely."

"As time went on and the earth became populated by humans some of us grew and split from them- adapted ourselves more to fit this world- as species so often do and lost some of what made us Them. But some of us human retained that quality over the years. Some humans are able to tap into that ancient genetic gift. Like grandma, like mom, like me and you. And Amelia, too. Not only us. They have been pulling those like us back through the rift for hundreds of years."

"Why would they put us here, then, only to take us back? I don't understand." Ray had the strange sensation that even if she explained, the logic wouldn't satisfy him. The coldness of Ravynn's tone was unnerving. She was delivering facts to him, but all emotion was removed. Details, facts, history, but the personal connection was estranged.

"Because they spotted these changes on Earth. And that the planet had become unsteady, unstable. All these things happening aren't random, Ray." She paused, and Ray scrambled to soak keep up.

"Chicken or the egg," she said quickly.

"What?" Ray was perplexed.

"You know the old saying, 'what came first, the chicken or the egg'?"

A tough lesson was coming. He grumbled. "Yeah, what does that have to do with any of this?"

"That's what's going on with the rift. And the end of the world. But which came first, Ray? They found the rift and began opening it to pull those like us through. The rift only worked through water; that was the conductor. But it seemed, the more they opened the rift, the more these strange things happened. Tsunami. Meteorites hitting Earth." She paused, as if for effect. "The 1839 India cyclone, 1881 Haiphong typhoon, 1887 Yellow River flood, even the 1906 San Francisco earthquake, and those are just some of the most recent."

Ray's body was frozen with the fear and realization. "All of those things, because of the rift?" His breaths became short and fast, and he struggled not to hyperventilate.

Ravynn continued, once again, unwavering, although Ray was obviously upset, "But the question is, did opening the rift cause the Earth to deteriorate, or did the deterioration of Earth cause the rift to open on the first place?"

"My head hurts thinking about this. Can't wrap my brain around it all." He brought a hand up to his forehead, squeezing on his temples with his thumb and middle finger. "So wait, the Earth has been 'dying' since they first opened the rift? You're telling me They are destroying the Earth?"

"We don't know for sure, Ray." Her tone carried a defensive tone, which took Ray aback because up until this point, most of what she said had been devoid of any emotion at all. And that she'd referred to them until now as *them*, not as *we*, as she just had, was a disconcerting shift. She continued, "When the Ancient Ones first opened the rift and started their experiments, strange things were happening. They sent all of those first humans through to Earth. Odd things started happening Under Another Sun, and The Council was called, and decided that the rift would no longer be used to send anyone else through. Not unless it was proved that the benefit outweighed the risk. Hundreds of years went by before anyone opened the rift again. Whether by accident or not, one defied the rules and opened the rift again after so long. That's when he discovered he could use the water funnel to pull us back through, back home."

"At first, he was severely punished for his actions. But then they realized what had become of humans on Earth, their evolution. While seemingly so very many had devolved- those without any of the gifts I'd referred to- according to The Council, there was a drastic split in mankind. These few newly evolved humans were so very close to them, yet different."

"You see, Under Another Sun, they had difficulties conceiving babies, and the population was dwindling. They discovered it was beneficial to pull some of us through to mix back into the population. Those of us from Earth have a much higher chance of procreation. We changed things for them, by mixing back into the population with them, and now they are thriving."

Ray wanted to ask her if she was one of those pulled back through and procreating, but she didn't give him a chance. She continued with her story. "Our original mothers and fathers were dying out. And we were their salvation. It was perfect. And now they are here, opening the rift, to save us from the devastation of Earth."

Ray's throat became very dry. He swallowed hard, and managed to whisper, "A crack in time saves ninety-nine."

"Yes, Ray. On that final day, they'll make one last pull. Open the rift one last time and save ninety-nine more. You, Ray, you will be there."

28

Ray rolled over in bed and glared at the clock staring back at him like his enemy. Not the clock's fault he didn't sleep most of the night. Tossing and turning. How do you solve an unsolvable problem?

The glowing numbers on the screen drove reality home. 8:37 a.m. Another night gone, another day to face. *The days are numbered.* He let out a long sigh and kicked the blankets off. *The countdown is on, and there's nothing I can do to stop that, but I can save my family. I've got to save my family.*

Over breakfast, Ray broke the news, as gently as he could.

"So, I had a bit of a discussion with Ravynn last night. It solidified what Matt and I discussed the other day. I have no idea how to tell you all of this- it's extreme- I mean—"

"No need to sugar coat things any longer, Ray. The world has flipped right upside down. Even though I fought you and the truth for so long, I had to come to accept that despite the fact that I didn't understand any of it, that didn't change things. I've lost my parents, we almost lost our house, my sister moved away. There is nothing you can tell me now that I can't handle. What I can't handle, is for us to keep things from each other or do anything to create distance."

Her speech was exactly what he needed to summon his courage. "The world is going to come crashing down all around us, very soon. We can't stop the disasters from happening. But there is something we can do to escape."

Elena stopped and set her forkful of eggs back down on her plate. "What do you mean?"

"Everything is speeding up. Disasters all around us. Every day the threat grows, the chaos grows. The world itself is winding down, it's falling down, and within a few days, won't be able to sustain life. That is what all of this has been leading up to."

A small voice chimed in, "Under another sun. That's where we're going. To see Mommy." Amelia stuffed her toast in her mouth.

"Amelia's right. We're going. Through the rift."

"Yup." Amelia nodded. "We'll walk under another sun," she sing-songed as she lifted her hand over her head and pointed up at the ceiling.

Reaching for his phone, Ray added, "I'm gonna call Matt. I think it's best he stay here with us. I want all my family in the same place, so it will be easier when we have to go. Things are going to get bad before they get really, really bad."

Elena nodded, and her silence was enough.

"Uncle Ray?" Amelia dropped her hand to the table and gawked at him, her eyebrows furrowed.

"What is it, little one?" Even though he was no longer pulling any punches with Elena, he wondered how best to communicate everything to Amelia. She was still a child, after all. He wasn't sure how much of it she truly understood. Yes, it was clear she was aware they'd be leaving. That they'd soon be joining Ravynn, but was she aware of the absolute destruction that was about to befall the planet and what that truly meant for all living creatures on earth?

"You said when *we* have to go. Mommy told you that we're leaving?"

"Yes. Under another sun. We're going to go through the

rift."

"Oh," is all she said. Her face crinkled into the beginnings of a frown.

"What's the matter? Thought you were happy to be going to Mommy?"

Eyes darted to the side, out the window as Amelia hesitated, clearly mulling something over. She never shifted her gaze back to him, her stare remained fixed. "All of us are going?"

Elena and Ray exchanged a glance, then Ray replied, "Of course. We're all family. We're all going. Nobody's getting left behind."

LATE afternoon, Matt gathered with the rest of the family in the living room; Amelia in his lap, and the TV on in the background with the volume off. Scenes of the former days' destruction flashed across the screen. Mt Vesuvius and its fiery eruption, indiscriminately eradicating everything in its path. Wildfires breaking out in Australia at frightening and unstoppable rates. In South Africa, on Seal Island, great white and seven gill sharks beaching themselves in the dozens. In Japan, off the west coast of Tokyo, a 9.1 earthquake had struck less than thirty minutes previous. Authorities warn of the possibility of a tsunami...

Every now and then, the TV flickered, momentarily turning to a snowy static screen, then coming back. Matt rubbed a hand back and forth over his daughter's back, to trying keep himself calm as well as her. Amelia was completely unfazed by everything going on. He, on the other hand, could use a fifth of bourbon. He marveled at his daughter's sense of calm as he kissed the back of her head and beautiful black hair. In those moments, she reminded him so very much of Ravynn.

Ray began his speech, "Tomorrow morning, we're heading to the beach. Where Ravynn... disappeared. We'll set up a camp and wait for her, wait for the rift to open. These last forty-eight hours or so are going to be the most intense. And as I've said, I think it's about to get much, much worse. We need to be ready."

"Right," Elena chimed in. "We'll have one last dinner here at the house, then pack up the rest of our things and try to get some sleep. If we can sleep." She reached for Ray's hand and squeezed.

The TV flickered again, and this time, so did all the electricity in the house.

Matt shifted Amelia from one knee to another. "Can we… I mean, should we… wait until tomorrow?" His worry was palpable.

The power flickered again, this time staying off for about a minute or so before coming back on. Everyone sat still, waiting, as if holding their collective breath.

The ongoing cycle of destruction on the TV halted, as the news flashed an emergency alert. The annoying, attention grabbing beep sounded from the tube. Ray reached for the remote and turned up the volume when the beeping stopped. "This can't be good." His stomach did a flip-flop. Even though he was aware that things were growing steadily worse, the reality of the situation playing out on tv did nothing to quell his anxiety.

--Emergency Broadcast System. This is not a test. Repeat. This is not a test. A long beep followed.

The President of the United States appeared wearing a very somber face. The TV flickered again.

"My fellow Americans. I come to you today with the gravest of news. What we have been dealing with for some time is unprecedented. The amount of sheer destruction this planet has endured over the past six months has grown immensely in its force and devastation. Each day, we endure yet another disastrous blow; volcanoes, earthquakes, tornadoes. There is no sure answer, no guaranteed outcome. What I most regret is having to inform you what this seems to be coming to: An unavoidable global catastrophe of massive proportions of the likes that we humans have never witnessed. Fires, rains, floods, tornadoes, earthquakes- all of what we have been experiencing- all are likely to continue to occur and escalate rapidly. My plea to you in these desperate times, my fellow Americans, is to seek shelter, hunker down, and pray that we will find a way to overcome these odds. These destructive events are likely to escalate in the next 24-72 hours. Continue to pray, and to hope. But be prepared for the worst.

My thoughts and prayers are with you all. God Bless."

The power flickered again, and the TV went out. When the power and TV returned, the President was gone. The video began on a loop, as the television repeated over and over the President's dire warning.

Outside the house, the wind whipped and howled, like a wild coyote crying out for the pack. The ground rumbled beneath their feet, reminding him more of the echoing of thunder at first. Then, all the glass in the house began to make a tinkling, shimmering sound. Elena clutched Ray's arm tight, fingernails pressing in.

"Don't panic yet," Matt soothed. "We're losing contact with the rest of the world. We were aware this would happen. We saw the warning in Ravynn's journal. Take a deep breath." He gained courage from his own calm tone. "We're ready for this." He sighed. "As ready for this as we can be. Water stocked up, earthquake and emergency kits loaded, spare clothes and necessities packed. We prepared." He nodded, as if trying to assure himself.

The electricity gave one last push, flickered and went out, and didn't come back on.

Elena mumbled, "Government officials, all the important people, they're all probably safe stashed in an underground bunker of some sort. Only the privileged." She grunted.

Ray eased her grip on his arm and gently took her hand into his. "We are the privileged. We are going to make it." His tone became more subdued, "I don't think they will."

The ground groaned as if in response. The house shook

and shimmied around and beneath them.

Ray took his hand back from Elena and stood. "While there's still light of day, we need to double check that we are organized. Bags ready. Camping gear. Food and water for two days. Car ready to go." They were prepared, but the double-checking gave him purpose, direction. And made him feel less helpless in those dwindling hours.

Matt got up, scooting Amelia off his lap. "We are ready, Ray. You've got a direct line to Ravynn." The attempt at levity left a bitterness in his mouth.

Ray added, "And she told us we'd be ok as long as we can get there."

"Then we believe her, believe you." Elena shot Ray a heavy smile. "No more doubts. Let's do this."

Matt grabbed Amelia's hand. "We're gonna be sure this one is all packed up. Can't forget clothes and maybe a stuffy or two," With that and a wink, they headed off to busy themselves.

In Amelia's room, she packed herself up while her father looked on. Little girl with a big purpose. She went to her dresser and pulled out her pajamas, a pair of slacks, a long sleeve shirt, her bathing suit, and brought them back all one by one, throwing them on the bed. Matt began folding them and packing them neatly into her roller suitcase.

"Sure you got everything you need?" He asked her. Regret raced through him as his little girl acted so grown up and realized all the time he foolishly missed. All the time gone that he'd never get back. His heart ached.

She nodded, very sure of herself indeed, and added, "I need one day of clothes. I get new clothes when I get to Mommy." She handed him a pair of socks. Then she slowly picked up her stuffed bear Shelly. Looking at the stuffy, she spoke delicately, her voice suddenly saddened, "I'm gonna miss you. Wish you could come, too."

Matt squatted down, putting his hand under her chin to raise her face to his. "You can take Shelly with you if you want, honey."

Her lips moved, seemingly trying to form words but she faltered. Her mouth turned into a pout.

"What's wrong? You know we'll be ok, right? And Shelly can come with us, there's room." He hadn't contemplated the mechanics of suitcases and luggage in general inside a rift, but he wasn't going to tell her that. He ran his hand across her cheek.

Her voice came out so delicately that the hairs on his arm raised. She said, "No. Not talking about Shelly." She flung her arms around Matt's neck and held on tight. All the rest of the hairs over Matt's body stood on end too. He was suddenly acutely aware that this trip might not be meant for everyone. He hadn't considered that possibility before. Up until this point, it had been fixed in his mind, absolutely decided that they'd all be going together.

Amelia pulled away and added, "We shouldn't wait to morning. We go tonight."

29

Ray turned the TV off and reached for the emergency radio. A hand pressed his. "Not yet. Let's eat, first. In silence. Nothing good is happening, we know that." He looked into Elena's imploring eyes. The weight of everything recent had taken a toll on her, and she looked like she hadn't slept in weeks. Like she'd aged several years in the past month. She'd never admit the toll it had taken, always trying to remain strong on the outside.

He agreed. "You're absolutely right." Her eyes softened with his words, the lines smoothing out. A moment of peace washed over her before Amelia snatched it away.

Leading Matt by the hand, she appeared in the doorway. The shadow of her small frame somehow towered over the room, commanding attention. The sturdiest of the entire family, she held herself straight and tall and spoke, "We should leave soon. Morning is not good." In that moment, her presence was not that of a seven -year old, but so strikingly similar to her mother, Ravynn.

Elena must have noticed as well, Ray thought, because her hand was on his arm and her nails quickly dug in. Her face stripped clean of color, like she might faint. He pried her fingers off himself one by one and spoke, "Why don't I start the grill? Then we finish up and leave."

The magnitude of the circumstances pushed down on them collectively, and each one in turn nodded their agreement. Even though Ray's family would be spared, he couldn't slip up. Couldn't dawdle or become complacent. *The world is falling down.*

"I can't eat all the food," Amelia grumbled, placing a hand over her belly.

A wayward smile crossed Elena's lips as she replied, "You don't have to, little bunny. Uncle Ray cooked up everything we had left." She shrugged. "Felt weird to waste it." She was right. Quite the feast was spread before them: sausages and hot dogs, chicken, asparagus and corn, sliced tomatoes and cucumber salad.

"Man, I could go for a banana cream pie right now," Ray laughed. "Hadn't had one of those in a while and its sounds damn good."

"Hush puppies. Steamed clams," Matt added.

"Filet mignon, anyone?" Elena laughed, and Ray embraced the levity, however fleeting.

Amelia was the first up. She disappeared in a flash and came back rolling her suitcase awkwardly behind her. "Let's go."

"Whoa, hold up, little one. Just a second." Ray went over to help her. Amelia had been the one all along who knew the most, regardless of how well she'd been able to communicate, and how often they'd listened to her or taken her ominous warnings seriously. It made him reconsider. "Know what? She's right. Let's get the rest of our stuff into the truck. Before it gets dark."

Elena began to fuss, picking the paper plates off the table when Matt stopped her. "Is there a need?"

Like a lightbulb, his words sparked a recognition, and she smirked. "You're right. In fact, you could not be any more spot on." She picked up her plate and flung the dish at the wall, the cob of corn smacking hard and leaving a buttery smudge.

A shocked silence followed but it didn't last long. Amelia bubbled over with laughter. "No throwing food!" Her little body shook with laughter. "Bad Auntie E!"

The laughter contagious, everyone soon followed. Chuckles, giggles, snortles and hiccups follow as the kitchen erupted into a food fight, though not with each other. With the walls, counters, floor. Matt picked up an untouched hot dog and flung the wiener up at the ceiling. *Thwack!* Then gravity took over, and the dog slapped down on the table, tipping over a glass of water. The water spilled over the side of the table onto the floor, and Amelia picked up her juice box, then hesitated, a question painted on her face.

Matt gives her the go-ahead nod, hoping to encourage her. She pointed the box at nothing in particular, spraying red liquid everywhere. She began to turn and swirl like a little whirling dervish, and the juice-box became a dancing sprinkler.

Ray seized a stalk of asparagus and challenged Matt to a duel that he happily accepted. Like expert fencers, they jousted and side-stepped each other, trying to strike the final blow. Matt went in for a hard belly shot and it looked like Ray was a goner. But the asparagus broke on contact, leaving Ray an opening to go for Matt's throat. He snuck behind, wrapping an arm around Matt and holding the asparagus to his throat. "Another move and this one gets the asparagus! If you think I'm kidding, go ahead and try me!"

Amelia clapped her hands in a fit of giggles.

Elena clutched a stalk of her own, stabbed it straight out towards the guys, placed her other hand firmly on her hip and declared, "Hello. My name is Inigo Montoya. You killed my father, prepare to die." She made a deep lunge at the twosome, and Ray let Matt go, both of them backing away with their hands up. She repeated herself, like a true Princess Bride fan, "My name is Inigo Montoya. You killed my father. Prepare to die!"

The antics momentarily pulled them away from the seriousness of the day, but it was short-lived.

The shortwave radio beeped and a voice came over the line,

crackling and afraid. "From Hawaii. Kilaluea erupting. Streets are turning to magma... lava... the mountain and shoots out of the ground. Like something from Armageddon. Anyone out there? Hello? What's... on? Anyone report. I repeat. Kilaluea is active Oh my--."

Elena gasped, bringing her hand over her mouth. "What are we doing?"

"A moment's reprieve. It's ok. But let's get the truck loaded up," Ray replied. "Get the things."

"We're pretty well set," Matt added. "Just Amelia's bag here, and whatever else you guys need."

The ground lurched beneath their feet and Elena slid through the juice on the floor and hit the countertop. Her hands came out before her to aid her. "Shit shit shit!" Elena only swore on the rarest of occasions, but this was a fine time for her cussing. Ray reached out for her and she recoiled, cradling her arm. "I hurt my shoulder again."

"Sorry, Auntie E," Amelia's eyes were full of regret.

"No, no. It's not you. That was fun. We needed that. Silly and playful. But these earthquakes are anything but." The ground grumbled and tried to drop out from under their feet.

Ray reached out for Amelia as they all spilled to the ground. He pulled her into him and used his body like a shield curled over her. Elena and Matt both slid on their knees on the wet floor, tucking themselves under the table.

Ray counted, trying to figure out how long the quake lasted. The counting also helped him keep calmer. One, two, three...

The earth moaned and grumbled, as if lamenting its own coming demise.

What was left of their glasses jumped out of the cabinets, raining down sparkling shards catching the last glaring rays of sunset. Ray drew Amelia in tighter, making sure her face and head were protected.

The earth strained hard to the left, causing almost a jumping sensation, and the plate of remaining veggies fell on his head, leaving an oily smear through his hair. Somehow, he was still counting and cursing under his breath.

A cracking sound banged at his ears as he reached one-hundred and forty-seven He lifted his head to spare a look. *Nothing inside the house*, he thought, though he was not positive. More like the sound came from outside. After the cracking, the sound of shifting soil, small tumbling rocks and earth ensued, and he had a pretty good idea what was happening. The earth was splitting apart. The rift was breaking the world down.

At around two hundred and twenty seconds, the ground stopped moving. No more crunching, shifting sounds. He held his breath and waited before moving. Not sure if more was coming soon.

The sound of a dog way off in the distance and car alarms went off. All three cars in the driveway were screaming their alarm. Ray wanted to join in on the scream-athon but restrained himself.

"I think it's safe to get up. Get everything else you need, if you need it at all, and let's get outside." Ray's authoritative schoolteacher commanding tone kicked in and everyone stood to attention.

On their feet, Ray lifted Amelia and handed her off to Matt. "Take her outside, I'll be right there. Amelia's suitcase is in the living room. Be right out." He looked to Elena. "Wait for me outside. Everyone, go."

The three made for the door and Ray headed to the living room, feeling ridiculous going back for a suitcase in light of the extreme events unfolding before them at such a rapid pace. He reached for the handle as the earth gave a little roll and he stumbled, but he closed his fingers around the handle. He swung it to his body like a football stuffed under his arm and headed back for the kitchen, where the door was open. For some reason Elena and Matt were standing still just outside the door, when Matt cried out, "Holy shit!"

As Ray got to the door, Elena let out a yip. "The driveway cracked open!"

Outside, the foursome stared at the opening in the ground. About six or eight inches across, and one side of the driveway was sitting up about four inches higher than the other. Ray peered down about a foot into the earth, and the sounds of cracking and shifting soil made total sense to him now. Like the earth was opening up to swallow them all.

Luckily, the Pathfinder sat on the other side of the crack, unaffected. Elena helped Matt get Amelia buckled into her seat, then climbed into the front. Matt climbed in the back with his daughter. Only Ray remained outside staring back at the house, which now sat at a slanted angle that it never had before.

He had to get into the truck, but his feet wouldn't budge. So many memories in that house. So much laughter, joy and pain.

Three months after they were married, they finally found the right house. Elena had insisted on painting the whole thing, mostly herself, since the original paint had been so hideous; that awful seventies green that somehow everyone during that time had been so fond of. Even the living room carpet had been that vomitous green shade.

Not only great memories came to mind, but the saddest as well. The night Elena woke up crying, shaking Ray awake. She was four months pregnant when those pains took hold. Looking down at the sheets, she gasped as she noticed them spotted in red. Later at the hospital, the doctors told her they'd lost the baby, and if that news hadn't been heartbreaking enough, she'd never be able to have kids again. That had sent Elena into a dark time that she had only recovered from when Amelia came to live with them…

Elena opened the door to the truck and yelled, "Ray! Let's go. What are you doing?"

"I'm coming," he said, with a break in his voice. "Sorry. I was saying goodbye." He noted the desperation in her eyes as he finally turned back to face her. He skipped over the crack in the driveway and flung the driver's side door open. "That crack."

"What?" Elena's eyes were wide.

"Sorry." He climbed in and slammed the door shut.

Elena reached over and stroked the back of his neck. "It's ok, I know. It was our home. But it's just stuff."

Her clammy hand gripped his. Tension was running high for everyone, the air thick with apprehension. "Got the emergency radio, Matt?" He looked back in the rearview and caught Matt's eyes glaring back at him. Ray started the truck and backed out of the driveway slowly.

Static. The shortwave radio came to life again: "This is Darren. Oroville Dam broke... the last quake. Marysville, Yuba City... Oroville inundated. The people—oh God. All those people— can anyone hear me?"

30

A stunned silence reached inside, grabbing hold of everyone in the car. As Ray drove along, the traffic got thicker, as did the tension.

"We should have left sooner," Elena muttered.

"We left at a fine time," Ray tried to assure her. "We left when we did. Can't change that now." He looked to her and forced a smile.

Elena nodded, knowing that it was one thing to be in the thick of it alone, but to see other people reacting to the news was quite another. Becoming real, more desperate, more final.

Attention pulled to the left side of the road, where Elena pointed at the gas station up ahead. "Glad we have gas already." The station was packed full of cars filling up, and a hopeful line of cars out into the street. Patience obviously running thin, horns were honking, people yelling at each other, hands waving frantically in the air. Elena rolled the window back up halfway.

Ray carefully maneuvered the truck around the line of cars waiting to turn into the gas station and kept on in the thickening traffic.

Another two blocks up was the local Safeway supermarket and traffic slowed again. Cars were parked everywhere, scatter-thrust and willy-nilly. People hastily loading up trunks and backseats. Here too, people screamed and yelled at each other; the frantic cries of despair.

Amelia asked, "Why are they fighting?"

Matt exhaled and responded, "People do strange things in desperate times like this. Often brings out the worst in humans. Really, they're just scared."

Elena brought her hand to her mouth and started gnawing away. "Ray, can't we go any faster? Get around them or something? I don't like this." Fear had gotten a hold of her too as she spoke, well aware there was nothing he could do that he wasn't already.

Ray looked from left to right, then forward again, hands wrapped white-knuckled around the steering wheel. He rolled his hands around the wheel, hard enough to cause the leather to emit a squeaky sound that made Elena cringe. "Where would you like me to go?" He asked, sardonically.

His sarcasm eluded her. "I don't know. But this is bad."

"I'm doing the best I can, Elena. There's nowhere to go, as you can plainly see, at the moment." He opened a hand and splayed it upside down, making a sweeping gesture. "We've got to move with traffic. But if you think you can do better—"

Elena paused, trying to control her anxiety. "Sorry. Not trying to pick a fight. I'm just frightened."

"We all are." He stretched his hand over and patted her knee.

"I'm not scared." Amelia bounced Shelley on her lap, smiling.

Fear mixed with a strange feeling of repulsion raced through Elena's veins as she viewed the little girl from the side mirror. *How can she be so calm? It's unnatural. Creepy.*

Elena slapped her hand over her mouth. *How can I think that about my niece? What's wrong with me? She just a little girl... an extraordinary girl.*

Casting her gaze back out the window and away from her

niece, she spied a couple grown men pushing each other, fighting over a package. The man wearing the baseball cap snuck in a cheap shot to the kidney, and the man in the flannel shirt buckled, but he didn't let go of his precious package.

A case of water was what they were fighting over. The tug-of-war raged on, and finally the plastic wrap holding the bottles of water together busted open and the bottles went crashing to the ground, rolling this way and that.

The two men, as well as other passers-by scrambled on the ground, grabbing as many as they could of the priceless commodity.

The man in the flannel jumped baseball cap guy, knocking the waters he'd collected back to the ground. Soon, they're wrestling and before they stopped and realized, there were no more bottles of water to fight over.

The sound of shattering glass yanked Elena's attention from the duo as a patio chair went flying through the front window of the store. A woman fell out after the chair, slipping and cutting her hands. A boy not much younger than Amelia screamed behind the woman. She turned and reached up and through the window to the child, her hands a ruin, blood streaming down her forearms and elbows.

"Ray…"

The truck accelerated, finally able to move past the chaotic scene. But the light ahead turned red and Ray was forced to stop the car. The car behind him slammed on the brakes and everyone jumped at the screeching tires across the asphalt.

Elena and Ray both whipped their heads back over their shoulders as a man in his sixties dramatically gestured his hands in the air, then flipped them the bird. Leaned out his window, wailed on the horn and shouted, "Go! What're ya waiting for? No time! Just. Go!"

Ray stepped on the gas and started to proceed when Elena yanked the wheel, jerking the truck to the right, tires jumping the curb.

Ray opened his mouth to speak but Elena pointed dramatically.

A hard-looking woman wearing filthy, threadbare clothes was standing off to the left of the truck in traffic. If Elena hadn't grabbed the wheel, Ray would've hit her.

The dirty woman held up a cardboard sign with words hastily scribbled across:

End of Days
Judgement is Upon Us

31

"That was close." Ray looked to Elena. He wiped the sweat from his brow and shook his hand out. Cars behind them grew impatient, honking on horns and yelling at them and the lady to move out of the way.

Ray rolled his window down a few inches and asked the lady, "Please get out of the road?"

The lady scoffed at him, either unaware of the dangers or unafraid. She lifted her sign higher and turned to face the rest of the traffic behind Ray.

Ray bit his lip, holding back a plethora of things he'd like to say to her. He opted for, "Lady, somebody's gonna run you down."

The woman brought the ball of her hand to her eye and rubbed wildly. "You don't see, do you?" Her eyes grew oddly wide as she stared at him, unblinking.

Patience wearing thin, Ray raised his voice, "Lady, you're gonna get killed."

She shook her head slowly as she approached the vehicle, plainly disappointed by Ray. "There is no one that will escape this. Mark my words. No human left unscathed." As she looked at him, really looked hard at him, Ray cowered under her gaze. There was no fear in her eyes, and probably none in her heart. Brazen, wild, she stared through him, as if he weren't a person, as if he weren't really even there.

No shoes cover her calloused, raw feet. Ray looked into her eyes and realized his earlier mistake. He'd been sure she was in her sixties, but now he gathered she was probably more likely in her late thirties. Blond hair disheveled, matted in places, thinner is some spots. Her face was lined, not with age, but more likely hard life on the streets.

Sadness washed over Ray as he looked on her with pity, and that piteous reaction reminded him of his childhood with his father. Before his dad was diagnosed, his episodes were almost exotic and fun to both Ray and Ravynn. To have an adult with the awe and wonder and unbridled lack of skepticism of most adults was refreshing. When Ray and Ravynn played make believe, dad would go right along with them, and often surpass their creativity and imagination. What they weren't aware of in those moments was that dad hadn't been able to dissociate reality from imagination. He wasn't playing along.

An idea popped into Ray's head and he decided to focus on the dingy woman. To see her. Her life, her past. Somehow, he couldn't manage. Like she was shrouded, covered in some kind of a sooty smudge. Like she was some empty kind of shell. The only thing coming off her was her desperation and firm belief that only God in heaven would be a savior in this time.

But she doesn't know about the ninety-nine.

A hard-rapping sound hit the rear passenger's side window and Amelia screamed. A man, eyes wide with fear bellowed at the window, "Let me in!"

Matt reached a hand out over Amelia in a protective gesture, even though the glass separated her from the man.

"Help! Let me in!" The man shouted again, slamming a fist against the window.

Matt yelled up to Ray, "Drive!"

Amelia was still screaming as the man pulled his fist back. Ray didn't wait for what might happen next. Not even looking at the man, he could read him. The energy came off him in waves, that guy was no good. Ray could see not long ago: Frantically fleeing, unprepared, when his car ran out of gas waiting in line, he grew impatient. He walked up to another car at the head of the line and ripped the woman driver out by her hair. She screamed and pleaded as he dragged her across the pavement, her blue capris tearing against the rough concrete. Her blond hair a tangle in the man's fist. He hadn't any shame, no remorse. No, this was not a man you stopped for.

Ray pressed on the gas and swerved back into the road. The tattered lady with the sign stumbled back, surprised but untouched, while the pleading man let his already wound up fist go and fell into the street.

Ray cringed and clenched his jaw as the car behind rolled right over the man, like they either didn't notice him, or didn't care. A faint crunching sound was heard, and Ray yelled to everyone in the car, "Do not turn around!"

The world is falling down, Ray thought.

Screams and cries from the backseat still erupting, Matt reached over and pulled Amelia from her seat. Now in his lap, he cooed at her, "Shh, you're ok. I got you. Nobody's gonna hurt you, baby girl. Daddy's here."

Ray eyed Amelia in the rearview mirror as she settle into her dad's lap. Cries replaced the whimpers and the whimpers faded to a sigh and she soon fell asleep.

Finally, at the beach, Ray pulled the truck off the road. "Let's get camp set up ASAP. Still got daylight to work with…"

Matt already had Amelia out of the car. Well rested, she perked up immediately. She dragged Shelly through the sand, off towards the water at an impressive pace, her little legs skittering along.

"Hold up, slow down," Matt called out. His pleas were in vain. He caught up to her right where the water began to kiss the sand. Lifting her off her feet into the air, she let out a squeal as her little legs kept moving. Matt couldn't help but laugh with her, and the stress of the drive out of town was evaporating.

A glance up and down the beach confirmed the emptiness, all except for a "Beach Buddy" camper a few hundred feet up the way. Not a person in sight, though.

Matt began to ask, "This… is where—"

Ray responded with a simple, "yes, where it happened." Matt turned to Ray as he dropped the tent packs in the sand. Matt lowered Amelia to the sand and her feet started going immediately, ready to take off before she hit the dirt. He faced her away from the water. "That way." He pointed. "Not in the water."

"Let's see how tall you can build a sandcastle," Elena called out, immediately distracting the girl from the water. As if by magic, or some strange power Matt was unaware of, Amelia plopped down in the sand where she stood and dug her hands in, pulling up piles of sand. A sadness crept into Matt's heart. If he'd been in Amelia's life the past year, he'd have tricks of his own to refocus her. What tools to use to distract her or calm her. But with a figurative snap of the fingers, Elena had been the one to do just that, not him.

Eyes tearing up, he looked away to the ocean. "This is where she left us."

"Yes," Ray replied, stepping up beside him, placing a hand on his shoulder.

"It's eerily quiet." A breeze rustled through Matt's hair as a wave crashed down on the shore. He ran a hand through his frazzled hair and then his palm across his teary eyes. "Besides the water. The whistle of the wind. Listen. What do you hear?"

Ray let his hand slide of his brother-in-law's shoulder. "Nothing."

"Exactly. Fucking weird, huh?"

Ray choked on a laugh. "Weird is totally relative, these days."

As Matt surveyed the beach, not only was it empty of people, but of any living thing. The sun was shining, low and bright on the horizon in the late afternoon sky, leaving a trail of orange and pink streaks in its wake. "Gonna be a hot one tomorrow," he said absently.

"You're right," Ray agreed. "Where are the birds?" No crying sounds or wings flapped in the sky.

Matt faced him now. "You think they know?"

Ray nodded his head in the affirmative without verbalizing.

Yet, the clouds began to shift, appearing to move lower and lower in the sky. A gradual thing, perhaps easy enough to miss, if you weren't paying attention, but Matt was. "Are those clouds actually getting lower or are my eyes tricking me?"

He waited, as Ray remained transfixed, staring up into the sky. "You're right. Like something is pushing down on them. But it's happening fast. I'm no meteorologist but it seems not right."

The horizon shrank as the clouds, which started as white and puffy, push down toward the ocean and began to fade to a grayish purple.

"Storm?" Matt asked.

Ray replied, "Let's get those tents up, huh?"

32

In the time it took to set up the tents, the weather had gone from pleasantly warm to scorching and muggy. The air draped itself on Ray's skin and coated him with a fine layer of perspiration. The breeze had died off completely and the only sound that remained was the sound of waves breaking against the shore. That might have been a calming sound if not for the looming threats of escalating destruction that hung over Ray's head, like those dark clouds forming in the sky above.

Clouds moved closer, pressing down from the sky. It had a claustrophobic feel, like the whole world was shrinking around them, shrouding them in a veil of haze.

A voice called up from up the beach, and Ray brought a hand over his brow to shield the sunlight from his eyes. No one was there. He wasn't quite sure what had been said, either. Like the sound had fallen flat in the air and died away into nothingness. "Is someone there?" Ray asked, not entirely sure he wanted anyone to respond.

"They're not normal storm clouds." A figure emerged from the haze, first just a misshapen silhouette.

Squinting, Ray tried to see this person through the ever-growing thickness, and as the person moved closer, the shape of a man appeared walking down the beach.

Concern for his family overcame Ray as the man approached. Who was he, what did he want? Ray reached his hand into the pocket of his cargo pants and fondled the handle of his pocketknife. His hand clasped tight around it as the man spoke again.

"I know you."

Soon as he said it, Ray recognized the man too. "The café."

"Yes. Malcolm McGregor." He stuck out his hand.

Ray released the knife and pulled his sweaty hand out of his pocket and wiped it on his pants before reaching out. "Ray Bradley." After a quick shake he pulled his hand back and scratched his head. "The clouds, you said?"

"Stratus clouds. Well, sort of." Malcolm laughed, and that action made him cough. The undeniable cough of a long-time smoker.

Ray sized the man in front of him up. Short, not fat, but heavy around the middle. His brown hair was thinning a bit on the top and at the temples, sprinkled with gray. The stubble on his goat-tee was full gray with a sprinkle of red. He had a warm grin, thin lips, and intense lines in his brow and crow's feet at his eyes. Ray figured him to be mid-sixties.

Malcolm slammed a fist over his chest and his coughing fit subsided. "Sorry. Yes, I was saying, weather should be cooling off but it's not. Hot and rather humid, wouldn't you say?"

Ray noticed the fine layer of sweat beading up on the man's brow.

Malcolm continued, "Don't think it's going to rain, though. They've got an odd movement, those clouds. Been watching the sky all day."

"Notice any birds?" Ray asked. "They seem to be gone."

"Mm-hmm," Malcolm said, nodding. "They took off this morning. Sensing the changes and all that. Took off inland in search of cover. Like a lot of living things did." He leaned in and waggled his eyebrows. "But you and I know there's nowhere to hide, don't we?" He scratched his belly and looked around the beach.

An odd one for sure. But he wasn't wrong. Although he seemed to be taking it a bit too lightly.

The questions began. "You by yourself up here?"

"Sure am," Malcolm replied. "Got no one." So abrupt and matter-of-fact, his answer startled Ray.

"Sorry to hear that." Ray felt like a jerk for asking.

"Nah, don't you be sorry. I'll be with my brother soon enough. Under Another Sun. He's been there for fourteen years. You believe that?" Malcolm slapped his thigh and another fit of coughing followed. When that stopped, he practically tipped over, overcome with laughter. His body shook, and his face turned red.

"What's so funny?" Ray asked, slightly irritated.

"I just now realized. Duh!" He smacked the heel of his hand to his forehead. "Who knows if they smoke over there? Or what they smoke. Oh, this might be a quick-quit kinda journey. Been meaning to stop for years, any-who."

Ray regarded him closely, not sure if he was harmless or off his rocker. Malcolm's lackadaisical way in light of all the disaster was disconcerting, but at the same time, Ray found himself a bit jealous. To be so calm and indifferent made no sense to Ray. Yes, they'd be saved, but the world would not be.

Malcolm laughed again. "You look like you're sizing me up, trying to figure if I'm gonna eat you for dinner or be your best friend."

Ray startled at the bluntness.

"I don't mean any harm. In fact, if you like, bring your family there up to the camper and we'll spark up a fire and roast some marshmallows." He shrugged. "Wouldn't mind the company."

"Hello." A small voice came from behind Ray. His niece stepped forward. "I'm Amelia. Who are you?"

Malcolm's face lit up. "Well, hello there, little lady. I'm Malcolm. Nice to make your acquaintance." He gave a deep and gentlemanly southern bow to greet her.

A smile beamed across her face. "You're going, too."

"Indeed, I am! My brother is waiting. Who's waiting for you?"

"My mommy."

"Well, I'll bet you she's gonna be so darn happy to see you." Malcolm looked past Amelia and Ray.

Over his shoulder, he spotted both Matt and Elena joining him.

"Hello there, Ray's family." He gave a nod.

Elena put on her happiest doubtful smile and said, "Hi. Nice to meet you. I'm Elena, Ray's wife." For the first time, Ray noted a solemnness cross Malcolm's face, but as he introduced himself to Matt, it had gone.

"Matt Higgins, Amelia's dad."

Malcolm reached out and took both of Matt's hands to shake. "So sorry for your loss, my friend."

Ray corrected the man, "Well, she's not dead. You know, she's Under Another Sun."

Elena gasped and grabbed Ray's arm tightly. "What are we talking about here?"

Ray filled her in. "Malcolm knows. He's going, also."

Elena's eyes grew wide. "Oh."

"One of the ninety-nine," Amelia added.

"Yes, indeed, you got that right!" Malcolm exclaimed. "I was telling Ray here that you all should come on up later and toast up some marshmallows over the fire with me. We ain't got nothing but time to kill, might as well eat marshmallows." He ended with a giant smile that Ray couldn't deny.

Amelia beat him to it. "Yay! Marshmelloooos!"

Ray turned to Elena who shrugged, and then Matt who nodded. "Sure. Sounds good. Thanks."

33

Nothing terrible was happening, but Elena had an awful sense of foreboding that she couldn't shake. Anxiety had found a permanent home deep within her mind and her gut. It wasn't Malcolm. Yes, he was a little weird, but nice enough. No, something more, something deeper that gave her a chill that no summer night or campfire could warm off. The world was ending, and they were toasting marshmallows with the strangest kind of stranger. Everything was too calm and casual. Like the world was taking one last nap, saving up its energy for one last push into finality.

Amelia leaned over the fire, her father holding her at a safe distance, as she roasted a marshmallow. There was such joy and satisfaction in her face that Elena had a hard time rectifying that with disaster that loomed.

The marshmallow browned slowly, as Matt directed Amelia to keep turning to get a nice, even toast. Of course, she didn't quite nail it, and one side caught fire. Elena was hypnotized as the soft marshmallow bubbled up and turned black under the flames. Completely helpless, it bubbled and burned until the melty mass slid off the stick. Elena couldn't help but relate to that marshmallow, in some way; sitting over that flame, waiting to catch fire and melt away. Amelia pouted as the marshmallow disappeared into the flames, and Malcolm reached into the bag and pulled out another, saying, "Try again. Nice and brown, don't let it catch fire this time. Not too close to the flame."

He handed the little girl a marshmallow and looked up at Elena before he finished, "Too close to the flame and you're gonna get burned."

Perhaps it was only Elena's anxiety playing tricks on her mind, but the fire shot an eerie shadow across Malcolm's face. All his features darkened and shrank into his face as she stared, unblinking. His eyes were small and beady like a bug's, his nose almost melting into his cheeks. Lips so thin they looked like they'd been drawn in by pencil. His brow began to grow and bulge out forward, almost Neanderthal. His eyebrows darkened and bent into a cruel V. Suddenly, this kindly man turned into a monster before Elena's eyes. She rubbed at them. A wave of nausea overcame her. *Blink,* she told herself. *Snap out of it.*

Something bumped her arm, and she jumped. Ray was jabbing her with his elbow. She turned to him, and he gave her a look that required no words; only a married couple who were so in tune with each other could read that kind of look.

'*You ok?*' The look said.

She gave the slightest of nods, a single deliberate blink.

'*You sure?*' The next look said.

This time she whispered back to him, "Ugh, just a touch of indigestion from all that food we ate earlier." Her smile was so forced it pained her. It wasn't a complete lie. She was a bit sick to her stomach. Had been for a few days. The illness grew more and more with each passing day, akin to the nausea one gets when on a boat for too long. At first, easy to dismiss, but as time went on, the motion creating more unsettledness and untrustworthy feet.

"Excuse me for a moment, gotta hit the men's room," Matt

said, getting up and shifting Amelia over to Elena.

"Me too. Be right back," Ray said. Before he got up, he shot Elena one more glance and she nodded quickly. *I'm good.*

Malcolm spoke, and when Elena looked at him again, his face had gone back to normal. Or rather, she realized, his features had always been that way. She cursed herself for letting her imagination run wild and frighten her. "Nice that you were able to get the whole family here."

"Not the whole family." A sadness reached into her heart and squeezed it tight. "Lost my Mom and Dad in the quakes and mudslides."

Malcolm lowered his head. "I'm so sorry."

Elena bit back the tears. "If not then, guess it would have happened in the next day or so." As soon as she spoke the words, she regretted them. So harsh and cold coming out of her own mouth. Why did she say those things? To fill the silence. Malcolm made her nervous, and she wasn't quite sure why.

"True, true. But a great loss to you just the same. My condolences."

She was so sick of hearing that phrase she thought she would puke. He was only trying to be kind, so she thanked him. She took a deep breath as she tilted her head back and searched the starless sky. The moon fought valiantly to thrust its dim light through the thick layer of clouds above. The chill crept over her again and she shuddered.

Malcolm's voice deepened as he spoke, "Well, just good you're able to get you all here, to the beach." He nodded his head, looked into the fire. "What a co-incidink that all four of you are bound for the rift. The ninety-nine and all that."

If she hadn't known better, she'd have thought there was some sort of intimation there that she couldn't quite understand. "Yes, about this ninety-nine. Interesting. Why only ninety-nine?"

Malcolm nodded, as if he'd been expecting this question from her. "As you may know, the rift, along with this world, is deteriorating at a rapid pace, see. Each time the rift opens, the tear in the fabric of earth rips a little bit more. And each time it rips, the Earth dies a bit more. Quite a pickle of a predicament, wouldn't you say?"

Elena didn't respond. She continued to stare at him, waiting for an actual answer. A wave of nausea rolled over her.

Malcolm continued, "How do I put this, let's see… Well, think about an elevator. Got it? Ok, so you can only stuff so many people into an elevator for it to be effective and get everyone to their floor, and not have those troubled cables snap and drop everyone to their deaths…"

Elena cringed at the analogy but nodded at Malcolm.

"Well, the rift is like that elevator. Hm, maybe more like a rickety old elevator but you get it, just the same. Well, this elevator can only go on one more trip, and can only take so many more people before it gives out and comes crashing down."

"But doesn't it seem callous for some other beings to choose who lives and who doesn't?"

Amelia dropped the marshmallow stick from her hand into the fire and piped up, her words severe in their delivery, "Mommy said not to talk about it."

Confusion and more anxiety gripped Elena, making her short of breath. Her words came out like a whisper, "Not to talk a—"

"Look at that!" Ray pointed to the night sky. What was dark and cloudy was now lit up by a strange orange glow behind the clouds. Like fire, but not quite.

Elena gasped. "What on earth?"

Malcolm coughed and answered, "The rift is taking its toll, for sure. Fire in the sky. Like the clouds themselves are on fire."

Horrible images ran through her mind all at once. Fire breathing dragons racing behind those clouds, setting them all on fire. Dipping and diving this way and that, streaks of orange danced behind the clouds, lighting them up.

She shook off the image and another came to her. A giant standing there behind the clouds, using its massive hands to tear a hole through the universe. Making the rift wider, like a wound, until the blood soaked into the clouds.

The Earth was dying.

34

"She'll be fine, sleep like a bug in a rug." Matt turned from Elena and gave Amelia a wink as he tucked her into the sleeping bag.

"You sure? There's enough room in the tent with us for her." Elena's voice was filled with doubt as she remained halfway through the opening of Matt's tent.

Normally, something like that would send Matt into a tailspin that most likely would end in him downing a bottle or so of bourbon, but bigger shit was afloat here. He knew she meant no slight, even though it was one. Really, he couldn't blame her. Did he think he could come in here after a year away from Amelia and be Super-Dad? He wasn't dumb. She was only looking out for the child.

"Ok, how about this? We flip a coin?"

Elena nodded. "If that's ok with you, Amelia."

Heavy lidded, the girl nodded back.

Matt slipped his lucky coin out of his pocket and held the object in his hand. Lucky because he always won with it. No, Matt wasn't really that lucky. He was a cheat. Double-sided coin. Always landed heads-up. He tossed the coin in the air and said, "Heads, she stays here with me."

He lost track of the coin through the beam of the flashlight and it landed on Amelia's sleeping bag. Amelia lifted her sleepy hand and looked at her prize. "Heads. Daddy wins."

Satisfied, Matt took the coin from Amelia and showed Elena the heads-side up. "See you and Ray in the morning. We're good. Nighty-night."

Elena ducked her head back out of the tent and Matt and Amelia were alone.

Matt let out a snicker and kissed his daughter on the forehead. "Can I tell you a secret?" He didn't wait for a response. "Both sides are heads." He put the coin in front of his daughter and flipped it over and then back again.

"Same sides!" Amelia giggled.

"Yup. Don't tell Auntie Elena though, she won't think it's as funny as we do."

Amelia pulled the sleeping back up to her chin and yawned.

"Ah-ha. Looks like sleep is settling in. Before you go to sleep though, I want you to have this. He opened her tiny hand and dropped the coin in it. Then he folded her fingers around the charm. "Always was good luck for me. I want you to have my luckiest of coins. So you're always lucky."

"Thanks, Daddy." Amelia yawned again, and Matt shifted to lay down next to her. He leaned on his elbow, hand holding his head up, watching his daughter fall asleep. Regret rushed through him for losing the past year. But in this moment, there was nothing he could do but soak in every breath of her, all that he'd missed.

Soon, his eyes too, grew tired and heavy and he set his head on his rolled-up hoodie. He listened to the night, but no living thing made a sound, giving off an empty and surreal quality. No crickets or night birds or any living thing scurrying, chirping, rustling.

The sounds of the night were disconcerting. Noises he couldn't identify. Almost like thunder, but not quite. A soft, high-pitched whine buzzed steadily through the night as well. The ground beneath hadn't been steady in days, and there was a constant shifting, no matter how delicate. Like the earth itself was groaning and murmuring its death song.

35

Elena zipped up the zipper door of the tent and faced Ray. "Amelia's off to sleep, and Matt is good." She crawled toward Ray and repeated herself. "He *is* good." At first, she'd doubted Matt, but then she was ok leaving Amelia with him. "He's sober. And sincere," she added.

"Come here." Ray lifted the flap of the sleeping bag up for her to crawl into with him. The ground grumbled and moaned and shifted underneath them, but they were growing strangely accustomed to the unsteadiness. They didn't startle, only righted themselves by leaning into the shift, although Elena appeared to be having more trouble with her balance than the others.

The Earth lurched again, this time more zealously, tossing Elena right into Ray's arms. She let out a nervous giggle and said, "I don't know if I can sleep."

He nuzzled his face into her hair and replied, "Ugh. Me neither. Wanna step back outside for a bit?" His hot breath on her neck frazzled her already shot nerves.

She nodded, and her hair tickled his nose.

Ray stepped out first, then Elena reached for his hand to

guide her out. The Earth shimmied a bit, making them do a little two-step. Outside, they both gawked at the night sky. Elena's hand closed around his bicep.

"It's ok." His words held no consolation.

She snipped, "No, it's not." She loosened her grip. "Sorry."

"It will be," he stressed.

"No, Ray. While you stepped away earlier, I asked Malcolm about the ninety-nine. Why there were only ninety-nine going through the rift."

"And what did he tell you?"

She shrugged. "I think more than Ravynn's told you, but still, not very much, I'm afraid. The whole thing seems very veiled."

"What do you mean?"

Elena explained to Ray much as Malcolm had to her, about the elevator, and how the rift was similar in that it could only carry so much more weight before it gave out completely.

He tilted his head and looked up to the night. "I guess that makes sense?" It seemed both he and Elena weren't completely sold on the explanation.

"And then Amelia came out and basically scolded me not to talk about it. That her mother told her not to. Ray, I love that little girl like she was my own, but when she talks like that... it truly frightens me."

The clouds were still dense and gloomy across the night sky, but the orange glow behind them had grown. The night was now like a sunset. The unrest Elena had was like the strange fire burning behind the clouds, festering and boiling inside her, coursing through her already anxiously busy mind one-hundred miles an hour. She wanted to itch at her skin. She needed to breathe but her lungs were squeezed tight from the stress, her intercostal muscles strained and pulled too tight. She took a quick assessment, realizing there wasn't a part of her body or mind that had no ache. The idea came to her to close her eyes and walk into the water, past the break of the waves, and keep going, disappearing into the darkness beyond. Letting go. Finding rest.

Something told her she would find no rest any time soon. Something awful plagued her, in the back of her mind. Like the word you're searching for that's on the tip of your tongue, this awful thing danced and darted, hiding deep in the recesses of her brain, shielding her from the cold reality. But what was she missing? Her fear held tight to her and wouldn't let her go. What if the calculations were wrong, and ninety-nine would not be saved? What if they couldn't open the rift one more time? What if they could, but not everyone made it through in time? What if… what if… what if?

Looks like something out of *War of The Worlds*," Elena murmured. "I keep expecting some kind of alien invasion. UFO's darting through the clouds."

"It would almost be easier to believe than the truth: the world is collapsing because of a temporal rift, and we're going to cross over into another world before it does. Just like Ravynn did a year ago." Ray reached his hand around her waist and pulled her closer. "This isn't science fiction; this is our reality."

No matter how Ray tried to console her, it wouldn't help. Fear and doubt had become part of her being, and they weren't about to let her go now that they had settled in and made a home.

His voice barely found its way through. "It's weird. And scary. But I trust Ravynn. She knows what's going to happen, and how to save us." His voice wavered as he ran the back of his hand down her shoulder, "Wait until you see the sky there. And the ocean. Breathtaking. The water is so crystalline, the colors so fantastic."

He told her, and Elena carelessly listened to all he'd seen there. The little glimpses of paradise they were headed to. "You'll see. It's a new beginning. And new possibilities." He laced his fingers through hers.

She replied, halfheartedly, "I'm sure it will be beautiful. Wonderful."

"So then why the doubt?"

She let his hand go and stepped away from him. She kicked

off her shoes and went towards the water, her toes sinking into the temperate sand with each step. She purposefully moved slowly, letting her feet ease in as far as they would, into the sand. The heaviness of it grounded her more. As if in a stark protest, the earth below groaned and shifted, reminding her not to trust it, that her feet and the ground she stood upon were not her friends. Every moment hinted a betrayal of assurance.

"Hey," he called out to her.

She called back, not bothering to turn around, "I need to feel the sand between my toes. The shock of the ocean as the cold water comes to lap at my ankles." One foot forward, she held for a moment, hovering above the water before setting it down in damp sand. "I have to feel something other than this uncontrollable fear." Tears clouded up her eyes and streaked her cheeks.

There was a hand on her shoulder suddenly, and it threatened to pull her out of her misery. She shook it off. "I want to feel in control of something. Does that make sense?" She didn't wait for his answer. She stepped into the water and caught her breath. Her ribs tightened again, but she pushed through the discomfort, taking a deep, painful breath. The salty air stung her lungs as she breathed it in greedily. She flung her head back and laughed at the sky like a madwoman. Forward, she moved, the cool water embracing her ankles, calves, knees and thighs. She gasped as the sea came up and met the warm place between her legs.

She kept going. Her shorts were completely soaked, as the water rose above her stomach and to her chest. Her shirt clung to her, and for the first time all day she was cold as the water receded, then pushed back against her body once more. The Earth took a sideways tilt, and Elena wavered in the water. Motion sickness swept over her again and threatened to purge her of all her dinner that sat unsteadily in her stomach.

She called upon what little sanity she had left to not keep going. To walk until she couldn't walk out any longer, submerged under the tugging shadows of the water. But instead, she stopped, stepped back until the water was above her knees, and collapsed. She sat there, her legs crossed, letting the waves come up and slap her in the face. The sharp, salty reality hit her again and again, but she continued to take each blow. To feel something.

Ray was calling to her. He was close, but he sounded so far away. Like they were worlds apart. To her it was like there was a gap that was impossible to bridge. Words fell deaf on her ears. They didn't matter, no matter what they were. There was no consolation for the despair that resided within her.

Ray held an unbreakable belief in his sister and her plan for the road to salvation, butt all Elena had was doubt.

36

Malcolm sat at the dying fire, watching the embers flicker and fade. Something quite hypnotizing and relaxing about staring into a fire. He was more relaxed than he'd been in years. Like everything in his life was leading up until this one final moment.

He robotically reached into his pocket and pulled out a cigarette, lit the smoke up. As he inhaled, the butt of it glowed an orange-red, not much different than those embers in the fire, nor the glow behind the clouds in the sky.

He took a long drag, the smoke filling his heavy lungs. On the exhale, the ground growled, dancing underneath him. What little of the burning wood there was left in the fire fell in upon itself; the embers popped as if excited by all the movement. Malcolm too, was affected by the moving earth, and the smoke in his lungs tickled him, stirring up a coughing fit.

He dangled the cigarette over the side of his chair, letting the ash burn while he caught his breath. A tap on his other shoulder surprised him, and he dropped his smoke to the ground.

To his left he found Amelia standing and watching him, her

hands locked behind her back. The glow of the fire lit up her face, and the hesitation was obvious. She took a step back.

"It's ok. Just surprised me, is all. What are you doing up?"

Amelia replied, "Can't sleep." She kicked at the sand.

"Too much going on." He waved her forward. "Lot happening. Who could sleep through it all?"

She stepped forward, moving to the side of his chair. "My Dad. He's snoring."

This got Malcolm laughing, and coughing again. "My Daddy used to snore something awful, too!" He slapped his knee. "So, what's on your mind? Care to parlay?"

Amelia squished up her lips but didn't answer.

"Excuse me. Parlay. Means chat, if you will," Malcolm clarified.

Amelia nodded. The invitation was all she'd needed. "I'm happy, but everyone else is sad." She looked down at the sand.

"I'm not sad," Malcolm coaxed.

Amelia lifted her head and a smile appeared on her delicate face. "No, you're not."

"No, I'm not," Malcolm agreed. "Not one bit. "A time is ending, and another time is beginning." He spoke to her like she was an adult, partially because he hadn't had much experience talking to children, and partly because she understood more than most. He waved the back of his hand towards the chair next to him, motioning for her to sit. "I'll see my brother again. And you'll get to see your Mommy. Those are happy things."

Amelia nodded vigorously. "And my grandma, too. And—" She brought her hand to her mouth and paused.

"You don't need to edit yourself here with me, young lady. Speak your mind. I know more than you think." He gave her a wink.

"Well," she began slowly. "My Mommy has a baby. A little brother for me." Her eyes lit up when she spoke about them. Malcolm smiled. Amelia continued, "He's almost brand new. I'm gonna be a big sister.

"And I bet you'll make a fine one, yes you will."

"Uncle Ray doesn't know," she admitted softly. "Mommy said not to tell anyone. Not Uncle Ray or Auntie E." She shrugged her shoulders clear up to her ears and put a finger over her mouth. "Secret."

"Guess he'll find out soon enough, won't he?" Malcolm gave a little snicker. There they sat like two odd pals exchanging secrets. "Wanna know something? My brother, well, he's got three kids over there."

Amelia's eyes lit up, and the glow from the fire almost made her appear cartoonish. All eyes, small face. "My grandma, um, she has kids too. But not Uncle Ray and Mommy. *More* kids." Her hands spread out to the sides. "Big family."

Malcolm nodded and picked up a stick and tossed the wood in the fire. The tinder crackled and snapped as it ignited.

"But your Uncle Ray don't know any of it. That right?"

"Mommy said it's too much."

"She's probably right. Your Momma is a smart one, I'm sure." Malcolm agreed. "I imagine it's hard keeping those secrets from your family, but it's best, you see."

"She said Uncle Ray doesn't understand. He thinks small."

Malcolm nodded, and his whole body bounced in his chair as if it too agreed. "Yup, I understand."

"So, I can't tell him. He has to see when he gets there," Amelia added.

Malcolm shifted to the side and stretched his legs out, crossing one foot over the other. "Some people can't see what's right in front of their faces. It makes them blind, in a sense. Nope, I think your Uncle Ray's not ready. Your Momma, she's a smart one, fer sure."

Amelia agreed. "So smart. She knows so many things!"

A thunderous clap boomed in the sky, coming from every and no particular direction at once. The world held its breath for a moment. The steady crashing of waves stuttered and halted, then came roaring down even harder.

Amelia and Malcolm both looked at each other, unaffected. "Not much longer now, he said."

"It's almost time," Amelia added.

"Can you keep your Momma's secrets a little longer, then?"

Someone came running up the beach before Amelia could respond, stopping short of the fire. Frantic, Matt huffed and puffed. "Amelia! You scared the hell—heck—out of me! You can't wander off like that!"

"She's fine, she's fine." Malcolm got up out his seat. "Having ourselves a chat."

"About secrets?" Matt's eyes narrowed. He grabbed Amelia and put her behind him.

Malcolm shrugged it off. "Well, yes—"

"What kind of secrets—what in the hell you—"

Malcolm placed a hand on Matt's chest, a soft gesture he was certain would either cause Matt to relax or take a swing at him. Malcolm could *feel* the distrust coming off Matt in waves and *see* it. The colors swirled around Matt, a glowing, surging, dark green pulsed out of Matt's body. If Malcolm didn't tread carefully here, Matt was going to beat him to a pulp. The violence surged through the distrust Matt was giving off as a blood red color which mixed and danced around the green. "Take a breath. We're fine, here." The words came off almost as a command, rather than a request. Malcolm's energy reached out to Matt and calmed him. He closed his eyes and pressed his hand firmer on Matt's chest. "I know your struggles. I see your hurts. But it wasn't your fault."

A soft murmur escaped Matt's lips, but no words followed.

Malcolm continued to read Matt. "You weren't supposed to be there that first night. You stepped into something you weren't supposed to." And then he shifted his thoughts to Amelia. "Your daughter's fine. And the secrets she keeps are her mother's. About this other side y'all are headed to." He bit his lip, not enjoying the taste of his lie. "Ravynn wants it to be a surprise."

He yanked his hand off of Matt's chest as if he'd been stung. Eyes flew open with surprise, and he stumbled back a step. "You know? And you're still—"

Matt stood tall and proud and stared the smaller man down. "About the ninety-nine?"

So shocked by what he read from Matt, he could only nod. His face contorted. "But, how?"

"It's obvious, if you care to notice. I'll admit, it took me a while to figure out. So far, Ray's so blinded by salvation and his love for his sister he's looking right through it, and Elena… well, I think she wants so strongly to believe in Ray that she's chosen to look past the obvious as well."

Malcolm stuttered, fidgeting with his words, "But why?"

Matt smiled, and then looked behind him at Amelia. "It's all for her." He swung around and picked his daughter up, beaming, pulling her in for a hug. He turned to walk away, but before he did, he glanced back over his shoulder to Malcolm, and added, "I'm no fool."

37

Matt set Amelia down so she could walk, but kept a firm grip on her hand, leading her back down to the beach to their tent. He'd been mumbling the whole time. "Honestly, I don't know what got into you. Can't just wander off. You're a little kid. He's a stranger..."

"He's not a stranger, he's Malcolm and he's going through the rift," Amelia replied, digging her heels in.

"Pick up your feet, Amelia. What on Earth do you think your mother would say about you wandering off and talking to strangers?" Matt cringed listening to himself. Ravynn was always the one punishing or scolding Amelia, and he was the one who let her get away with almost anything she wanted. But Ravynn wasn't here.

"She'd like Malcolm." Amelia yanked her hand out of Matt's and stopped in her tracks.

Matt turned around, about to reprimand her more, when Amelia pointed off into the water.

"Is that Auntie E? What's she doing in the water like that?" Amelia didn't wait, took off running in Elena's direction.

"Will you stand still for one second?" Matt rolled his eyes

and took off after her. "Slow it down!"

"Auntie E! Auntie E! What are you doing in the water?" Amelia stopped short of the shoreline.

A strange thing was happening as she stood there. Matt caught up to her and stopped by her side where Ray joined them.

Ray called out, "Elena, get out of the water."

"I can't, Ray. Not yet." She held the stubbornness of a child in her demeanor.

Matt chimed in, "Elena, I really think you should listen to Ray. Get up. Get out."

Perhaps Elena was unable to observe from her low vantage point in the water, but Matt and Ray surely had the full view.

Matt forgot all about chastising Amelia as he realized what the waves were bringing in. The orange sky behind the clouds shed enough of an ominous light on the water to illuminate what was being pushed ashore. Carcasses.

Dead seals washed in on the tide.

"Elena!" Ray called. "Get out. There are… things in the water. Dead things."

Too late.

The next wave tossed a dead baby seal right into Elena, knocking her backwards. She screamed, coughed as she swallowed the water, and scrambled backwards like a drunken crab, howling the whole way.

The baby seal wasn't the only thing washed ashore. More seals came soon after. A sea lion joined the macabre parade, along with a Hawksbill sea turtle amidst a blur of fishes. Every one of them washed up onto the shore. Dead.

Amelia scurried over to Elena, careful to stay out of the water. She called to her aunt, "The fishes know there's nowhere to go."

Elena and Amelia's roles reversed. Elena sat on her hands and knees in the wet sand, attempting to stand, but either lacking the strength or the will.

From the distance, Amelia reached out her hand to help, but Elena didn't take it. Her face grew dim and vexed, her lips pursed, her eyes narrowed. "Well, you just know everything, don't you?" She slapped her hand at the water, like a child throwing a temper tantrum. Her hand came across a fish, and she slapped it away. "You knew about this! You knew about the birds! About Vesuvius!" She balled up her hand and shook her fist at Amelia.

Matt could take no more. "Hey! Don't talk to her like that! She's just a kid!" He stepped in between Elena and Amelia. He wasn't sure what she was going to do next, but he prepared to intervene. "She's your niece."

Elena was overcome. "Just a kid, huh? I don't know any kids that could do... that could..." She couldn't finish. Shaking her head, she stumbled over her words.

Amelia spoke to Elena in a composed tone that was beyond her years. "It's ok, Auntie E. I know you're scared." She stepped forward, this time into the water, with her hand still outstretched, unaffected by the dead things around her. Or perhaps she cared more for her aunt than a moment's discomfort as a carcass shifted past her through the waves. "I'll help you up."

Ray came up behind Elena and scooped her up from under her armpits. He righted her to a standing position, all the while talking to her, "Elena, calm down. I know you're upset, but it's not Amelia's fault. You love that little girl..."

"Unacceptable," Matt spat at Elena. "No matter what." He turned to Amelia, went down on one knee, and explained to the little girl, "Auntie Elena is just really scared. Tired and worn out. She didn't mean to get mad at you. Yell at you. She loves you." He smiled at his daughter, but her face remained blank. "Remember when you used to get so overtired and then you'd cry but you wouldn't understand why you were crying?"

Amelia nodded, but looked past him at her Aunt, who was now crying into Ray's shoulder.

Matt placed his hand under his daughter's chin and tilted her head back towards him. "It's like that, honey."

"It's ok, Daddy. I know Auntie E loves me. I love her, too."

Relieved, he pulled Amelia in for a big hug. "I'm so proud of you. You're so smart. And so brave. Like your Mom."

Amelia pulled out of the hug slowly, staring deep into her father's eyes. It almost looked as if Ravynn was staring back at him, not his daughter as she said, "Regular people don't see it. I do so I'm not afraid. And I know it's almost over. I'm going home."

38

The sun sneaked into the sky before Ray was aware it was morning. Hard to tell with the fiery-orange streaks washing through the sky and clouds. Day wasn't true day, yet no longer night. A fitting end, Ray imagined. If this was to be the last, why not have it be both day and night?

The clouds had crept lower from the sky, shrinking the horizon and threatening to blot out the beach. The humidity sat heavy, coating Ray's skin in a misty layer of sweat.

Elena had fallen asleep, sobbing in his arms, but her sleep hadn't come easy. They had all foregone the tents, as being enclosed ended up making them more claustrophobic. They'd huddled in front of Ray's tent instead, blankets thrown in the sand and watched the sky until their eyes couldn't stay open any longer. One by one, they'd drifted off, Amelia and Matt, the sobbing Elena, then Ray. Or at least, Ray thought he'd slept. He wasn't sure.

He couldn't believe Amelia was able to sleep at all as she lay there so peacefully. Or maybe he could. Everything had been so normal to her, the whole time. She was the only one who never thought anything odd about the events unfolding.

If you grew up in a world, in a time of such strange occurrences, of such tumultuous chaos, and those were the normal for you, why would you be affected?

She was the only one through all the chaos who remained steadfast. The only one who was resolute. So, she slept, through the winds and the shaking earth and the maddening sky above, and the world about to fall down all around her.

"She is everything I never knew I could do in life," Matt

said, catching Ray's eye. "She's perfect. The only thing I am truly proud of in this world." He laughed. "In this world." He shook his head and looked around. "Look at this world. What it's become. It's such a human thing to take everything for granted. To take life for granted. You think you've got all the time in the world. Like the world just sits there and waits for you to decide what to do. That's priceless." He laughed. The bitterness and sadness in those words were palpable. All the time he'd wasted in the bottom of the bottle, not facing life or the world around him. It literally took the end of the world for him to sober up and face it all. "We thought that life would go on and on and on. That this planet would keep on supporting life. Keep on keeping on…" He seemed to drift, lost, looking at his daughter with such sadness in his eyes.

Ray agreed, "We do. We did take it all for granted. But we've got another chance. Not that there is no sadness in this end but hope for the future and what we can have. When we get there. When we get to Ravynn."

Matt gave Ray a smile that was too distressed to be genuine. Like his smile was a frown in disguise. "Sometimes we see only what we choose to see," Matt said.

Elena rolled over, off Ray's lap into the sand. Moaning, she rubbed sand off her face as she sat up. "Is it morning?" Her eyes squinted. Her lips pursed.

"It's… well, it's not night any longer," Ray replied as she sat up rubbing at her swollen eyes. She looked like shit, but Ray wasn't about to tell her.

She turned away and rummaged through a pack. "Ah-ha! Breakfast of champions." She pulled a plastic baggie of blueberry muffins from her pack. She handed a couple of them to Matt and he scarfed his down in two bites, then set Amelia's aside. He got to his feet and stretched, looking off into the ocean.

As Elena reached to hand one to Ray, the earth lurched underneath her and spilled her into the sand once more. Righting herself with a nervous chuckle, she said, "Balance sucks."

She grabbed Ray's shoulders to steady herself and he noticed her hands shaking. At first, he thought nothing of it, but as the earth went back to stillness, she continued to quaver.

He placed his hands over hers and stared up into her eyes. "It's ok to be scared."

"No. I'm not scared." She took a deep breath. "I'm terrified." She lowered her voice so as not to startle Amelia. "I can't help it. After everything that's happened up until now. And everything that's coming. Uncertainty can be the scariest thing of all. How will it all unfold? What will we experience before Ravynn gets here? What will we have to endure?"

"It'll be ok. You'll see. Ravynn is coming for us. We'll be safe." He tried to assure her, although getting through to her felt akin to chipping away at a solid mass of ice; so cold, and could he break away enough to find his way inside? He wasn't sure if she didn't want to believe or if she couldn't. He wasn't sure which was worse.

"I know. I hear you. I do." She clenched her teeth to keep them from chattering. "It's cold, pass me that blanket?"

He obliged without calling BS on the cold part. The fear was painted all over her face and ran up and down her shaky body covered in goosebumps. "We'll be ok," he repeated, staring up into her frightened eyes.

"Yes, I hear you. But I want to… I need to tell you how much I love you, Ray. How sorry I am for all the doubts and—"

"Whoa, whoa," he interjected. "Let's not do this. There's no need. I know. I understand. In your shoes, I probably would have done the same. It's all in the past, so let's look to the future."

A hiccup escaped her as she tried to choke back the tears. "I'm just so fucking scared, Ray."

"Shh. It will be ok."

"I know, I know Ravynn is coming. But nothing is promised. Nothing is absolute. And we've already taken so much for granted. I love you—"

"I love you too, Elena. Shh. Come here." He wrapped the

blanket around her and pulled her to him, wrapping his arms around the bundle of her. He rocked her back and forth like he would a small child, for whatever comfort he might give her.

A gust of wind picked up and howled over the dunes. The wind kicked up and swirled sand into the air; like little sand tornadoes they whipped and beat around. Shielding his eyes, Ray leaned over Elena, and Matt's fatherly instinct kicked in as he darted back and covered Amelia's sleeping face with the hoodie he'd used as a pillow. Ray sat with his eyes closed, and his hands over his face. Little grains of sands came through and nicked at his face and arms. Like thousands of little knives, they gashed fine lines into his skin. "Into the tent! Everyone!" Matt scooped up Amelia and shoved her inside, then reached back for Elena. The sand swirled and kicked up angrily around Ray and Matt before they both tucked inside the tent made for two along with the others.

Inside, it grew hot rapidly. The tent was entirely too cramped for four people. Something had to give. "I hope this windstorm dies down soon." Ray wiped at the sweat on his face with the back of his arm. Not a great decision, he soon realized, as the sweat stung the fresh cuts. He winced.

"Let me help you with that," Elena said. She dug her way through his pack, finally pulling out a bottled water and a spare t-shirt. She ripped the shirt into shreds. "Let's get both of you cleaned up." Although the distraction had been painful, a diversion was just what Elena needed to snap out of her funk and into action. Opening the water bottle, she splashed some and doused the shirt. She dabbed gently at the little cuts on Ray's face first, then handed him the rag and let him finish his arms, as she helped Matt with his face.

"Thanks, Daddy," Amelia murmured. He pushed Elena's hand away and looked at his unscathed daughter.

"No cuts, no nothing?" He asked her. The tent pitched and buckled each time the wind changed direction.

She smiled and shook her head. "Nope." She took the shred of shirt from Elena and finished wiping at Matt's face. "Does it hurt?"

"Nah, not too bad."

The tent bucked in on them from a burst of wind but withheld. Ray wasn't sure how long it would, though, as the fine grains of sand that cut at them now sliced at the tent. Was probably a matter of time before the dirt found a way through. Ray secretly scolded himself for foolishly parking his car in an actual parking spot and not having driven it and parked right there on the beach. It would have provided a much better shelter in this storm.

Amelia moved in closer, studying Matt's face. If Ray and company hadn't been in such tight quarters, he wouldn't have heard her whisper to Matt, "You were a good Daddy."

The howling winds outside the tent reminded Ray of the old Irish legend of the banshee. He closed his eyes and chills streaked up and down his body, despite the oppressive heat inside tent. His mind created the vision of her, coming over the dunes, wrapped in a dress of tattered cloth the color of sand, hair the color of the sea, eyes dark pits of despair. Frail, thin, and long her body was, like skin and bones, her gangling fingers ending in claws outstretched. The keening went on and on, moving closer, then farther away, as if she were searching the beach, or warning of impending death.

39

The keening ceased, as did the winds. The tent was silent and too hot inside, but Matt was wary to open it up yet. He grabbed the zipper, his fingers closing on the metal, and began to pull up and open gradually. He listened, half-sure that the winds would start back up and kick into his face again. He heard nothing. Nothing but the sound of the waves crashing onto the shore. He wasn't sure what he was listening for, exactly. What sound would make him sure it'd be safe to leave the tent? What sign would lead them forward?

Amelia leaned over his shoulder and he stopped. "Hold on a minute," he said to her.

She was already standing, her little head leaning on the back of his shoulder. "In my sleep, Mommy told me it's almost time. She'll be here soon. Be careful."

"How soon?" He asked. "Careful of what?"

A rapping sound, knuckles on tapping on the outside of the tent, startled him. A shadow stood in front of the door. Matt couldn't find his voice. "Wh-who's there?"

"It's Malcolm. Come on outta there, kids, winds are gone,"

the voice called back through. "Y'all ok in there?"

Matt sighed, a bit irritated with himself for jumping in the first place. Did he really think that was going to be Ravynn standing there on the other side, knocking? He unzipped the door and flipped it open. A gust of air, not cool, but cooler than in the tent, came through. Amelia pushed by him and out first.

As he climbed out, she was already in full rant, talking to Malcolm, "And then the sand cut his face up pretty good. Daddy's too. But not me. Look!" She tilted her head from side to side to show him. "Mommy said it's gonna happen soon. She's coming. To take us home. We need to be ready. And stay safe and careful…"

"Okay, okay," Matt said, patting her on the shoulder. "Don't wanna talk the man's ear off." He turned to help Elena out, and Ray followed.

"God it was so hot in there, thought I was gonna pass out!" Elena stood, wiping damp hair off her forehead. She pulled her sticky shirt out and released it several times, trying to air out.

"Glad it didn't last too long," Matt added. He took a step forward and almost tripped over Elena's backpack that sat in the sand, completely covered from the winds, as was everything else they'd left out. Matt and Amelia's tent that had started only a few yards away had been yanked out of the sand by the winds and tossed to the shore. There it sat, with all the dead fishes.

The sky had darkened, the day growing more ominous. The orange streaks behind the clouds still remained, but there was a threat of rain brewing as well. Inky, bulbous clouds crept across the sky, blotting out the sun, and a shadow swept into Matt's heart. He couldn't escape the sense of foreboding.

There was a stink in the air, too. The sour smell of decay wafted up to Matt when the warm breeze came in off the crashing waves. His stomach flopped. With this heat, the odor would worsen quickly.

Malcolm pointed back across the shoreline. "Pretty

interesting, right?"

"Not sure I'd say interesting," Elena chimed in.

"Well, thinky here." Malcolm continued. "Dead things washed up on the shore. Look, the beach is coated with 'em. But what's missing? Anybody tell me?"

"Birds," Amelia said, flapping her arms.

"Ding! Winner!" Malcolm said, beaming. His tipped his empty palm up, sweeping his hand to and fro. "All those dead creatures on the beach, and no birds scavenging. They should be circling or darting this way and that out of the waves, having a feast. But where are they, indeed?"

The Stygian cloud grew swollen and sank lower in the sky. Matt didn't like the look of it. He fished Elena's backpack out of the sand. "Looks like it's gonna storm. Let's plan on taking some cover, don't wander too far off, anyone." He hated the idea of scouring through his tent among the carcasses. He wondered if there'd be anything left inside worth saving anyway.

"Why don't you all gather up your goodies and packs and come on up to the camper. Much more room than that tent. Play some cards or something."

Matt's gut reaction was to give him a firm no-way-in-hell. Something creeped Matt out about him. Most likely, Matt considered, it was an envy about how cool and calm Malcolm was. About everything. Not only a coolness, it was almost *excitement*. Ocean life covered the shoreline, dead, and soon everything else on this planet would be joining them, and this guy wanted to play cards. Disregarding his own feelings on the matter he turned to consult Ray and Elena.

Elena shrugged, but Matt was sure he sensed the same kind of apprehension coming off her.

Ray answered for them all, "Great. Thanks. You're right, it would be better than tents. The way that windstorm whipped around, it's a wonder the tents are still standing. We accept your invitation, thanks. Let's grab what's left of our belongings and head out."

40

Elena thought that Malcolm's camper, though a bit of a cramped space for five, was quite spacious after being stuffed in the tent like sardines in a can. The cleanliness, however, or lack thereof, was another thing entirely. Upon stepping up into the camper, she wondered if the man was a slob, or his disregard for order was a new thing because the world was ending. She guessed the latter.

"Don't mind the mess none," he said, huffing, picking up stray pieces of clothing and flinging them into a pile on his bed in the corner. Cans of food sat on the countertop, opened and empty. A chocolate bar, half eaten, sat on a seat, melted from the heat.

"It's fine. Actually, very nice. We thank you for your hospitality. Very comfy," Elena said. She tried to hide the disgust.

"Well, now you're just blowing smoke up my arse," Malcolm replied. He slapped his thigh and burst out laughing, which in turn became a fit of coughing. Lungs rattling and wheezing through the effort.

You're the only one blowing smoke, Elena thought. The camper reeked. Like a filthy, dank ashtray with too many butts wasting away inside. The thought made her belch, but she caught herself. She sank down in a chair by the too-tiny table. She jumped up and pulled a pack of smokes from under her rear, then sank back down into the seat, thankful that was all she sat on in this mess.

"You look a little pale, you ok?" Ray asked.

"Feel a bit off. Little dizzy. Nauseated, too."

Maybe it was the heat, or the stench of dead things in the air, rotting away on the beach. Or perhaps the stale cigarettes. She ran the back of her hand over her forehead, testing for a fever. Clammy, but not hot. She wanted to go home. To her own bed. Climb in and sleep off this nightmare. Wake up to air-conditioning pumping so cool she'd have to pull all the blankets up around her head.

So many things she wanted, she'd never again have. She wanted to talk to her Dad, hear his voice, no matter what he said. She wanted to hug her mother and drink a bottle of wine with her sister. Wanted to be in a classroom with students all around her, learning and fidgeting and protesting and taking tests. But none of these things would ever happen again.

"Maybe I need some fresh air." She got up to leave. "Not that there's any fresh air out there." She swung the door open and went to step down.

Malcolm called over to her. "We're losing out footing on this earth, see. Everything's changed, and now our bodies are feeling it too. Birds have been feeling it for some time. Why they fell from the sky and ran away and hid, instead of gobbling up all those fish parts on the beach. Humans are less aware than other creatures, so it took us longer to feel it. And you, Elena, are more sensitive than most."

With that, she chose not to respond, but stepped down and out of the camper. She missed the step and fell into the sand.

Ray came hustling out after her and helped her to her feet. "He's right, you know. I don't feel it as much as you, but it's there. Like the Earth and I aren't friends, anymore. Don't have that same attraction, if you know what I mean." He waggled his eyebrows at her, and she thought it was a sweet attempt to make her feel better.

'Thanks. You're a dork." She leaned in and kissed him on the cheek. She looked up to the sky and gasped.

It's so dark. Those clouds, s-so angry looking," she stammered. The one dark cloud that had blotted out the sun not long ago had swept across the sky, devouring all the other clouds and covering the sky with a big black blanket. The sun's glow could barely be seen through the murky film, casting midday into a twilight setting. The orange streaks still danced behind the clouds, but now they moved slower, as if they were getting stuck in the sludge of the darkness.

Off on the horizon, little waterspouts flit and moved about over the ocean. They'd spin frantically down toward the water then disappear, leaving the water to drop back down into the ocean. Like angry little ballerinas these little funnels hopped and jumped and danced over the ocean. "You see that?" she croaked.

"Yeah."

"Are those the funnels, like the lady on the water used?" Elena grabbed Ray's hand. "Is it time?"

"No, that's not it. Those are like little water tornadoes."

"Oh." Elena wasn't sure if she felt better or worse that now wasn't the moment. The time of Ravynn's arrival. Was it strange that she took comfort in little tornadoes?

Underfoot, the earth rumbled, a long continuous growl like an angry dog warning to stay away from its bowl. The sky too let loose a roaring rumble to match the earth's. Thunder. Not a few seconds later, lightning streaked across the sky; a color and effect of lightning she'd ever seen. The orange streaks in the clouds were drawn to the lightning and hopped on its back for a ride. Orange lightning.

Little droplets began to tap at the top of her head. Cool, tingling water drops falling from the sky. Small relief. They began to fall faster and faster, and Elena was relieved to wash the sweat from her body. She let Ray's hand go and spread her arms wide out to her sides, tipping her head back to the sky.

The rain beat down harder and faster, but she didn't budge. It was the most welcome reprieve she'd had in days.

That respite didn't last.

The drops turned into a pelting barrage of rain. Something larger, and harder than a raindrop slapped her on top of her head. "Ouch!" She opened her eyes and covered her head with a hand. "What in the—"

"A crab hit you!" Ray grabbed her by the hand and pulled her back against the camper. "From the sky!"

"It's raining crabs?" Elena asked, pushing her back as firmly against the camper as she could. She closed her eyes to keep from crying and a sob got stuck in her throat. She wasn't sure how much more of this she could take. How far would it escalate before Ravynn came?

"Not just crabs, look!" Ray pointed in front of them and to the ocean. Several little critters, crabs, plankton, seaweed, all began to drop from the sky with the rain. In the background, out over the ocean, the water tornadoes grew larger and more violent, sucking up the ocean like a crazed vacuum as they swept along.

The ocean gave off little splashes here and there where the sea matter landed. In awe, she gawked as these things fell all around them. She gasped as she caught a glimpse of Ray's outstretched hand. "Ray! Your hand!"

She yanked at him and he pulled his hand back to cover. But what should have been normal raindrops were anything but. Much more viscous, and a disconcerting shade of red.

"Is that blood?" He asked, his voice panicked.

"Oh God. It looks like blood. What if it's dangerous?"

"It doesn't hurt. It's just gross."

"What if it's laced with something awful? God Ray. Take off your shirt and wipe that off."

He stripped his shirt off over his head and wiped furiously at his arm. The liquid smudged, leaving red streaks up and down his arm.

"Wait!"

Elena reached for the door to the camper which was

already open, with three heads sticking out. Malcolm and Matt pressed side by side and Amelia tucked her head out from behind Matt's hip. "Pass me some water, quick," Elena shouted to anyone that would respond.

Malcolm dipped back inside and popped his head back out, with a water bottle in his hand. Elena grabbed the water from him and hurriedly poured the contents all over Ray's arm. "Do you feel anything weird? What if it's poisonous?"

Ray wiped away the red streaks and grabbed Elena's hand. He turned her around and helped her up the step into the camper, Malcolm and Matt and Amelia stepping back. "Calm down. It's ok. It was just red water. Red rain. Look," he said, holding out his arm in the safety of the camper. "Looks fine. My skin's not melting or burning or stained or anything."

Elena grabbed hold of his arm and pulled him closer to inspect. She flipped his arm over and back again. Once she was content that there was no damage, she muttered, "It's raining blood. I need to sit down."

Malcolm cleared a space on the nearest seat, which happened to be the one with the melted chocolate bar. He swept the candy onto the ground in one quick movement and gestured for her to sit.

Dazed, she sat down in the melted chocolate seat.

Malcolm leaned across from her and smiled. "It's not blood. I really don't think it is, anyway. The sky, the streaks, remember? They were orange and fiery behind those clouds. This must be the product."

"Small consolation," Elena whispered. "Who knows what it's made of?"

"I am fine," Ray insisted.

The sound of the bloody rain and critters from the sea tapped and slapped and slammed into the top of the camper, seemingly coming in waves. In moments it sounded like just rain, the tap-tap-tap a steady rhythm, then after a few minutes, the sound became uneven, things smacking into the camper mixed with the rain.

Within about five minutes, the chaos stopped.

41

The earth was quiet.

All was still. For the first time in a very long time, nothing was happening.

The ground had ceased the angry growling and rolling. Hadn't the movement been consistent since before Ray and his family left their home for the last time? No matter how roughly or calmly the earth moved and shook, it had been active for some time. Ray almost couldn't figure out how to stand on his own anymore. His brain kept telling his body to give in to the movements and autocorrect, but now there was stillness.

He looked to Elena, who had turned a pale shade of green. Opposite the effect it had on him, the ceasing of motion was taking a harsh toll on her. Like a person stepping off a rocking boat and onto sure-footed land, Elena couldn't find her balance. Even sitting, she shifted and rocked back and forth. She brought her hands to her head.

"Come, come. Outside. The air will help. And seeing the horizon," Ray urged her. Malcolm, Matt and Amelia were already outside waiting. They too, were as hushed as the earth. Ray helped her out of the seat slowly, letting her find her legs.

Almost like a toddler, she took one shaky step after the next. He stepped out of the camper and turned, reaching his arms up to her. She gave in and let him lift her out, into the sand. "I've got you."

As he turned and set her next to him, he understood the long silence.

Everything had changed. The awful bloody rainstorm must have washed it all away.

The sinister clouds had shifted and were now literally disappearing in front of their eyes. Poof.

His gaze lingered and the clouds, the whole world around him began to blur. A wild distortion, colors wrapping and bending into each other. *So familiar.*

Through the fuzzy lens, he observed these clouds, confused. Not moving as normal clouds do- but what was normal these days? Each one, instead of following each other across the sky, crashed into the next, from left to right, up to down, each cloud seemingly eating the one next to it, as if once one met another, they fought for their own lives, to the death, consuming the other, absorbing the other into itself. *I know this. I've seen it before.*

Poof, they'd disappear, as if sucked out of the sky by a huge invisible vacuum. A spinning, transparent vacuum. *In a dream, I've seen this.*

"Not a dream," Amelia answered his thoughts out loud. "It's the beginning. It's time."

Malcolm nodded, stepping forward to the shoreline, ignoring the carcasses he waded through. He called back without turning around, "The beginning of the end."

Ray responded, without any thought, "The calm before the storm."

Amelia chimed in once more, "The world is falling down."

The darkened clouds remained but a memory. The storm had washed all evidence of them away. In their place, exquisite, white, cottony clouds swirled and collided into each other, like strange bumper cars in the sky. Inevitably, they would absorb each other, growing into enormous, fluffier clouds. The fiery orange streaks no longer danced behind them. They'd retired or run their course; produced the blood rain and moved on.

A fair, cobalt blue had been painted across the sky that only Van Gogh could've imagined. As the clouds continued to do their dance, shifting and eating their way across the horizon, the sky grew bluer, if that could be possible, and the sun shed the most golden of rays across the beach.

Elena propped herself up leaning against Ray and muttered, "It's the most beautiful thing I've ever seen. My eyes almost hurt."

Ray glanced to his side and found tears streaking down Elena's face. The splendor before them had struck them all. He was overcome by the vision above him, but most of all by the vision beside him. The woman he had loved since the moment he laid his eyes upon her. Even though her skin still held its greenish pallor, and her hair was matted to her head from sweat, she was still the most beautiful things he'd ever seen. He wrapped his arm around her waist and pulled her in closer. Her small frame pressed into his side, giving him her weight, trusting he'd keep her steady in a world that had plucked her balance away from her. "I love you," he whispered.

"I love you, Ray."

This was *the* moment. There was a pull, an urge, a desperate need to go. To be somewhere else. Under another sun. Not only that, but an absolute knowing that this place was no longer for him. This thing called Earth was on its last leg; its demise imminent. Everything leading up to this point: the meteorite, the floods, mudslides, tsunami's, earthquakes, wildfires, volcanoes, all but a hint of what was to be the final curtain call. He was awash with a mix of emotions, too many conflicting sentiments at once. A thankfulness for the salvation of his family, and an overwhelming anguish for all those families who never stood a chance.

"I think it's about time. I mean, I think I can feel it." Ray led Elena forward toward the shoreline.

"The pull. It's coming," Malcolm agreed.

"I can't feel anything," Elena said.

"Me neither, don't worry." Matt scooped his daughter up into his arms. "You feel anything different, Amelia?"

She smiled. "Mommy's coming." She fidgeted with something in the palm of her hand.

The world around Ray swelled and contracted with him, with each breath he took. On his peripherals, colors blended into each other, like his surroundings were slowly melting away. Like the world was aware of its own disintegration. The sun's incandescence burned through the slender layer holding this world together at its shredding seams. Almost as if he could see in between worlds. But each time he shifted his gaze, side to side, it changed. Staying scarcely outside his line of vision. The lines of existence here on this planet fading away.

It wouldn't be that easy, gentle or pretty.

"Can you see the lines?" He asked without thinking. "Like our reality is crumbling away."

"Until all that's left is nothing..." Malcolm uttered.

Elena shivered next to Ray. "I can't see any of that. Only the impossible blue skies and weird clouds bumping and eating each other. No melting, no fading..."

"That's ok," he soothed. "We're here. We're together. And it's time."

Off in the distance, the horizon shifted. At first, Ray wasn't sure of what his eyes perceived. The skyline moved, came closer, like it was some live thing, crawling forward to meet them. Shrinking.

"You see?"

Amelia responded, "She's close." She opened her hand and showed Matt what was inside. His lucky coin. She held it out towards him, a suggestion.

Matt shook his head at Amelia and folded her hand back around the coin. "You keep it. Good luck, remember?" He smiled and winked.

Amelia shook her head, "I don't need luck, Daddy." She pushed her hand out forward again, but again he made sure her fingers were closed tightly. He lifted her hand to his lips and gave it a light kiss, then placed her tiny hand over her heart.

"Always keep it close," he said softly.

The horizon pushed forward, inch by inch toward them. The sky and water line blurred as if they were one. The blue of the sky matched the blue of the water, and the waves pushed up, up, higher and higher into the sky.

Something small began to spin as it thrust itself out from the horizon. Two something's, in fact. Tiny little circular spinning objects. But Ray couldn't exactly call them objects, no. They were devoid of any definitive shape or color.

Tiny funnels of water. Not like the tornadoes from earlier. These moved from the distance out towards them, pushing in a horizontal motion, not vertical like a tornado should.

The water tunnels.

"She's coming!" Ray yelled, his voice crackling.

"Mommy!" Amelia squeaked.

The two funnels rotated outwards toward them, growing from mere inches to feet. Around and around they spun, growing closer and larger.

Ray looked up, and not a cloud remained in the sky. All that was left was a blue so strong and profound the effect stung his eyes. The sun still shone brightly, but now instead of normal rays, the sun pulsed, causing the beams to thrum and undulate in an outward manner.

The ground, too, began to quiver to the same rhythm as the rays, the same rhythm as the funnels coming toward them.

The shaking of the ground escalated to a furious level. Ray's teeth rattled in his head. He held tighter to Elena's hand as she turned her head and retched. She wiped her mouth with the back of her other hand. "I'm good."

She looked anything but. There was little time left anyway, and Elena would soon be able to rest. Once they got to their destination. Finally, they would all rest.

"See y'all on the other side!" Malcolm yelled out. He started moving away from them, farther up the beach, matching the movement of one of the funnels. About thirty yards up, he stopped, and walked into the water, past the dead fishes splayed about the beach.

That was the last Ray would see of Malcolm on this side of things.

42

Elena cried as a multitude of feelings washed over her. She felt awful for all the doubts and fights with Ray. All the times she questioned his sanity and told him none of this was not possible.

Elena, Ray, Matt and Amelia all locked hands on the beach as the funnel grew closer.

The spinning vortex reached up and out of the water completely until it rested right above, hovering. Water rolled and gushed around in a spherical motion, and an opening began to generate inside. The visage of Ravynn formed, and at first, she appeared like she too was made of water. Waves rippled and bent through her shape, light bathing her and soaking through her form. She solidified more, her body becoming more real within the funnel. Her long dark hair whipped out behind her, it too, caught up in the swirling.

I can see her. She is real. Ray was right. Everything, every doubt of sanity, every moment of fear, every nightmare, all led us to this moment.

Ravynn looked more ethereal floating there within the funnel, more defined. Her hair was almost black, a dramatic sight against her cool white skin. Her green eyes sparkled, as if they held a million secrets inside, twinkling. More than a woman, more than a human.

Tears spilled down Elena's cheeks as the final moments-the realization set upon her. The culmination of all the struggles, all the bizarreness, all the worry and sleepless nights had arrived. Fatigued, all she wanted to do was close her eyes and sleep. Find a peaceful spot somewhere Under Another Sun and be still.

Once we get through the rift...

MATT couldn't believe his eyes. There she was. Ravynn. His wife that he'd lost and mourned a year ago stood before him. He lost his breath at the sight of her. The proximity of her. The reality of her. His heart squeezed in his chest so tight he thought he'd die. If only for this moment, to witness her beauty and the life within her, he was certain he *could* die happy.

Second chances. Like the one he never got with her were before him now. Possibilities. In the decay of a perishing world, she shimmered. The *Woman on the Water*. Just like all those years ago, under the bridge when he rescued Ravynn. To think that woman was her grandmother, calling her home. Bringing her to another world, where she and her mother could live on.

Matt had stopped all that then.

But now, there was nothing standing in between him and his *Woman on the Water*.

RAY wept, too, as his tortured past year flooded his mind. All the nights he had dreamed of her, all the times she came to him through the water, calling to him, challenging his sanity.

The battles and struggles with Elena, the doubt she had in her eyes, the fear that he was not only losing his sanity, but his family and his job. It all bubbled to the surface. All the proof in the world now stood before him. His sister, Ravynn, in the ever-growing funnel.

The ground shook and threatened to toss them all. Yet the sky above remained crisp and blue. So serene, so tranquil. The juxtaposition of the stillness and the chaos coming together. So beautiful. The last goodbye.

The funnel stopped moving forward and stopped growing. It had reached its location. Ravynn spread her arms wide, ready to embrace them. Her welcoming gesture tugged at him. Physically. Something had a hold on him, something tied between him and his sister that held them together and urged him forward. An impalpable force.

He mechanically moved forward, not thinking. Salvation lay ahead. Like Ravynn had all those years ago under the bridge, he realized if he could get to her, everything would be ok. In those moments, he began to finally comprehend what she'd experienced, and how easy it had been to go through the funnel. The innate pull from the planet that had always been his home.

Ravynn's eyes shifted to Amelia. Matt moved into the water, carrying his daughter. The water went up to his knees, and the earth shook under him, threatening to toss him aside. He trudged forward. Matt stood before the funnel with Amelia in his arms. He took a step forward, but the ground shook again and tossed him into the water. "It's getting worse. Get Amelia inside," he said as he handed off his daughter to Ray.

Ray scooped Amelia up and took one shaky step up, to move inside the funnel. His mind was sure he'd go right through and splash in the water. That's what logic would dictate, but his heart carried him forward. He progressed, ever so gingerly at first, not yet trusting those first few steps, even though they were indeed solid. The excitement rose within him, his heart rate increased as he realized he'd be able to walk straight across it to Ravynn.

His foot didn't go through the sheer pathway. It landed on what was quite solid, despite the appearance. Solid as walking on a cement path. Sturdy and sure. All he had to do was put one foot in front of the other and trust. He looked down to the ocean beneath, the water swelling around under him. Nothing was shaky any longer. All was still and calm within the funnel. He looked up and Ravynn stood right before them. He couldn't make out anything behind her; it was as if the funnel swirled tightly behind her, obstructing any clear view. No matter. She was here.

Ravynn reached out and took Amelia from him. Amelia beamed and giggled and kissed her mother's cheeks.

Ray turned to go back to Elena and Matt, to make sure they got in as well, but he felt a warm hand take his. Ravynn had a firm hold on him. Her touch was of absolute safely and calm. Suddenly, Ray was weary. The safety and surety enveloped him and hummed in his ears, coaxed him forward, to Ravynn, to the other side.

He wasn't ready. He tried to pull away from Ravynn, to get to Elena and Matt, to help guide them inside safely. "Let me go. Let go, Ravynn. Not yet." His heart broke uttering the words, "I have to help them inside."

Ravynn said no words, only kept a firm hold of him. The pull was not only from her, but from the other side. That invisible force would not let go, tugged on every part of his being. Once home had a firm hold, it would never let go. Earth was no longer home, and in fact had been but a placeholder all this time, until he could be where he was meant to be. This all became both beautifully and painfully obvious as he looked on Matt and Elena.

Up to that point, his only thought was getting Amelia to Ravynn. Forward and onward. Never once had he feared that Matt and Elena weren't but a step behind him. He now realized his error. He yanked with all his strength, tried to pull his hand free from Ravynn. She would not budge. Like she was planted in stone, she was immovable. Inhuman strength, her resolve unbroken. She would not let go.

A crack in time saves ninety-nine...

How could he not have known that would happen? How was it not ever a thought? Why would Ravynn never have told him? Had she not hinted that everyone would be safe? Had he only assumed? Or did Ravynn tell him what he needed for her to get him and Amelia to safety? He replayed every piece of their conversations since she first came to him. Tried to find some clue he may have missed. How his sister had misled him, or how he had misled himself.

Stuck, unable to help, Ray could do nothing but helplessly witness Elena and Matt try to take those first steps up into the funnel, but the 'magic' of the water did not hold them. Their feet went right through, as if there were never a sturdy thing to step on. Stumbling, they both plunged, splashing into the water. Again, they tried, to no avail. The funnel was not made for them.

The earth outside the funnel shook, as Elena and Matt were hurled about in the water. Elena panted for air and instead gulped a mouthful of seawater. She coughed and spit it back out, gasping for air. Inside the funnel, everything was still. Nothing moved.

You're running out of time...

A crack in time saves ninety-nine...

Ray saw an image, Elena's face so contorted in abject horror and despair he was sure he'd die seeing it. His heart squeezed as if a giant hand had reached into his chest and crushed his lifeforce. His airway constricted and his head swooned. His body meant to collapse to the ground, to give up, but Ravynn and the pull would not allow for it.

Elena howled, a blood-curdling soul-crushing scream, reaching out to Ray who was only steps away, but already a world apart inside the funnel. Helpless to join him- both Elena and Matt struggled to fight the growing waves and furious earth that juddered beneath them.

Ray tried again to move back to them with a step, but his feet wouldn't go in that direction. There was a solid tug at his body to keep him. Ravynn's hand on his were so warm, almost burning.

Not only Ravynn held him from getting to them, but the force that was there under the bridge that Matt fought so hard against to save Ravynn was here. A firm grip was upon Ray and a realization struck him so hard he gasped. Ravynn was never meant to be saved by Matt, was she? She was always meant for the other place. And so was Ray...

43

Elena splashed through the water toward Ray and the funnel, with utter futility. Elena too, felt a force holding her back. She shrieked again, as Matt pulled her to him. She fought him, fist closed, hammering on his chest. "What are you doing? We have to go!" She screamed. "We have to go now! Inside!"

Her eyes pleaded him to let her go. Let her go to Ray even though it wasn't possible. She was suddenly keenly aware that she was never meant to be saved, never one of the ninety-nine. How could she have missed that? Ravynn's cryptic warnings and incomplete answers to Ray fooled them all and got them to this place. A place where she was never meant to come to. She was only a catalyst, a pawn Ravynn used to motivate Ray and Amelia to this point. If Ray had the slightest inkling that Elena wouldn't be able to get through the rift, he wouldn't go. *Ravynn. Brilliantly deceptive.*

Matt's face was indecipherable. Unyielding. How? How could he? Did he know? Had he figured it all out before this moment? Had he known he wasn't meant to be saved?

A terrible doubt crossed her mind and she questioned if Ray had known this whole time too? But that couldn't be. He would never. Panic and horror welled up inside her as she gazed up to Ray in that tunnel. How could he have?

His face contorted in agony, as he realized the futility, his gross miscalculations, at the same time Elena had. In that moment, she knew that he'd been ignorant. That he'd been fooled by his sister. They had both assumed she was always meant to join them and walk Under Another Sun. Ravynn had tricked them both.

Her attention was pulled past him to Ravynn, who uttered no words, but her gestures spoke volumes. As she held one hand of Amelia's and kept a firm grasp on Ray, she tilted her head slowly to the side, her eyes intense, and slowly pulled Ray and Amelia in closer. She shook her head in the negative at Elena. Her eyes were full of empathy, but other than that she was stoic, unflinching. Something profound exchanged between the two women using no words at all. Gratitude from Ravynn for caring for her daughter, for being a mother to her when Ravynn could not. A genuine appreciation that only mothers could share. The recognition faded away in a heartbeat, and she turned to an even nothingness.... stone cold.

The earth convulsed again. This time so much more violently, but Ray and Amelia were beyond that. In the space with Ravynn, they were protected, shielded from the catastrophe unfolding mere steps away and all around them. For that, Elena was grateful.

Elena glanced back to her husband, their eyes meeting one last time. A glimpse of their unraveling history; an exchange so heavy, so full of love and sadness, hope and regret. Every moment of their life together passed between them in that one look.

The earth shook with such cruel intentions that Elena couldn't see. Her body lost its ground, unable to find solid footing and she fell into the water again, thrashed about by the furious waves.

MATT fumbled, reaching through the water, frantic to grab a hold of Elena and pull her to him. He flashed back to that night under the bridge when he pulled another girl to him, trying to save her. Young Ravynn in his mind was before him once again, and he tried to pull her so close one last time, but that otherworldly force was yet again fighting him. The woman under the bridge was fighting him. Oh, how beautiful she was, he thought. *Never truly meant to be mine. Never meant to belong to anyone. Like an angel.* Ravynn, his angel.

He couldn't help but smile. Amid the screaming and flailing and the unsteady earth shaking and roaring, he held still in the water. He had made a choice, and he'd understood the implications. The sacrifices that had to be made for his daughter to survive. There was no other way.

Elena in his arms, he gazed upon his long-lost wife, and he smiled. He had found peace at last. The vision of Ray, Ravynn and Amelia in front of him, safeguarded within the funnel was now growing ambiguous and indistinct. Like they were fading away. Melting far, far away from the violent and doomed place. He tried to take a mental snapshot of them there, one last thing to hold onto in a world where everything was crumbling before him. Before they disappeared, as if they were standing in between two worlds, he exhaled in relief. No matter what happened to him here, his family would be fine.

They were gone.

He could once again hear Elena's shrieks and pleas as they stood alone to face their fate. Her cries grew louder as the earth curiously began to quiet, as if giving her one last chance to grieve and wail. There came a strange swooshing sound, soft at first, but steadily growing more ferocious. He had the sudden acute awareness that he and Elena were no longer crouching in those tumultuous waters, but only in sand. It took but a split second for him to acknowledge what was about to happen. He glanced up at the spot once more where Ravynn,

Ray, and Amelia were moments before, and saw the third most beautiful thing he'd ever seen in his life. A wave. His mind quickly tried to find a measure for its height but couldn't comprehend. It towered, scraping the sky and clouds above.

He drew Elena's face into his chest and held her there securely to shield her from seeing what was coming. The quiescence was both a fright and a welcome. The only sounds remaining were the mix of his own heartbeat in his ears and Elena's sobbing. He raised his face up to this monster, not in defiance, but in acceptance, a welcoming gesture. There was no other way. This was his fate. He welcomed it with a calm he'd never experienced before. He had finally realized his purpose. He saved Ravynn all those years ago, and it was a fluke, as she was supposed to go then. But they had a beautiful child, and he had the chance to save his daughter. Both of his girls were now safe, and where they belonged. And both of his girls had saved him, too. He would have died years ago, a hopeless alcoholic, unable to get his disease under control, if not for this purpose, for their love and salvation.

44

Moments before Ray went through the rift, he was overcome by guilt of losing Elena and leaving Matt behind. Duped by a sister he always trusted. A sister who would have never steered him wrong. Yes, she saved him and Amelia, but at what cost? His sister, the one he grew up with and knew better than anyone would never have been this reticent. So callous, with such blatant disregard for human life.

He was reluctant to go, but the funnel was spinning itself down slowly, getting steadily smaller. He looked to his sister and shook his head, the tears clouding his eyes. His head wouldn't stop its shaking, and his body soon followed.

She put a firm grip on his hand and pulled him in. "We must go now," she said, and there was an icy insistence in her voice he'd never known before. "Now."

"But—"

Ravynn shook her head and tugged harder. Closed her eyes and spoke, "The earth is dying, Ray. It will take two more days for total destruction. The planet itself will be ripped to shreds by forces beyond comprehension. The rift has finally taken its toll. But *human* destruction is happening much quicker." She opened her eyes and regarded him, but Ray sensed no compassion coming off her. Like she was reporting facts, detached. She tilted her head and glared at him, her look cutting through him. She confirmed what he knew and feared deep inside, "They are already gone. Matt and Elena. It was quick. There was nothing that could be done for them. But we must go now. I am sorry." Something in the very corner of her eye twitched, and Ray hoped it would betray her emotions. He waited for a single tear, or a slight downturn of the mouth, but nothing else, no other sign came.

He couldn't turn back. He understood what she said was true, although he couldn't escape the nagging sense that somehow his escape was not an escape. For the first time, he was afraid of what was really on the other side of that rift. What could lie there that turned his sister to ice. Made her so apathetic watching her own husband and Elena's deaths. Sheer indifference, not self-preservation.

He hunched with remorseful defeat and acceptance, realizing everyone's fates had been sealed. Like those people he'd seen outside the café. Their lives that had been, that had to end. No other way. He stopped resisting her pull and stepped further inside the shrinking funnel.

A crack in time saves ninety-nine...

In that moment, he wished he'd been wrong. Wished that all his talks with his sister after she 'died' in the tsunami had been a delusion. A fantasy of a sick mind. If he could've gone back and chosen it, he would have gladly faced an illness he'd grown more certain and afraid of every day. Would have chosen to face schizophrenia like his father. Even in the worst of the disease, being unable to discern reality from fantasy would have been better than this. Because then, Elena and Amelia would be safe at home and Matt would still be alive. And all of those billions of people, too. The planet. Life.

She smiled at him, at his defeat, and reached out with her other hand to take his. Amelia behind her, holding her mother's dress as it whipped in the whirlwind. Ray licked his impossibly dry lips that tasted of both salt and a queer betrayal, and asked,

"Who   are   you?"

Acknowledgements:

I want to take a moment to thank a few incredibly special
people who have helped to make this all possible.
It wasn't long ago that I had every doubt in the world about
my writing career. We all do. We doubt, we fear, we question.
I believe this is just part of the creative process, part of being
an artist.

Then there is a moment where things change. Whether it is a
single definitive moment, or a combination of things that make
it impossible to doubt your path any longer. I am lucky to
have had that a-ha moment. That feeling of *this is exactly what I
should be doing.*

During this with Under Another Sun and leading up to my
publishing journey, there were those very special people who
listened to me cry, whine, and celebrate. Every single amazing
idea I had I needed to tell them, every doubt I had they pushed
me through. This is by no means the entire list, but a list that I
hold dear to my heart.
A quick thank you to my Mother and Father, who gave me life
and the endless support to express myself any way I chose. A
little bit of their art exists within mine, though mine tends to
lean towards the darker side of things.
Mike and Steph, thank you for always being there and
humoring even my most grandiose ideas.
Thank you, April, Carolina, Jess, and Michelle.
Thank you, Kate, for being my fearless beta reader and honest
friend. How many margarita happy hours have there been
during this process?
And thank you Med, for being that person that there is no one
word to describe - confidant, fellow author, cheerleader,
sounding board, tech-savvy brain-boy, and all-around
extremely patient person ☺

ABOUT THE AUTHOR

D.M. Siciliano grew up in a small town in Massachusetts. She
rediscovered her passion for storytelling after ending a brief
stint in music., unable to push away her artistic urges.
Living in California wine country has brought out her
creativity, as she published her first novel in 2019, and has
several other manuscripts currently in the works.
She is an active member of the Horror Writers Association.

Find out more about D.M. Siciliano at DMSiciliano.com

Other books by this author:
INSIDE

Made in the USA
Monee, IL
04 October 2020

43764632R00194